BIRTHRIGHT

BIRTHRIGHT

STRANGER MAGICS, BOOK TEN

ASH FITZSIMMONS

BIRTHRIGHT. Copyright © 2020 by Ash Fitzsimmons.

Print Edition ISBN: 978-1-949861-24-2

Cover design by BespokeBookCovers.com

www.ashfitzsimmons.com

PROLOGUE

C'era una volta...

That was how the stories began when I was small—*once upon a time*. Kings and queens, princes and princesses, knights and damsels in need of rescue, ogres and trolls and hungry wolves, enchanted beasts and voiceless mermaids in disguise. And always, there was magic in those stories: books, carpets, lamps, rings, roses, wands, words. Put the right item in the right person's hands—maybe an evil *stregone*, jealous of a beautiful princess, or a good *fata* who could wave a wand and turn a girl's rags into a ballgown—and wonders resulted.

These stories—lovely, horrifying, or weird as they may be—are reserved for children, who are young and gullible enough to believe in nonsense like magic. Adults are far wiser, but still, they retell the tales. In so doing, they indulge themselves, returning to a time when they, too, believed in the impossible.

But adults, for all their wisdom, forget that the stories had to come from *somewhere*. That once, not so very long ago in the grand scheme of things, the wisest believed in things unseen and dangerous, and they knew, without question, that magic was not to be trifled with.

This truth has been forgotten by most people, who are so much wiser and cleverer than their forebears. But those of us who perceive magic in its many-hued splendor, who have reached out and changed the world through concentration and force of will, we remember the old stories. They're mostly wrong, those stories, warped far beyond fact by too many tellers' embellishments, but they all carry a spark of truth. A warning.

Magic is very real, and sometimes, people are not who and what they seem.

C'era una volta...

Long, long ago, before the mortal realm's great empires began to rise from the riverbanks and the sands and the jungles, a centuries-long war raged across Faerie, one of the two adjoining realms. Sometimes, Faerie's conflict would spill over into the mortal realm through one of the many gates between them, holes torn through the barrier dividing the realms. Every so often, the chaos would touch even the distant Gray Lands, the third realm, whose magic was strange and useless to the fae. The combatants were curious creatures: eternally youthful, immensely powerful, often capricious in their cruelty, and peculiarly cursed by an allergy to silver and iron.

While Faerie ripped itself apart—and no one still alive save the realm can name the cause—three of its children with great strength and talent for enchantment gathered armies about themselves and began to battle each other for supremacy. To end the war, Faerie herself brokered a truce among the Three, giving them unmatched power, setting them as queens and king over their respective courts, and tasking them with maintaining the peace. And it worked.

For a time.

Faeries raided the mortal realm, causing havoc and taking what—and whom—they liked back through the gates, toys to play with until they tired of them. They scattered half-blooded children across the two realms, immortal creatures with vast power but largely human sensibilities. Mortals gifted with talent for magic began to arise as well and banded together against the fae threat. Though their power was weaker, they learned to use wands and other tools to channel it more effectively, and they developed the techniques that would become the rudiments of spellcraft.

Eventually, the three-way truce in Faerie fell apart. Mab's court was driven out for rising against the others, Oberon's was forced into the mortal realm by its ancient, restless king, and Titania's remained to enjoy the spoils. And then, one by one, the Three were killed and replaced. Coileán inherited his mother's court in Faerie, Eleanor left academia to lead her father's home from its wandering, and Valerius reluctantly took his mother's in hand to bring an end to its warring. The new Three reached an unofficial peace with the other non-mundanes in the two realms: with the Fringe, weakly gifted witches, faeries of diluted blood, and the witch-blooded result of their joining, many of whom made their home in Faerie; with the Dark Company, the mortal realm's mercenary shapeshifting spies; with the Arcanum, the governing body of wizards and those witches they allowed to remain within their ranks; and with the Minor Arcanum, wizards and witches who had quietly decided they could do without the Arcanum's bureaucracy. Together, they held their collective breath and waited for Nath, Lady of the Gray Lands, to make her move on the mortal realm.

It was only a matter of time.

C'era una volta...

A thousand years ago, when the wizards of the world battled each other in petty turf skirmishes, Simon, called the Magus, rose up and subjected the others to his will, creating the Arcanum out of chaos and forging order where there had been war. For generations, the Arcanum maintained stability among mortal practitioners of magic, led by a grand magus and his or her council of magi.

In 1970, a promising wizard named Gregory Harrison was chosen as grand magus. He led the Arcanum for almost thirty-six years, and then he handed it off to his young protégée, the talented Helen Carver. But Helen's selection was highly contested. Her half brother, Aiden, was himself half brother to Coileán, by then a king in Faerie. Worse yet, she had eloped with a young man who was not only *not* a wizard, but had also recently learned that, mundane though he seemed, he was kin to Coileán and Eleanor in equal measure. A large faction of the Council, led by an influential magus named James Mulligan, rose up in secret, imprisoned Helen, and went after the Fringe, killing the fae-blooded among them and kidnapping the witches as hostages. Mulligan's gambit worked, for unlike their predecessors, Eleanor and Coileán were half-blooded and so possessed a capacity for mercy, and they stayed their hands to save the captives' lives.

But Helen had a daughter, Roslyn, who was raised within the Arcanum but whispered to in secret by Faerie herself. When she learned the truth about who she was and what Mulligan had done, she freed her mother, who then, in alliance with the courts, freed the hostages and sought justice. Mulligan was executed, but the judges who considered the rest of the conspirators took pity and recommended that they be bound, prevented from using magic but allowed to live. Helen agreed, and then she resigned, leaving in her place Arnold Lowe, a magus who had worked throughout the Mulligan years to save the Fringe.

Though a decent man and a talented wizard, Arnold wasn't nearly as watchful of the bound probationers as he should have been. By the time he passed the office to Bertram Wold ten years later, many of the probationers had joined forces with a small army of rogue faeries, and they took as their hostage Faerie's consciousness. To save the realm, she killed herself and passed her power to Roslyn—and Roslyn, in turn, gave Val his birthright in order that he might bring the rogues to heel as their king.

When the proverbial dust settled, it was clear to the Council that Bertram wasn't fit for his position, and

Arnold didn't want it back. With no successor in place, witch-blooded Fotoula Pavli made a bid for grand magus. Some of the magi balked. After all, her father had been executed for killing dozens of wizards, while her mother was *Mab*, one of the original Three. Worse still, her protective half brother had just been handed their mother's court. But there was no one among their number stronger or more talented than Toula, and so Grand Magus Pavli she became.

But when you take power by force, you need force to hold the throne—and as Toula would soon discover, not all of the Arcanum would willingly subject itself to a "mongrel's" rule.

C'era una volta…

One rainy June weekend, a young man named Gianni came up from Rome to a multi-artist show in Paris. He brought with him six of his best canvases and a sketchpad, hoping to sell a painting or two and be inspired by the city. When he'd finished setting up his stall, he looked across the aisle and saw a young woman kneeling by her plastic tubs, carefully unpacking the beautiful clay pots she'd nestled therein. She looked up at him and smiled, and his knees went weak. Rather than collapse, he bravely ventured to her side and, in his halting, broken French, offered his assistance with her setup.

Her name was Lucie, she was from Nice, and she spoke roughly as much Italian as he did French—which is to say, barely any. But his eyes made her heart flutter, he was cute when he tried to pantomime his intentions, and she was pleased for the help.

They traded phone numbers and e-mail addresses, just in case.

The show was a great success for them both. Gianni sold all his paintings, Lucie sold most of her pots, and both picked up commissions from new patrons. As Lucie packed away her remaining wares, Gianni suggested that they accompany each other to dinner, and she agreed.

They found a café, where they ordered moules-frites and a bottle of chardonnay to celebrate, and they stumbled through the meal and laughed at their hapless attempts at eloquence. Maybe it was the wine, or maybe Paris has a magic of its own, but they couldn't keep their eyes off each other, and their parting that night was bittersweet.

Gianni went home and immediately signed up on a language-learning website, intending to improve his French and write to Lucie. But the next morning, he found a message from her in his inbox—poorly rendered by an online translator, but still comprehensible. He replied and hoped the translator was more effective in the other direction. It wasn't, but within a year, the two of them had learned enough of the other's mother tongue to no longer require its services.

They met again in Paris, and that time, they left together.

Neither had any family to consider, and so they were quickly married in a civil ceremony. They moved into a little flat in Rome, which was drafty in winter, hot in summer, and politely described as "cozy," but they had a spare room to use as a studio, and they were as happy as any young couple desperately in love can be. Soon enough—maybe through chance, maybe by accident— they learned they were to be parents, and they added a secondhand bassinet to their tiny bedroom. In the old Italian tradition, they named the baby for Gianni's late mother.

And that is where I enter this story.

CHAPTER 1

By my third night on the street, I was famished.

Some of the picture books I'd read made running away seem like fun, a quick jaunt into the wide world with a bindle and a sandwich. Maybe the hero would find some scary woods and scurry home to his mother for safety, all grievances forgotten, and she'd give him a hug and a snack, and that would be that, a happy family reunited with no one the worse for wear.

But I wasn't going home. I *couldn't*. I was in big trouble, and for the last three days, my every waking moment—and most of my dreams—had been devoted to hiding from the well-intentioned adults who would have dragged me back. That hadn't left much time for finding food, however, so I crept from my hiding places in back alleys and behind stinking rubbish after the sun went down, waiting for the evening crowds to thin before I began scavenging in the bins.

Unfortunately for me, the crowds never seemed to be in a hurry to leave. January wasn't peak tourist season in Rome, but I heard plenty of funny accents as I skulked around the city, silently watching couples with bikes and middle-aged tourists who'd been disgorged from busses as they posed in front of old buildings and yapped at each other, dripping gelato on the pavement. Some got drunk at night, and I saw one man almost run down when he weaved into the road. Another drunk mistook me for a beggar and tossed me a few coins as I stood frozen in place in the shadows outside a streetlight's glow, hoping he'd pass me by without asking where my parents were. I picked up the gift when he left, but it wasn't going to do me any good; he'd left me barely a Euro, and besides, I couldn't just walk into a store alone and try to spend it.

I was five. Five and a half, when asked, and tall for my age, but officially, I was still far below the point when children can reasonably be expected to keep themselves out of trouble, and I knew it. Zia Giulia always held my hand when we were out in public, squeezing my fingers too tightly as we passed through crowds as if she feared the current of people would snatch me away like a swimmer in a riptide. I wondered why she bothered—given how often I annoyed her with my noise or mess, I doubted that she would have minded if someone had carried me off. She wasn't really my zia, anyway, but we had no better term for our relationship, and sometimes, she could be kind. Zio Luca was another matter, and the reason why I was hiding in an empty alley on a cold Sunday night.

My stomach growled like an angry dog, but I had nothing to put in it. The nearest rubbish bin was made of black-painted metal and taller than me, and when I hoisted myself over the top to look inside, I could see little but cardboard boxes with plastic spouts and a nest of shredded paper. There were a few cafés in the next block, and I decided to hunt over there when the night stilled and the warm light of the plate-glass windows went dark. Until then, I had no choice but to be hungry.

Cold, on the other hand, was something I could fix.

I'd done it the previous night, when the wind picked up in the wee hours and cut through my thin jacket. A rubbish bin was sort of like a fireplace—it contained the fire, at least—and as I'd discovered in spectacular fashion a few days before, all I had to do to start a fire was think about it. I still didn't know how I could do that, and my brief life on the run hadn't given me much time for contemplation, but the fire had been lovely and warmed my hands and face until a police officer almost caught me and I fled.

Double-checking the alley for unwelcome observers, I took a few steps back from the bin, held out my finger like a match, and whispered, "Brucia."

A force like rushing water ripped down my outstretched finger, and suddenly, the paper in the bin burst into flames—much larger flames than I'd intended, and I jumped back in alarm as they shot up from the bin in a violent, almost columnar, conflagration. Before I could try to undo the damage, however, the fire died as quickly as it had been born, and I barely heard the approach of quiet footsteps over the blood pounding in my ears.

"Impressive," said a voice from down the alley, and I whirled around to see a stranger silhouetted against the streetlights. I couldn't make out much about him—he seemed smaller than Zio Luca, or at least not as fat, and I didn't recognize his accent. A tourist, I supposed, not a police officer, but still, I tried to hastily plan an escape. The back of the alley was blocked with shipping cartons, but if I was quick, maybe I could dart by him and disappear into the night...

But I was still too scared by the unexpected fire and the company to make a run for it, and so I stayed frozen by the bin, watching the stranger approach and fighting the tremor in my jaw.

When he neared, he looked into the smoldering bin and sniffed deeply. "Olive oil. No wonder it burned so well. Did it hurt you?"

I shook my head and willed my legs to move, but they wouldn't listen to me.

"Can you do it again?" he asked, stepping back a pace. "Show me how you made that."

Finally, I recovered my voice, or at least a squeaking facsimile of it. "I...I didn't..."

The stranger crouched beside me, and even in the faint light, I could tell he was smiling. "I saw you. That's an impressive trick for someone your size." When I continued to stare at him in paralyzed fear, he cupped one palm, and a brilliant orange fireball bloomed in his hand, a flower made of dancing flame. "It's all right," he whispered. "You're not in trouble."

I squinted in the sudden glow, but at least I was able to get a better sense of my companion. An adult, obviously, but younger than my zio and zia, maybe the age of the nice playground supervisor at my nursery school whose wife sometimes dropped in with their tiny twin babies. His hair was short and brown, lighter than his eyes, which were soft as they studied me. One of his canine teeth was crooked, and I could see a dimple when he smiled at me over the flame, but I kept returning to his eyes. There was nothing about them that should have given me pause, but somehow, they seemed wrong, like a perfectly fitting piece inserted from another puzzle.

"Go ahead," he urged. "Or I will, if you prefer. The night's cold enough as it is."

I'd never done it with an audience, which made me more nervous about replicating my trick, but I stood well away from the bin, pointed at it again, and muttered the fire into being. It flared as before, but the man flicked two fingers, and the blaze subsided to a safe level. "Very nice," he said, extinguishing his fireball, then warmed his hands over the bin. "Who taught you to do that?"

I thought again about running, but the fire *was* warm, and since the man had shown me his secret, too, I decided to push my luck. "No one," I said, shuffling closer. "It just happened."

"Mm. And this wouldn't have anything to do with why someone such as yourself is alone on the streets at this time of night, would it?" He paused, but when I gave no reply, he knelt beside me and murmured, "Why are you alone? Where are your parents?"

"Dead," I mumbled.

He seemed taken aback. "Then who should be looking

after you?"

My eyes began to prick. The stranger was too close, I couldn't run, and he was going to drag me back...

As I fought tears, his brow knit, and then I felt...*something*...moving through my thoughts. If I concentrated, I could follow its rapid trajectory as it bounced among my memories. There was Zio Luca, smacking my bottom and legs for breaking a glass, and there he was again, yanking me over his knee when I was three and wouldn't go to sleep, and again, and again, and again...

And then the thing in my mind seized upon the last time. Zia Giulia had allowed me to paint in the kitchen after dinner, and I'd accidentally squeezed a green glob onto the rug. She'd cursed and started to clean it up, telling me how lucky I was that my zio wasn't there to see what a mess I'd made again, but before she'd finished, Zio Luca had come home early from the bar where he spent most nights with his friends, angry at the world and stinking of alcohol. Catching Zia Giulia on her hands and knees with a rag and me standing silently by, he'd put the pieces together and marched toward me, pushing up his sleeves. I'd run to my little bedroom at the back of our flat, hoping that removing myself from his sight would do the trick. Instead, he'd burst through the door a moment later with a thick belt in his hands—a gift from Zia Giulia, who knew how much Zio Luca liked the old American Western movies and had found a real cowboy belt for him. The buckle was almost the size of my hand and sharp around the edges. I'd started babbling an apology for my accident as soon as I saw him in the doorway, but he hadn't slowed, he'd just kept winding the belt around his hand...

...and something had thrown him across the room, straight into my dresser, shattering the mirror above. The cheap furniture had splintered where his bulk had fallen onto it, but he'd been too drunk to feel the impact. Rising from the wreckage, he'd continued toward my bed, shouting about how I was going to learn this time, I was going to *behave*...

The dresser I hadn't fully understood—that force had manifested so suddenly that I'd barely realized it had come from me. But I'd felt the twinge of power thrum down my arm when I'd pointed at him and begged him to stop. In the next instant, Zio Luca's clothes were on fire, and as he'd screamed and flailed, making matters worse for himself, I'd gone into survival mode. Snatching my jacket from the floor and the one photo I had of my parents and me from the ruins of my mirror, I'd darted past screaming Zia Giulia, out the door, down the stairs, and into the night.

By the time the strange sensation in my head disappeared, I was crying in earnest, and I felt the man wrap me in a careful hug. "I won't take you back," he promised, holding me as I sniffled. "But you can't stay here, little one." When my breathing slowed, he released me and said, "You're hungry."

It wasn't a question, but I nodded anyway and swiped at my eyes.

The weird sensation flashed through my head again, and a flat box appeared in the man's hands. "This should be close," he said, almost apologetically, and offered me the box. When I lifted the lid, I found a steaming pizza inside—extra mozzarella, baked ham, and nothing else, the way I liked it. I looked at him in surprise, but only for a second before I plopped onto the concrete with the box and tore into the perfectly thin slices, which were just hot enough to burn my mouth. I didn't care. My ravenous stomach was awake and shouting, and I almost choked in my hurry to fill it.

When I came up for air, the man passed me a stack of napkins and sat beside me while I attacked a fresh slice. "What's your name?" he asked.

I swallowed hard and gasped for air. "Maria."

"Only Maria?"

"Corelli," I said, and burped, but the man didn't seem to mind.

"I'm called Val," he replied. "So, now that we're acquainted, what are we to do about you?"

At the moment, I could think only as far as the pizza in front of me and the warmth of the burning rubbish at my back, and I shrugged as I ate.

"You have a special talent, you know. Has anyone ever told you you're a...maga? Is that still the word?" He thought briefly, then sighed. "Close enough, I suppose. You're a maga. Probably a gifted one, judging by that," he added, nodding at the bin.

I shook my head.

"No? Not entirely surprising. Your parents, what about them? Maghi?"

"I don't know." I wiped my hands as clean as I could—they'd been grimy before, and the layer of sauce and crust crumbs hadn't helped the situation—and pulled my folded photograph from my pocket. "That's Mamma and Papà," I said, showing him the snapshot, "and that's me." I pointed to the dark-haired bundle in my mother's arms as if it weren't already obvious. "Mamma made pots. Papà painted. Zia Giulia never said they were maghi, but maybe she forgot."

"I see." He waited until I put the picture safely away, then said, "I have a proposal for you, Maria. My sister is a maga, and she knows most of the others out there. If I take you to her, she could tell if you have family who could care for you. Keep your fires under control. Would that be acceptable?"

The notion was exciting, but I saw an immediate problem. "I don't have any family. Mamma and Papà didn't have any brothers and sisters, and my grandparents are dead, too. That's why Zia Giulia took me in."

"Who's not really your zia, correct?"

I nodded. "We lived in a flat in her building. She took care of me when Mamma and Papà went to Switzerland,

and then they didn't come home, and so I lived with her."

Val frowned in thought. "You're certain they're dead?"

I took the photograph out again and showed him the back, where Zia Giulia had written our names. She'd listed my birthdate, but for my parents, she's put down two dates each, and the last ones matched. "Zia Giulia said they were going to an art show, and the train crashed."

He studied the dates, then gave me back my picture. "I'm sorry. You never knew them."

"No," I said, shaking my head. "I don't remember them."

"Four months is far too young," he agreed. "But let me take you to my sister—you might have distant cousins you don't know who would be happy to have you, and you wouldn't need to return to your...zio," he said with distaste.

If it meant a permanent escape from Zio Luca, I was prepared to do almost anything. "Now?" I asked, eyeing the rest of the pizza.

Val considered the dark sky above us, then gave me a more critical examination. "In the morning. Come home with me for the night. You can bathe and rest...and you can finish that there," he added, catching my focus on my dinner. "Yes?"

Had I been older, less exhausted, and better fed, I might have listened to the internal warnings cautioning me against going anywhere with a stranger, let alone one who could summon fire and food at will. But that night, faced with the choice of long hours in the cold darkness or the prospect of a bed, I threw caution aside and packed up the rest of the pizza. "Do you live close?"

"Not exactly," he replied, pushing himself off the ground. "I came over for a walk. It's good to clear your head, and the city's interesting at night." With that, a jagged flash like lightning shot through the air just beyond the fire bin, and the world seemed to split in a widening circle. It was night on the other side, too, but I could see what appeared to be white stone walls and neat vegetation suggestive of a garden. "Ready?" he asked me as I clutched the pizza box to my chest.

By then, it was too late for second thoughts. I nodded, and as he took my hand, he extinguished the fire, then led me through the hole.

The place on the other side *was* a garden—some of the flowers' true colors were revealed in the flash as the hole closed behind us—but it seemed to be contained on all sides by walls and columned walkways. I looked up and gasped, and Val chuckled as he realized the cause of my surprise. "They're pretty, aren't they?" he said.

Spread above me were thousands of stars, more than I'd ever seen, born as I had been under the constant glow of city lights. They twinkled and glittered like a picture in one of my storybooks, impossibly numerous and brilliant, a bottle of diamond dust spilled across bluish-black velvet.

"Come with me," he said after giving me a moment to soak in the view, then led me down a succession of lamp-lit breezeways and through more gardens, most of which I missed in my effort to keep my eyes on the panorama above. Soon enough, we stopped in front of a wooden door carved with a delicate palm frond motif and stained the color of deep mahogany, and Val ushered me inside. "It's not perfect," he said, lighting the sconces on the wall with a twitch of his finger, "but it should suffice for the night."

The room was, in a word, palatial, from the greenish slate floor to the high ceiling, which was covered in a starry mosaic almost as impressive as the real thing above it. The wide four-poster bed was hung with a gauzy white canopy, and the matching linens looked plush enough to swallow me. Two of the other three walls were set with doors: to my left, I could see an attached bath, while straight ahead, the doors had been left open to admit the breeze from yet another garden. A pair of sheer curtains was the only thing separating the room from the night outside, but they seemed sufficient, and I realized it was quite a bit warmer there than it had been in Rome.

As I gawked, Val pried the pizza from me and put it on a wooden table, then pulled out one of the pair of chairs and patted the green cushion. "Finish your meal," he suggested. "I need to make some calls."

I climbed up without hesitation and tucked in—somehow, the pizza hadn't cooled, but after everything else I'd witnessed that night, I wasn't bothered. While I ate, Val stepped to a corner of the room and removed a little phone from his pocket, then had two brief conversations in a language I didn't recognize. When he finished, he returned to the table and took the other chair. "My sister's excited to meet you," he explained, "and someone's on her way to help you with your bath."

By then, the pizza was almost gone, and I was satiated enough to wonder if I wasn't being horribly rude by not offering my host a piece. "Are you...hungry?" I asked, pointing to the dwindling pizza and praying he'd say no.

To my relief, Val shook his head. "I've eaten. But before Bonnie gets here, there's something I need to do." He shifted his chair closer to mine, then put his fingertips on the sides of my head and smiled reassuringly. "Very few here speak Italian. This will help you."

A soundless flare went off behind my eyes, painless but disorienting, and I jerked and dropped my slice. Val released me and said, "Sorry, I know it feels strange, but there's no way to explain what that's like to someone who hasn't been through it."

"What did you do..." I began, then realized the words sounded wrong.

"I gave you the local tongue, that's all," he soothed. Switching back to the familiar words I knew, he added, "Your native tongue is still in your head—I merely added to it. Did it hurt?"

"No..."

"Good. It won't feel as odd to you in a few—ah," he

said as someone knocked at the main door, then called in the other language, "Come in!"

The woman who hurried inside looked to be about Val's age but shorter, a brown-eyed brunette who'd pulled her honey-streaked hair back into a loose bun. She seemed frazzled, her blouse clean but slightly wrinkled over blue leggings, and she was already rolling up her sleeves before she'd shut the door. "I'm sorry, my lord, I was in bed," she began, but he beckoned her closer and cut her apology short.

"And I'm sorry for waking you. Bonnie, this is Maria. Could you—"

"Oh, you're a *mess*," she interrupted, and *tsk*ed as she took in my unwashed tangles and dirty jacket. "Bath time, little miss. Move it," she ordered, pointing toward the next room.

"It's best to do as she says," Val murmured, and watched as I climbed down from the table. "You'll be all right?" he asked Bonnie.

She gave him a look of incredulity. "I'm pretty sure I can manage one little girl," she said, and shooed me along.

The marble tub was sunken into the bathroom floor and roughly the size of the bed. As I started disrobing, it instantly filled with warm water, and a cushion appeared on the edge for Bonnie. "In you go," she said more gently. "Can you swim?"

I nodded and shucked off the last of my grimy things, and Bonnie helped me into the bath, which immediately began to go gray around me as the dirt rinsed off. "Duck your head under, let's deal with that mop of yours," she said, and I held my breath and sank until I was sitting at the bottom of the tub, which was perhaps a meter deep. Surfacing, I wiped my eyes clean and stood by the edge as Bonnie rubbed shampoo into my hair, and then she asked, "Are you a bubbles sort of girl?" I turned to her and beamed, and with a casual flick of her finger, the surface of the tub changed to rose-scented foam. "Thought so. Okay, let's rinse that out and see where we stand…"

Two shampooings, a round of conditioner, and a thorough scrubbing later, Bonnie let me swim in the tub for a few minutes before coaxing me out and into a towel. Somehow—by magic, I would realize in retrospect—my hair seemed to have dried on its own. It was once again chestnut and wavy, but like everything else, it now smelled faintly of roses. Bonnie presented me with a set of pink and white nightclothes, the softest I'd ever worn. Dried, dressed, and with teeth brushed for the first time in days, I was hustled off to bed, and Bonnie tucked me in. "Stay here," she said, smoothing my hair from my face as I squirmed deeper into the thick mattress. "Don't go wandering, now. We'll be back in the morning to get you."

As I yawned, she surprised me by bending over to kiss my forehead. "Get some sleep, sweetie. I'm sure you need it," she said, then let the sheer bed curtains fall and took her leave.

I never heard the door latch behind her. Clean, full, and exhausted, I was out almost as soon as I closed my eyes.

I woke to warm sunlight and a cool morning breeze. Disoriented, I panicked, bolting upright in bed before I recalled the night before and where I was, then caught my breath and relaxed. This was Val's house. Bonnie said they'd be back, and then I would meet Val's sister, and she'd help me find my family. Calming, I climbed off the bed and took care of business—the stepstool Bonnie had pulled from thin air remained in place by the bathroom sink—and then I splashed water on my face and got a good look at myself for the first time in days. I seemed clean enough—I thought I'd better brush my hair before going anywhere, and maybe my teeth—and best of all, the last traces of the black eye Zio Luca had given me a week ago had faded to pale yellow.

When I'd first started nursery school, I'd been upset

that everyone else seemed to look like their parents, and I didn't. But now I was happy not to look like Zio Luca, whose brown eyes squinted in anger in his ruddy, fleshy face whenever I messed up, which seemed to happen with greater regularity those days. Zia Giulia was sallower, and though her platinum hair was pretty, it was brittle and didn't match her dark, permanently arched eyebrows. Having studied my one photograph for hours, I'd decided that I looked rather like a chubbier version of my mother—same hair, same nose, same mouth, a bit too large for our faces—but I had my father's eyes, round and hazel, fringed with long lashes. Sometimes I'd wondered if they would think I was pretty. Zia Giulia mostly complained about the way my hair snarled.

Satisfied, I wandered into the bedroom, but there was no sign of Val or Bonnie, and I didn't want to go back to bed. My clothes were neatly folded on the table, clean and fresh, but the pajamas Bonnie had given me were comfortable, and I wasn't ready to change. Instead, I peeked out at the garden beyond the curtains, a walled enclosure that appeared to open onto other rooms. Tall trees I couldn't name offered shade in the corners, and the neat flowerbeds lining the walls were filled with blooming bushes. I walked out on the flagstones in my bare feet, resisting the urge to pick the flowers, and then I turned my attention to the burbling fountain.

There were smaller flowerbeds at the base of the fountain, a three-tiered circular stone piece in the middle of the garden that cascaded into an artificial river of sorts, which flowed out of the garden and between the connected rooms. I traced its path with my eyes and saw another fountain in the distance—perhaps, I reasoned, they were all connected, and one could get around Val's house by boat. The low stone bridges across the fountain channels might make that difficult, but then maybe swimming was an option.

As I looked down into the channel, a glint of gold

caught my eye, then a flash of red among the green at the bottom. Fish, I thought—but no, not *real* fish. The mosaic lining the channels was alive with waving aquatic vegetation and darting fish, colorful shapes that moved within the neutral background tile as if they were true animals and plants, and I squealed as a few of the nearest fish seemed to peer out at me.

I had to take a closer look. Nightclothes and all, I slid into the channel, gasped at the cold water, then held my breath and ducked beneath the surface to play with the fish. They hid or swam away when my shadow fell over them, but soon, they seemed to regain their courage and emerged, swimming back and forth below me as I glided up and down the fountain.

And that was how Val found me: soaked, shivering, and chest-deep in the channel, having surfaced to breathe just as he stepped into the garden. Suddenly remembering that I had places to be that morning and was now a bedraggled mess, I stopped in my tracks and looked up at him, desperately trying to come up with an explanation that wouldn't make him angry. "Fish," I managed, pointing to the water. "There are fish—"

His look of surprise dissolved into laughter, and he reached down to pull me out of the fountain. "Yes, there are," he said, grinning. "Maybe I should have warned you. My sister made those, by the way, so we can blame her for your morning swim. Hungry?"

Suddenly, I was dry again, and Val coaxed me back into the bedroom, where a covered tray was waiting on the table beside my clothes. I gobbled the eggs and toast, too grateful to not be in trouble to complain that I didn't care for wheat bread, and then Bonnie stopped by to tidy me up. "That'll do," she said, tying my hair back with a ribbon. "Much more presentable. You have fun in England."

"England?" I echoed, wide-eyed. "How are we getting to…*oh*," I mumbled, seeing that Val had already opened another of the strange rips in the air.

Bonnie chuckled and patted my shoulder. "You'll get used to it, hon. Go on, now."

Val took my hand again, and we stepped through the hole into a meeting space, a windowless, stone-walled room dominated by an oval wooden table and six matching chairs. After closing the hole, Val cracked the door and peeked through, then opened it wider and motioned for me to join him. "Thank you for working us in, Toula," he said, heading across the spacious office toward the woman behind the desk, and I followed in his footsteps as I tried to make sense of her.

Val had said his sister was a *maga*—a wizard, to use the English term—and seeing her in person, I could believe it. She appeared to be about his age, but whereas Val seemed fairly ordinary—well, but for his eyes, which were no less strange by daylight—Toula looked the part, a tanned woman in a deep purple robe, which fell open to reveal a black T-shirt and leggings beneath it. She wore her black hair in a pixie cut only slightly longer than Val's, but she had streaked it with electric blue highlights that brought out her eyes, which didn't share the indescribably odd quality of her brother's. Still, I hung back, suddenly shy, and reached for Val's finger for reassurance. Noticing my touch, he looked down, smiled, and pulled me forward.

"This is Maria Corelli," he said by way of introduction. "Maria, this is Toula Pavli, Grand Magus of the Arcanum—"

"Toula's just fine," she interrupted, and motioned toward a couch and a pair of stiff-backed chairs. "Have a seat. We need to talk."

Puzzled, I followed Val to the couch, and Toula, carrying a folder of papers, took one of the chairs. "It helps to know Fringers," she said as she settled in. "They did a little digging last night for me."

"Oh?" said Val.

"*Oh* indeed." She slid a printout across the table. "Birth certificate for one Maria Corelli, parents Gianni Corelli and

Lucie Dubois, born in Rome. You're five, sweetheart?" she asked me.

"And a half," I mumbled.

"Then that's the right certificate. And here's a marriage certificate for Gianni and Lucie from Florence—he's an Italian national, she's French." She added a second piece of paper to my birth certificate. "You said they were artists, Val. I've got listings from a few shows in central and southern Europe with their names on them, and a couple of headshots…"

By the time she had their pictures on the table, I was off the couch and straining to see. "That's them! Papà and Mamma!" I exclaimed, and hastily pulled our family photograph from my pocket. "See? That's us."

Toula glanced at my photo and nodded. "Glad we're on the right track, then."

While I stared at my parents' pictures, Val asked, "Do you know of any wizards with those names?"

"No, but that doesn't mean anything," said Toula. She cleared her throat, then pulled a paper from her folder and held it to her chest. "Maria…do you know how your parents died?" When I nodded, she handed the paper to Val. "Train derailed outside Geneva. Looks like it was a freak accident. There were thirteen fatalities, including her parents."

He scanned the page, then put it face-down on the table. I couldn't see much through the thin paper, but the dark splotch in one quadrant made me think there was a photo there.

"So Maria moves in with Giulia Rossi," Toula continued, showing us both the next page. "Here, she's listed as Maria's legal guardian. And here's her marriage to Luca Zullo about a year later."

"Zia Giulia and Zio Luca," I confirmed.

Again, Toula hesitated, then handed Val another piece of paper. "Three days ago," she murmured.

Val read it over, frowning, then gave it back to her

without letting me see it.

"What's that?" I asked, looking back and forth between the adults for an explanation.

It was Val who finally broke the silence. "Maria," he said quietly, taking my hand, "you're never going back to Zio Luca. Everything will be fine."

But I could hear in his tone that he wasn't telling me everything. "What's wrong? What was that paper?"

"Val," Toula cautioned, "she's *five*."

He studied my face for a long moment, then traced the remnants of my black eye with his fingertip. "Luca cannot hurt you anymore. He, uh..." Val cleared his throat. "He died."

"*Died?*" I whispered, shocked. "Like...like Mamma and Papà?"

"Yes."

Death might have been a hazy proposition to some of my peers, but I had a decent understanding of the concept, thanks to Luca's frequent reminders about my parents' fate. Still, it took me a few seconds to slot together the puzzle pieces.

I'd last seen Luca in our burning flat. Fires killed people. And I'd started the fire.

Val's grip on my hand tightened as my eyes opened wide. "This is not your fault. You were defending yourself."

"But I didn't mean to hurt him! I...I didn't, I promise, I..."

As I started to cry, Toula came around the coffee table and rubbed my back. "It happens," she said softly. "Most of us find our talent gradually, learn how to control it, but if we're young and go through something really bad, really scary...sometimes, it comes all at once, and it's not pretty when it does. You're not the first, kid." A wad of tissue appeared in her hand, and I wiped at my eyes. "What we're going to do is figure out who your family is, and then we'll get you into one-on-one lessons so this doesn't happen again."

I still couldn't quite understand what I'd done, but the adults were being strangely reassuring about it, and so I sniffed and tried to calm down. When my breaths were no longer quite so hitching, Toula returned to her side of the table and held out her hands. "This won't hurt," she assured me. "Ask Val if you don't believe me. I'm just going to have a look at your background and see what matches I can pull."

She began to mutter incomprehensibly, and in a few seconds, a brightly glowing green orb appeared in front of my face, spinning slowly over the table. It wasn't solid, but rather a network of lines and swirls and spirals connected in a random jumble.

"Yeah, *that's* a wizard," Toula declared, "and with that sort of intensity, I wouldn't be shocked if…" Her voice petered out, and with a flick of her wrist, the orb ceased to rotate. "Hey, Val, take a look at this."

He rose and joined her, and he appeared surprised when he followed her finger. "Witch-blooded?"

"Ever so slightly. I doubt it's affecting her, but still, good to know. Now, let's see what we get when we look at her parents…"

The orb split in two, but as it did, it faded from brilliant green to dark blue.

Toula whistled low. "New-blood. *Shit.*"

"What does that mean?" I mumbled.

Seeming to remember my presence, she looked past the orbs at me and explained, "New-blooded wizards don't have long family lines in the magical community. *Really* new-blooded ones are kind of rare. It doesn't mean you're any less talented," she hastened to reassure me, "just that you're the first in your family."

"You can't help her, then," said Val.

Toula sighed and shook her head. "I'm sorry, honey, I really am, but I don't have the answers you were hoping for. Being first-generation new-blooded means that you almost certainly don't have any family in the Arcanum."

"She's not just new-blooded," Val reminded her.

"*Right.* Spontaneous witch-blood—I've never heard of that happening, but given how distant the fae line is…"

"Anyone you know?"

"Can't tell at this distance. I can check, but it's going to take me a minute."

"I'm in no hurry." He returned to the couch and patted my knee. "Don't worry, we'll figure something out," he told me as the orbs split over and over, each division containing a blue orb with an ever-stronger streak of red. "Toula will know what to do. This is mostly academic."

"Satisfying our curiosity," she agreed.

Finally, she split the orb for the last time, and it divided into red and blue halves. "Okay, let's see," she said, flattening the red one, then paused, scowled, and tapped the quartz ring on her left hand until an identical red lattice appeared in the air beside mine. "Guess who?" she muttered.

Val's eyebrows rose. "Mab?"

"Yeah. I've pulled a few signatures from our more distant nephews and nieces, so maybe there's a match in my bank…"

The red and blue orbs re-fused into the mixed lattice, and Toula flipped through sample after sample until she landed on a winner. "Well?" Val asked. "Who was it?"

Toula's teeth raked over her bottom lip for a few seconds before she met his gaze again. "You."

He laughed in disbelief. "*Me?* I've never fathered a child! Something's wrong with that ring of yours—"

"I had to go back seventy-five generations to hit you. This would have been a *fairly* long time ago, and your partner would have been mundane."

"Impossible. The only mortal I've ever been with was my wife, and…" He paused, his expression shifting from incredulity to horror. "No. No, that can't…surely, I didn't…"

"The ring's as accurate as it's ever been," she murmured. "I can't sit here and tell you without question that you had a child with Caecilia, but if she's really the only one…yeah, it looks that way."

By then, Val appeared stricken. "Excuse me," he mumbled, rising from the couch, and disappeared into the anteroom from which we'd come.

When the door closed behind him, I looked to Toula in confusion. "What's wrong? Did I do something—"

"No, honey, you didn't do anything," she said, and waved her hand until the orbs disappeared. "He's just had a surprise, and—" She paused at the sound of a knock on the door, then rolled her eyes in frustration and rose. "Sorry, one second."

There was an old man at the door when she opened it, and after speaking to him briefly—I couldn't understand their language—she turned to me and said, "Just a moment, Maria, I'll be back. Don't go anywhere."

The door slammed, and I sat alone in the big office, confused and scared. For several minutes, I studied the pictures of my parents again, but then, with only the ticking clock and my thoughts for company, I slid off the couch and went next door to check on Val.

I could tell he'd been crying—his eyes were swollen, and his face was blotchy and wet—and he was sitting in a chair, staring at a spot above the floor, when I let myself in. Hesitantly, I crept closer and whispered his name. He lifted his head as if dazed, and I fought the urge to run out the way I'd come when his eyes turned on me. "I'm sorry. I'm really sorry," I began, feeling the words tumble over each other in my rush to expel them. "I didn't mean to—"

"You did nothing wrong," he mumbled, and reached for me. I moved closer, and Val pulled me onto his lap.

"You're upset," I said, pivoting to face him.

"Sad."

"Why?"

He released a slow breath. "A very long time ago, I

married the most wonderful woman I've ever met. But soon after, I went away to war, and when I was out there…something happened. Like you and the fire."

"You hurt someone?"

"Saved him. It didn't matter, the men with me were scared. They made me leave. I couldn't go home—I would have put my family in danger if I'd gone back. But I never knew until now that she…that we…had a child."

"You never asked her?" I replied, confused.

"I never saw her again. And I abandoned my own child."

True, I wasn't a great judge of adult age, but Val appeared to be youngish. "You could find your child. Everything's on the computers, you could look there."

But he shook his head sadly. "I'm much older than I seem, little one. My child is long dead. But he or she must have had a child, and that child had a child, on and on, because one of those distant children's children is you."

My pulse quickened at the news. "We're family?"

Val paused, considering that, then slowly nodded. "Yes. Yes, exactly."

Before I could press him further, Toula came in. "*There* you are! Sorry, it apparently takes half a dozen magi to schedule a damn Council meeting." She leaned against the wall and folded her arms. "So, here's my thought. Maria can be raised as a ward of the Arcanum."

"Like you?" said Val.

She made a face. "I'll see that she's treated better. But we'll keep her here, get her the training she needs, and when she's ten, we'll slot her right into classes. As long as no one finds out about her, uh…*tainted* blood, she should be fine."

"You couldn't raise her?"

"Not well. The Council and the Conclave have me running at all hours…and besides, that would blow her cover if I let it be known I was taking in my grandniece. Even *distant* grandniece," she muttered. "No, it'd be best to put her with a young couple and be done with it."

I could tell by the look on his face that the idea sat poorly with Val. "Could Helen teach her what she needs to know for now?" he asked.

Toula nodded. "Sure, any magus could. It's not something I'd have to personally oversee."

He turned from her and looked me in the eye. "Would you like to come home with me? To stay, I mean. I'll take care of you."

"Really?" I said, beaming.

"Whoa, now, let's not be hasty," Toula interjected. "She needs training—"

"Which you just said Helen could provide," he countered.

"You're busy."

"I have aides for a reason."

"And you don't know the first thing about raising a kid!"

His face remained impassive. "If a twenty-year-old can figure it out, then so can I. Anyway, surely the Stowes will have a few tips."

"Val…"

"I brought Maria here to find her family," he interrupted, tightening his grip on me. "She did. And now I'm taking my granddaughter home."

"Just think this over," Toula urged him. "Take a day or two and consider—"

He lifted me into his arms and stood. "I am *not* abandoning another child," he said, and opened a hole back the way we had come. "Thank you for your help. I'll call Helen," he promised her, then carried me away.

Toula was a good sister, and she was thorough. At her insistence, Val allowed her to draw blood from both of us, but she returned empty-handed, unable to locate any hidden great-grandparents of mine or any other descendants of Val's. "As far as I can tell," she admitted to him, "unless someone's hiding *really* well, Maria's the end of your line. I might be able to find some distant cousins of hers if I keep digging, but right now, as it stands…"

"She's home," he replied.

"Be that as it may, when she's old enough, she's going to have to come back and get an education."

But that wasn't an immediate concern of mine. While the adults talked about my future, I sneaked out of Val's office and into the nearest courtyard to look in the fountain. The fish twinkled in the mosaic below, and without a care in the world, I jumped in.

CHAPTER 2

There may be better ways to grow up than as a virtual princess at the heart of Faerie, but I can't think of any.

It didn't take me long to understand exactly where in the pecking order I'd landed. Val—and by tacit agreement, he was always Val to me—was a king among the fae, and he made it abundantly clear to his staff and the rest of the court that I was not to be harmed. The other two monarchs, Eleanor and Coileán, reacted much as Toula had when he introduced me, but they warmed quickly enough, and every now and then, while I was still going through my pink and frilly phase, Eleanor would take me aside and whip up dresses that were properly swishy. Bonnie, who was of a more practical bent, just shook her head, but she helped me tie bows and fix crinolines, then cleaned off the stains I inevitably accumulated.

Bonnie was Val's chief of staff, in charge of keeping the rest of the aides in line and his schedule organized, and she added me to her slate of tasks without complaint. But while she made sure I was tidy and looked after me in her gruffly maternal way, Val doted. I spent my first few days there either in his office or in the adjacent garden, playing under his watchful eye, and I suspect that he would have been content to let me keep his odd hours until help arrived in the form of Martin and Rohese Stowe, thirteen-time parents who came at Eleanor's request to offer Val some guidance as to the management of small children. Sitting in the garden, brushing my new doll's hair—which always regrew, no matter how I cut it—I overheard snippets of their conversation. They insisted that I needed structure: rules, chores, a bedtime, a balanced diet.

To his credit, Val listened, though he was seldom strict with me. I tried to please him—I knew too well from experience what happened when adults around me were unhappy with my behavior—but my new reality didn't fully set in until the first time I broke something of his.

Val had stepped out of his office for a few minutes, leaving me unattended with my growing pile of toys, and my eye caught the sheen of the bronze sword mounted in easy reach behind his desk, just above a decorative table with a pair of low vases. Intrigued, I took a closer look, then climbed onto a chair to pull it free. It clattered out of my grip onto the stone, and, spooked by the racket, I hurried down to retrieve it and put it back. But the blade was heavy, far too big for me to wield single-handed, and so I awkwardly dragged it with me as I ascended the chair once more. Getting it into its mount was another story, and I grunted and strained as I tried to lift it into place. Unfortunately, I made the rookie error of wrapping my hands around the sharp edges, and when it slipped in my sweaty palms, it cut one of them open. I cried out and dropped the sword, and as it fell again, it knocked against one of the vases, sending it to the floor in a shower of colored glass.

Before I could begin to hide the evidence, Val returned and found me standing on his chair, clutching my bleeding hand and staring in fear at the mess I'd made. I thought he would beat me, but instead, he cleaned my wound, built a quick enchantment around it to heal the cut, then easily rehung the sword and waved the vase whole and back into its position. "I'd be happy to show you what to do with one of those swords," he said as I trembled on the couch, anticipating the blow, "but you'd need something smaller for now."

The expected beating didn't arrive, and I slunk around for the rest of the day, waiting and hoping he'd forgotten.

When there was still no sign of punishment by the time I climbed into bed, I'd recovered enough of my nerve to apologize for the vase. "An accident," Val said with a shrug, tucking me in, then paused and gave my face a more careful examination. I felt the intrusive sensation again in my mind—soon, I would recognize that as his search through my thoughts—and when it retreated, his shoulders slumped. "You thought I would...*no*, Maria," he sighed, pulling the blankets to my chin. "You hurt yourself. You learned. Why would I add to that?" Seeing my continued uncertainty, he bent closer and murmured, "No one will ever again do to you what Luca did. If he weren't dead, I would kill him myself. Sleep well." And with that, he cut the lamps and left me to unquiet dreams.

Perhaps Val wasn't the most orthodox of parental figures, but I can't say he didn't try.

True to his word, he arranged matters with Helen Carver, a former grand magus, who came over every day for weeks to assess and train me. At her suggestion, he also made arrangements with Wanda Fitzgibbon, a petite, gray-haired, soft-spoken woman who served as one of the Fringe settlement's therapists. Thanks to the Mulligan years, the Fringe's counselors had no lack of experience with traumatized children, and so, every day after my lesson, Helen would take me into town to Wanda's office of brightly colored plush couches and potted flowers to talk. Wanda always had cookies on hand, which endeared her to me, but what I found more intriguing was her conversation with Val when he picked me up after my first session. "For this to work, she has to know this is a place where she can speak freely," Wanda warned him. "If you go poking around"—she tapped her temple—"that's no longer the case. Do you understand?"

King or not, Val knew when to acquiesce, and Wanda became my trusted sounding board for years, helping me come to terms with what I'd done to Luca and navigate my relationship with my inexperienced but eager guardian.

It was fortunate for Val that he had willing help, as I arrived as damaged goods. I was clingy and desperate to please, and despite Val's reassurance, I cringed in anticipation every time I put a toe out of line. The adults around me walked a tightrope, stressing the importance of learning control while insisting that I wasn't bad for having fought back, and Wanda did her best to guide me as I struggled with what I had done. Gradually, she coaxed me into talking about my memories of my zia and zio, insisting that it was normal to miss them. While I did miss Giulia, the only mother I'd ever known, the one emotion I could summon concerning the Luca-shaped hole in my life was relief—and as I shared more of my past with Wanda, she began to understand why.

I didn't like to remember my zio. My earliest clear memory was from a summer evening when I was three. Zio Luca had been sitting on the steps of our building, drinking cheap wine and laughing with his friends. I'd been playing tag with a neighbor boy my age on the sidewalk, and I tagged him too hard. When he fell, he scraped his knees and began to bawl, and his father scooped him up and carried him inside. His evening interrupted, Zio Luca glared down at me and dragged me into our flat without a word, and the door had barely latched behind us before the beating commenced. Sloppy with drink, he hit me far too hard, and I finally tried to slide off his lap between blows. Instead, he caught me by the arm, but he pulled it the wrong way, and the next *crack* I heard wasn't on my legs but rather deep in my bones.

Zia Giulia told the doctors that I'd fallen from a stepladder. The look she gave me promised a world of punishment if I contradicted her account, and so I held my tongue and tried to stop crying while they fit me with a pink cast.

The night after Wanda dredged that memory up from the abyss in which I'd tried to hide it, I dreamed of Luca again, hitting me over and over...but when I looked at his face, it was blackened and smoking, burned to the bone in places, and I realized his lap was on fire, *I* was on fire, burning, choking, surrounded by the flames that smelled like drunk sweat and roasting meat...

I woke in a blind panic, panting in the darkness on drenched sheets, and I cried out and flailed at the blankets until a glowing hand pulled them away to disentangle me. "It's over, you're okay," a voice soothed, and I found a blonde stranger in jeans and a frumpy gray sweatshirt perched on the bed beside me. That would have been disconcerting enough, but the fact that the woman's radiance was throwing shadows on the wall left me wide-eyed and motionless with fear. Sensing my distress, she smiled and gently brushed my wet hair from my face. "I'm Ros, sweetie," she murmured. "You had a bad dream, that's all. Nothing to worry about."

It took me three tries before I managed to whisper, "You're very bright."

"I know," she replied, briefly grimacing. "Can't do anything about that. Do you want a drink of water?"

I nodded, and a glass appeared in her hand, complete with bendy straw. She eased me upright, and while I drank, she flipped my pillow and dried the evidence of my perspiration. When I finished and my heart began to slow, the glass vanished, and Ros tucked me in again. "I used to have those dreams, too," she said, leaning close to me as if confiding a great secret. "Just remember that he can't hurt you."

I watched her rise from my bed and smooth out the depression she'd left in the blankets. "How did you make them stop?" I asked, squinting a little as I stared at her.

Her smile seemed almost sad. "I don't really sleep anymore. But yours will get better—give it time," she said, and vanished.

In the morning, when I asked Val about my midnight visitor, he seemed unsurprised. "She's the consciousness of the realm," he explained over breakfast. "Ros won't harm you." When I remained unconvinced, he added, "She's Helen's daughter. I promise, she doesn't mean you ill."

If I'd been older, I might have been distressed at the notion that Ros was aware of everything that happened in Faerie and could pop by at any time. But I was five and a half, the contours of my mental map of the universe were still fuzzy, and so I accepted that she was a part of life, just as I accepted that magic was real and something I could learn to tame.

Still, the nightmares continued—sometimes my zio and fear and pain, but more frequently, I'd find myself in dark woods or on empty streets, running from a nameless terror and knowing I'd been abandoned, that help would never come, that everyone I knew was gone forever. After one such dream, I woke in tears and ran from my room, desperate to find Val, but the villa was quiet, the gardens empty and silent but for the bubbling fountains. Barely conscious of where I was going, I made it outside the walls and into the wide mountain meadow in which the complex was nestled, and I ran barefoot through the tall grass, half blind with panicked tears. The loud crack of an opening gate behind me pulled me to a halt, and as I turned, Val hurried through and hoisted me into his arms, murmuring comfort as I sobbed. After a moment, he created a blanket around me and carried me back into Coileán's office, where the Three had been meeting. "Thank you," he said, and I looked up from his wet shoulder in time to see Ros disappear.

Val held me until I fell asleep, and when I woke the next morning, he was in a chair beside my bed, watching me. "You're safe, child," he said, taking my hand as I reached for him. "I would never leave you, Maria, I swear it."

I knew that he meant it, and nothing he did gave me reason to doubt his sincerity—I wasn't in the realm a month before I had him wrapped securely about my little finger. Still, no matter how much I talked with Wanda or how many times Val caught me running from my room in the middle of the night, I couldn't quite dislodge the deep fear that my good fortune was temporary—that everyone would abandon me in the end.

My fear wasn't entirely unfounded.

I asked Val only once if I might see Zia Giulia again. He seemed hesitant, but that night, he walked me past my old building, now covered in tarps and scaffolding as the fire damage was being repaired. A poster in the front window announced that the building was for sale. I unlocked the front door with our combination and ran upstairs to our old flat, but it was nothing but plastic sheeting and paint cans, and the stairwell was empty. Of Giulia, there was no sign.

Years later, I dug through enough records until I located her in Florence, married again and with three children of her own. If she ever tried to find me, the documents were silent.

All through that first spring and mild summer, I worked with Helen to tame my wild talent. She showed me how to focus on my breathing as a tool to tamp down strong emotions, and we practiced daily until I learned to calm myself to a place where I was once again in control. "Spellcraft takes precision," she explained. "If you act on impulse instead of planning it out, you won't get a good result."

"Like Zio Luca?" I mumbled.

"Well, yes, but not in the way you're thinking," she said gently. "Someday, once you've had enough practice, you'll be able to cast successfully by reflex. Shields, bolts, all of that combat stuff will become second nature in time." She thrust out her arm in demonstration, and a complex shield seemed to erupt from her hand, a precise, glowing construction of active magic. "Now you try."

I mimicked her movements, but what came forth was small and jagged, a jumble of haphazardly flashing reinforcements that looked more like a knotted necklace chain than a proper shield. Before I could grow too frustrated, Helen moved to my side and began to teach me, coaxing order from the chaos until my shield resembled a cut-down version of hers. I couldn't hold it together for long, but she smiled with satisfaction when it fell apart. "A good effort," she decreed. "*That* is why we learn to focus. And the more you make shields like that, the quicker they'll come."

I tried again to summon one forth, but my second attempt was only marginally better than my first, and I sighed in disappointment. "It's still messy."

At that, Helen squatted in front of me and waited until I met her eyes. "Do you know when I made my first shield, Maria? I was seven, and I was far ahead of my classmates. Most wizards don't even start learning to do what we're doing until they're ten or so. Be patient, honey. Heck," she said, ruffling my hair as she stood, "we haven't even started playing with wands yet."

"Wands?" I asked, intrigued. I'd had one once, a piece of glittery plastic with a silver star and purple streamers on the end, but I'd lost it with the rest of my old life.

"They make casting easier," she explained. "But seeing what you can already do without one, I think we should wait a few years before putting a wand in your hands."

"But—"

"Nope. The other part of learning to focus is getting you to the point that you don't accidentally lash out with a spell. You've got to show me you can be responsible before I arm you."

Chastised, I finished my lesson without protest, though I brought the matter up with Val at bedtime. But even he balked at the notion of outfitting me with a wand. "We're going to do whatever Helen thinks best," he said as I brushed my teeth. "And if she doesn't think you're ready, then I'm not going to argue with her."

I spat and rinsed out my mouth. "What if I just got a little one?" I wheedled. "For practice?"

"They aren't toys," he replied, and shepherded me to bed. "You'll grow into one soon enough." I frowned up at him, stymied, and he chuckled as he handed me the small menagerie of stuffed animals with which I'd taken to sleeping. "Let me tell you a secret," he said as he tucked me in. "The best wizards don't need wands. Helen doesn't use one, does she?"

"No…"

"Then learn from her." He kissed me goodnight, waved the lamps off, and opened the door, but he paused before taking his leave. "Wanda thought keeping a light burning in here might help. Want to try it?" I nodded, and after brief consideration, he gestured toward my bed. The canopy began to shimmer like stardust, gently pulsing in soft busts of color, and I snuggled in among my animals to watch the show until my eyes grew heavy and I fell into mercifully dreamless sleep.

When September rolled around and the Fringe settlement's school went back into session, Helen decided that I could be let loose around other children without serious risk of maiming. To say that the school staff were less than thrilled at the prospect would be a gross understatement, but whereas the more vocal parents had once been able to drive out Ros and even the principal's quarter-blooded son for safety reasons, they backed down when Val announced that I would be getting an education, and that was that. Those Fringers not born in Faerie had come there as refugees twenty-five years before, and Val didn't hesitate to quietly remind the holdout protesters of their precarious footing in the realm.

By the same token, it was also drilled into me that I was not to use magic at school under any circumstances short of a dire emergency. Duly warned, I settled in for my first weeks of formal instruction—all in Fae, or at least the creolized version common in town. The original evacuees had spoken dozens of languages, and while all had been given the local tongue to assist with their resettlement, most spoke their first language at home. Their children had grown up multilingual by default, and anyone with an ear for languages could pick out snippets of English, Chinese, Spanish, Hindi, Russian, and more among their slang. If the eleven other children in my class knew where I'd come from, they didn't seem to care, and by the end of my first week, I was beginning to learn the nuances of their vernacular on the playground and over lunch.

I turned six on my second Friday in school, and Bonnie saw to it that I had cupcakes for the occasion. She also surprised me with a cake at breakfast—almond-flavored with chocolate frosting, my favorite thing to have come out of the villa's kitchen—and Val watched bemusedly as she set the candles alight. "It's tradition," she explained. "And once a year, this counts as a balanced breakfast."

I blew the candles out and licked the chocolate from the bottom of each as Bonnie did the honors. "Pretty big occasion," she said, sliding a generous piece of cake in front of me. "You've got to start counting on *both* hands now, huh?"

I held up one hand and my other thumb and grinned before diving into my sugary breakfast. Bonnie took hers to go, leaving Val to prevent me from gorging myself while the responsible parties' backs were turned. Between bites, and hoping for more celebrations in the near future, I asked him when his birthday might be. "First of June," he replied, producing espresso from the ether.

"You didn't have a cake," I pointed out.

"I did not."

This struck me as odd. For all else she might have done, Zia Giulia always made sure that I had *something* sweet for the occasion, and I couldn't imagine willingly forgoing the opportunity to indulge. "You don't like it?"

"Oh, no," said Val, "this is quite good. But once you've had enough birthdays, you tend to let them go by without much notice."

I couldn't imagine such a scenario. "How many?" I pressed, and tried to think of a large number. "Forty?"

"More than that."

"Forty-five?"

"Higher." He put down his fork and regarded me curiously. "How old do you think I am?"

At that, I could only shrug and guess. "Fifty?"

Val laughed and shook his head. "If I've counted accurately…two thousand, two hundred forty-one."

I stared at him, then at my cake, and tried to conceive of how much larger a cake he would require to fit that many candles, let alone what sort of breath control it would take to blow out a conflagration of that size. Suddenly, six didn't seem very old at all.

Before I could puzzle through the full ramifications of that information, Val leaned toward me and whispered, "All right, Bonnie isn't looking. Seconds?"

I nodded, happy to be part of the conspiracy, and wolfed down the next piece to make it to school on time.

That evening, Val took me back to Rome, to his favorite gelateria, and we sat on a fountain and watched the weekend pedestrians go by as we ate. "You're lucky, Maria," he remarked, digging in with his little plastic spoon. "We didn't have this when I was your age."

I wasn't sure I wanted to imagine a world without gelato. "Why not?"

"No real way to freeze it. Every now and then, you'd find crushed ice with fruit or honey, but nothing like this." He licked the spoon clean and smiled with contentment. "Certainly not bacio. I wish we'd come up with it."

Val had told me almost nothing about his past until then, and curious, I pressed him. "Where did you come from?"

"Here. It didn't look anything like this back then, but…well, that's time for you."

The old stone buildings around us seemed immutable, and I frowned at Val. "What did it look like?"

He hesitated, then put his dessert aside and took my hand. "We're not going anywhere, and this is just illusion," he murmured, "so don't panic. Want to see?"

I held on tight and nodded, and the city…*blinked*.

Light returned once again to the sky as the buildings around us changed to a series of three-story edifices, their lowest level accessible via arched entrances. Balconies hung from some of the higher floors. The concrete and asphalt below our feet was replaced by a stone plaza, and across the way, I could make out street vendors' stalls—fruit and fish, perhaps. Strangely dressed men and women milled about, shouting children ran among them, and a pair of dogs barked at each other from competing balconies. Six men walked by, straining under the weight of a wooden litter, and the crowd slowly made way.

I stood, gelato forgotten, and would have ventured into the crowd to explore if not for Val's insistent tug on my hand. A few seconds later, the vision cleared, and I was back in the noisy nighttime square, standing near the edge of the pavement. "I didn't want you walking into traffic," said Val, pulling me back to our fountain seats.

I plopped down beside him, wide-eyed. "That was *here*?"

"Perhaps. With the way the city has changed, it's difficult to tell. But that's a place I remember."

Replaying what I'd seen, I retrieved my gelato and picked through the sensory impressions before finding one that bothered me. "I couldn't understand what they were saying."

Val glanced up at the streetlights, then back at me. "The language changed, too. Everything did."

He seemed suddenly melancholy, and I gripped his finger. "Will you show me again? I won't walk off."

"If you like," he replied, then brushed my temple with his free hand. "And here, if you want to listen…"

Once again, I felt the strange, painless explosion as Val inserted another language into my mind. "Let me give you the proper tour," he said, the words foreign yet familiar, and the night vanished around us.

But nothing good lasts forever, even in Faerie.

"You're off your game today," said Helen, stopping me as I haphazardly threw a stack together. My wards were coming along to her satisfaction—after four and a half years under her tutelage, I was performing far beyond what could be expected of a ten-year-old wizard—but my mind was wandering that afternoon. "Somewhere you'd rather be?"

"No," I mumbled, letting the half-constructed stack fall apart.

"If your friends went swimming or something—"

"It's not that," I snapped. The mention of my classmates only worsened my mood.

Helen gave me a long look of consideration. "Did you have a fight with Val?"

I shook my head, then folded my arms on the table and rested my chin atop them.

"So what's the matter?" she asked, mimicking my pose.

Sighing, I did as Helen had taught me and fought for calm, keeping my emotions on a short tether even though I wanted nothing more than to throw the furniture into the walls to blow off stress. "Val told me I'm not going to school in town this year. He's sending me away to Glastonbury."

"It's time."

"I don't *want* to go! I like it here! All my friends are here, and…and…and why can't I stay?" I finished lamely.

She didn't flinch in the face of my outburst. "Because there's no finer place than Glastonbury to learn spellcraft."

"But couldn't you keep teaching me?"

"Sure." She shrugged. "The mechanics, at least. But you need to meet other wizards your age, Maria, and I can't duplicate that here. Val's right to send you over."

My eyes began to prick, and I blinked hard to hide the evidence. "I don't want to go."

"It's not forever," said Helen, squeezing my shoulder. "And you'll only be a day student, right? You're not boarding, are you?"

"No…"

"See? Just a few hours a day, honey. This isn't the end of the world." With that, Helen rose from the table and stretched. "I think we've done all the good work we can do today. Why don't you go enjoy the sun?"

But I was too anxious to do more than try to read in the garden. My new school started in three days, earlier than the Fringe school, and as Val hadn't given me much advance warning, my mind was working overtime. I hadn't been back to the mortal realm without him since I'd moved to Faerie, and suddenly, I was to go to England, of all places, with a class of strangers. In the last two days, Toula, who was natively fluent, had given me the necessary language, and Val had taken me late one night to see Dr. Powell, the Arcanum's in-house medic, for a course of vaccinations. The look she'd given him once she realized how far off schedule I'd slipped spoke of naked frustration, and she'd jabbed me at least half a dozen times before letting me leave.

Val had done his best to make the change sound exciting. As grand magus, one of Toula's first initiatives had been to overhaul the Arcanum's educational system, which theretofore had consisted of night classes in the installations with the occasional bit of remote instruction. Instead, she built an entire school within Arc 2, the castle where the Arcanum kept its headquarters, incorporating both mundane and magical classes. With the subjects integrated, young students weren't stuck with hours of mundane homework after hours of night school. The Glastonbury experiment had yet to run a class of students all the way through—my first year was only the school's eighth—but many of the older graduates had gone on to university, and still others had stayed to do independent research or work as Council aides until they were twenty and, at least by the Arcanum's reckoning, adults. With the early success of the program, Toula had built a dormitory and invited boarding students from regions too off-synch with Glastonbury to make scheduling practicable, but some of the more far-flung students still made the daily commute, and a few of the teaching magi were on hand every morning and evening to open the necessary gates.

I wouldn't be boarding, Val assured me—I'd be coming home every night, even if Faerie's days were less than predictable, and "night" could very well be high noon before long. But that did little to reassure me. In Faerie, I knew that Ros kept an eye on me and that Val would drop anything if I needed him. In Glastonbury, I'd be on my own, operating with a cover story about commuting from Italy—and Toula had warned me that for my sake, I couldn't let on that we were acquainted, let alone kin. "I want them to see you for the wizard you are," she'd explained. "That means leaving Val and me out of the picture."

And though I'd expressed in the clearest of terms how little I liked this idea, Val put his foot down. I was going, and the plan wasn't up for discussion.

The night after my aborted lesson with Helen, I stared at my twinkling canopy, unable to shut off. I'd picked at my dinner, and though Val assured me I'd like Glastonbury, I wasn't buying it. My bedtime companions had by then been whittled down to a stuffed brown dog, and I stroked its lifelike fur as I tried to will myself to sleep. Just as I'd decided to throw in the towel and sit in the garden—stargazing was at least as restful as what I was doing in my bedroom—I caught a flash to my left and rolled over to see Ros heading toward me. "Something you should see," she said without preamble, and a projection like a screen appeared over my head, blocking my canopy from view.

I realized she was showing me Val's office, and there he was with Toula, sitting on the couch and drinking coffee. "What are they—"

"Shh, watch," Ros interrupted, and I did as she bid.

"There's nothing tying her to either of us," said Toula, crossing her legs. "'Corelli' won't set off any alarms, and there are enough commuters from Arc 3 regions that she'll blend right in. Arnold and two of the Inner Council know, and that's it. And Frank, but he'll keep his mouth shut. She'll be fine."

But Val frowned in thought as he sipped his coffee. "Helen says there's a touch of enchantment in her work. If someone notices—"

"It's not much. We've talked." She paused, then asked, "Did Ros have anything to do with that?"

"No. She says Maria's fae blood reacts to the realm. And has Helen told you what she's capable of?"

"Ahead of you, big brother," Toula replied. "I'm going to pretest her tomorrow, see what sort of wand she can handle. If the kid's already on pine, I'd rather know now and doctor one up to keep that a secret. There's no sense in calling extra attention to her."

Val drank again, wrapping his hands around the mug and staring at the wall. "What if we waited a year? Let Helen continue to work with her, make sure she's ready to—"

"It'll only be harder for her if we wait. Put her in now while everyone is new and clueless together." She hesitated. "Unless you plan to keep her here forever, she needs to understand the Arcanum."

"*You* don't even fully understand the Arcanum," he muttered.

"I understand enough."

"And the Conclave?"

Toula groaned and leaned back into the couch. "Can we not talk about that? Please?"

Val watched her over his mug. "Bad news?" he asked, softening.

"More defections. The Morse and Conrad boys I expected, but Arc 1 says we've lost a few of the folks who used to run in Russell Mulligan's orbit. I thought they'd learned from his example, but apparently not."

I scowled at the projection, trying to make sense of their conversation, but before I could ask Ros for clarification, Toula changed the subject.

"So, have you given any thought to what we talked about regarding Maria?" she asked, turning back to him.

Val flashed a quick grimace. "Not as such..."

"Marcus Valerius—"

"She's not yet ten!" he protested. "Surely we don't need to plan her future tonight, do we?"

"No," Toula conceded, "but I want to know how much pushback I'm going to get if baby girl eventually decides she wants to go to college or get a job or...I don't know, join an ashram in Tibet."

"An *ashram*?"

"Pick your favorite hypothetical. Are you going to raise hell if she graduates and doesn't immediately come home?"

Val pushed himself from the couch and headed for the open door onto one of the gardens. After staring into the night for a long moment, he murmured, "I'm terrified."

"She's going to be fine," said Toula.

"You can tell me that for the next ten years, and I'll still be terrified. If she were to need me..." His voice, already low, faded out.

Toula rose and joined him at the door. "She's growing up," she said gently. "There's nothing in the first-year class that she can't handle, I'm sure of it. You've got to let her stand on her own." When he made no reply, she touched his shoulder and leaned closer. "She's mortal. If she wants a life in that realm, she has to make it now. Don't hold her prisoner."

"I wouldn't, I want her to be happy," he protested, "but…"

"But?"

Val struggled for a moment before he answered her. "What if she doesn't come back in time?"

"Like…she stays over until she's seventy or so? Have you met our nephew's wife, by any chance? Badger seems to be doing just fine."

"I know, I know," he muttered, "but…still."

Toula gave him space to compose his thoughts, then said, "Maria's going to grow up, Val. She may even grow old. It has to be her choice. I mean, unless Ros is feeling generous…"

"She won't."

"You've already asked about the deal?"

"Years ago. She says it's too risky."

Her forehead furrowed. "Ros doesn't feel confident enough yet to try, or what?"

"Maria isn't sufficiently fae," he quietly explained. "Ros said it was excruciating for Aiden and Joey, and they were so much closer. 'Lava bath' is how Joey described it, actually. Ros said that if she made the attempt with Maria, the pain alone would probably kill her."

The two were silent for a while, and finally, Toula cleared her throat. "You know, the Stowes thought for years that they'd lose their daughter, and look at Vivi now. Happy, healthy, still quite mortal, and not going anywhere. At this rate, I think she might run the Fringe settlement until the end of time."

"We spoke," said Val, still staring into the darkness. "The Stowes advised me to send Maria to Glastonbury, let her make her own decisions."

"And you're not happy?"

"She's not yet ten. How can she know what she

wants?"

With that, Ros cut the feed, and I sat up in bed, blinking at the sudden shift in light. "I wanted you to understand that Val doesn't like this any more than you do," she said, leaning against a bedpost. "But it's for the best. Give it a try—you might be surprised, you know."

"Wait," I called as she began to fade, and she brightened again. "What were they talking about? What deal?"

"I was hoping you wouldn't catch that," Ros muttered. "Uncle Aiden is technically a fifty-fifty witch-blood, and my dad's only one-sixteenth fae. You wouldn't know it because my predecessor was able to make some modifications, if you will. I've tried to think of a way I could do the same for you," she said, sounding apologetic, "but every scenario I come up with ends in disaster. I'm sorry, honey."

"It's okay." I shrugged, not fully comprehending. "Hey, Ros?"

"Mm?" she asked, once again pausing in her departure.

"What's the Conclave?"

"Oh, boy," she muttered, and took a seat at the foot of the bed. "So, you know that my mom was briefly grand magus, right?" I nodded, and she made a face. "You've heard about what James Mulligan did?"

Again, I nodded. Even the sanitized version was gruesome: he'd had a good portion of the Fringe murdered, kidnapped and tortured more of them, and locked Helen away in stasis, stealing unborn Ros from within her when she was powerless to fight back.

"Well, once Mom got free and Coileán and Eleanor offered backup, Mulligan and his cronies went down. Mulligan was executed, everyone else was bound and put on permanent probation. You follow?"

"Yeah…"

"So Mom stepped down, and Arnold Lowe took over as grand magus, and then he handed it off to Bert Wold.

But by then, some of the probationers—including my loving grandparents," she muttered—"teamed up with Coileán's daughter—"

I frowned. "He has a daughter?"

"Not anymore. She was leading part of what's now Val's court. Anyway, they attacked the realm, my predecessor sacrificed herself, I got this gig as omniscient busybody, and Toula told the Arcanum that she was volunteering as the next grand magus, and anyone who disagreed could fight her for it. The Council magi are many things, but no one was that stupid. '

"She's that strong?"

"In wizard terms, she's *scary*. But since she took the job more or less by force, and since she's a witch-blood with questionable parents, a decent chunk of the Arcanum wasn't thrilled to have her at the helm, especially once she started executing the probationers who'd joined up with Moyna. I mean, in fairness, they *did* violate their probation, but that doesn't matter to a particular subset of the Arcanum that…well, you'll see soon enough, I'm sure," she muttered. "Suffice it to say that while Toula was getting settled in, most of the remaining probationers and others who just don't like having her around fled the installations, joined forces, and dubbed themselves the Conclave. They sent her a formal letter and everything, claiming they were a new arcanum and demanding official recognition."

"Did Toula go along with it?"

"That's the sticky bit," said Ros. "Technically, the Arcanum doesn't recognize any wizard organization but itself—it was formed by conquering all the others, see? But there's another group out there, the Minor Arcanum, much less organized, and they were a massive help to the Fringe during the Mulligan era. Toula, if not the Arcanum, recognizes them. Now, what's she supposed to do about the Conclave?" She shrugged. "If she takes the hardline approach and goes after them, she'll upset the Minor

Arcanum, but if she recognizes them, she'll look weak."

"What happened, then?"

"A whole lot of nothing. Toula's biding her time," Ros explained, and stood. "It should blow over before too long, anyway. All of the known crafters live here, and since none of them are working for the Conclave, those wizards will either have to go wandless or re-assimilate eventually. But that's not a problem for tonight," she said, and began to fade out. "Get some rest, Maria, and don't worry about Glastonbury. You're going to be fine." Just before she disappeared, she added, "If something *does* goes wrong and you're in a pinch, look for Frank. I'll let him know you're coming."

That was poor consolation—I knew Frank only by the little I'd gleaned from Ros, and what I knew *of* him was that he was a full-grown dragon, apparently hiding somewhere around Arc 2. I'd seen dragons in Faerie—half a dozen of them lived near Coileán's palace, and on occasion, one would fly north over Val's territory—but I was leery of lizards of any size, much less the rideable kind, and so I decided to give Frank a wide berth.

Alone with my thoughts, I stared up at the gentle lights of the canopy until I succumbed to uneasy sleep.

CHAPTER 3

The person who designed the participant bleachers in the castle's competition room did so without much regard for anatomy. Even at my size, there was little legroom between the rows, and the wooden bench pressed against my bones. I wasn't the only one shifting uncomfortably—the other thirty-one kids in my year fidgeted as badly as I did, prodded by a combination of sore bottoms and nervous energy.

I had no reason to be anxious. Toula and Helen had tested me two days before, and after making me try out a variety of wands, they'd agreed that I could start with maple and amber. I'd had no idea whether that was good or bad until Toula left and Helen explained the wand system to me. "Solid wand for a mid-level wizard, very high-end for a child," she'd said. "I tested to maple first, and so did Ros." She'd hesitated, then added, "We did put a pine wand in your hand, and you pulled that off, too, but maple's a better starting point."

"What's wrong with pine?" I'd asked.

"Nothing. Wands don't get any weaker than that, and it's one step away from doing wandless work." Before I could protest that I did wandless work with her all the time, she'd said, "Equipping a first-year with a pine wand would be an extraordinary measure, and I don't think you want that kind of attention."

She was right—I had enough on my mind just keeping my story straight without dealing with wand scrutiny as well.

Toula told me that she didn't care for the wand ceremony—all it did was give the incoming class performance anxiety—but tradition dictated that we be subjected to it, and she chose her battles. The more comfortable spectator stands above the floor level were stacked with parents, siblings, and other family and friends proudly waiting to see what their first-year could do. There was, of course, no one there to watch me, so if I managed to tumble down the bleachers, at least I wouldn't be an embarrassment to anyone.

We'd been seated alphabetically for the event. The boy to my right spent the entire waiting period chatting with another boy in the row behind us—his longtime best friend, from the sound of it—but the girl to my left was quiet and, at least by our standards, still. When we glanced each other's way at the same time, she smiled nervously, then looked at her feet.

Trying not to be rude, I gave her a quick examination out of the corner of my eye. She was slight and pale, her hair barely darker than dandelion fluff and braided to her waist. A stray short lock had escaped, which she kept tucking behind her ear. Her eyes were a deep green, and the space between and below them was sprinkled with freckles. Noticing me watching her, she turned in her seat and mumbled, "Hi."

"Hello." Though I'd practiced my new English with Helen the day before, the words still felt funny in my mouth. "I'm Maria," I offered.

"Kitty." She cocked her head and studied me in turn. "Spanish?"

"Italian."

"Oh. Why aren't you going to school at Arc 3, then?"

"This one is supposed to be better." I replayed her question, comparing her accent to the voices around me, then guessed, "Australian?"

"American," she said, giggling.

"You're boarding?"

Kitty nodded. "Too many time zones. It's easier this way."

"Didn't want to go to school at Arcanum 1?" I asked.

At that, Kitty's expression briefly clouded. "My mom...she's really busy, and I've got a baby sister now, so she's *super* busy, so..." She shrugged. "Boarding school's best for everyone."

She didn't sound convinced.

"Where's your family sitting?" she asked, turning and craning her neck to peer at the seating in the upper level.

"They aren't," I replied. "Only me."

Kitty regarded me curiously. "Busy?"

"No, um..." I ran through the story I'd rehearsed, making sure I had it straight one last time, then said, "I'm...new-blooded. That's what you call it, yes?"

She nodded. "Very new?"

"The first. It's just my grandfather and me, and he wants me to have an education, but he's, uh...not a wizard..."

"Mundane," Kitty supplied.

"Thanks. And he thought coming here would be uncomfortable."

I didn't have Val's mental talents, but from the look on Kitty's face, I'd sold it.

"Yeah," she muttered, "sometimes people can be jerks. But you don't live with your parents?"

"They're dead."

Though I stared ahead at the table stacked with wand boxes, I saw Kitty's face begin to color from the corner of my eye. Instead of attempting to retract the question, however, she mumbled, "My dad died back in June."

When I turned to her again, I found her once more examining her shoes, newish Mary Janes with a hint of purple sparkles in the leather. "I'm sorry."

She offered a noncommittal shrug. "At least I have Mom. You've lost both of yours."

"Yes, but I was too young to remember them," I

countered. "It probably hurts more when you know what you're missing."

Kitty considered that, then barely nodded. "I lived with Daddy on our farm in Tennessee. Mom has to stay in Montana at the silo, but Daddy liked the old farm. He grew sunflowers," she said, and the ghost of a smile crossed her face. "But right after school let out for vacation, I went out to get the mail—it's about a quarter-mile from the house to the mailbox, see—and when I got back..." Her voice faltered.

"Accident?" I murmured.

She shook her head. "Aneurysm. Probably didn't hurt. So then I went to Montana with Mom and Beth—that's my baby sister, Beth—and Mom set it up so I could go to school here."

"What about your sunflowers?"

"They're someone else's now. Mom sold the farm. She said she didn't have time to take care of it."

I turned to look into the crowded seating for a hint of a face like Kitty's. "Did she bring your sister?"

Kitty's voice was far too calm to be natural. "She couldn't make it. Her job's very important, and Beth's too young to stay alone, so..."

When Kitty fell silent, I nudged my knee into hers, and she looked up, startled. "Then I suppose I could cheer for you, and you could cheer for me, and maybe no one will notice the difference."

That earned a small grin. "Yeah?"

"Yeah."

"What if we mess up down there?"

"How could you possibly mess up?" I asked. "As long as one of the wands works, isn't that enough?" My stomach clenched as an unpleasant thought occurred to me. "We're not getting graded on wand skills already, right? Or was there summer homework I was supposed to do?"

"No, there's no homework," said Kitty, eyeing the

wand boxes. "But if you don't get a good wand...you know."

"Uh...no?"

"Right, new-blood," she mumbled, as if reminding herself that I might be slow on the uptake. "If you don't get a good wand, it'll be embarrassing. Everyone's watching, and they'll see—"

"Your mother isn't here," I pointed out. "No pressure."

"Maybe."

"Well," I said, nudging her again, "whatever happens, we're all leaving here with wands."

Before she could argue with me, the lights flickered, and Toula walked out toward the table of boxes, accompanied by a gray-haired man in a black robe and glasses. "That's the grand magus," Kitty whispered. "And that's Magus Lowe. He used to be grand magus when we were really little."

I recognized the name from my last talk with Ros, but I played dumb. "You know them?"

"*Me*? No, just their faces."

We watched quietly, fidgeting on our uncomfortable benches as little as possible, as Toula made her welcome remarks. All too soon, she concluded, gave us a reassuring smile, and picked up a clipboard from the table. "Let's see...Colby Abernathy? Great, there you are," she said as the pudgy boy two seats to Kitty's left rose. "Come on down, let's get you equipped."

Helen and Toula had explained the process to me, but I watched with interest as Toula produced a series of cubes in the middle of the room, ranging in size from a paving stone to Val's personal weaponry locker. "Let's give this one a try," she said, putting a long wand in his hand, and gestured toward the cubes. "Anything you want. Lift one, spin it, set it on fire, whatever floats your boat."

Colby took aim at one of the midsized cubes and mumbled, and it exploded like a popped balloon. He jumped back in alarm, and Toula patted his shoulder as the parents good-naturedly twittered. "Too much wand. Here." She exchanged the stick in his shaking fist for one she'd pulled from a red wand box. "Ash. Try again, it's okay."

He preemptively flinched as he casted, but the box rose that time and began a slow rotation, and Magus Lowe scribbled on the clipboard. "Ash it is," said Toula, raising her voice for the benefit of the parents, and the gallery applauded as Colby, beaming, made his way back to the bleachers on unsteady legs.

Next up was a boy with the unfortunate name of Mortimer Burnside, who also walked away with an ash wand. As he tested the models out, Kitty gave me a quick, whispered tutorial. "Ash and phoenix blood is good. The grand magus started testing them with oak and unicorn horn—that's the one in the blue boxes—and it's *okay*, but not great."

"What's the difference?" I asked, feigning ignorance.

"Wand strength. It's kind of like eyeglasses, or so my dad said," she explained. "If your eyes are great already, you don't need a strong prescription. Magi and wizards like them use pine wands, and those barely do anything."

"Why not give them a stronger wand?"

"Messes up your casting. Like, it overcorrects. Say you're trying to start a fire. If you use a wand that's way too strong, your spell goes haywire, and you might make an explosion instead. Or, say, if you're doing something delicate, like building a ward, too much wand might make you break it."

Kitty pointed to the laden table. "If you're really good, you'll get one of the old willows—those are the purple boxes, they're all recycled—or there's a new one that's been going around, birch with composite cores. Orange boxes, I think. They're like willow wands, but they don't have merrow in them." She grimaced at the notion. "And if you're really, *really* talented, you'll get a maple wand," she concluded, pointing out the black boxes on the far-right end of the table.

"What about those?" I asked, indicating the yellow boxes at the opposite side.

Kitty's shoulders tightened as she glanced at them. "Dragonscale," was all she would say, and before I could press her for an explanation, Toula had called her name.

"Katherine Connolly?" Toula smiled and beckoned her to the front. "So glad you're here," she said, taking her by the shoulder, and scanned the crowd. "Where's Magus Stanhope sitting?"

"Couldn't come," Kitty said, shrinking under Toula's touch. "My sister—"

"Of course," she said too quickly, and smiled again at Kitty as if nothing were amiss. "Let's see, now…how about we try one of these?"

It seemed that Toula was starting everyone with an oak wand, and Kitty held hers as if she'd caught a venomous snake by the tail. "Just breathe," said Toula, giving her shoulder a last squeeze of reassurance, and stepped back while Kitty took aim at one of the small boxes. I saw Kitty's lips move, and her wrist flicked like she was cracking a whip, but nothing seemed to happen—the box remained stubbornly where it lay, unharmed. Flushing, Kitty tried again on an even smaller box, but it, too, remained apathetic to her frantic attempt at casting.

"It's okay," Toula soothed, taking the oak wand from Kitty, and Magus Lowe opened one of the yellow boxes and handed its wand down the table. "Give this one a try," she said lightly. "Sometimes it takes a few minutes before you find a good fit."

Kitty clutched the new wand and stared at the cubes, her right arm trembling. She raised the wand and sighted down the smallest of the bunch, the one barely larger than a brick, and her lips moved as she cast.

When nothing happened, the room, which had begun to mutter in concern, fell silent.

She jabbed the wand toward the box as if fencing with an unseen opponent and whispered, "Move." When that garnered no result, she pleaded, "*Move*," with more frantic intensity, but the box remained perfectly still.

The rumbling of the crowd resumed, but its voices had taken on a new tenor. Kitty had flushed scarlet, while behind her, Toula and Magus Lowe were shooting each other questioning looks. After half a dozen unsuccessful attempts, Toula stepped toward Kitty again, but then, with a furious, wordless cry, Kitty focused everything she had on the tiny box—and slowly, it rose a few wobbling inches above the floor before dropping and tumbling to a halt.

Kitty still held the wand out, panting and shaking with the exertion, and the spectators began to converse more loudly. Still, I heard Toula when she wrapped her arm around Kitty and said, "Good effort, sweetie. It'll get easier."

I started to clap when Kitty turned back toward the bleachers, as did a few others out of courtesy, but the applause was weak and quickly fell apart beneath the louder commentary, which echoed around the room in condemnation. Red-faced and hunching her shoulders, Kitty bypassed our bleachers and headed straight out the door, and no one moved to stop her. I started to go after her, but Toula's voice reminded me that I still had a part to play: "Maria Corelli? Your turn."

After watching Kitty's disastrous performance, I had a moment of stage fright as I approached the table, but Magus Lowe winked at me before Toula moved me into position before the boxes. "Okay, now," she said, all business, "let's try this one first."

From the color of the wood, I recognized the wand she'd handed me as an oak model, and I turned to her with concern. "Don't be scared," she said with a little smile, followed quickly by a quiet voice in my thoughts: *Sorry we have to go through this rigmarole, but I can't just "guess" that you need maple. Really, it's okay if you blow the boxes up.*

Toula's mental intrusion was delivered with far less finesse than Val's were, but no one else seemed to have heard her, and I played along. Facing the boxes, I held out the wand, focused on the largest, and tried to nudge it skyward. From practicing empty-handed with Helen, I knew how much force would be required for the task...but I didn't factor in the amplifying power of the strong wand, which channeled the power I shot through it like a magnifying glass in the sun.

I dropped to the ground in alarm when the box exploded into flame, and Toula quickly extinguished it. "Right, that's too much wand," she said, and handed me another as I climbed off the floor and dusted the knees of my trousers. "When you're ready, Maria."

I waited until Toula had remade the box I'd torched, then aimed again with the new wand and tamped back the power. Unfortunately, I still managed to overload the wand, and the box went sailing off through the room until it spun like a helicopter rotor and shattered, raining sawdust over the competition floor.

The crowd was muttering again, but at a more excited pitch.

While Toula produced another replacement box, Magus Lowe handed me a maple wand. "Easy does it," he murmured, leaning toward my ear. "Your nerves are ramping you up. Focus."

That time, I started with barely anything, testing the wand until I was confident that nothing was about to shower me in flaming wood, then whispered the box into the air. It hovered obediently, and I sent it into a controlled rotation. Helen was right—the wand *did* make casting a bit easier—but in truth, after four years of wandless work, I felt off my game as I made the necessary adjustments to keep the spell intact.

"And I think we have a winner," said Toula, patting my back. "You can drop it, kid." While the parents applauded, she passed me the black wand box and gestured toward the bleachers. "Good work," she whispered. "Go relax."

But when I started back toward my classmates, I saw that Kitty's spot on the bleachers was still empty. With Toula distracted by the next contender, I slipped out of the hall.

She hadn't gone far, and it hardly took a detective to locate her. The stone walls of the high-ceilinged subterranean level amplified every sound, including the noise coming from the women's toilets across from the competition hall, and I let myself in as quietly as I could. I needn't have bothered with attempted stealth—the cubicle at the far end of the room was closed, and I had a fairly good guess as to who was sobbing on the other side of the latched door.

Leaving my new wand on the sink, I approached her hiding place and knocked. "Kitty? It's Maria. Are you all right?"

"Fine," she mumbled through her tears.

"That doesn't sound like fine," I replied, and slid down against the wall, facing the closed door. "Want to talk?"

"No."

"Well, you can't stay in the toilets all night." She made no reply beyond sniffles, and I tried again. "There's supposed to be snacks when it's over—want to go upstairs? We could get the first shot at the food if we're there early."

"I'm not going," said Kitty, and tore off another wad of tissue paper.

"But there's sure to be *cake*."

"Go on, then."

I sighed and stretched my legs, enjoying the freedom from the tight bleachers, even if it meant sitting on the floor. "You're planning to move in here? Just put a bed in the corner and be done with it? I mean, you'll have to come out for class eventually…"

I stopped talking as the latch slid back, and the door opened on Kitty's wet, blotchy face. "I don't want to be here," she said, swiping at her runny nose. "Daddy wasn't going to make me go. I was going to stay at school with my friends, he knew that I...I..."

The end of that thought was lost in a fresh wave of tears, and I got up to pass Kitty a handful of paper towels. She buried her face in them until she regained some degree of composure, then honked and looked up at me, chin trembling. "I'm not supposed to be here," she managed between the hitching aftershocks of her crying jag.

"Your name was on the list," I pointed out.

She plopped onto the tile and tucked her knees to her chest, and I joined her. "I'm a witch," she muttered. "*Barely.*"

"You got a wand—"

"Dragonscale! And *that* almost didn't work!" She lowered her head until the threatening tears retreated. "Daddy was an old-blooded wizard. Mom's an old-blooded *magus*—she's the second in command at Arc 1, that's why she's so busy. And I'm *this* close to a dud," she said, holding her thumb and finger a millimeter apart. "Daddy said I didn't have to study magic, since I can't do anything anyway, but Mom made me go here. I told her I could just go to school in Montana and skip night classes, but she wouldn't let me. Said I had to work harder. Told me not to...to embarrass..."

I fetched more paper towels, and Kitty dried her face. "You know what?" I said. "You pointed a stick at a box, and it levitated. Most folks can't do that."

"Didn't go far," she mumbled.

"But it *went*! Do you know how many people would give anything to do what you just did?" I asked, sliding closer to her until she looked me in the eye. "Think about it."

"You don't get it, you're new-blooded. Witches are embarrassing," said Kitty. "Maybe that's why Mom doesn't want me around. She doesn't have to watch me screw up if I'm over here."

I thought of my now former classmates, children of Fringers who could manage only the barest rudiments of magic, if that, and started to tell Kitty that it would be okay, that she didn't need magic to get by—but I bit my tongue in the nick of time. "Well, your mother's missing out on the cake tonight, and that's her loss," I said, and pushed myself off the floor. "Can you show me the dorm? How is it?"

It was a blatant attempt at distraction, but Kitty was amenable to persuasion. "Pretty nice," she replied, and finally left her cubicle. "The older boarders don't come in until tomorrow, so it's quiet now."

"Show me," I urged, linking my arm around hers. "Come on, while everyone else is busy."

In my hurry to lure Kitty out of the toilets, I forgot my wand on the sink, but she noticed it and pulled me to a halt. "Is that yours?" she asked, pointing to the black box.

"Ooh, thanks," I said, tucking it under my free arm. "I might need that."

She stared at me, flabbergasted. "You got a *maple* wand?"

"I got a stick, and so did you. So, are you in bunkbeds or what?"

Kitty's mouth opened, and she seemed poised to protest for a few seconds until she sighed and followed me into the hallway. "No, they're regular beds. And there's no closets—everyone has a little wardrobe thingy and a footlocker, and that's it."

"That's *all*?"

"And a desk and chair. I barely have room for my books," she grumbled, guiding us toward an elevator.

"What books? I thought we get those tomorrow."

She pushed the button and shrugged. "I brought all of mine from home. No place for them in Mom's apartment, you know."

Putting it mildly, Kitty was a bibliophile. Stacks of paperback and hardback books lined the wall by her desk, and I could only imagine what she'd put on her computer. Even without hundreds of books, her room was cramped, mostly filled by a twin-sized bed topped with a navy duvet. Lying on the edge of the bed, it was possible to reach across the room and touch the wardrobe. The view was nothing special, just a glimpse into the castle's massive central courtyard. The girls shared a communal bathroom—all but the eighth-years, who had larger rooms with en suite facilities, Kitty informed me with undisguised envy.

She had only a single photograph on her desk, a picture of her and a beaming blond man in a brass frame with an enamel sunflower in the corner. An arrangement of perfect sunflowers sat beside it in a squat vase, the petals preserved by the spell I could see flickering around them.

We hid in Kitty's room for the next hour, her on the bed and me in her desk chair, talking about our new classes and Tennessee and my imagined life in Rome with my thoroughly mundane grandfather. She had just turned on her computer to show me photos from the old farm when someone rapped twice at the door. Before we could formulate a plan, Toula stuck her head inside and smiled. "Everything okay, girls?"

Kitty froze, then mumbled, "Yes, Grand Magus."

"Glad to hear it. Oh, and I wanted to make sure you two didn't miss out on this," she said, and dropped a pair of chocolate cake–laden plates on the desk. "Plenty more downstairs if you're hungry."

Toula saw herself out, and then, not quite believing our luck, Kitty and I dug in. Once we'd licked up the last crumbs, my stomach was still growling, and Kitty looked longingly at her empty plate. "Come on," I coaxed. "I don't know anyone, you don't know anyone, so let's go steal food."

Though hesitant, she followed me back to the

reception room, where the crowd had thinned into knots. Those of our classmates who'd escaped parental supervision stood together in twos and threes, gorging themselves on sweets. Kitty and I helped ourselves to the remains of the spread, and we were wandering off in search of a quiet corner when someone said, "Oi! You two!" Turning, I found Mortimer standing behind us, grinning evilly. "Where'd you go?" he asked. "You missed it!"

"Missed what?" I replied.

"Quentin Tartt got scared and was sick. *Everywhere,*" he said, raising his eyebrows. "The floor, the table legs…Magus Lowe…"

Kitty grimaced. "*Eww.*"

"I know! Hey, try the fudge," he added, and hurried off to join a group of boys.

I glanced at Kitty, who mumbled, "He's probably new-blooded."

"Or the fact that someone threw up on a magus is a lot more embarrassing than your wandwork," I countered. "Where was the fudge?"

She picked a brown square off her plate and gave it a contemplative chew. "Here, I'll show you. I'm going to need more."

CHAPTER 4

It was obvious to my class that Kitty was a witch in only the most generous sense of the term. A wand in her hand was barely more effective than a twig pulled from one of the courtyard trees, and even when she followed instructions to the letter, her spells only worked one time in ten. But whatever Kitty lacked on the magical side, she more than compensated for it in her mundane studies. She devoured books, whatever the topic, and she *synthesized*. While the rest of us flipped through our underlined pages, looking for answers when prodded, she could carry the discussion of the previous night's homework—and she often did, buying the rest of us time. By the third day, when she interrupted Colby's ineffective search through his science book with a long, complicated question about the magic-conducting properties of trees, the rest of us had caught on to her ploy, and she had our gratitude.

On the fifth day, Quentin gathered us up before first period and passed out half-sized notebooks. "My sister's class built these," he explained. "Write a name, then write the message beside it, and it'll go to that person's book. Or there's a 'message all' symbol inside the front cover. Just copy that, and it'll do the trick." He passed the last one to Kitty with a hopeful smile.

Computers were strictly forbidden in the classrooms—the risk was far too great that a miscast spell could fry them—and since our teachers had made it clear that any telephones they saw would be confiscated, the notebooks became our class-wide messaging system. To our general relief, Kitty was a willing collaborator, jotting down notes as needed to keep the lessons running, and she was generous in helping us avoid making fools of ourselves. Of our teachers, only Ms. Veracruz, who was dragging the first-year class through introductory Latin, seemed to catch on, but after seeing how much less we accomplished on the one day she made us take notes on loose leaf, she relented. That was a blessing—I was fluent in a late pre-Classical form of the language, thanks to Val, but my knowledge hadn't come with a firm understanding of the grammatical rules, and Kitty was far better than me at keeping the mechanics of the declension charts straight.

The one place where Kitty couldn't be of use was in our practical magic class, the period in which we met in a practice room with Magus Lowe for supervised wand usage. While magic theory was taught by Magus Forester, a crotchety old man who droned when he spoke and had to squint through his bifocals to see even the front row of desks, practical magic was one of the better-liked classes, in large part thanks to the teacher. Magus Lowe knew his technique and spent much of the early lessons correcting our faulty first attempts at wandwork, but he was encouraging and paid attention to our strengths, and he paired us appropriately. Often, he put me with Natalie Gutman, a strong birch-wielder who was the closest thing I had to an equal, but to our mutual surprise, he sometimes paired me with Kitty. After one such class, he stopped me at the door and pulled me aside to explain, "I know you can do it. She needs the practice."

I didn't mind. In short order, Kitty had become my closest friend in Glastonbury. Being around her was like trying on a new pair of shoes that had already been well broken in. We laughed at the same jokes and complained about the same teachers. I didn't mention her magical ineptitude, and she didn't mock my eclectic English pronunciation.

At first, we said little about our home lives, but after

the first weeks, once I started coming over early to eat breakfast in the castle's dining hall with Kitty, she began to open up about her past, dabs of information that started to coalesce into a larger picture—a loving father, a frequently absent mother, a childhood spent running through fields of flowers that towered over her head. The Connollys had been horticulturalists for generations—most seemed to have a knack for the sort of craft that made things grow more vigorously, plus a disdain for political games that kept them well away from the Arcanum's hubs. But during the Mulligan years, when nearly all wizards were forced to move into the installations, the Connollys hadn't been exempted—and their young son, Orson, had fallen for a classmate, Eva Stanhope. They were in their early twenties when Mulligan's regime ended, but though they were free to leave, they lingered in Montana for a time, as both had secured positions as Council aides to the magi left behind when the new Inner Council moved to Glastonbury. After a few years, however, Orson's pining for the fields of his childhood finally grew to be too much for him, and he moved home to Tennessee, while Eva remained in Montana, soon becoming a magus in her own right. The two visited each other on occasion—Kitty had never heard them speak of divorce, which was frowned upon in Arcanum circles—but they lived largely separate lives. They had Kitty when they were on the cusp of thirty, and the prospect of a family must have seemed wonderful to Orson, whose parents were killed shortly after moving away from the silo in a four-car pileup. A few months after Kitty's birth, Eva had tasked Orson with the child-rearing duties while she tended to the daily problems of the silo, and so Kitty's mother had become more of an infrequent houseguest than a fixture in her life. Compounding matters, though Eva's parents had called and visited their young granddaughter, they had died when she was small, succumbing to heart attacks within days of each other. In the end, Kitty had lived as an only child of only children in a de facto single-parent house, and she had been as shocked as anyone when her parents had Beth, a surprise baby born ten years after her big sister.

In return, I gave Kitty the least fabricated version of my family life that I could. I told her what I knew about my parents, but I omitted my years with Giulia and Luca, instead segueing straight to a loving, lonely grandfather who picked up where my parents left off and sent me to Glastonbury once a wizard noticed my budding talent. I described a roomy flat in Rome and tried to mentally map a route between my imagined home and my "old" school, careful to note the highlights along the way. It wasn't difficult to plot myself through the city, as Val, having decided that I needed more than a passing familiarity with my birthplace, had taken me back dozens of times to show me the notable sights.

(And, on one memorable occasion, to humiliate the obnoxious faux gladiator who posed for tourists near the Colosseum and tried to goad passersby into a fight with toy swords. Val had left him dazed and bruised on the sidewalk, and I'd learned that day that even a plastic weapon can be highly effective in the proper hands.)

I hated lying to Kitty, especially as she began to trust me with her story, but I had no choice. My future in Glastonbury depended upon my ability to keep the truth about my family a secret, and so I smiled and spun half-true tales about a life I'd never lived.

"You look tired," I said one morning, sliding my plate of eggs and bacon onto the table across from Kitty. "Up late?"

From the size and color of the circles under her eyes, it looked as if Kitty hadn't slept at all, but she smiled and drank her tea. "Just didn't sleep well, that's all. Did you want to go over math while we eat?"

My Achilles heel that autumn was fractions, and Kitty,

who seemed to enjoy multiplying the damn things for sport, was happy to check my work and explain my mistakes—and since her tutoring made more sense than our maths teacher's rambling lessons, I took her up on it.

It was well known, even among the first-year class, that almost any teacher who answered to "Magus" shouldn't be teaching a mundane subject. Fortunately, most of the teachers were ordinary wizards, and many had a knack for the classroom. But there were exceptions, and for some reason, eighty-year-old Magus Humphries insisted that she teach maths to a room full of first-years. Magus Lowe, who oversaw the school, had a tender streak, and I suppose he saw no harm in making an old woman happy.

As I waited for Kitty to compare our answers, I looked up and saw a lone diner in a black robe slip into a seat at a small, empty table near a window. I'd noticed him before—a young, thin man with curly brown hair and half-moon glasses who always sat alone with his plate and tablet, reading and eating breakfast in silence. While he settled in, Magus Lowe passed by and wished him good morning, but after a nod and a quick response, the man's attention returned immediately to his work.

"Is he one of the upper-level teachers, do you think?" I asked Kitty.

She glanced up from my notebook, eraser in her mouth. "Who?"

I pointed over her shoulder, and with all the subtlety a ten-year-old could muster, she quickly looked behind her. "Magus Wold?" she whispered, eyebrows raised. "I don't know. I've never seen him grading papers, so…"

Though I recognized the name, I feigned ignorance. "He seems lonely. No one ever eats with him."

Kitty put down her pencil and leaned across the table, and I met her in the middle, our foreheads almost touching. "He was the grand magus when we almost lost magic altogether," she murmured.

"Huh?"

"We were two, and I'm sure your grandpa wouldn't have known anything about it. Uh…" Her brow furrowed as she thought. "I told you about Grand Magus Mulligan, right?"

"Yeah…"

"Well, a bunch of magi ended up on probation after he was executed. They didn't do anything while Magus Lowe was grand magus, but just after Magus Wold got the job, some of them teamed up with this crazy group of faeries. Daddy said they tried to take over Faerie *and* the Arcanum. Anyway, they were holed up on these boats off the coast near here, and when Magus Lowe and everyone got to them, they found Magus Wold out there. He said they'd forced him to go, and he wasn't convicted of treason or anything, but…" Her voice trailed off, and she sat back and shrugged. "Daddy always called him Weasel Wold."

While she continued to look over my homework, I again considered the magus, who ate mechanically with one hand and scrolled through his tablet with the other. "If they let him stay on the Council," I told Kitty, "he can't be bad."

"I wouldn't know—Mom never talked about the Council with me," she muttered, then tapped my notebook with her pencil point. "More importantly, look here. Two-thirds and three-fourths are *not* five-sevenths, Maria."

As September wound down, Kitty's fatigue only worsened. Her dark circles became permanent additions to her face, and I had to nudge her awake in class on more than one occasion. She still insisted on helping me with maths in the morning, but she did so with a cup of strong tea in one hand, drinking as if her life depended on it.

When I caught her asleep beside her breakfast tray one Monday, I dragged her into the toilets and prodded the truth from her. "It's some older kids," she admitted as she splashed water on her face. "Fifth-years, sixth-years, a few older than that. They're…jerks."

Her tone suggested she had a stronger term in mind.

"What's going on?" I asked.

She sighed and patted at her cheeks with a paper towel. "Bunch of old-bloods. They come by and…mess with me. At night, after bed check." Seeing that I wasn't going to let her out of the room without an explanation, she said, "They have this club or something, call themselves the Old Guard. It was little things at first—they asked me if I was sure I was Magus Stanhope's daughter, if I'd been dropped on my head, stuff like that. Then they started in on how I don't belong here…" She paused, and one hand squeezed the sink until her knuckles turned white. "You know, the usual. There's no place for witches in the Arcanum, I should go away to make things better for everyone else…they said it's insulting that they have to be around me."

"Kitty—"

"I know they want me to go home, but it's not like I can just leave, right? Mom's not going to want me back in Montana. I *told* them she's the one who sent me here, and if they don't like that, they can take it up with her. But that didn't help." She bit her lip. "They've started messing with my stuff. When I got back to the dorm yesterday, my bed was soaking wet, and I had to take care of that. And my clothes disappeared for two days last week—everything but the sweatshirt I left in my footlocker. I think some of my books have been leaving, too. Woke up last Monday, and all my weekend homework was a pile of ash. I mean, I don't leave my computer alone anymore—it stays under my pillow at night, just in case."

"Kitty," I protested, "you have to tell someone."

But she vehemently shook her head. "Tattling will just make it worse, and if I make a scene, Mom will get upset, and…you know." She shrugged. "I'm sure they'll get bored eventually," she said, though she didn't sound convinced.

I folded my arms. "You have to tell one of our teachers, at least. Why don't we go to Magus Lowe and—"

"*No.* I can handle this. Promise me you won't say anything."

"But—"

"Maria, *promise me.*"

I didn't like it, but I gave Kitty my word and followed her back into the dining room. As we walked in, I overheard tittering from a table to my left, and I spotted a group of older girls bent over their plates and cutting their eyes to Kitty. My friend cringed and looked away, and for her sake, I resisted the sudden urge to march over and demonstrate a few of the techniques Helen had taught me. I wasn't confident that I could best all six of them, but Helen and Val had worked with me enough that I was certain I'd have a decent shot of walking away intact. But Kitty had moved on, aiming for her abandoned breakfast, and with a parting glare for the girls, I joined her.

October rolled in with a lingering dampness and a strong cold front that drove those of us from more temperate climates indoors. Kitty seemed no better rested with the new month, but she hadn't brought up the Old Guard again, and I didn't press her. We started the week as usual: our class passed notes during our mundane subjects, let Kitty take the lead in theoretical magic (as she was the only one who could be counted on to have completed the dry reading), and paired up to fling spells at each other under Magus Lowe's sharp eye. But near the end of the day, our history teacher handed us an unpleasant surprise, a short research paper due by Halloween. "This will be fun!" said Mrs. O'Moore, who smiled entirely too brightly for the news she was delivering. "I'm sure there's some facet of world history you're eager to read about. At least five pages, at least ten scholarly sources, and if you don't know if a source fits the criteria, come see me."

"Beats another test, at least," Kitty said that afternoon as we spread our books out in our favorite study room. The library was pocked with those rooms, little nooks with tables large enough for four to ten, which could be reserved for a week at a time. Kitty and I had religiously re-upped our reservation, and by that point in the term, we considered the room our private study—especially as we received keys to close it up when we weren't around, saving us from having to drag all of our textbooks with us during the day.

"I don't know," I groused as I opened my English reader. "What do you plan to write about?"

"Considering my options." She glanced at the time on her phone, then looked out the sliver of window at the gray sky, which was quickly darkening toward nightfall. "Hour until dinner. Think we can cram everything in by then?"

"I think I'll be working at home tonight," I said with a sigh, and propped my chin in my palm to read.

As had become our routine, Kitty and I parted company around six, when she went to the dining hall and I headed in the direction of Magus Lowe's office, ostensibly to ask him to open a gate for me. In truth, I had a preferred closet for the task, and I'd grown so accustomed to making the trip that I could be home in under a minute. The time in Faerie wasn't quite aligned with Glastonbury—there was still a glow in the west when I came over—but Bonnie had my schedule down to a science, and she saw to it that the kitchen always had dinner waiting for me, even if Val was otherwise occupied.

That night, he joined me for an early meal, nodding sympathetically as I griped about the least pleasant parts of my day and coaxing me to eat more vegetables. As dessert came out, the conversation veered toward Kitty. "Is she sleeping these nights?" he asked. "Or is her insomnia still troubling her?"

"She's working on it," I said around a mouthful of

pudding.

Val gave me a long, measured look, the kind that told me he knew exactly what I wasn't telling him, but he didn't pry—well, not vocally. I knew he snooped through my thoughts on occasion, especially if I seemed upset without apparent cause, but generally, he kept any commentary on his discoveries to himself. We both saw through his farce of ignorance, of course—I didn't yet have the strength or skill to keep him out of my head—but I appreciated the illusion of privacy.

Tuesday was much as Monday had been, but for Mortimer's cracked rib in Magus Lowe's class, the result of Natalie's good bolt and his sub-par shield. Kitty and I decided to both do papers on aspects of ancient Egypt so as to maximize our research time, and we spent our afternoon study session combing the stacks with the help of vague directions from the reference librarian. Once we had half a dozen books—a good start, in Kitty's assessment—we divided the pile and agreed to compare our notes in a week.

Still, the history paper wasn't my most pressing priority, and so I was almost ready for bed before I realized that I'd left my books in the study room. Grunting in frustration at my carelessness, I slid on a sweatshirt over my pajamas, shoved my feet into my tennis shoes, and opened a gate into a dark corner of the library, hoping to avoid detection.

It worked—at nearly eleven, the library was all but dead, save a few lights under the doors of other study rooms. Not trusting my luck, I skulked in the shadows, holding my breath every time I thought I heard the rustling of fabric or the riffling of pages. The last thing I wanted to do that night was come up with an explanation for my presence long after the day students had been sent home. But fortune was kind, and no one noticed me as I quietly unlocked our study room, intending to grab my forgotten books and go.

What I found on the other side of the door, however,

stopped me in my tracks. The light falling in from the corridor showed me a rudimentary camp on the carpet beneath the table: a backpack pillow, a jacket as a blanket, and Kitty, staring fearfully at my silhouette in the doorway. I hurriedly closed the door and turned on my phone's torch, the better to see what I'd stumbled across, and she squinted as she sat up. "What are you doing here?" I whispered, crawling under the table to join her. "I thought bed check was at nine."

"It is. I missed it," she whispered back, drawing her legs up as I sat beside her. "I didn't have a bed to be checked into."

"What?"

"My bed's gone. The wardrobe, the desk, the footlocker...all my books..." Her breath hitched on the inhalation, but she held herself in check. "Gone, all of it. I...I started carrying my picture of Daddy and me last week, just in case, but they...they..."

"They what?" I asked, seeing her eyes well in the phone's glow.

"They took my...m-my sunflowers," was all she managed before she covered her mouth and cried, trying to stifle the ragged howl that threatened to escape.

I hesitated, hoping not to make matters worse, then touched her knee. "Old Guard?"

Kitty nodded and buried her head.

Seeing her hiding there in the dark study room, surrounded by the few possessions she had left, I felt something red and sharp and reckless flare within me. "Take me to the dorm," I told her. "Show me which ones are the Old Guard. I'll make them give it all back."

She sniffed and wiped her nose on her sleeve. "There's too many, and they're all older than—"

"I don't care. Just show me which ones to go after."

But Kitty shook her head. "Not tonight, it's late. Maybe it'll all be back tomorrow..."

"All right, maybe, but you can't sleep here," I

protested.

"I'm okay," she tried to assure me. "The door locks...and what are *you* doing here, anyway? How'd you get back?"

"Forgot my books," I said, dodging the rest of the question. "Look...my bed's more than big enough for two. Want to sleep over?"

She continued to wipe her wet face with her shirt. "Really? Your grandpa wouldn't mind? It's already midnight in Rome, isn't it?"

Suddenly realizing the ramifications of what I'd just offered, I turned off the torch and found Val's number. "Let me phone him and ask, yeah?"

Praying that Kitty's knowledge of Italian was limited to pasta dishes, I dialed and waited only a few seconds before Val picked up. "I'm sorry," I began, slipping into my mother tongue. "All of Kitty's things have been taken, and she's sleeping under a library table. Can she stay with me tonight?"

Val said nothing for a moment, and I'd begun to think the connection had dropped when he asked, "Do you trust her?"

"Yes."

"Then stay there. I need to clear this with Toula."

He hung up, and by the light of the screen, I could just see Kitty's hopeful face. "He's asking the grand magus," I reported. "Probably wouldn't be a good thing if no one here knew where you were, right?"

"The grand magus gave your *grandpa* her number?"

"For emergencies," I fibbed. "We're to wait here until she decides what to do."

The decision was a long five minutes in coming, and when Toula called me, the edge in her tone suggested that Val had explained to her what I'd promised Kitty I wouldn't share. "If you're sure about this," she told me in poorly accented Italian. "Tell her whatever she needs to know, but if this gets out..."

"She won't let it," I replied though my palms had begun to sweat as I put my phone away. "Right, then," I said to Kitty, scooting out from beneath the table, "you can come home with me. But, uh…there's something I need to tell you first."

She grabbed her belongings and slid her jacket on. "You're *awesome*. What's up?"

"I…um…" I could barely see her by the phone's illumination, but still, I could feel the weight of her eyes on me. "I…don't live in Rome."

"Oh? Okay. Suburb?"

"Not exactly. And before I say anything else, you must promise me that this stays between us. *Seriously*. No one else can know."

"I swear," said Kitty, bemused.

"Not a word—"

"I mean it, I swear. What's the big secret?"

Checking to be certain that there were no feet visible in the thin bar of light beneath the study room door, I slid close to Kitty and murmured, "What I told you about my grandfather and me…I made a lot of that up. I, uh…I actually live in Faerie."

"You *what*?"

"Since I was five," I said in a rush, trying to stop her before she could throw a fit. "My parents died, my guardians weren't great, and my grandfather…he's not *directly* my grandfather. There are a few generations between us. But you'll be safe, nothing bad is going to happen—"

"Hang on, stop," she said, cutting short my rapid reassurances. "Are you…you're not *fae*, are you?"

"Witch-blooded," I mumbled, tensing for the blow. "Very slightly."

I cringed, waiting for Kitty to disavow me and our friendship, but instead, she exclaimed, "*How*? You cast so well!"

"Very, *very* slightly witch-blooded. And I had a good

teacher before I came here. But if you'd rather not go, I'll—"

"It can't be any worse than this," she said, hitching up her backpack. "Who's opening a gate for us?"

I waved one open beside the table and looked at Kitty in time to see her eyes widen as the lights of my bedroom came into view. "How did you…" she breathed.

"I don't really need a wand. Please don't tell anyone," I said, then ushered her through and collapsed the gate behind us.

Kitty stood in the middle of my room, mouth agape, and stared at the details I'd almost come to take for granted—the sumptuous canopied bed, the starry ceiling mosaic, the door open to admit the breeze from the night-dark garden. "Wow," she finally whispered.

Before I could respond, my phone beeped, and I saw a message from Val: *Working late. I will stay away. Do whatever needs to be done. Toula understands.*

"Put your things anywhere," I said, sliding my phone into its place on the nightstand, and kicked off my shoes. "Hope you won't mind if I don't do the Egypt reading tonight."

But Kitty had already poked her head into the garden and was marveling at the starry panorama. "This is gorgeous!" she exclaimed over the noise of the fountain. "This is your *room*?"

"Yeah," I replied, and tossed my sweatshirt onto a chair. "Bath is through the door over here. I'm going to bed."

Kitty slipped back inside, then considered her backpack and made a face. "Any chance that you've got an extra toothbrush?"

Envisioning it as Helen had taught me, I whispered a toothbrush into existence and handed it to Kitty, who looked at it as if I'd just passed her a holy relic. "Toothpaste is in the left-hand drawer," I said, then flopped onto the bed and burrowed.

By the time Kitty emerged, teeth clean and face damp, I'd found my usual hollow and barely felt it when she climbed into bed beside me. "This is amazing," she mumbled, rolling onto her side. "There's so much magic here. Maybe even I could cast..."

"In the morning," I yawned, and waved the lights out.

It was still dark when my phone alarm blatted, and Kitty, by then a barely visible lump under the blankets, grumbled in her sleep beside me as I shut it off. "I'll shower first," I offered, giving her a few more minutes of peace.

On leaving the steamy bathroom, I was surprised to find her awake, leaning up against the headboard and blinking blearily at the contours of her surroundings, which were coming into focus thanks to the light from the garden. "Sleep well?" I asked, heading for my closet.

"Yeah. Pretty well." Her morning voice was an octave deeper than usual and crackled. "Hey, Maria?"

"Mm?" I asked, opening the closet door.

"Did I just dream it, or are we in Faerie?"

"Will you be upset either way?"

"Since that was the first decent night's sleep I've had in two weeks, no," she said, and stretched. "But if my mom ever knew I'd spent the night here, she'd have a holy *fit*."

I slipped into the closet to change but left the door cracked open. "Good thing you're not going to tell her, then, eh?"

"Right. I don't want to die," she replied, and grunted as she extricated herself from the bedclothes. "Borrow your shampoo?"

Once we were both dressed and mostly dry, Kitty stepped out to see the garden in the pale morning light. "Beautiful," she murmured, scanning the trees and bushes.

"Did you look into the fountain?"

She followed my finger and laughed in surprise when the fish darted out from hiding in the mosaic grasses. "Are they—"

"Just part of the tile. I might have gone swimming to investigate the first time I saw them," I replied, and grinned.

"I don't blame you." She crouched beside the fountain channel, watching the fish for another moment, then rose and cracked her back. "So this...this is really Faerie? You're not pulling my leg?"

"This is Faerie," I confirmed, guiding her back into my room. "You can sort of tell by the amount of ambient magic, yes?"

"I'd noticed." She ran her fingers through a bluish blob of untapped potential. "Mind if I try something?"

I shrugged, and Kitty pulled her wand from her backpack. She closed her eyes in concentration, held out her wand, and began to mutter to herself. Two seconds later, a shield bubbled out from the tip of her wand—a poorly constructed shield, but large by her standards. She opened her eyes and smiled in wonder before letting the shield fall apart. "That was *fast*."

"Casting's easier here. It's helpful if you're trying to work out something from class."

"Lucky." She packed her wand and the rest of her few things away, though that didn't take more than a minute. Kitty's clothing from the day before had done triple-duty as her pajamas and that day's outfit as well. "So," she said, zipping her bag, "is your grandpa around?"

"Probably." I frowned. "Why? Need something?"

"No—I just wanted to thank him. Daddy always said you should thank your hosts, so...uh...but if that's a problem—"

"No, no, he's probably eating. Come on," I said, and grabbed my own backpack. "Quick walking tour."

Kitty dragged her feet as we made our way through the villa—not out of reluctance, but because she was too busy gawking at the gardens to keep up. I tugged her along as needed, then pushed open the door to the smallest dining room, where Val was sitting with coffee and a stack of papers. He looked up at the intrusion, surprised, and shot me a questioning glance as Kitty came in behind me.

"Sorry to interrupt," I began, switching to Fae by force of habit. "Um…this is Kitty. She wanted to say hi."

To my relief, he didn't seem upset. "So, *you're* Kitty," he said, his English strongly accented but intelligible. "Welcome. Did you sleep?"

She nodded, and when she spoke, her voice sounded unusually shy. "Yes, sir. Thank you for having me."

"Certainly. If your furniture has not returned by the end of the day, come back with Maria. Or as you like," he offered, cutting his eyes to me. "She knows now, so if you want to have her over, I don't mind."

I smiled, and Kitty quietly sighed—with relief, I assumed. Manners aside, it took a lot for a witch to confront an unfamiliar faerie, let alone before breakfast. "Thanks. We'll be off," I told him. "If we're in the dining room as usual, no one should notice."

"Agreed, but Toula wants to speak with you two first. Stop by her office on the way, hmm? And Kitty?"

She straightened, clutching her backpack strap. "Sir?"

Val barely twitched a finger, and the wrinkles fell out of her clothes. "Better?"

"Better," she agreed, surveying the result, and smiled at him as I opened the gate back.

"Try to behave yourselves," he called after us, and before the gate closed, I heard a parting thought: *Tell her not to be afraid. I won't bite.*

CHAPTER 5

"**R**ight," said Toula as Kitty and I took a seat on her office couch, "here's how this is going to go. Ms. Connolly, you're going to tell me *exactly* what is going on in the dorm and who's involved. Ms. Corelli..." She frowned at me, then shrugged. "Eat your bagel. I may have questions for you, too."

Kitty had already bitten into the bagel Toula had offered her, and it didn't take a genius to recognize a stalling tactic. When she could reasonably masticate no longer, she swallowed, though she looked a little sick. "It's no big deal, Grand Magus—"

"Bullshit. Tell me about the Old Guard."

The unexpected profanity threw her, but Kitty recovered and began to poke a hole in her paper napkin with her thumb. "They're old-blooded, that's all I know."

"How many?"

She paused. "At least ten."

Toula picked up a notepad from the coffee table and clicked her pen open. "Names."

"Grand Magus, I—"

"*Names*, Kitty."

She sighed and continued to tear up the napkin. "I don't know them all. They're older than me."

"Just do the best you can," Toula coaxed.

After a long moment, Kitty mumbled, "Heloise Stout. She comes around the most."

"Stout," Toula repeated as she wrote the name. "Her mother's a Parsons. Families don't get much older than that."

"Lewis Hines," she continued, widening the hole. "Caroline Boynton. Griffin McClure."

"Mm-hmm," said Toula as she transcribed. "Any others you know?"

"There's someone named Tabby…"

"Tabitha Solomon."

"And there's this other guy, I think they call him Trey."

"That," said Toula, looking up from her notepad, "would be Leonard Rossi the third. American, right?"

Kitty nodded. "That's all the names I know."

"Fine." Toula put her pad and pen aside and took a sip of coffee. "What I'll do is call them in here and grill them until I get to the bottom of this, and we'll get your room back in order—"

"Please don't," Kitty quickly interrupted. "Please, Grand Magus, it's no big deal."

"It *is* a big deal. I don't give two shits about how inbred your fellow students are—they have no right to make your life hell."

"It's just—"

"Honey," she said, cutting Kitty off with a raised eyebrow, "I went by your room early this morning. It's still empty."

"But they'll bring it back, I'm sure—"

"Correct me if I'm wrong, but your master plan last night was to lock yourself in a study room and sleep on the floor, right?"

Kitty's cheeks began to color. "You heard about that?" she muttered.

"I needed a damn good explanation before I okayed your field trip to Faerie," Toula replied, "and that's me knowing where you were headed and trusting that you'd be sent back in good condition. So yes, Val had to convince me that the trip was warranted. He's concerned about you, by the way."

"He is?" she asked, surprised.

Toula leaned back and crossed her legs. "He can be a little protective. There may have even been an offer made to assist me if I chose to go after the Old Guard last night. Honestly, he told me enough that I was almost ready to take him up on it."

I saw the flash of betrayal in Kitty's face before Toula stepped in. "Maria hasn't said anything. He's old, and he's nosy when it comes to her, and when he wants to know something, he doesn't always bother to ask. Judging from what I heard, *she's* worried about you," she continued, nodding in my direction, "and I am, too. So I'm going to have a little chat with this so-called Old Guard—"

"*Please* don't," Kitty begged. "If there's a fuss, Mom will get mad at me."

"Why? None of this is your fault," Toula began, then paused to study Kitty's expression, a grimace of fearful desperation, and sighed. "Let me help you, sweetie."

Kitty shook her head. "They'll stop eventually. I'm just going to ignore them."

Though she seemed unconvinced, Toula bit into her bagel and chewed thoughtfully. "Okay," she said after a moment, "if you're set on this, I'll stay out of it for now, but if it escalates, I *will* step in, and Eva can deal with herself. Agreed?"

"Thank you, ma'am," Kitty whispered.

"Sure. And on the off chance that your little friends aren't bored of you just yet…if you need to go home with Maria again, you have my permission. Just try not to get killed over there."

I snorted in indignation. "You make it sound like the villa is booby-trapped."

"I'm not worried about the villa," said Toula. "But do me a favor and don't go exploring, girls. Explaining your disappearance isn't a conversation I want to have with the Council."

Pressed for time before the first bell, we finished our bagels on the way to class, and I licked the traces of Nutella off my fingers as we took the final staircase. Kitty was quiet as we settled in, and though I caught a few of the boarders regarding her questioningly, she ignored them and opened her textbook. Glancing toward her desk, I saw private messages begin to appear in her notebook, but her scribbled responses seemed perfunctory, and she forwent conversation in favor of class participation—at least one of us was feeling eight a.m. maths.

Midway through the period, however, she sent me a private note: *Do they all look that young?*

I cut my eyes her way, but Kitty was focused on copying a problem from the board.

Without glamour, yes, I wrote back. *But their eyes don't always match the rest of them. You can tell.*

I noticed, she replied after volunteering yet another correct answer. *Your grandpa looks younger than my daddy did.*

You get used to it.

Before she could respond, a message went out to the entire class from Natalie, who, like Kitty, was a boarder from the States: *Kitty's ignoring me, so has anyone seen her furniture? What the heck happened?*

Half a dozen pencils flew in quick order.

NO. I walked past going to the bath, and I saw it was empty, replied Gwinn O'Shea. *I thought you'd packed and left, Kitty.*

Heard about it, wrote Javier Navarro, another of the boarders. *Some of the fifth-years were laughing, but I couldn't tell what happened.*

What happened??? added Colleen, a day student.

The pencils stilled for a moment as Kitty asked a question about the long problem Magus Humphries was working. But once the matter had been clarified, Kitty resumed writing in her other notebook, ignoring the discussion.

After a moment, Tom Whitby, our lone Canadian, chimed in. *There's a group of old-bloods in the upper classes called the Old Guard. They're not real fond of new-bloods or anything else. One of them started talking to me back in September before he realized my wand sucks.*

It doesn't <u>suck</u>, Colby quickly replied.

You're not the one on oak, Tom wrote. *Anyway, I have cousins in the upper classes. They told me to stay away from the OG. And last night, my cousin Nate came to check on me and said the OG were going after Kitty.*

No one needed further explanation. Though it was widely acknowledged among us that Kitty was a witch, one didn't just *say* that in front of the class.

Finally, with a little sigh of exasperation, Kitty joined the conversation: *Ignore them, they'll stop.*

Okay, but where are you sleeping until they do? asked Natalie.

I'm fine, Kitty replied, and that was all she would say on the subject.

Her belongings were still missing after class, and the snickering down the corridor in the girls' dorm told me the site was being watched. Kitty looked around her empty room for a moment as if hoping the furniture would spontaneously reappear, then hitched up her backpack and started for the staircase out of the tower, her shoulders tight. "If it's no trouble…"

"It's not," I said, and followed her down.

Instead of holing up in our study room as usual, we gathered our things and left from a gate I opened in an empty classroom. Safely back in my room, and with far more daylight than we'd left in Glastonbury, Kitty cleared a spot at my table and began to unpack. "Got a plug?" she asked, pulling her computer from her bag. "I didn't charge last night."

"By your feet," I explained, taking the seat across from her. "That thing you're kicking is a generator."

"Oh." She bent down to attach the cord. "Guess there's no electricity here, huh?"

"Not in the walls. That's just there for my computer."

She lingered beneath the table, considering the box. "Solar?"

"No. There's a tight little enchantment that drives the engine, and it makes enough juice to run what I need."

When Kitty popped back up, she was frowning in bemusement. "You got magic to play with electronics? *How?*"

"*I* didn't do anything," I replied, opening my maths book, "and the engine is pretty basic. There's a guy here who's good at running machines without zapping them, and he set me up. Built my computer, too," I added, giving it a pat. "There's a shield on it to help keep it safe here, if you look closely."

She did, whistling in appreciation. "That's *nice*."

"If you're going to be coming around," I said, glancing at her unprotected computer, "we should probably go see him. You know, make sure yours is shielded, too."

Just then, I heard Bonnie's familiar staccato double-tap at the door, and she poked her head inside. If she was surprised to find Kitty with me, she gave no indication. "Have you two eaten, or were you planning to do so here?" she asked in English.

My stomach reminded me that it had been hours since lunch. "Here, thank you," I told her. "Oh, uh…Bonnie, this is Kitty."

But Kitty had perked for another reason. "American?" she inquired, surprised.

Bonnie grinned. "Not originally, but I was a Texan for a long time. You're from…Tennessee, right?" she added with a squint.

She nodded and smiled like she was meeting an old friend. "Yes, ma'am."

"And they packed you off to England, huh? How's that going?"

Kitty made a face. "I'm here, aren't I?"

"Good point." Bonnie came in and closed the door.

"Well, then, let me make things a little easier for you, hon," she said as she approached. "Linguistics first…"

It took Kitty a moment to recover from getting Fae enchanted into her mind, but her eyes lit as she realized the potential. "That's great!" she exclaimed, trying out the new tongue. "Can you do that with Spanish, too?"

"Sí," said Bonnie, "but it's best to pick it up from a native. You get a better understanding of the nuances that way. Now, on to more important things: where's your luggage?"

Kitty gestured toward her emptied backpack. "That's all I've got. The folks who took my stuff haven't given it back yet."

She tutted. "We'll have to do something about that, then. Stand up, let me get a look at you…okay," she said as Kitty did a slow twirl, "little smaller than Maria, we can handle that." With a flick of her wrist, a variety of clothes appeared on top of my bed, and Kitty's eyes bulged. "Those should all fit," said Bonnie, "but take a look, see what you like, see what needs tweaking…"

She didn't have to tell Kitty twice. With a muffled squeal, Kitty ran for the bed and started picking through the offering, beaming like a child in the final scenes of a sappy Christmas movie. I plodded through my maths homework while Kitty modeled and Bonnie tailored, and Kitty gushed her gratitude as Bonnie packed it all into a new suitcase for her. "Can't very well have you running around naked, child," she remarked, then patted Kitty's shoulder and turned to go. "Dinner should be almost ready. Wash up, girls."

That night, with the lights out and the garden door open as usual, I burrowed down beside Kitty and felt myself slide toward sleep, pushed toward the precipice by the dry reading I'd just completed for our papers. Before I could fall off the edge, however, Kitty rolled over to face me and whispered, "Maria?"

I grunted in query.

"Did I do okay tonight? I didn't, like, *upset* anyone, did I?"

My eyes cracked open in the darkness. "You were fine. Why would you—"

"I don't know, but you hear about how touchy faeries can be, and how things get messy in a hurry if they're mad at you, and..." She sighed and shifted against her pillow. "So...I'm okay?"

"I wouldn't worry. Val likes you."

"You think?"

"I know."

I'd spoken to him plenty of times before then about my new friend in Glastonbury, but with Kitty at the dinner table, unprotected from mental intrusions, Val finally had a chance to do some exploring on his own. Over the course of the meal, I caught flickers across his face as he riffled through her memories, forming his own impression of her...and by dessert, he was silently peppering me with questions, keeping up two concurrent conversations. I didn't have the talent to speak directly to his mind, but I knew to push my responses to the top of my thoughts, and he picked up what I wanted to convey. He approved of her—and, I noted when his questions turned toward Magus Stanhope, he made no attempt to hide the shade of anger coloring his indignation.

Regardless, Kitty seemed uneasy. "I didn't offend him when I called him Mr. Corelli?"

Val had laughed at that—quietly, but with genuine mirth. "No," I assured her. "It takes real effort to offend him."

"I didn't know what else to call him," she protested, still trying to defend herself. " 'Hey, Maria's grandpa' seemed kind of rude." She paused, then asked, "Why do you call him by name, anyway?"

"What do you mean?"

She snorted. "If I'd ever tried to call Daddy by his first name, I'd have been in a world of trouble."

"I don't know," I replied, and flipped onto my back to stare at the hypnotizing lights of the canopy. "Suppose it's easier than trying to find a word for exactly how we're related. That gets unwieldy."

"How?"

To simplify things for Kitty, I ran through the English terminology Toula had given me, looking for a match. "He's my seventy-second great-grandfather," I finally explained. "There's no easy word for that."

"*Whoa*," she whispered. "That's...like—"

"Ancient, I know," I agreed. "But we're each other's family, and Val..." I shrugged beneath the comforter. "He's Val."

Kitty was quiet for a moment, then softly said, "He's immortal, right? He'd have to be."

"Yeah."

"Are you?"

"No." I yawned as I rolled back to face her. "I'm almost entirely human, yes? You've seen me cast."

"Well, *yes*," said Kitty, "but I didn't know if you got any...you know...perks."

"Not exactly," I replied, deciding I was too tired to work through the murky details of the tiny thread of enchantment in my craft. "But I got Val."

"You're lucky."

"I know."

"No, you don't," she said, and flipped away from me. "He's not going to up and die on you."

Kitty didn't resist when I slid against her, and after a few minutes, her chest ceased its silent hitching as she fell asleep.

Kitty's room remained empty when we checked on Thursday morning, then again on Friday. When nothing had changed by that afternoon, she came home with me for the weekend. Finding her at breakfast Saturday, her clothes slightly rumpled from their time in her new suitcase, Val accompanied us back to my suite, then created a door in the wall between my bedroom and the empty one next door. "Before you two grow sick of each other," he explained with a little smile, then left us to move Kitty's things into the closet. For the rest of the morning, we ignored our homework to play at interior design, and I put to use the skills Helen had taught me to modify the guestroom—skills that I didn't yet dare to exhibit in Glastonbury. Kitty took it all in stride, suggesting color and fabric modifications while I warped the world around us, and then, when she had things almost to her liking, she pulled her wand from her bag and pointed it at the tufted silk throw pillow on her bed. After a solid half-minute's concentration and a string of what sounded suspiciously like muttered cursing, the pillow's color shifted from deep violet to royal blue, and she clapped in triumph.

Bonnie, who had been passing by, popped in at the sound of Kitty's cheers and smiled in bemusement. "Everything good?"

"I did it!" Kitty crowed, jabbing her wand toward the pillow. "I cast! It *worked*!"

To her credit, Bonnie didn't bother to ask about the scope of Kitty's spell. "Atta girl," she said with a thumbs-up, quickly followed by, "Don't you two have reading to be doing?"

We spent the afternoon at work, migrating between our rooms and the garden until the sun set, and then Val took us out of the villa and across the wide meadow to the western gap in the mountains. The sliver of moon was setting early above the sea, and Kitty stood beside me in the tall grass, her wind-tossed hair almost silver in the starlight, raptly drinking it in. Val considered her for a moment, then opened a gate down to the distant shore, the narrow spit of sand at the foot of the cliffs, and motioned us through. "Go on," he told Kitty, who regarded the gentle waves with uncertainty, and motioned a shield into being out past the breakers. "There's nothing there to harm you tonight."

She stepped onto the beach, then kicked off her shoes, rolled her leggings up to the knee, and ran into the night-black surf, shrieking with glee and cold and the excitement of the saltwater blowing in her face. I looked up at Val in silent enquiry, and he murmured, "She's only seen the sea once. I thought she might enjoy the distraction."

"Come *on*, Maria!" Kitty called over the roll and hiss of the waves. "Get in here!"

"Thank you," I told him.

Val briefly pulled me close and kissed my forehead, then nudged me toward the water. "Of course, carissima filia. Now, you should go to her before she drags you in."

By Monday morning, when we returned to school, Kitty seemed almost comfortable around Val—not quite at ease, but relatively confident that he wasn't going to incinerate her if she put a toe out of line. I had gleaned enough to realize that her understanding of Faerie and its politics was minimal; her dad had warned her about the place and the natives, but he hadn't gone into detail. That suited Val, who never seemed to crave ceremony. Kitty's personality was beginning to fully bubble up again as she gained sureness in her safety, and if she found it odd that he had a staff tending to the sprawling villa, she let it slide. I knew she was finally settling in when she left the framed photograph of her and her dad on her nightstand, safe from the potential harm in Glastonbury.

"I'll be working late tonight," Val told me as we took our leave. "Go to bed before dawn, hmm?"

"*Fine*," I said, sighing melodramatically, and he chuckled as he closed the gate behind us.

Kitty and I got to class shortly before the bell, and we'd barely settled in when a slew of questions began appearing in Kitty's notebook. She opened her textbook with nonchalance, ignoring the incoming queries until Ms. Veracruz was busy at the board with another of her endless declension exercises, then forwarded the messages to me.

All came from boarders: *Where have you been? Did you go home? Are you okay?*

And, more worryingly, *The OG is pissed.*

When Kitty answered them, she looped me into the conversation. *I went home with Meria. Everything's fine. And why are they mad?*

Tom responded first—a quick sketch of a face with a straight line for a mouth and a quirked eyebrow. *No bullies at your last school?*

Not in my class.

Lucky, he scribbled. *They don't like it when their favorite targets hide from them.*

Kitty huffed her indignation. *I'm not hiding, I'm just avoiding them until they give me back my stuff.*

Same difference, Gwinn chimed in.

As Kitty protested, Javier cleared his throat on the back row. *Hide, avoid, call this whatever you like. What the heck does the second sentence mean?*

And with that, class was back to normal. I fielded the question, and Kitty rolled her eyes when I glanced her way. *This isn't that hard*, she griped to me. *Do they just not do the reading?*

Neglecting to mention the instantaneous crash-course I'd had in Latin, I shrugged, kept my mouth shut, and tried to pay attention to the board.

Not until the end of the day did the matter of the Old Guard arise again. As Kitty and I headed for the library, Natalie and Gwinn pulled us aside and lowered their voices. "You can stay with one of us, Kitty," Natalie offered. "No need to go all the way to Italy."

"Yeah," Gwinn chimed in, "I've got a cousin in the seventh-years. She'll make a bed for you, no worries. And if we're quiet about it, the Old Guard might not even know you're back."

Kitty's shoulders began to hunch. "Thanks, uh…but those rooms are small, you know, and—"

"And she's expected for dinner, anyway," I added, giving her an out.

That satisfied our classmates, and we retreated to our study room to work. But Kitty seemed restless, drumming her fingers on the tabletop and frowning at her book. Looking up from my maths homework, I noticed her staring at the same two pages for five minutes, then asked, "Are you all right?"

Kitty scowled as she raised her eyes from the words she clearly wasn't reading. "Do you think I'm a coward?"

"Why would I think—"

"I should face them. Tell them to give me back my things."

I dropped my pencil and gave her a long look. "You want to take on a bunch of upperclassmen by yourself? That's a *dumb* idea."

She barely paid me any mind. "Ignoring them isn't working. Bullies will back down if you confront them, that's what my third-grade teacher told us," she murmured. "I just need to show them that this isn't okay, and they'll stop."

"You *need* to let the grand magus handle this," I countered. "They're bigger than you, they're more talented…think about it, Kitty." She seemed to deflate as I spoke, but I pressed on before she could get any other great ideas. "I know you want them to stop, but taking them head-on? Really?"

"I can't hide at your house forever," she muttered.

"You're not *hiding*, you're sleeping over," I replied, trying to draw a distinction.

But she remained restless, and a few minutes later, she

pulled her water bottle from her bag and stood. "Need a refill. I'll be back," she said, and let herself out.

I continued to work, but when I got to the end of maths with no sign of Kitty, I realized she'd been gone far too long to have merely trekked to the water fountain. "Stupida," I hissed at myself, and then, eschewing caution, I opened a gate into Kitty's dorm room.

The room was still empty of both furniture and people, but I heard raised voices from down the hall and hurried into the corridor, where Gwinn and Natalie were huddling, wide-eyed. "What's going on?" I demanded.

At least my classmates were too distracted to notice that I'd come from nowhere. "Kitty stormed in here and started shouting for Dahlia," said Natalie.

The three of us cringed at the thump of flesh hitting wood.

"Who?" I asked.

"Dahlia Leighton," Gwinn supplied. "Of the Yorkshire Leightons?"

"Her mom's a magus, too," Natalie explained. "*Old* family. She's running around with the Old Guard idiots in here."

I understood then why Kitty had neglected to mention her name to Toula, but I didn't have time to dwell on it. Leaving Gwinn and Natalie in relative safety, I ran down the hall toward the yelling, tracking it to a single eighth-year bedroom. The door wasn't even closed, and I had mere seconds to take in the situation before the Old Guard noticed me.

The eighth-years' dorm rooms were at least twice the size of the first-years', but even still, the place was crowded. Students leaned against the walls with their arms folded, a few holding wands. Kneeling on the rug by the bed, struggling to stand, was Kitty, disheveled and panting for breath. Her tangled hair partly obscured her face, but not enough to hide the fresh swelling of an upcoming black eye.

"I just want my flowers," she said, woozily clutching at the low bedpost. "Give them back. I didn't tell the grand—"

A bolt from an older brunette's wand made her yelp and curl into a ball, and her assailant looked at her with an expression of slight interest and amusement—the same look one might see from a child plucking the wings off a fly. "When are you going to get it through your thick skull that you don't belong here?" she asked as Kitty tried again to rise. "We've been nice"—the rest of the room snickered—"but since that hasn't worked..." She lined up the next shot, then glanced at the door and saw me standing there, empty-handed and horrified. "What do *you* want, girl?"

At that, my anger finally boiled over, and with it came a commensurate drop in prudence. Forgetting for the moment the role that I was supposed to be playing, I flung a wave of force around the room, throwing the onlookers up and against the ceiling, then dropped them. Caught unawares, they were too surprised to shield themselves against impact, and they fell onto the furniture, the floor, and in one boy's case, the radiator. While they were stunned, I swept in, threaded my arm around Kitty's back, and pulled her to her feet. "Come on," I said, half-dragging her into the hallway, then met Natalie and Gwinn again as we aimed for the staircase. "Taking her to the infirmary," I lied. "You might want to lock your doors."

The others scrambled away, and when the coast was clear, I ripped open a gate straight into Val's office and hustled Kitty through.

Val wasn't there, but as I guided Kitty to the couch, I heard indistinct voices coming from the direction of the central courtyard. He was holding court, I deduced, and there was no telling how long he would be busy hearing grievances. "Stay where you are," I told Kitty, propping a pillow between her head and the armrest. "I'm going to find Bonnie."

Kitty was quietly crying, though from her injuries or frustration, I couldn't tell. "Maria," she mumbled, "I told them—"

"It's okay," I soothed, and pressed her flat when she tried to sit up. "Be still, I…" Her face was red and swelling, and there was no way to know what sort of damage she'd sustained beneath her clothes. "I'm going to get help. Lie down, don't move, I'll find someone to look at you—"

I turned at the sound of an opening door and found Val hurrying in from the breezeway. The door closed quickly behind him, but not before I caught a glowing glimpse of Ros in his wake. "Move," he told me, and started to inspect the extent of Kitty's injuries.

He sounded brusque but not angry, and I stood behind the couch while he worked. "She got in a fight with the Old Guard," I explained as he began to throw together a healing enchantment.

"Not much of a fight, was it?" he muttered, and pulled a wet rag from the ether. "There's blood up here at the hairline, but I think it's superficial…"

Kitty flinched as Val prodded her cut. "I told them they could keep everything," she mumbled, wiping at her eyes. "And I told them I asked the grand magus not to do anything. I just want my flowers back."

Val sat on the coffee table and added a numbing thread to the enchantment he'd woven around her. "What flowers?"

"My sunflowers. They came from the farm, and Daddy…Daddy made them so they wouldn't wilt…" Kitty's eyes welled again, but she bit her lip and tried to hold it in—and then she frowned at Val. "What…"

From the intensity of his stare, I knew he was rummaging through her mind. "No matter," he said, and rose. "Maria, a word?"

I followed him into the breezeway and closed the door. "I'm sorry, I didn't mean to interrupt," I began, but he waved dismissively.

"I don't care about that. Toula has to know what's happened, whether Kitty approves or not. Can you make your friend see reason, or do I need to intervene?"

"I'll talk to her. But there's another magus's daughter involved, that's why she's been quiet about it—"

"How much of that beating did you observe?" Val interrupted.

"Just the end. I, uh...I snapped and threw everyone around," I mumbled.

"*Good.* You didn't see much of what they did to her."

He pulled out his phone, but I tried to stop him before he could make the call to Glastonbury. "Can't we run this by Kitty first? If her mom has to get involved—"

"She has at least three broken ribs," he said, scrolling through the list. "Enough is enough." He dialed and waited, and I heard Toula's voice rendered tinny by the speaker. "Get over here," he said without preamble. "You have a problem."

I had seen a spectrum of Toula's less pleasant moods in the years I'd known her—irked, perturbed, frustrated—but never had I seen her so angry as she was the next morning. Hers was a glacial sort of anger that day, cold and still but powerful enough to rend the land beneath her, and I found myself avoiding her line of sight. Sure, Toula was family, and she might have nominally been Arcanum, but she was also half fae, and her displeasure had gone far beyond mere annoyance.

From the way she shifted at my side, I sensed that Kitty felt the same instinct of preservation that drove me toward Toula's peripheral vision.

Val had insisted that Kitty remain in Faerie that day— she was healing nicely under his enchantment, though her bones were still knitting and her swelling subsiding—but Toula was firm, and so back she came. Gone was the enchantment, too, so as not to blow my cover, and although Toula and Magus Lowe had done what they could to replace it with a spell, Kitty was far from comfortable. She breathed shallowly through her mouth, doing what she could not to tax her aching ribs and swollen nose, and with the discoloration on her face, she looked pitiful.

Kitty hadn't been thrilled when I let her know what Val had done, but by the time Toula arrived, she had resigned herself to snitching. Holding an ice pack to her eye, she went down the list of the Old Guard for Toula, spilling every name she knew. When all she had was a face, Toula plucked it from her thoughts and assigned an identity.

"You get used to it," I'd told Kitty later that night when she'd pressed me for information about how, exactly, the adults around us were slipping into our heads. "I can't do it," I'd hastened to reassure her, "but Val's old, and the grand magus—"

"Is the grand magus," she'd finished, sounding like she was in the middle of a bad cold. "It's still weird. How do you have any privacy?"

"He doesn't dig for *everything*. My therapist insisted. But you'll know when he's in there."

"You can't block him?"

"No. Not yet, anyway." I'd pulled together a coaster for her damp ice pack and left her to sleep, though I'd kept the door between our rooms open, just in case.

Kitty had slept fitfully, bothered by her aches and bad dreams, and she scowled at the Old Guard assembled in Toula's office through puffy, shadowed eyes. The others looked no more pleased to have been called in before breakfast—Toula had sent a cadre of security to escort them from their dorm rooms, and some were still dressed in barely more than pajamas. Their expressions had been a mixture of feigned innocence and confusion when they were escorted into the office, but on seeing Kitty sitting near Toula's desk, their masks had begun to crack.

Toula didn't yell, but then again, she didn't have to. "I want to know two things," she said, folding her hands on her desk as she stared the Old Guard down. "First, I want to know where Ms. Connolly's belongings are. And once you've told me that, I want to know what gave you the goddamn right to beat the shit out of a ten-year-old."

Her vocabulary had become slightly politer than it had been the previous evening, but not by much.

Some of them shot each other nervous glances. A few focused on their feet. Finally, after an awkward silence, Dahlia looked Toula in the eye and spoke up for the group. "Her things are gone. As *she* should be."

"Gone?" Toula repeated, tilting her head ever so slightly. "You hid them, or you destroyed them?"

"Destroyed," she replied, defiance written on her face. "The witch doesn't belong here."

A quiet sniffle told me Kitty was fighting back tears, and I squeezed her hand.

"That's not your decision," said Toula. "And need I remind you that your mother and Kitty's mother are *colleagues*? Her family's as old-blooded as yours, for whatever little that means." She stood and leaned over her desk, pressing her palms against the blotter. "You don't get to decide who lives here, who works here, who studies here, little girl. *I do*. And I'm telling you fucking miscreants right now that the next person to do *anything* to a student you've decided is beneath you, in all your great wisdom, will be expelled. Should that come to pass, I *will* have your wand. Have I made myself perfectly clear?"

A few of the Old Guard nodded sheepishly, but Dahlia kept her chin high. "*You* don't belong here, either," she said with disdain. "A dirty mongrel—"

"Who is *this* close to dangling you out the window by your big toes and seeing whether you bounce. Want to try me?"

Obnoxious as she was, Dahlia was neither stupid nor suicidal, and she slunk out with the rest of her fellows.

When the sound of their footsteps faded, Toula sighed and turned to us. "Honey, I'm sorry," she told Kitty. "I'll replace what I can, if you'll just tell me what they took." She considered Kitty's swollen face for a few seconds, then added, "Later. Why don't you take the rest of the day off, hmm? Go back to bed." She waved a gate open and came around her desk to collect Kitty. "Maria…"

I perked in anticipation of the invitation.

"Take good notes today, okay?"

"Yes, Grand Magus," I mumbled, and scowled at the gate as it zipped closed behind them.

Toula allowed Kitty to stay out until Friday, giving her time to heal and her nerves time to settle. Kitty had fretted on Wednesday, wondering if her mother would object, but Toula assured her the matter had been addressed, and Magus Stanhope wouldn't cause a problem. Indeed, her mother never called Kitty to chide her—but then again, she didn't call to check on her, either, and I wondered how Toula had explained the situation.

While Kitty was away, Toula saw to it that her room was put back in order, including copies of most of her stolen books, but the one thing Kitty truly wanted was beyond Toula's power to remake. She could have filled the room with sunflowers, but the perfect blooms Orson Connolly had ensorcelled for his daughter were history. Though Kitty didn't mention them again, I knew she felt their loss keenly, but there was nothing I could do to help her.

When I came home from school on Thursday, I was pleased but not surprised to learn that Val had sent Kitty to spend the afternoon in Wanda's comfortable office. After taking stock of the situation, Wanda had recommended sessions twice weekly, either with her or with an Arcanum counselor, as Ros quietly confided to me that night when Kitty was asleep "I mean, come on, the kid lost her dad four months ago," Ros whispered, arms folded in consternation, "her mom has basically ghosted, and she got beaten up. Therapy sounds like a decent plan." She paused then and gave me a long look. "And should you be asked, you know none of this, capisci?"

Kitty seemed to be in decent spirits on Thursday night, but the next morning, with her bags packed for her first weekend back in the dorm, she picked at her breakfast and said little. As I shoved down the last of my toast, Val came into the dining room and handed Kitty a gray metal sphere the size of a large marble. "One of the crafters in town put this together," he explained. "A single-use spell, preloaded and ready. The crafter assured me that even a true mundane could trigger it with concentration."

"What sort of spell?" she asked, carefully rolling the sphere across her palm to see the faint etchings on the metal.

"That will open a gate into this realm." He sat and stared at her until she met his gaze. "And should you find yourself repeating recent events, I expect you to use it. Yes?"

Kitty nodded and slipped it into her pocket. "I'll take care of it, I promise."

"I'm more concerned that you take care of yourself," he replied, and waved a gate open. "Don't be late."

She dragged her new bag across and hurried toward the dorm to unload it before class, but Val held me back before I could follow her. "Stay away from the Old Guard," he murmured. "Even if they say nothing, someone will have noticed what you can do. Avoid them, Maria."

"I'll be careful," I assured him. "And they won't try anything. You didn't see their faces when Toula finished with them."

"I hope you're right," he replied. "If not...if they turn on you..."

"I can defend myself."

"Presumably. But if not, forget your cover charade. Come home. We'll manage the repercussions." He stooped to look me in the eye. "I'd rather have you in one piece and exposed than sneaked back broken…or worse."

His hug was brief but fierce, and as he sent me on my way, I hoped I looked more confident than I felt.

CHAPTER 6

For the next three weeks, it seemed as if Val had worried for nothing. The Old Guard gave Kitty a wide berth, the dorm was quiet, and we could all get back to the business of trying not to fail our classes. Kitty continued her quest to become valedictorian, prodding the rest of us along as needed, but as the term ramped up, my stress began to come out during Magus Lowe's class. He still paired me with Kitty most days for our practical sessions, but when the lessons turned toward the rudiments of combat, he finally tested me with a minor melee. "You're just shielding, now," he cautioned me, then let Natalie, Quentin, and Colby fire their best bolts. The exercise wasn't difficult for me, but it was a relief to do real magic after holding back for so many classes.

On our way to English, Tom caught me by the elbow and said, "That was impressive."

"Just practice," I fibbed.

"That's more than *practice*," he scoffed, wiping his sleeve across his sweaty face. "They're talking about you in the upper classes, you know."

My stomach tightened, but I tried not to let on. "Oh? Why?"

"What you did with the OG." He slid closer to me in the corridor and lowered his voice. "Rumor is you threw everyone in the air. *Empty-handed*."

"I was angry," I said, clenching my backpack strap. "Scared. That's all."

"It's true, then?"

I glanced at him in time to see his little smile. "Maybe."

"No need to be embarrassed," he replied, elbowing me in the side. "If I could do that, I'd do it *all* the time. Long line in the dining hall? Boom. Teacher getting on your nerves?" He forked two fingers and made a zapping noise.

I laughed. "If I did that, I'd be in *so* much trouble."

"But you could," he said, and grinned again. "Own it, Corelli."

While I appreciated Tom's support, I tried to maintain a low profile, holding back even when Magus Lowe allowed me to open up. Soon, however, I realized that the rumor Tom had mentioned had circulated in our class as well—and I could feel the others looking at me when Magus Lowe began to tell us about the Games.

Our first year would be the fifth round of the annual end-of-term event, a three-day opportunity for us to show off in front of our parents and peers. Students from our class up to the group turning twenty were invited to come to Glastonbury from all the installations and compete in a variety of events designed to showcase our budding skills. There would be a competition for technical craft, Magus Lowe explained—generally wardwork—and one for rapid casting, plus an academic bowl. But the most popular event—judging by the amateur bookies, at least—was single combat.

"You won't have to fight eighth-years or graduates," he assured us, meriting a few quick sighs of relief. "What we do is pit contestants against their classmates—you'll be fighting other first-years from across the installations. Every year will have a winner. Now, the winner gets to progress and fight in the next age group, if he or she wishes, but there are prizes for every level. There'd be no point in making you fight kids twice your age."

Mortimer—who, by that point in the year, was doing everything in his power to convince the rest of us to let him be Morty, with mild success—raised his hand. "Is this optional, Magus?"

"Oh, completely. You can go out for one event or most of them…or none, if you're not feeling confident."

I noticed a few heads swivel toward Kitty.

"But even if you don't win, I'm sure your parents would like to see that you've learned something this year," he continued. "Talk it over with them. This isn't a decision to be made today. And while you'll thinking about it, let's pair off for drills…"

Before I could slip away from the circle with Kitty, I heard Natalie mutter beside me, "Nothing personal, but I don't want to fight you."

"Ditto."

She snorted and tapped her wand against her palm. "Says the one on maple."

"Says the one on birch," I retorted.

Natalie shrugged. "Just promise you won't throw me into a radiator, huh?"

I smiled weakly and nodded, but I reminded myself to keep my talent under control. The less I warranted attention, the less likely it would be that anyone would look too deeply into my background. We all knew how the Old Guard felt about witches. I could only imagine what they would attempt if they learned there was another mongrel in their midst.

As the calendar ticked over to November, Magus Forester, our theory teacher, made an announcement. "I'm going on holiday this weekend," he told us Thursday morning. "Our youngest is having her fifth baby, and despite my assurances to the contrary, Mrs. Forester thinks our presence is required at the blessed event. But never fear, I've written detailed lesson plans, and I will leave you in the hands of a capable substitute on Monday—and I expect a good report on my return," he added, glaring in warning through his bifocals. Even if he couldn't make out our individual faces, the effect was sufficient.

But as fate would have it, Magus Forester's grandchild couldn't wait for the weekend, and an unfamiliar woman with a pleasant face and gray-streaked brown hair was sitting at his desk when we filed in on Friday. "Good morning," she said, standing as we came to attention, then tucked her hands into the draping sleeves of her crimson robe. "I'm Magus Leighton, and I will be your instructor today."

Kitty and I exchanged a quick look. Friday theory was a two-hour class—bad enough already, but worse with the looming possibility that our substitute would put names and faces together.

Magus Leighton opened the slim black binder on the desk and pursed her lips as she flipped through its pages. "This is *dull*," she said, and snapped the binder closed. "Shall we leave the boring bits for Don, then? I've got something more interesting in mind—more practical, at least. No one uses Pendergast's Focus these days. There are far better options...but that one may have been fresh when your Magus Forester was in school," she added with a faint smile. "Old habits and all. Now, I'm going to give you a lesson that may save your life someday."

We leaned forward, curious if not immediately concerned.

"How many of you know of the courts?" she asked, sitting on the edge of the desk.

My stomach sank, but I raised my hand with the others.

"Mm. Good," said the magus. "And how many of you can tell me anything useful about the Three?"

The hands stayed down that time, and she smirked in acknowledgement. "As I thought. Understanding Faerie isn't a simple undertaking, but you *must* know your enemy. It's imperative. And should you be unfortunate enough to find yourself confronted by one of those monsters, you will need an arsenal of tricks to defeat it. Let's begin your arming process."

I slid lower in my chair, willing my face not to color,

and focused on my notebook so as not to accidentally catch the magus's eye. No note came from Kitty—but then again, since our substitute could actually see what we were doing, no one in the room seemed eager to take chances.

Magus Leighton surprised us by pulling a tablet from her robe's inner pocket, then whispered a command to project the screen onto the whiteboard behind the desk. She stepped to the side so as not to obstruct our view as pictures of three people deeply familiar to me appeared. "On the left, Coileán, called the Ironhand," said the magus. "Known glamours are mostly age variations on the base you see here—he'll make himself look older, but almost always with these features. He's killed dozens of wizards that we know of, presumably more." She waited until the classroom's gross pencil movement slowed, then continued. "In the middle, Eleanor. Less of a pest than Coileán, but more creative with her glamours. Reports indicate that she favors a male appearance when she walks this realm, so good luck identifying her at first glance."

I bit my tongue. Eleanor never seemed anything but herself around me, and I doubted she'd have a need to disguise herself in the mortal realm. On many occasions, Val had allowed me to join them at dinner when he had the other two over unofficially, and when the wine began to flow—I was only ever given a sip—they inevitably tried to top each other's stories. Coileán had his share, but Eleanor, who had lived much of her life as a man out of convenience, had a wilder couple of centuries before she fell in love with academia, and some of her reminiscences left the others rolling. "But honestly," she'd once added, hiccupping through her laughter, "should I ever try to go male again, take me to have my head examined. You only *think* you have more fun."

"And then," said Magus Leighton, "on the right, Valerius. Old and skilled at combat, but otherwise largely a cipher. But what we *do* know is that his mother was Mab, who was so intolerable that the other two courts cast her and her court into the Gray Lands—"

Not true, I wanted to say, but swallowed the remark.

"—and then Mab had a much younger daughter." She tapped the screen, and a fourth image appeared, just below Val's. "Our own *beloved* grand magus," she said, the words drenched in sarcasm.

Some of my classmates began to whisper in confusion behind me. I raised my eyes, chancing a glance at Kitty, and was greeted by a look of shock. With the magus focused on her computer, Kitty pulled her notebook into her lap, and I lowered mine in time to see her scrawl: *He's a king?!?*

Yes was all I had time to write before her pencil flew again.

You know the grand magus, then? You actually know her.

We're keeping it quiet. Please, Kitty.

I know, she began, then stopped writing when the screen changed to just a shot of Toula's official portrait.

"Let's take a little diversion," said Magus Leighton. "There's no other way to say this: Toula Pavli is a mongrel."

"Yes, there is."

She peered at the back of the room, looking for the source of the interruption. "Who spoke? Stand."

I turned and saw Morty go to his feet. "Witch-blood, Magus," he said. "That's the right word."

She let him stew for a few seconds, then put her tablet on the desk and folded her arms. "Your name?"

"Morty Burnside, Magus."

"Burnside…" She squinted at the ceiling. "Not a terribly old family, is it? Any relation to the American general?"

"Distant cousin, Magus. And my mum is a Quarles."

One eyebrow quirked. "Not one of the better ones, I trust, if she married a new-blood."

I cringed for Morty, but he seemed unbothered. "Dad's

fifth-generation," he replied with a slight shrug. "Hardly matters at that point, does it?"

Magus Leighton smiled, but there was nothing kind in her expression. "Ah. A new old-blood," she said, drumming her fingers on her arm. "Oxymoronic, isn't it? How many of you are new-blooded, then?" she asked the room. About a third of us raised our hands, and she snorted. "Blood used to be given its proper consideration, and new-bloods knew their place. But I suppose I digress…and sit, boy," she added, waving her hand at Morty before retrieving her computer.

Well, that was rude, wrote Kitty.

You know that's Dahlia's mother, right?

Ugh.

"As I was saying, the grand magus is a mongrel," Magus Leighton resumed, looking at the projection. "This is truly a low point for the Arcanum. There was a time, not very long ago, when we did not have a mongrel problem. Do you know why?"

We shook our heads.

"Much depended upon where a mongrel was born. Those born in Faerie were usually killed young, as I understand it. Those born within the Arcanum either met the same fate or were employed as crafters—out in the world, naturally. The idea of allowing those things to live among decent wizards…" She shuddered. "It wasn't *done*, and we were better for it."

Gwinn stood and lifted her hand. "Why, Magus?"

Magus Leighton gave her a once-over, then cocked her head. "Why what?"

"Why not let them stay?"

She chuckled and motioned for Gwinn to take her seat. "Mongrels are inhuman. *Subhuman*, really. That they exist at all is a problem—with rare exception, they're untalented. I realize you're young, but I assure you that if you ever tried to pursue a relationship with a mongrel, your parents would strenuously object." She sighed and glared at

Toula's picture. "Most seem to understand their position. They leave us, perhaps do work for us, and let their blood die with them. Some think they're owed more, however. Some actually *breed*. And then some decide they're worthy of a magus's chain."

She gestured toward the projection. "Pavli was raised in Arc 1. Your grandparents may remember her father, certainly your great-grandparents would, mass-murdering new-blooded fiend that he was. And to have combined *that* with Mab? Why the Council didn't kill her as a liability is a mystery to me, but now we're stuck with her—our grand mongrel, if you will," she said, smiling at her own cleverness. "She stole the office, you know. Marched in with her brother. The threat was clear, and too many magi were cowards. Personally," she continued, turning to face us, "if I had my way, all mongrels would be sterilized, if not eliminated outright. Best solution for all of us...yes, what is it?"

Kitty had risen and stared Magus Leighton down. "If you killed off all the *witch-bloods*, then who would make our wands?"

"A fair question," she replied. "And you are?"

"Kitty Connolly, Magus."

"Indeed?" She paused. "Eva's girl?"

"Yes, Magus."

"Hm. Well, I suppose she *is* rather busy with the baby."

Kitty's face was a mask. "If you got rid of all the crafters—"

"Yes, yes," she said with an impatient wave. "Tell me, what do you know about crafters?"

She bit her lip in thought. "They're, uh...Fringers? I think that's the word. And I *think* they're all in Faerie—"

"The courts control them," Magus Leighton interrupted. "Restrict their output. There was a time when crafters were beholden to us, but the current batch fancy themselves our equals. As does the rest of the so-called Fringe," she scoffed, shaking her head. "Witches and lesser bloods and mongrels—we'd be better off without them, you know."

I had thought my stomach was roiling only from hunger, but the longer our substitute spoke, the surer I grew that it was threating to do far worse than growl.

"Excuse me, Magus," said Kitty, "but you didn't answer my question. What would we do for wands without them?"

The room held its breath as the two of them stared each other down, but after a brief pause, Magus Leighton smiled. "Glad you asked. Mongrels aren't actually necessary for wand production. With the proper training, a wizard can craft as well as any mongrel—probably better," she said, allowing her smile to widen. "There was a wizard some centuries ago known as Erik Niger—and take this down," she added to the rest of the room—"who wrote a treatise on the subject. He predated the Arcanum, but his work—"

"Is a myth."

The magus twitched as if she'd been pinched, then glared at the right side of the room as Gwinn rose. "What did you say?"

"Erik Niger is a myth, Magus. Gwinn O'Shea," she offered before Magus Leighton could demand it of her. "My sister Fíona is an archivist now, and she wrote her eighth-year thesis on Erik Niger. She says he's just a story, and even if he weren't, anything he wrote is long gone. She told me about it last summer, when I asked her about the wand ceremony—"

"*Sit*," Magus Leighton interrupted, and both Gwinn and Kitty sank into their chairs. "Don't you know it's poor manners to contradict your instructor?"

Gold star for G appeared in our notebooks from Tom, who sat in the back and generally had the sense to keep his mouth shut. I would have added to the conversation, but the longer I listened to Magus Leighton's voice, the more certain I was that I needed to leave.

"Whatever your sister told you is but one inexperienced archivist's opinion," the magus continued. "There are older, wiser individuals within the Arcanum who say just the opposite. And since it is possible to make wands without mongrels, the best thing—the *kindest* thing— would be to eliminate them. They are, quite simply, abominations. But now, unless anyone else has a comment, we'll continue with our discussion of faeries and the best ways to fight them..."

The projection changed from Toula's portrait to a hairless, wide-eyed corpse covered with swaths of weeping, smoking sores, followed quickly by a chorus of gasps and *eww*s from around the room.

"An extreme example," said Magus Leighton, smiling grimly at the image, "but one of my favorites for demonstrative purposes. This faerie was caught near Arc 3 back in the 1950s. A young one, fortunately. Someone knocked him unconscious, and the guards had the bright idea to clamp him in armor. If you've been to Switzerland, you've probably seen their old armor gallery—truly a fine collection. Anyway, before he regained consciousness, they wrestled him into one of the suits of plate metal. This was the result. Iron, you see, is *incredibly* effective against the fae, and steel will also do the trick..."

That was as far as I made it. The look of horror and anguish on the corpse's ruined face was enough to push my stomach to the brink, and I leapt from my desk and bolted from the room.

Fortunately, the toilets weren't far, but I barely made it. As I was sick over the bowl, I heard the door open, and then hands pulled my hair away from my face as I retched and cried. "Breathe," said Kitty, then passed me a wad of paper towels. "Here, want to wipe your mouth? I'll get you some water."

I was still kneeling by the toilet, not trusting my emptied stomach, when she returned from the sink with her refilled water bottle. I clutched it with both hands, my arms shaking, and drank until my throat no longer burned with acid. "Too much, huh?" she murmured, flushing the evidence away. "I don't blame you—"

"She wants me *dead*. If she knew…"

I don't know how bad I looked curled up on the bathroom floor, but whatever comfort Kitty had been preparing to speak died on her lips. "Go home," she said after a moment's pause. "I'll tell her you went to the infirmary. Bring you the notes and homework tonight, okay?"

"You heard what she—"

"Yeah, I did. And you're a mess right now. Go. I'll make your excuses." She pulled me to my feet and gave me a quick hug. "Keep the water bottle, I'll get it later."

Nauseated and sniffling, I opened a gate from the cubicle into my bedroom, then slipped through and collapsed onto my bed. A breeze was blowing in the garden past my open door, adding the rustling of leaves to the steady burbling of the fountain, but all I could hear was Magus Leighton's voice: *Abominations. Subhuman. Mongrels. Eliminate them.*

I didn't want to close my eyes, knowing full well that my mind would continue to show me the magus's favorite demonstrative if I did—and that it was trying its best to merge the stranger's face with Val's. And so I rolled onto my side, pulled the blankets to my chin, and stared at the shifting shadows on the wall while I waited to stop shaking.

"Maria. *Maria.*"

A familiar voice and a brusque hand on my shoulder pulled me back to consciousness with a yelp, and I tried to make sense of my surroundings. I was in bed—yes—and I must have been asleep—okay—but it was still daylight, and I was wearing shoes, and Ros was standing beside me…

The morning's events came back in a rush like floodwater, but before I could begin to explain to Ros why I was home so early, she said, "I know, I get it. Pull yourself together, babe." As I struggled to sit up and untangle myself from the covers, she added, "Sorry for the rough wakeup. I was going to show up in your dreams, but I figured you'd rather leave those quickly."

I nodded, latching on to fragments of threatening, half-remembered shadows. "Magus Leighton said—"

"I know what she said. You're not the first witch-blood to see that side of the Arcanum, trust me." Ros waited until I swung my legs free, then said, "I didn't tell Val you were back—thought you wanted a little time to yourself before he jumps in and starts swinging."

"Thanks," I mumbled, brushing my staticky hair from my face.

"Yeah, well, that plan went to hell. Kitty came over, and he's stormed off to find Tcula, maybe kill a magus. Coileán's gone along to keep him in check, but..." She grimaced. "Good luck, buddy."

"Kitty told—"

"Of course she told. And she's got a broken arm, to boot, so if you'll come with me—"

"*How?*" I asked, jumping out of bed. "What happened?"

Ros's mouth tightened. "I'll let her explain. Come on, Eleanor left her with Aiden," she said, and I ran through the gate she opened for me.

Coileán's younger brother kept the greatest concentration of sensitive electronics in all of Faerie in his apartment, and it was understood that the best way to get to him without incurring his anger was to keep gates well away from his workshop and control room. As such, Ros dropped me just inside the main door in a stone-walled vestibule that matched the rest of Coileán's castle. I hurried down the short hallway toward the sitting room, where Aiden had set up a big-screen TV, and found him beside Kitty, who was wrapped in a plaid afghan on one of the plush couches. "Hey, Maria," he said, beckoning me over. "Rough day?"

"What *happened*?" I demanded.

Kitty's right arm was in a sling, and a fine network of enchantment surrounded it from shoulder to wrist. She lifted the mug in her left hand in greeting, and I smelled chocolate. "Looks like I'm not going to be competing in the end-of-the-year combat tournament," she said, and sipped.

"*Kitty*."

She put the mug on the table, wincing as her arm shifted. "Class got rough after you left. Don't worry, you're not in trouble—Magus Leighton believed me when I told her you'd gotten sick. But I'm sorry, your stuff is probably still at your desk—"

"Never mind my *stuff*, what happened to you?"

"Sit down, kid," Aiden interrupted, rising from the couch. "And here." He produced a second mug of chocolate and passed it to me as I took his vacated seat. "Be careful and don't bump her—that arm's going to be soft for a while. Have either of you had lunch?"

"I'm not really hungry," I mumbled.

"Uh-huh. Well, one mongrel to another, you're not going to do anyone any favors by starving yourself, so I'll work on pizza, and you two catch up, okay?"

Aiden slipped off down the hall, and Kitty lowered her voice. "He doesn't really need to work on it, does he?"

"Nope. Start talking."

She frowned in thought, then gingerly retrieved her mug, took a sip, and began.

Kitty had returned to class, explained the situation to Magus Leighton, and been allowed to take her seat without further questioning. The rest of the room had started writing notes to her—it wasn't every day that someone ran away to puke—but she'd provided no real details, blaming my condition on questionable breakfast yogurt.

Magus Leighton had continued with her lecture, and Kitty had taken careful notes, particularly as there hadn't been any preparatory reading. But as class continued and Kitty chimed in with her usual high level of participation, the magus began to grow annoyed.

"Daddy never told me much about the courts, exactly," she explained, holding her mug close, "but he thought I at least needed to know about the other groups out there. He taught me a little about the Fringe, the Minor Arcanum—you know, who they are, what they do. I guess, you know, in case I turned out to be a witch," she added, shrugging her good shoulder. "And he told me the grand magus is witch-blooded, but it never seemed to bother him. I didn't realize it was such a big deal until I spent last summer in Montana."

Kitty had a mind for detail and trivia, and the lecture soon devolved into a dialogue between her and Magus Leighton, as the rest of our classmates were either ignorant of the correct answers or unwilling to risk a dressing-down by the magus. But though Kitty was able to provide the answers the magus had in mind, the magus soon tired of hearing her voice.

"At first, she stopped calling on me," Kitty recounted. "And she started randomly calling on people, so I tried to help with notes, but that didn't work too well. So then, she went on about the Fringe conspiring with the courts to take the Arcanum apart, and I said that wasn't right, my dad told me they'd joined up when Grand Magus Mulligan kidnapped all those witches, and she lost her temper."

"She yelled at you?" I asked.

Kitty's mouth twitched. "At first."

What followed was a blistering lecture from Magus Leighton on respect—respect for one's elders, for instructors, and for magi in particular—and then things took a more personal turn. "You're barely even a witch, aren't you?" she snapped at Kitty. "Everyone on the Council knows about Eva's dud. Did they give you a wand at all, or just a nice little stick to make you feel better?" She waited until Kitty pulled her dragonscale wand from her backpack, then took it from her, tossed it into the air like a baton, and smirked as she handed it back. "There's a core, at least. Maybe you *are* a witch. Witches in particular should show proper respect, you know." She leaned over Kitty's desk, staring her in the eye. "And they should know their place. That's not here. I don't care who your mother is, you have no business wasting your classmates' time."

But Kitty stood her ground. "The grand magus says otherwise."

"And as I told you, Pavli is an upstart mongrel." With that, she straightened and smiled at the rest of the class. "Well, since you're having a difficult time focusing on a lecture today, let's try a technical exercise to wake ourselves up, shall we?"

With the class following behind her like nervous ducklings, Magus Leighton selected an empty practice room and ushered them inside. As they gathered around her in a semicircle, she asked, "How are your shields coming along?"

"She showed us this complicated technique," Kitty told me. "Much harder than the stuff Magus Lowe has been teaching us. And then she told us she was going to see how well we'd been paying attention." She sipped her chocolate and pulled the afghan more tightly around her shoulders. "We were going to play a game."

Magus Leighton pointed to Kitty and sent her to the middle of the room. "Since you've been so eager to participate, dear," she said as Kitty shuffled into position, "I'm certain you won't mind being our first volunteer." When Kitty was in place, the magus told the others, "Now, let's see how well Ms. Connolly can reproduce the shield I just showed you. On my signal, she'll have a ten-count to shield, and then you'll have a chance to punch through it."

The others looked uncertainly at each other, then at Kitty and her dragonscale ward. "Um, Magus?" said Natalie, stepping out of the pack. "I want to go first, please."

"Wait your turn."

Quentin stepped up and raised a finger. "Magus, Kitty isn't meant to do melees. Magus Lowe said—"

"This is not his class," she snapped, "and any wizard worthy of being in this school can surely shield. Your time starts now, Kitty."

"I tried," she said into her mug. "Really, I did. I knew I couldn't make her technique work, so I went with the usual ones, but you know how long it takes me to make a good shield."

I nodded in sympathy.

"And I pulled one together. Better than I'd expected— I actually blocked the first shots," she continued. "I mean, everyone was throwing softballs, but still…it held, see?"

"You're getting better at it."

"Not quickly enough," she muttered. "Magus Leighton got impatient, I guess, since no one was hitting me hard, and she jumped in."

The magus's bolts came in a rapid-fire burst, strong and unblockable, and ripped through Kitty's shield like nails driven through wet tissue paper. One slammed into her right arm, splintering the humerus. With the shield shattered, Kitty dropped her wand and grabbed her broken arm—but Magus Leighton kept up the barrage.

"You are *useless!*" she yelled, marching toward the center as Kitty knelt and tried to cover her head. "Weak! Pathetic!" By the time she reached Kitty, she was practically frothing, and she pulled Kitty to her feet by her shirt. "You have no right to be here," she said, flinging specks of spittle onto Kitty's face. "And if you *ever* attack my daughter again, I'll show you what a real wizard can do, you little—"

The rest of her tirade was cut short when Magus Lowe

ran in and started bellowing for Magus Leighton to back off. Seeing Kitty's dangling arm, he cursed out his colleague in loud, colorful terms, then shepherded Kitty to the infirmary.

"He was teaching the fourth-years next door," Kitty explained. "When Magus Leighton was focused on me, Gwinn and Tom ran out to find help, and they made him come. He said Tom was yelling that she was going to kill me."

"I think he had the right of it," I muttered.

"At least she just gave me bruises and a broken arm. Could be worse. Magus Lowe left me with a medic, and she put a healing spell on my arm and sent me to bed for the rest of the day."

"But Val's work is better?" I ventured.

"Well, yeah, and I was worried about you."

"I'm not the one with the sling!"

"Maybe not, but you're my friend, and...and you've been looking out for me," she mumbled. "A *lot*. And I wanted to explain why I wouldn't have notes for you—"

"Forget the notes. She could have hurt you a lot worse than she did. If Magus Lowe hadn't been there..."

"Don't remind me." Kitty took a long drink of chocolate, and a twinge of pain crossed her face as she adjusted her seat on the cushion. "So I still had that preloaded spell that Val"—she paused and cleared her throat—"*Lord* Valerius gave me, and I used it to come over."

My eyes widened. "The spell on your arm—"

"Broke when I crossed, yeah. Forgot about that. So that hurt like the dickens, and I didn't know where I'd landed—I was standing on a big lawn next to a castle—and this glowing woman appeared out of nowhere—"

"Ros."

"That's what she said..." she replied, hinting for more information.

"She's, um...well, she's the realm's consciousness,

more or less. She knows when anyone comes through—"

"My niece is nothing if not nosy," Aiden interrupted, carrying a large pepperoni pizza into the room. "You two get started on this," he said, waving a pair of plates and a stack of napkins into existence on the coffee table. "I'm still tweaking the cheesy bread."

When he disappeared into the kitchen again, Kitty lifted an eyebrow. "Runs in the family?" she murmured.

"Wouldn't surprise me." I loaded our plates, and Kitty traded her mug for one, balancing it on her lap while she ate left-handed. "So, Ros found you?" I asked as my stomach, calmer after my nap, remembered it was empty.

Kitty nodded as she chewed through a mouthful of dough. "She didn't let me get two words out before she dragged me into the castle. Said I needed to see…uh…your grandpa right there."

"You know, if he lets you call him Val, he means it."

Her skepticism was evident, but it faded from her face as she tore into the slice. "Like I said, Ros brought me in here, and we stopped outside this closed door, and she said they were meeting, but she'd make the interruption, and she went ahead before I could ask her to wait."

I tried to imagine Kitty's reaction at that moment— aching from the unensorcelled arm and her fresh bruises, shaken after the morning's events, and then realizing she was about to walk in on the Three uninvited. True, I'd done so on numerous occasions when they met in Val's office, but I'd never had cause to fear them. I didn't know what else Magus Leighton had told the class after my departure, but from the look on Kitty's face at the memory, she'd been at least queasy when Ros interrupted them.

More than queasy, came Ros's whisper in my mind. *Poor kid was shaking. I thought she was in shock from the arm at first.*

I kept my face still, trying not to let on to Kitty that I was receiving additional commentary to her play-by-play. "They weren't upset, were they?"

"Not right away. Ros called me in, and they were together, and they looked up…" She bit into the pizza, stalling while she assembled her thoughts.

But Ros beat her to it. From her omnipresent vantage point, I saw the scene play out: Kitty slumped by the door, clutching her arm, Ros beside her, and the Three sitting across the room with a litter of papers spread on the table between their couches. Coileán jerked in surprise at the sight, Eleanor put down her teacup, and Val was on his feet in seconds. "I'm sorry to bother you," Kitty said in a rush. "Maria got sick today, and she went home, but I think the magus really upset her. We had a substitute—"

"Moon and stars," Val interjected, striding across Coileán's office, "your *arm*. What happened?" Her lip trembled as he approached, and seeing her fear, Val paused. "You're safe, child," he murmured, then closed the distance. "Sit. I'll patch the arm, tell me how it broke."

Kitty stammered out the beginning of an explanation, but once Val finished enchanting her arm into mending, he took the shortcut and looked for himself. I saw a selection of emotions flicker through his eyes, but the one that lingered was rage, quiet but white-hot. "What is it?" Coileán asked as Val stood and turned to the others, and when he mentally repeated what he'd gleaned from Kitty, their eyes flew open wide.

"You'll excuse me. I need to speak with my sister," he said, waving open a gate.

Eleanor and Coileán traded looks, and he rose and jogged after Val. "I'll, uh…help," I heard him say before the gate closed.

In the end, it was Eleanor who delivered Kitty into Aiden's safekeeping. After he'd wrapped Kitty up on the couch—her shaking had only worsened—Eleanor had quietly told him the salient points, including his brother's whereabouts, then asked him to keep an eye on Kitty until Val returned.

When the vision cleared, I knew I'd given myself away,

as Kitty was regarding me strangely. "Thought you couldn't get in my head."

"I can't," I told her. "Ros decided to play middleman."

"And we have cheesy bread," Aiden announced, emerging once more with a plate of gooey, garlicy manna. Producing a plate for himself, he plopped into a recliner with a couple of slices and a few breadsticks. "Passable?"

"*Really* good," I mumbled around a mouthful of pizza.

"There's a time and place for authentic Neapolitan style, but if you want comfort food, 'cheap American delivery' is unbeatable, in my humble opinion." He tested his work, groaned happily, and pushed back in the chair until the footrest popped up. "You guys want to watch a movie or something? I've got an old Wii, but with the bum arm, I don't think that'd be entirely fair."

Kitty chewed thoughtfully, then swallowed and cleared her throat. "Um…sir, did you say you're—"

"Witch-blooded? Yeah," Aiden finished. "Didn't find out until I was fifteen, and Montana raised me as a dud, so believe me, *I get it*. And speaking from experience, the best thing to do with a break like yours is try to sleep through the initial re-knitting—you'll be a lot less uncomfortable after that, numbing enchantment or not." He sat up a little to see her better. "Heard you've been spending time over here with Maria."

"Yes, sir."

"Is your computer shielded?" Kitty shook her head, and Aiden sighed. "Well, that's unfortunate. The fastest way to ruin a computer, other than chucking it in the bathtub or beating it with a sledgehammer, is to keep it around active magic."

"They don't let us have them in class—"

"If they were smart, they wouldn't let you have them unprotected in the building. You don't have yours here right now, do you?" he asked, sounding almost hopeful. When Kitty shook her head again, he leaned back and readjusted his plate. "Next time you're over, bring it by, and I'll get some protection in place."

Kitty's brow furrowed. "But if you did that, wouldn't it fall apart every time I brought my computer back through from Glastonbury?"

"Nope. The force at the border breaks magic on living things. It won't affect your gear—I mean, if it did, more than half the folks in this realm would end up naked every time they crossed from that direction."

She glanced down at her shirt, one of Bonnie's creations, and nodded in relief.

Aiden considered her for a moment, then quietly said, "I've known a lot of good, smart, brave people who couldn't cast like a magus if their lives depended on it. If Toula thinks you can hack it at Arc 2, then trust her. Hell, *she* gets it," he added. "She was pretty heavily bound until she was in her thirties. Not everyone starts with a fancy wand." He sat up again and grinned. "You think you have it bad? My sister tested at maple out the gate. Ever heard of Grand Magus Carver?" Kitty nodded, wide-eyed in recognition, and he chuckled to himself. "Try living up to that when you can't even cast a shield. They didn't bother testing me—I've never been able to use a wand."

"But you're—"

His fingertips sparked, and a green ball of flame bounced from knuckle to knuckle. "This came later. What I'm trying to say is that you're not the first to have a rough time growing up Arcanum, and if you get to the point that you're about to punch a wall…like I said, I've got a Wii."

He looked up at a sudden pounding on the door, then twitched a finger to unlock it. "Den!" he called. "Is anyone dead?"

Toula and Val came down the hall almost in tandem, so neither saw it when Coileán, who followed a few paces behind, looked at Aiden and mimed wiping his brow.

"*Shit,*" Toula hissed on catching sight of Kitty. "I am *so* sorry, honey." She slid the pizza to the side and perched on the coffee table directly in front of Kitty and me.

"Okay, time to be absolutely honest with me. What did Leighton say about witch-bloods?"

"That we should be eliminated," I muttered.

"Or...um..." Kitty scowled into space, then jerked as Toula rifled through her thoughts

"Sterilized? She said all of that in front of a room of first-years? *Really*?" She rolled her eyes to the ceiling and huffed in agitation. "Inbred bitch. I'll have her chain by Monday."

"Are you sure that's wise?" Coileán began. "With the Conclave—"

"This isn't about the damn Conclave," Toula snapped. "This is about a magus on a racial purity kick attacking a child. Imagine if a magus had started throwing bolts at Aid when he was their age," she added, glancing at the recliner, then pointed to Kitty's broken arm. "Francine could have killed her."

He lifted his hands in pacification. "I know, I'm just saying that you don't need more enemies in the Council right now."

"She and I have never been friends. And if I stand back, close my eyes, and let old-blooded wizards run over witches again just to keep the peace, then I'm no better than Greg. That's a devil's bargain I will *not* make."

"Um...Toula?" I ventured.

"Yes, sweetheart?" she replied, still glaring about the room as if she was waiting for Magus Leighton to jump out from behind the couch.

I tried to choose my words carefully. "The magus had a lot to say about you, and...uh..."

She cut her eyes to Val. "I got the gist of it. Don't worry about me," she said, giving my knee a pat. "If Francine Leighton wants to hurt my feelings, she's going to have to do a lot worse than that."

"But she—"

"What she expressed isn't exactly an uncommon sentiment in certain quarters of the Arcanum. The place is a snake pit on a good day, but I've made it this far. So don't you worry about her—and don't worry about yourself, either." She clasped my hands between hers and offered a reassuring smile. "There are only half a dozen people with Arcanum connections outside of this room who know what you are, honey. You're not going to get ambushed by a pitchfork-waving mob of magi."

But Val seemed uncertain. "Half a dozen? Beyond Arnold…"

"Bee," she replied, counting on her fingers, "so we can presume Daisy as well. Ros said she'd mentioned the situation to Frank. A couple other magi I trust. No one's going to out her." Her gaze swiveled back toward Kitty. "I mean, unless—"

"*Nope*," insisted Kitty, shaking her head so vehemently that she caught her hurt shoulder and yelped.

Toula winced in sympathy and gave her good arm a quick squeeze. "That's what I figured. And if you want to spend the night over here and let that heal, I won't say anything."

There was no point in getting the assignments from our classmates—neither of us had our books with us, nor did we particularly wish to go back for them. But before dinner, Toula slipped across to retrieve our bags, then returned with three slips of paper in hand. "Excuses from the infirmary for you both," she said, passing one to each of us, "and your homework. I know you don't want to get behind over the weekend," she added with a meaningful stare, and we grudgingly nodded.

By Monday morning, Kitty was on the mend, if still somewhat discolored, but Val seemed reluctant to break the enchantment and send her on her way. "I'm okay," she protested. "Doesn't even hurt."

"Because it's been numb for almost three days," he pointed out, then handed her another metal sphere. "A replacement. The next time you're drafted into serving as a target, use it before the spells start flying, yes?"

"Thank you," she said as she tucked it away, "but I can't just trigger that in the middle of class. I'd blow Maria's cover."

"Maria," he replied, giving me a long look, "knows how to protect herself. You do not."

"But—"

"Secrecy is useful to a point, but I know what Aiden went through. Don't hesitate."

As usual, Val held me back once Kitty was on her way through the gate. "You're stronger than they are," he said, lifting my chin. "Don't let them upset you."

"I'm sorry…"

"For what?" He stooped and pulled me close. "You're ten, you're learning. And I am very proud of you, Maria." Releasing me enough to see my face, he murmured, "I'm sorry that Kitty was injured, and Toula's promised to address the situation. But she's also well aware that if anyone does that to you, there will be blood. Understood?"

I nodded, and Val nudged me back to Glastonbury.

CHAPTER 7

Though the grand magus wielded great power within the Arcanum, Toula wasn't omnipotent in personnel matters. Without evidence of treason or another serious offense, she couldn't simply remove magi from the Council at will. Magushood was for life, and per the Arcanum's rules, the removal process involved the presentation of the case to the rest of the Council and a vote on the matter.

But there were ways around the rules if one knew where to apply pressure.

Over the weekend, Toula confronted Magus Leighton about Kitty's injuries. With Magus Lowe backing her and recounting in detail what he had witnessed, she demanded our substitute's chain and resignation. Magus Leighton balked at first, but as Toula later told Val (and Ros then told me), the magus knew she couldn't win against the full Council. Sure, some might have agreed with her "death to mongrels" spiel, but few would ever sanction an attack on a child, let alone a *magus's* child, no matter how untalented she might be. And so, on Monday morning, as we halfheartedly translated one of Ms. Veracruz's lengthy passages, word began to spread that Dahlia's mother had resigned her position. By lunch, there was no doubt, and Tom ran to our long table to breathlessly announce that he'd had confirmation from his older cousin. Magus Leighton was a magus no longer—and Dahlia Leighton was nowhere to be found.

As Kitty's shoulders began to unclench, Gwinn gingerly patted her back and smiled. "That's that, then," she said with a little smile. "Surely the rest will leave you alone now, eh?"

Kitty nodded, but as the two of them began to talk about our latest maths assignment, I turned my attention back to my meal. I propped my elbows on the table and ate my sandwich, staring into space...and then I noticed that I was being watched by a pale man eating alone two tables over.

If my observer had been almost anyone else in the room, I might have looked past him, but the man was striking in his coloration—or, more accurately, his lack thereof. Kitty's blonde waves were close to platinum, but the man, though apparently young, had a full head of white hair, which he'd pulled back in a low ponytail. His eyebrows blended into his face, and his lips seemed nearly bloodless. I could see nothing of his eyes; even in the relative shade of the dining hall, he wore a pair of sunglasses with small, round, gray-smoked lenses. The rest of him seemed ordinary enough—a black ribbed sweater and a plate of chili-topped fries—but then his glasses met my gaze, and one corner of his mouth ticked into a slight smile.

And then he stood.

And *stood*.

The pale man was enormous, at least a head taller than the men walking near him and quite a bit broader than most. He had to stoop to retrieve his tray from the table, and then he wandered away through the noon press, out the main doors and, presumably, into one of the auxiliary dining rooms.

I continued to stare after him until I realized Kitty was calling my name. "Sorry, what?" I said, blinking to focus on her.

"You okay?" she asked. "Lost you there for a minute."

"Fine," I said, and forced myself to smile. "Maths coma."

Natalie groaned into her soup, and Gwinn and Kitty

rolled their eyes. But while the conversation soon turned to the distant weekend—Natalie was trying to drum up interest in the boarders' planned outing to the cinema—I couldn't help but wonder who the pale man was and what he'd found so interesting in our direction.

By Tuesday morning, three more of the Old Guard had disappeared.

On Wednesday, the count was up to ten.

The whispers continued—if anything, they were louder than ever—but their tenor changed. Instead of jokes about Magus Leighton running away to work in a call center and ensorcell impossible customers, I started to hear more worrisome mutterings: *Gone. No warning. Middle of the night.*

And then, quietly, *Conclave.*

Whole families disappeared that week, parents and children alike, all under cover of darkness. We lost two from my class, a local girl named Alice and Omar, a boy from Arc 5, the Giza installation. Both were old-blooded, and neither came to first period Thursday morning. No one knew much about Alice's living situation, but Omar's room had been a popular meeting place for the first-year boys, and suddenly, it was empty but for the furniture. Neither left a note or answered the messages we sent.

To make matters even more uncomfortable, the pale man continued to appear.

He never approached, and he never removed his glasses, but I could almost feel the pressure of his stare—a few tables away in the dining hall, at the end of the corridor, in an armchair in the library. I thought of broaching the issue with Toula, but after the previous weekend, I didn't want to put another matter on her plate. The watcher didn't seem threatening, after all, just...there. Not curious, not intimidating—*present.*

With all the goings-on in the castle, I was eager to escape for a few hours to see a movie on Saturday afternoon. I wasn't the only day student to sign up for the outing—Magus Lowe, who had agreed to chaperone, coordinated gates to bring a dozen or so of us back into the installation, and then another teacher passed out cards for the bus. The cinema was on the other side of town, not a terribly long ride, but still, the notion of riding out beyond the castle's walls proved popular.

Kitty and I sat together, squished toward the window to watch the town go by. I played with the strap of my purse—for once, I needed funds, and Toula had procured a prepaid debit card for me. Kitty had a similar setup, and she'd judiciously parceled out the pocket-money her mother had given her at the beginning of the term. We talked about the snack options and the movie, the sequel to a cartoon I'd never seen, and Kitty filled me in as well as she could while we wound our way through Glastonbury.

Once we reached our stop, we filed off the bus and found Magus Lowe waiting alone. Our group was too large to take one bus without drawing attention to ourselves, and the first wave—mostly older students who were catching an earlier film—had disappeared into the building. As we passed, Magus Lowe played with his phone, though his slight nodding suggested he was taking a head count.

The problem with field trips of any sort was that officially, our school didn't exist. Off of the castle grounds and out of the camouflaging bubble of enchantment, we were just a mob of kids and teens who happened to be sharing the same space. Our ostensible chaperones kept their distance, which was probably for the best whenever there was a magus involved, as we'd been warned not to address them as such off-campus. We weren't allowed to have our wands with us, either, but since we were planning to be largely unsupervised and armed with food missiles in a dark theater, that was almost *certainly* for the best.

Feeling like very grown-up ladies about town, Kitty and I bought our tickets and headed inside to queue for popcorn. As we waited, I glanced around the lobby, watching the trailers for the impending slew of December films. Just as I decided that the cashier in our line couldn't move any more slowly if he were encased in cement, I heard an unfamiliar voice in my head say, *Lady Maria.*

My head jerked, and the voice quickly added, *Show no reaction. There's a bank of posters to your left—look at those.*

Gripping my purse in my sudden fear, I did as the speaker bid. *Good girl*, the voice continued. *No need to panic yet. I'm going to get you out of here.*

I pushed my question to the top of my thoughts and hoped the voice could read them. *Who are—*

A friend. And since your buddy has a target on her back, you're in danger by proximity.

What danger? I protested, looking around in spite of the voice's instructions. *It's just the cinema—*

A man and a woman are standing ten people back from you in the queue. They plan to sit near Kitty and make it look like she choked during the movie. Maybe an allergic reaction. They're carrying wands, by the way. Don't look.

I forced my eyes forward. *How do you—*

Know? They're nervous, and it's practically broadcasting. The voice paused, then said, *Here's the plan. I'm standing near the drinks machine. Look up, notice me, and bring her along to say hello. Be deliberate about it.*

I don't even know your name!

Seriously, stop panicking, it'll make you sloppy. And I'm Frank.

Frank? I thought, confused, and cut my eyes toward the meeting place.

There was the pale man, leaning against the wall and sipping from a bottle of water. He still wore his glasses, and as far as I could tell, he was watching another screen of previews.

Ros said she told you I'd be around, he replied. *Did she forget?*

Suddenly, I recalled where I'd heard that name. *No, but...*

He must have been able to make sense of my sudden jumble of thoughts, as I detected amusement in his reply. *What, you thought I'd sleep out back or something? Difficult to do the work if you can't fit in the building.*

But—

Explanations later. Get over here.

I was no actress, but I tried to sell it. "Oh, hey!" I said to Kitty, plastering a fake smile on my face, and pointed across the lobby. "That's my friend over there!"

Kitty glanced around me to follow the direction of my finger. "Who's *that*?"

"Frank. Come on, I want you to meet him."

She protested when I pulled her out of the concessions queue, but I dragged her over to Frank and waved. "Hello!" I called as we neared. "How are you?"

He twitched in feigned surprise, and the glasses dipped toward me as he straightened. "Ah, Maria! Good to see you," he said, his voice so low-pitched that it nearly rumbled. His mouth moved into an approximation of a smile. "And this is…"

"Kitty," she said with faint bemusement. "Um…are you…"

"What are you seeing?" he interrupted, and I flashed my ticket. "Hey, me, too. Mind if I join you? It might be crowded, so why don't we grab seats, and I'll hold them while you get your popcorn."

Kitty seemed unconvinced by this plan, but she trailed along when I followed Frank. He bypassed our theater, however, and then, after a quick check inside, pushed us into the deserted men's toilets near the back of the building.

"Long story short," he told Kitty, "you've got assassins on your tail. Don't worry, I'll make a distraction."

Before she could say more than, "*What*?" Frank located the smoke detector on the ceiling, puckered his lips, and blew a thin jet of flame into the air. The detector began to blat as the white tiles around it blackened, and with a quick hiss, the sprinklers came on.

"Stay with me," said Frank, leading us next door into the women's toilets, then set off the smoke detector in there as well. As Kitty gaped, flabbergasted, he took the extra step of pulling the fire alarm in the hallway, then pointed to the emergency exit. "That way. I'm in the car park."

Overwhelmed as I was, I didn't know what to expect outside the cinema, but the black Ford sedan that beeped at Frank's touch of the key fob came as a surprise for its sheer mundanity. I hopped into the front seat, Kitty took the back, and Frank pulled onto the road with worrying speed. "No need to brace yourself," he said, giving me a quick glance as I clung to the door handle. "I know what I'm doing."

"You're licensed?" I asked, tightening my grip when he swerved into the fast lane.

"No, but I've been driving since I was seven," he replied, and shrugged. "Two pedals, sometimes three, a stick, and a wheel—it's not *that* difficult."

"Seven?" Kitty echoed weakly from the back as she fumbled with her belt. "Someone let you drive at *seven*?"

"Job training," said Frank. "And that was seven years ago, so I've had practice since—"

"You're *fourteen*?"

He grinned at the rearview mirror. "It's not my fault your species takes forever to grow up. But we can talk about that later," he added, and darted down an alley. "You're in deep shit, kid."

Kitty tugged her chest strap tight and glowered toward the front. "Would someone *please* tell me what the heck is going on?"

"In brief," Frank replied, whipping into oncoming traffic to pass a bicyclist, "Toula asked me last weekend to keep an eye on you for a few days. Said you'd got a magus fired, and she was worried about retaliation. I'm useless with a wand, but most of the folks in the castle don't know that, and size has its advantages. No one tried anything during the week, but I started picking up on an undercurrent last night in the library—"

"But I didn't go to the library last night," said Kitty.

"Got to do my own work *sometime*. Anyway, a few of the rank-and-file were trying to be inconspicuous in a study room—no one I've dealt with, but I'm sure Toula knows their faces. I picked up on enough to be concerned, and when I saw you were part of the movie trip, I came ahead of you. Helps to know where the Arcanum fleet's keys are kept," he said, giving the steering wheel a pat. "As I said, there are assassins after you. A pair of them back there, to be exact. Armed." He sped past a compact car and zoomed onto a thoroughfare.

"Someone's trying to *kill* me?" Kitty cried. "*Why?*"

"Yes to the first, and as for the second, you tell me—I try to avoid Arcanum politics,' said Frank. "But it's nothing to worry about now. I'll have you back to the castle in no time, and we'll go straight to Tou…oh, *fuck*."

He glared at the mirror, and I turned to see another nondescript car speeding up behind us. "Is that—"

"Yeah." His tone was suddenly more clipped. "Right, then. Ros says you're talented, Maria."

"Somewhat…"

"Shield us."

"What, the whole car?"

"Only the parts you'd like to keep intact. And hurry it up. Passenger's pulling a wand."

For once, panic was my ally, and the shield that flew from my fingertips rapidly expanded to surround our vehicle. I barely had time to reinforce its construction before the woman behind us leaned out her window and began firing bolts our way. They ricocheted, but I cried out with the strain of holding the shield together under the assault.

"I've got a better plan," said Kitty, bracing herself as Frank sped around a corner and down a tight alley. "Gate.

We drive straight into Faerie—they probably won't follow us."

"Can you make a gate?"

"Maria can."

"You *can*?" Frank glanced my way as I grunted with a fresh shield impact. "Damn it, no one told me that..."

"Want a gate?" I panted. "I'll have to drop the shield—"

"No. Hold it steady," he replied, and depressed the accelerator. "Besides, if I drove into Faerie with the two of you in the car, I'd probably kill you both. *And* destroy our ride."

"Huh?" said Kitty.

"Ensorcelled," he absently explained, sliding back into traffic and running a red light. "I'm quite a bit larger when the spell breaks. Being in my proximity at that moment would be a bad idea."

We flew through town and out the other side, heading for the fields around the hidden castle, but the other car stayed with us, matching Frank turn for rapid turn. I hoped the approach to the installation would give our pursuers pause—even when the barrier ward was disengaged, the road was disguised as a dead end with a chain-link fence and a deep creek beyond it, not the sort of thing most drivers wanted to plow through. But they didn't slow, and I suspected they knew the secret as well as we did.

As Frank raced through the camouflaging ward toward the main gate, white-knuckling the wheel, I heard his voice again in my head: *Is the shield permeable from this side?*

"Yes," I mumbled, aching deep in my bones as yet another bolt slammed into my spell.

Good.

Without warning, Frank spun us around on squealing tires and drove straight toward our pursuers, lowering his window. When we were almost upon them, he slid to the left, turning the head-on collision into a tilt, and angled his head just outside the car.

The couple behind us had been on the offensive the whole time. I didn't have it in me to shield to that extent *and* strike, and Kitty was no help, particularly empty-handed. As such, they didn't have a shield for us to contend with—and their car was vulnerable to the blast of fire Frank shot at them as we passed. The driver had his window up, but the flames came far too close to the petrol tank, and with a boom that rocked our car even as we hurried away, the assassins' vehicle exploded.

Frank kept driving until we were well clear of the scene, then whipped the car around again and stopped. "Problem solved," he muttered.

"Oh, my God," Kitty whispered behind us, barely audible above the idling engine. "Oh, my God. You just…"

As I stared at the conflagration, something old and buried crawled out from the corner of my mind that I tried to keep walled off, something black and amorphous but for the needle teeth it sank into my psyche. My heart raced, my chest heaved, and as I sucked at the air, I could smell the smoke and burning petrol wafting through Frank's window…and with it, another smell I knew from my nightmares, roasting meat with overtones of sour beer…

I didn't realize I was screaming until Frank released me from my seatbelt, pulled me out of the car, and carried me away from the scene. Pressing my face against his shoulder and turning to block my view, he murmured comfort to my mind until I could focus enough to understand that Luca wasn't coming after me. Disoriented and ashamed of my terror, I burst into tears, and I didn't stop until Toula, who had run down with the castle's security force to see why there was a sudden bonfire in the road, pried me from Frank's arms and pulled Kitty and me into her office by gate. "We'll handle this," she said, then opened a second gate into Val's office. He looked up from his work, surprised at the intrusion, and Toula nudged the two of us through. "They're safe. Problem outside," was all she said, and the rip closed behind us.

Val hurried around his desk and gave us a quick examination: Kitty, wide-eyed and pale; me, still weepy and shaking. "What happened?" he demanded.

"I...I'm not sure," said Kitty, hugging herself, "but I think someone tried to kill me, and someone named Frank...uh..." She swallowed hard. "He burned them alive..."

Val didn't ask permission before he plucked the pertinent details from our memories. Cursing with a vocabulary that even Ms. Veracruz would have admired, he threw blankets around us both and ordered us to stay on the couch, then pulled out his phone. "Hello, Wanda?" I heard him say as he paced across the room, running his free hand through his hair in agitation. "Someone just tried to murder the girls. Would you come over, please?" He paused, then muttered, "Of course," and waved a gate into existence.

My therapist poked her head through, then tentatively crossed and gave her surroundings a cursory inspection before heading toward the couch. "We're going to need privacy," she told Val. "Is there somewhere—"

"Use my office," he said, opening a gate into Toula's. "I'll return."

Wanda was fae only by the most generous of definitions, but she had mastered a sort of magic all her own. By the time Val reappeared with Toula that evening, I was feeling almost like myself again, and Kitty had even laughed at a bad joke. "Don't hesitate to call me," she told us as Val opened a gate back to town. "Nightmares, panic attacks, weird thoughts...I'm here."

Murmuring his thanks, Val saw her on her way, then leaned against his desk and massaged his forehead. As the gate closed, Toula took the opening and sank into the chair Wanda had just vacated. Her formal blue robe fell open, revealing the T-shirt and ratty leggings beneath. "So," she began with a weary sigh, "I have good news."

Val snorted, but she ignored him.

"The two who came after you today," she told Kitty, sliding a printout across the table, "were Pauline Norris and Kirk Haverfield. They lived in Arc 1 until about two years ago—Conclave defectors," she muttered. "And both were Council aides here around the time that Francine Leighton was hired. By all reports the three of them were chummy. Kirk and Pauline were in the Leighton wedding, incidentally." She sat back and folded her arms. "The Inner Council's conclusion is that this was a one-off event. They saw their old friend lose her chain, learned why, and decided to do her a favor."

"*Or*," Val interrupted, "this was a first attempt. If the Conclave has a grudge against Starhope—"

"They don't," she replied tersely. "Eva's as inoffensive to the Conclave as they come, and our intel backs that up. She had nothing to do with Francine's removal, anyway. So, and not to be rude about this, Kitty," she continued, "we don't anticipate this happening again because you're just not that important. I know that sounds terrible, but it's a good thing. You're not a valuable target. If this was a planned Conclave hit—and I can't imagine why it would have been—then they've lost two assets already on you. They won't waste more."

"You assume," said Val.

"I make that assumption based on our best information," Toula retorted, "and in case we're wrong, I'm ramping up security on the castle. The girls will be safe—"

"That's not enough."

Briefly, she closed her eyes and sighed as if searching for patience. "A freak incident, that's all."

"A lightning strike is a freak incident." He pushed himself off his desk and took the empty chair beside her.

Though he kept his voice level, I knew Val well enough to see the tension in his face, and I saw it reflected in Toula's features as well—twin thunderheads rumbling on opposite horizons and heading toward a collision.

"Two wizards shot at *my child* today," he said, staring her in the eye, "and you're telling me you can keep her safe?"

"Let's be accurate. They were shooting at Kitty, not Maria."

"Yes, and if Maria hadn't shielded and they'd destroyed the car, I'm certain that would have made absolutely no difference."

"It's over," said Toula, a note of testiness breaking through the forced calm of her tone. "There is no current threat—"

"You don't know that."

"I *do* know—"

"You do *not*," Val snapped. "You cannot. As long as the damn Conclave exists—"

"And what more would you have me do?" she countered, finally giving vent to her frustration. "I'm walking a fucking tightrope in a hurricane—sorry, girls," she mumbled—"and I'm doing the best I can."

"It's not enough."

"Then why don't you enlighten me?" Her blue eyes narrowed in anger. "I can't just carpet-bomb them, and even if my conscience would allow it, the Council never would."

"You are the—"

"First among equals on the Council. I'm not a queen, and I *don't* get to unilaterally decide to massacre everyone who runs from the Arcanum, so get that out of your head." She paused to take a long breath. "Don't you sit there and judge me, Val. I've made mistakes, sure, but you're far from perfect."

Val's hand clenched on the arm of his chair as he pulled his temper under control. "All I am saying is that you need to adopt a more aggressive approach to the Conclave. You'll never have security until you fix this problem."

"And then something else will rise up to replace it," said Toula. "Peace isn't forever. You think this is guaranteed?" she asked, spreading one arm. "I bet Titania felt the same way at one point. Mab, too. Hell, at least the Conclave has an agenda. Your people start shit because they're *bored*."

"They're your people as well."

"That may be, but I'm not the one babysitting them. And don't start lecturing me like you have all the answers—you *don't*. Absolute monarchy must be fun, but that's not my reality."

"You think this is *fun*?" he countered.

As they glared at each other, I glanced at Kitty, who shot me a quick grimace. Hoping I wasn't about to ignite anyone's short fuse, I cleared my throat and scooted forward on the couch. "It's okay, Val," I began, resisting the urge to shrink back into my seat when both of them wheeled on me. "I like my school, and I'll be careful, and...and Kitty's going back, isn't she? I mean, they weren't even after me, they were after her..."

My voice trailed off under the force of his stare, and I heard in my mind a thought that he had the decency not to utter: *I'm sorry for what's befallen her, but she's not my primary concern. You are.*

I swallowed hard, racking my brain for a winning tactic, and settled on, "If I don't go back, Magus Leighton wins."

"This isn't a game," Val protested. "I don't care what points she scores as long as you're *safe*."

"Oh, yes," Toula cut in, "because Faerie is known far and wide as the absolute safest place in the universe."

"At least no one's shooting at her!"

"*Yet!*"

"Okay, seriously?" interrupted a voice from the other side of the room, making Toula and Val jump. "You all need to step back and chill."

Val gave Ros a long, hard stare as she approached. "This doesn't concern you."

"Like hell it doesn't." She perched on the far arm of the couch, bathing half of Kitty's face in her radiance. "I talked to Frank while you two were running around like headless chickens in Glastonbury."

Val's eyes widened in indignation. "*Headless—*"

"Yeah, lot of action, not much of a game plan. While you were off chasing ghosts, I got Sam to call Frank to get the rest of his impressions. You were too panicked to pry everything out of him."

His mouth flapped as he sought an answer, and then he sat back, peeved but momentarily chastised. "Explain."

"Gladly. Toula's almost certainly right that this was a one-time deal—Frank didn't pick up on anything suggesting a larger plan or other involved parties, and he was listening. And come on, those two were amateurs. Trying to off someone in a crowded theater, knowing there were other wizards on the premises? Frank said they were wearing facial prosthetics—they weren't even talented enough to whip up decent disguises and hide the spell. So unless someone gets word that the Conclave has turned those two idiots into martyrs and plans to attack the castle, I think the girls are safe enough."

"You can't know that," Val began, but Ros lifted her hand to cut short his protestation.

"One hundred percent? No, of course not. But I *do* know that Maria shielded a moving car today, and since we're all sitting here, I'd say she made a damn good shield empty-handed. Do you have any idea what that says about her talent, Val? Honestly?"

"She's strong, yes—"

"Many adult wizards can't do what she did," said Ros, "let alone someone her age. That's a magus-level talent in the works, mark my words. Mom will back me up on this."

Val glanced at Toula, who nodded silently.

"I know you want to do right by her," Ros continued. "And I know you're scared to death that she's going to get hurt. But if you're serious about acting in Maria's best interest, you'll send her back to Arc 2. She needs the training."

For a moment, he seemed to waver before his resolve strengthened again. "But what if Helen—"

"I'm not just talking about technique. She's not going to learn her way around the Arcanum if she tries to do it from a distance. Heck, you saw how well I did," she added with a soft laugh. "Unless you intend to hold her here forever, you need to do the right thing. The unpleasant thing. And before you try to tell me I don't know what I'm talking about, this isn't just Ros's opinion. This is Faerie's collective wisdom weighing in."

Val stared past the couch and into the corner for a time, his face occasionally twitching as he mulled that over. Finally, he shifted in his chair and turned to Toula. "One more chance. She goes nowhere unaccompanied, and she comes home immediately after class."

"That's fair," said Toula.

"Hey, wait—" I tried to interrupt, but the adults ignored me.

"I'm serious," Val continued. "She's not to be in any situation that could turn into an ambush from the Conclave or its friends. Understood?"

Toula glared back at him. "If you think I would knowingly put Maria or any of the other kids in danger, you've lost your mind. But yes, she'll go straight to class, then back here, if that's what you want."

He nodded. "And the same for Kitty."

"Hang on, you can't—"

"We've seen the security situation in the dorm. She'll be safer here, and then I won't lose sleep wondering if Maria's sneaking back across." He gave Ros a long, knowing look, and a slightly guilty expression flickered across her face. "And since they could have been killed while under Arcanum supervision this afternoon—"

"*Nominal* supervision," Toula interrupted. "A public theater isn't a highly secure environment, you know."

"Be that as it may, they'll be safe here."

Agitated, Toula closed her eyes and rubbed her forehead. "You realize you have no right to make this demand, yeah?"

He shrugged. "I'm looking out for Maria's best interest."

"And what am I supposed to say if Eva finds out that Kitty's moved off campus, hmm? How do you see that going down?"

Val glanced at Kitty, who waited nervously by my side, then back at Toula, and murmured, "Do you envision that being a problem?"

She paused, then muttered, "No. But Val—"

"You know I'm right."

Still visibly displeased, she finally turned to the two of us. "Well, girls? How does that sound?"

Kitty and I looked at each other, and then she grinned and slid off the couch. "If someone could get the gate, I'll go pack."

I enjoyed having Kitty in the next room, and not only because maths made sense when we worked on it together. Now that I'd embarked on a proper Arcanum education, my former classmates in the settlement kept their distance. Their parents had never been happy with my presence in school—no matter how nicely I played, I was a danger to their children—and though I still sent messages to a few of my friends, no one ever suggested that we hang out. Ros, speaking from experience, had warned me that this would happen, but that knowledge did little to lessen the sting or the loneliness. But with Kitty around on the weekends, however, I didn't get bored, especially as there was so much she had yet to see.

We began spending our after-school hours in town at one of the three coffee shops, which offered overstuffed couches and a steady supply of cookies, even if the owners did keep an eye on younger patrons' caffeine intake. As November gave way to December, some of the storefronts began putting up lights and decorations—our preferred coffee shop opted for an oversized menorah in the window—and our conversation turned to the upcoming winter break. Kitty seemed appalled to learn that my Christmas festivities were limited to midnight Mass—when I moved over, Joey, Ros's dad, had made the case that I'd been raised Catholic to that point and should at least make an occasional appearance—but having never experienced the tree-and-gifts bonanza Kitty described, I didn't miss it. Still, she felt the need to find presents for her mother and baby sister, and so, at Ros's suggestion, we ended up in the settlement's lone pottery studio one Saturday. Stuart Purcell, the artist in residence, kept a variety of unfinished ceramic pieces on hand for novice experimentation, and he set Kitty up with a bowl and a variety of glazes. She was pleased with the result—a little unintentionally brown where the colors ran together, but overall a solid first effort—and carefully packed it with a stuffed bear in her suitcase on the night before the end of the term as she made preparations for Montana.

But after the last day of class, as Val and I were eating dinner, Toula rapped on the door and walked in with Kitty, who still dragged her bag after her. "Things are, apparently, rather busy at Arc 1 right now," said Toula. "Would it be a problem if Kitty spent the break here?"

I pretended not to hear anything when Kitty cried herself to sleep that night.

The next morning, I was surprised when Helen stopped by and found Kitty and me playing Monopoly in our pajamas. "Ooh...do you guys have any idea how many friendships that game has ruined?" she asked, then pointed to the door behind her. "Get dressed. I want to see what

Arnold's been teaching you."

We threw on clothing and met her in the field outside the villa, a relatively safe, if flammable, practice area. "Hi," she said to Kitty as I dropped my jacket and water bottle in a pile. "Don't think we've met. I'm Helen."

"Kitty," she replied, then stopped and looked at her strangely. "Uh...you look..."

"Familiar?" Helen offered. "Are the magus portraits still hanging outside of Toula's office?"

Her eyes widened in recognition. "You're Grand—"

"*Really*, just Helen is fine," she said, grinning, and turned her attention to me. "All right, Maria, shield up. And put that wand down, you don't need it."

For the next hour, Kitty sat in the grass and watched as Helen put me through my paces, alternately shooting and shielding, and all the while barking exhortations to improve my form. When I was a red-faced, sweaty mess, she let me take a break and sat beside Kitty. "Not bad. I was hoping to see more by now, but Arnold said he hasn't been able to work with you as much as we'd like. Val said you're coming home earlier these days—I think we should resume one-on-one instruction, hmm?"

"Sure!" I replied between gulps of water. Letting loose felt great, even if I was exhausted with the exercise.

"Okay, we'll work it out," said Helen, and stood again. "Your turn, Kitty."

A look of fear crossed her face, and she shook her head. "No, um...I can't do—"

"I'm not going to pummel you," Helen said gently. "Let's find out what you *can* do, and I might be able to help."

Hesitantly, Kitty climbed to her feet, then took up her stance and gripped her wand. "Shield," Helen instructed, and waited until a small but neat construction bubbled forth from the wand tip. "Hmm...slow," she said, running one hand up and down the shield's length, "but fairly solid. How're you feeling?"

Kitty was already sweating with the effort. "Fine."

"Uh-huh. You can drop it. How's your aim?"

For the next ten minutes, while I caught my breath, Helen methodically tested and analyzed Kitty's casting ability. "I've got an idea about how to proceed," she told us, "but not until this afternoon. See you after lunch."

We returned to our game for the rest of the morning—Kitty wanted an aspirin after the workout Helen had given her—then did as ordered, only to find that Helen hadn't come alone. "Hi, Badger!" I called, running to close the distance between us. "What are you doing here?"

One of the few remaining members of Val and Toula's family was their nephew, Seamus. Though half fae, he had taken up residence in town with his wife, Badger, an exceptional wizard and one of the Fringe's coordinators. Both former police officers, the two had spent most of the Mulligan years spiriting Fringers to safety in Faerie...and then they'd lingered in the mortal realm for another decade, as a deal that Badger had brokered with Nath was the mortal realm's surest defense against an invasion from the Gray Lands. Only a heart attack in her late sixties had finally convinced Badger to give up her vigil and go to Faerie. While Ros couldn't make Badger truly young again, a glamour gave her an appearance closer in age to her husband's boyish looks, and she and Seamus built a life together among the people they'd rescued. Crime was seldom a problem in the settlement, and so the two of them made up the entirety of the underused police service.

Badger wore her dark hair bobbed, and the wide red headband she used to hold it out of her face covered much of the white stripe that had given rise to her nickname. Like Helen, she had come in sweats, but she also had a pair of rolled-up yoga mats sitting by her feet.

"Hi yourself," she replied, lifting a hand. "While Helen does bad things to you, I'm going to work with Miss Kitty...this way, now, don't be shy," she said, beckoning Kitty closer, then nudged the mats with her foot. "We're just going to work on focusing techniques, nothing painful." She stuck out her hand, clasped Kitty's, and grinned. "Focus is key when you don't have much oomph behind it. Let's see what you can do."

"Not a whole lot," said Kitty, picking up a mat and following her out of Helen's line of fire. "I'm, uh…a witch…"

"And I grew up on a shadow alder wand," said Badger, "so more or less the same. The Fringe has techniques that the Arcanum doesn't bother teaching, so let me show you a few tricks."

By the end of the winter break, Kitty could hold a shield together for ten minutes at a stretch. Not a great shield, and not a particularly thick one, but a solid piece of spellcraft nonetheless. Badger was pleased with her progress, and Kitty seemed to leave our lessons with a spring in her step, even as I limped to the shower after Helen's more physical lessons.

Restless on our last night of freedom, I wandered into the garden in the wee hours, hoping a few laps around the fountain and a little night air would put me back to sleep. I hadn't been outside long before I saw my shadow appear and turned to find Ros behind me, glowing against the darkness. "Can't sleep," I explained.

"I hear you." She fell in step with me and shoved her hands into her pockets. "You're coming along well. Mom's being tough on you, but she's satisfied."

"That's good." I paused to kick a leaf into the fountain channel. "And Kitty's better, isn't she? Don't you think?"

Ros kept her silence for a moment, then nodded. "The realm's having a positive effect on her. It happens. Most of the Fringers are stronger now than when they came over."

"So…if she stays here long enough, do you think she'll become a wizard?" I asked hopefully.

But Ros shook her head. "Kitty is many things, Maria.

A wizard will almost certainly never be one of them. But she *is* getting stronger—don't crush her dreams just yet," she said, and disappeared.

I returned to bed and stared at the glowing canopy until my eyes grew heavy. Ros knew a lot, I decided, but she didn't know *everything*, and I wasn't about to give up on my friend.

CHAPTER 8

The school year varied across the Arcanum installations, and as the June days warmed and lengthened, my classmates who'd come from the States spoke longingly of proper summer vacations. Arc 1's calendar kept pace with the local school, and when we were returning from our half-term holiday, Arc 1 was almost finished for the year. "A blessing in disguise," Magus Lowe told us when we griped about the situation. "If nothing else, you'll be in better shape for the Games."

That was small consolation, considering that some of my classmates' friends and cousins had June plans at the beach or theme parks, but still, the Games was a bright spot on the horizon. The last three days of the summer term were guaranteed to be free from exams, and the older kids hinted at a dining hall lunch menu that leaned heavily toward pizza and ice cream in celebration.

At the beginning of July, Magus Lowe put out the signup sheets for the Games and explained the rules during class. "Technical casting, rapid casting, academic bowl, and single combat," he said, pointing to each sheet of paper in turn. "The casting contests both begin on Wednesday, and technical will run into Thursday morning as well, but those rounds will be just the oldest contestants, so you can still do one of the castings and academic bowl. Combat is all day Friday, and it has to be single-elimination to keep things moving, so you may as well sign up and give it a shot—we've certainly had surprises. All right, try not to shove each other…"

He stepped aside while we rushed the table, pencils out, and scribbled our names. When the dust settled, the sheets were fairly lopsided. Few had elected to go out for the academic bowl—Kitty was the unspoken favorite, and only two of the boys had chosen to challenge her. Rapid casting, which I had picked, had far more takers than technical casting, which required patience and planning. And then there was the combat sheet, twenty names strong. To no one's surprise, Kitty had declined the opportunity.

When the period ended, we packed to head for lunch, but Magus Lowe held me back for a moment until the others left. "Helen's been keeping me apprised," he said, gathering the signup sheets. "You're aware that the combat contest is non-lethal, yes?"

"Yes, Magus."

He glanced at me over his glasses. "That includes unintentionally lethal force. I'm not going to tell you to lose on purpose, but I expect you to rein it in appropriately. Friendly competition, understood?"

I nodded and shouldered my bag. "Bolts and shields only, then?"

"No," he admitted after a moment's thought, "you can be a little creative. But my dear, there will be several bouts going on in that room simultaneously. If someone were to, say, start a wildfire on the floor…"

He left that thought unfinished, but he'd said enough. "Understood," I replied, and hurried on my way, the fingers of my wand hand twitching in memory.

The other competitors arrived on the Monday before the Games commenced, brought by gate at times convenient to their local schedules. First through were the groups from Arcanum 7, a bunker located outside of Alice Springs that oversaw Oceania, and Arcanum 4, the Mongolian installation that served much of Asia and parts of Eastern

Europe. Next came Arcanum 5, the Giza group, which supported wizards throughout the Middle East and Africa—a political situation that satisfied few outside of Egypt, but as the installation system had been established by a Canadian grand magus of old-blooded European extraction in the 1960s, Africa and the Middle East hadn't been given proper consideration. Magi from Sub-Saharan Africa in particular perennially argued for the establishment of an installation closer to home, much as Southeast Asian magi fought to break away from Arc 4's territory.

Arcanum 3, which handled the parts of Europe that couldn't bear to move to England, popped over around lunchtime. Late in the afternoon, we saw the team from Arcanum 6, the fantastic Brazilian treehouse installation, and finally, after dinner, Arc 1 arrived from Montana. Though most of the newcomers proceeded immediately to the assigned guest dorms, we found a handful in the dining hall at all times during the first day and night, either battling insomnia or trying to adjust to the local clock. While the teachers and chaperones from the various installations chatted amicably enough, the students kept to their own groups at first, doing little in the way of cross-installation interaction beyond shooting likely contenders glares and whispering behind their hands. The exceptions were the older students from Arc 7, a rowdy band of Australians, New Zealanders, and other Pacific Islanders who were *thrilled* to have escaped the depths of winter for a few days and eager to try Glastonbury's finest cheap liquor stores. Some of their counterparts in Arc 2 offered to serve as tour guides, and by Tuesday night, a mixed band of older teenagers from around the world—even some of the cliquish Arc 1 group—were gallivanting about town, apparently giving little thought to the morning's competitions.

As I soon learned, they knew what they were doing. The youngest classes started first, and by the time the eighth-years were up, the revelers were mostly sober. Having heard accounts of midnight carousing and an impromptu courtyard Disney singalong from the boarders, Kitty and I watched with a little awe as the older students called forth complex wards and spells powered by dozens of interlocking stacks.

I lost Wednesday's competition in the first round, bested by a Sudanese girl known among her classmates as "La Machine" for her precise, rapid-fire casting. Her wandwork was impressive, but I admit that I wasn't sorry to see her taken down when she competed against the second-years. Kitty, who hadn't competed, was more generous, and she offered congratulations in the few words of French she knew. La Machine was a gracious winner, beamed at Kitty's attempt, and clasped her hand. She and half of her Arc 5 classmates ended up joining a dozen of us for lunch, and though most of our conversation consisted of gesticulating and grinning, we sat together to watch the afternoon's events. As the hours passed, the Arc 3 group merged with our pack—at least a few of them could communicate with the francophones from Arc 5, and one German kid spoke passable Arabic. Slowly, the Arc 6 first-years migrated into the herd, encouraged by the snippets of Spanish, French, and Portuguese coming from our end of the bleachers, and then the Arc 7 pack arrived with snacks stolen from the dining hall, including five cheese pizzas. Finally, the kids from Arc 4 slid our way, encouraged by Arc 7's proffered pies. Several were nearly fluent in English or Arabic, and they joined in the mass conversation of limited topics— name, hometown, upcoming contests. Only the Arc 1 group kept to themselves—a few watched us curiously, but none strayed from the safety of the Montana clump. It was their loss. Val had agreed that Kitty and I could stay and eat dinner in Glastonbury, and the mixed first-year classes sprawled over four tables, doing the best we could with our limited language skills, laughing at each other's clumsy attempts, and finally toasting Amina—La Machine—and a Japanese boy named Masaji for their wins.

Though Thursday morning had two events, the spectators remained in the competition hall for the last of the technical casting. While the older students finished their rounds, the academic bowl commenced in ten classrooms, where each age group sat down with a written examination as an elimination tool. After lunch, the top ten from the first-year class took up spots behind podiums in the competition hall, buzzing in as one of the magi from Arc 3 posed questions. Unlike the students, the magi had worked out linguistic spells, and so both the competitors and the spectators could understand the magus as he quizzed my peers in rapid Hungarian. My classmates and I cheered when Kitty won for our age group, and she performed admirably when she squared off against the second-years, though she only placed eighth in the buzzer round. When she returned to the bleachers, it was to a wave of congratulatory back slaps and fist bumps. She smiled and thanked her well-wishers, though I noticed her glancing toward the Arc 1 group. All of the silo magi had made the trip, but though Kitty had spoken to her mother in passing that morning, Magus Stanhope was nowhere to be found.

"She's embarrassed," Kitty said that night, flopping onto my bed and staring at the canopy. "I mean, she has to know I'm not competing tomorrow."

"But you *won* today," I reminded her. "Why would she be embarrassed by *that*?"

"You can train any mundane to answer questions," she muttered. "Knowing about magic and being able to work with it are two different things, right?"

I tried a different angle. "Maybe your sister was being fussy, and she took her into the hall."

"She left Beth with a babysitter in Montana. I asked her." Kitty sat up and scowled at the wall. "I wanted to give Beth her Christmas present today, but I guess it'll have to wait until the weekend."

Kitty had packed her bags several days prior for a month's vacation at Arc 1, assuming she'd be spending the night with her mother on Friday and leaving with her after the awards brunch on Saturday Having seen how the winter break—and spring break, and every other holiday that year—had turned out, I didn't know whether Kitty had been hasty in packing, but I wasn't about to broach that topic with her. She spoke of her plans for the silo with utter certainty, excited to show her mother how far she'd come with Badger's steady coaching and spend a few weeks with her little sister, and I hoped for her sake that she'd make it back across the pond.

The bookies' money for single combat was on Hunter Crowe, a twenty-year-old graduate of Arc 1's program. Though he and most of his year were adults by the Arcanum's estimation, they were given one last chance to compete, as a few of their cohort were still nineteen. Hunter had been working as an aide to Magus Stanhope for the last two years, but the rumor was that he spent every free hour in the silo's practice rooms, honing his skill. He'd won combat in his age group ever since the Games began, and he'd competed against the tenth-years in his seventh before being eliminated.

But Hunter and his year didn't deign to spectate at the beginning of the morning, and I didn't give them much thought. Two-thirds of the first-year class had signed up for combat, and I sat on the narrow bleachers on the floor of the competition hall, watching as the first bouts came to their conclusions—sometimes swiftly, sometimes after a prolonged struggle and miscast spells. The magi on the floor served dual roles as referees and guards, calling matches and casting as necessary to keep the effects of one bout from hurting the competitors nearby. The haze of active magic on the floor was thick and colorful as a laser show, and even from our vantage point, sometimes the only way to see who had won was when a magus raised a competitor's arm in victory.

Though she was meant to be in the spectator bleachers, Kitty had slipped down to sit with me as moral support. I caught her glancing at the upper tier once or twice before I picked her mother out of the Arc 1 contingent, a thin woman with a violet robe and a honey-blonde bob. Part of me took Kitty's excuse for coming to the floor at face value, but another part wondered if she wasn't hiding with the competitors to avoid her mother's disappointment.

I had noticed Toula sitting in the middle of the crowd, surrounded by members of the Inner Council and their assistants. The rest of the spectator bleachers had filled early, and while I awaited my turn on the floor, I scanned the crowd, guessing at the unfamiliar magi's home installations. A group of older Australians set up a chant when one of the Arc 7 students won—judging by the volume, I assumed the victor was a chanter's little sister— and looking just past them, I noticed a man sitting by himself near the top of the bleachers with his arms folded. Not a magus—they all seemed to have donned robes for the occasion—and given the sparseness of the spectators around him, presumably not a chaperone. I couldn't make out his features beyond gray hair, dark-rimmed glasses, and a slight paunch beneath a brown shirt, but then he seemed to look back at me, and one corner of his mouth ticked upward.

You thought I would miss this?

I did a double-take, then turned around to bring my face under control. Val was unrecognizably glamoured, and when I felt the familiar sensation of his mind reaching for mine, I did nothing to hide my surprise. *Toula is aware*, he told me. *Not thrilled, but aware.*

I could lose in the first round, I thought, and waited while he picked up on my message.

I doubt it.

Before I could speak further, Magus Lowe called my name, and I hurried across the mats to meet my opponent, a skinny boy from Arc 4 who wore streaks of purple in his black shag. We nodded to each other and took up our stances, wands extended at the ready, and then Magus Lowe dropped his hand, the signal to begin.

I shielded immediately, and as I'd expected, the boy went on the offensive. His first bolt was strong enough to make my arm flinch, but the second was weaker, and by his tenth shot, he was rapidly losing steam. I took a risk, dropped my shield, and fired a quick volley of bolts that knocked him off his feet, and his wand flew from his hand. As I advanced on him, he looked around, saw that his wand was well out of reach, then crossed his wrists in an X above his face, the agreed-upon sign of surrender. Magus Lowe lifted my arm to end the bout, and then, while my opponent picked himself off the floor, I retrieved his wand and offered him the handle. Though visibly disappointed, he accepted it with a slight smile and a nod of acknowledgement, and we returned to our bleachers.

First round, hmm? came Val's comment from the nosebleed seats. *You could have ended that in under ten seconds.*

I got a drink of water and watched the next pairs run out. *Maybe if I'd shot first. But that's risky—I don't know most of these people.*

I wasn't suggesting that. Shield, then shoot through it.

We haven't been taught that yet.

You have, he countered, then relented as I showed my frustration. *Your contest, your strategy. Do what you must.*

I continued to watch as the first round of eliminations wound down, and then one of the referee magi flashed the results on screens visible to us and to the spectator balcony. The surviving contestants' names were listed alphabetically until a random number appeared next to each—58 for me. The list rearranged itself into numerical order, then split into pairs.

With only four bouts running simultaneously, it took a

few minutes until I met number 57, a girl from Arc 3 with the beginning of a knot on her forehead. She smiled weakly as the magus positioned us, and I tried to size her up in the seconds available to me. Injured in her first round, ash wand...

As soon as the magus's hand dropped, I let fire a single strong bolt, which slammed into her wand before her shield could come forth. She dropped the wand with a surprised cry, then quickly signaled her surrender. When we started back to our seats, she slid close to me and whispered, "Grazie."

It was a pleasant surprise to hear Italian, though her accent gave her away as Swiss. "For what?" I replied in kind.

"You could have hit my wrist instead of my wand." She gingerly tapped the swelling on her head and muttered, "I'm already due for the infirmary."

"Feel better," I said, but before I could leave her side, she grabbed my arm to stay me.

"There's talk about you. First-year to beat. That's a maple wand, isn't it?"

I nodded, and with a little squeeze, she released me and headed for her chaperone.

The round ended, and once again, the names appeared and were paired off. I took my turn in the group of thirty-two, of sixteen, of eight. At the semifinals, we competed one pair at a time, and though my opponent from Arc 6 got off a few good shots, I walked away the victor. Finally, Magus Lowe called the last round, to Arc 2's delight: Natalie and me.

She frowned as we took our places and readied our wands. "This was what I was hoping to avoid," she said below the noise of the crowd. "We're still friends, right?"

"Of course," I replied, and glanced at Magus Lowe.

He nodded to us both, and then his hand fell.

For the first time that day, I knew what to expect from my opponent. Natalie was fast and tough, but she was predictable: she would shield for a few beats, getting the measure of her adversary, then go on a quick offensive. It was a solid strategy, but there was a crack in her wall. Natalie's shields were beautiful, thick and able to absorb almost anything thrown at her, but they were somewhat small, often only extending to her knees. Under ordinary circumstances, that was no problem—she had learned to move her shield in class to compensate for its size. But this wasn't class, and I knew how to exploit the opening.

As Natalie's shield coalesced, I lunged forward with a spell, aiming for her ankles. Instead of striking, however, my bolt hooked and boomeranged, catching her like a tripwire and throwing her to the mats. Natalie yelped in surprise but managed to hold on to both wand and shield. She scrambled back to her feet putting a bit of distance between us, and sighted me down while I stood unshielded, practically begging her to take a shot. We circled each other like wrestlers searching for the right moment to strike until the lure of my bait proved too tempting. Natalie dropped her shield and readied the expected bolt, but before her lips finished moving, I breathed a word and flung her toward the rafters.

The spell she had been planning turned into a cry of fear, but I held her steady, ten meters above the ground, forcing power into the spell keeping her aloft. I had her in an impossible position: if she'd shielded, she would have fallen, and from the look on her face, Natalie didn't trust herself to stick the landing. With no good alternative, she dropped her wand and crossed her wrists, and I gently lowered her to the mats while the crowd roared its approval.

I handed Natalie her wand when she touched down, and we hugged. "Holy *crap*," she whispered in my ear. "How much have you been holding back?"

"Some," I admitted, and broke away so that Magus Lowe could lift my arm.

"That wasn't *some*," she retorted, but she clapped for

me along with the crowd, and we returned to a hero's welcome from the Arc 2 contingent on the bleachers.

"Ten minutes," said Magus Lowe, adjusting the screens. The projection, which had been flashing my name in red, switched to a long list of unfamiliar names, and mine slotted in with the other C surnames near the top.

"Knew it," said Kitty, passing me my water bottle. "Ready for the second-years?"

I gulped down water until my stomach protested. "What are the odds?"

"What do you mean?"

Someone cleared his throat behind me, and I turned to find Tom waiting with a notebook. "Current odds on you are twenty-five to one. Care to make a wager?"

"Are you *crazy*?" I snapped.

"No. And I've got five quid on you, so don't let me down, Corelli," he replied, then joined the rest of our year in vacating the lower bleachers, making room for the second-year competitors. Kitty remained, however, rising only to get me a refill while Magus Lowe announced the rules for the benefit of the fresh competitors.

The random number generator had been kind, and I had a few minutes to rest before my first round, a girl from Arc 1 who was quick on the draw but lousy at shielding. She blushed as she accepted her wand from me, and I felt for her—it had to be embarrassing to lose out of the gate, especially to a younger student. My second opponent was tougher, a girl from Arc 7 whose bolt left my elbow numb for a moment, but she went down with a shot to the gut that threw her almost into the next group of fighters. One by one, I worked my way through the ranks, taking out a boy from Arc 5, another from Arc 4, and finally one of the Arc 2 girls, who shook my hand before we parted. "If I'm going to lose, at least someone from the home team should win," she whispered, briefly tightening her grip.

When the screen switched to the final pair and I took to the mats opposite a lanky boy from Arc 6, the room held its breath. He and I shook hands, and when we began, he struck immediately. But by that point, Helen had hit me enough times that my shield was almost instantaneous, and it held. Still, he didn't let up, and he didn't seem to tire as bolt after bolt slammed into my construction. I kept my defenses strong, but I assumed that his plan was to wear me down—it had worked for him in the quarter- and semifinals, after all.

As we danced around each other, I heard Val in my mind: *End it, Maria.*

Wearying of the bout, I abandoned caution and took his suggestion. I held the shield steady with my wand, then whipped my left hand forward, whispered power into its momentum, and flung a bolt through my shield. Defenseless and unprepared for retaliation, my opponent caught the full force of the strike, and as he staggered back, I dropped my shield and leapt into an offensive. In seconds, I had him on his knees, and a final blow blasted his wand from his hand.

When the red haze of combat cleared, I realized that Magus Lowe was lifting my arm again, and the first-years were chanting. I stumbled back to the bleachers as they clapped and shouted above: "*Corella! Corella! Corella!*"

Kitty was waiting with water and a sweat towel, and I willed my limbs to stop shaking as I drank and dried off. While the second-years filed out, Tom made his way down through the press and clapped me on the back. "Have I told you you're my favorite?" he said, and showed me his notebook, which was updating itself with the latest odds. "Look at that. Only fifteen to one on you next round."

"That's good?" I mumbled into my towel.

"Oh, yeah. Smaller is better, see? That Crowe guy has even odds to win it all." He paused as more text appeared, then laughed aloud. "Two hundred to one on you making it to the finale, *five* hundred to one on you winning. How about it, want to make a classmate rich?"

"How about I focus on surviving the third-years, huh?"

"That's the spirit," he chirped, and left me to lick my wounds before the next round.

By the lunch break, I had cast my way through the fifth-years, and I could barely eat for the press of well-wishers in the dining hall, who crowded around my table as if watching me gobble a sandwich with trembling hands was fascinating. Kitty did the best she could to bring me food—my stomach had turned into a bottomless pit, and every bite only served to remind me of how exhausted I was—but she had a nearly impossible time navigating the crowd until Ms. Veracruz, who was in possession of a booming voice that didn't match her petite frame, cleared a path and shooed some of my spectators away. When I'd done what I could to satiate my appetite, she hustled Kitty and me into her classroom and locked the door behind us.

"Sit," she said, pointing to the rows of desks, then headed for her supply closet at the back of the room. I plopped into my usual seat, and she returned with a first aid kit. "Roll up your sleeves," she ordered. "Let me see those cuts."

"What cuts?" I asked, but did as ordered. To my surprise, my arms were crisscrossed with red lines, a few of them as yet unscabbed.

Ms. Veracruz *tsk*ed and muttered beneath her breath, and a bowl of water and a rag appeared on the desk. "Adrenaline is a powerful thing," she said as she cleaned my wounds. "It gives you strength when yours is failing, and it can make you insensate to injury. But you're coming down now, and you're going to be sore pretty soon." She patted my left arm dry, then pulled a packet from the box. "Aspirin. Take it, it's not against the rules."

While I dry-swallowed the capsules, she doused my cuts with stinging antiseptic spray. "I'm sorry, Maria," she said as I winced. "Using a healing spell right now might be construed as an unfair advantage, and I'm sure you don't want to be disqualified." She blew on the largest of the cuts until the burn faded. "There, that's better. How's your torso? Anything bruised?"

When I regarded her uncertainly, she waved down the shades and motioned me to my feet. "Take your shirt off."

I had developed several large bruises, in fact, including one on my ribcage that made me yelp when she prodded it. Ms. Veracruz did the best she could, including an application of tape along my sore side. "Right, then," she said as I dressed, "that appears to be the worst of it. You'll be stiff after lunch, so do some gentle warmups before your next round."

"Thank you," I told her, sliding from my desk. "Really, I mean it…"

She smiled to herself as she packed her kit. "Magus Lowe said you might need a bit of patching. Happy to pitch in. The Arc 1 group is *insufferable* when they win. Be careful out there, now," she added as I opened the door. "Shield up, Ms. Corelli."

Soon enough, I was back on the bleachers, somewhat limbered but feeling my bumps and scrapes. "Okay?" Kitty whispered as Magus Lowe went through the rules for the sixth-year class.

"Close enough," I muttered, then rose in the first wave of eight to fight.

The start of the tenth-years' round was delayed half an hour that afternoon. Officially, the referee magi needed a break before the real fireworks started. Unofficially, Magus Lowe and Ms. Veracruz wanted to inspect my damage.

After nine levels of competition, I was a mess. My arms had sustained further cuts from bolts and worse, and the back of my right leg was raw with the burn I'd taken in a hard, fast landing on the mats. I had a tender spot at the base of my skull, a sore knee, and at least one broken rib, per Magus Lowe's assessment. As I downed a liter of orange sports drink, he gently manipulated my joints, and then Ms. Veracruz gave me more aspirin to dull the worst of the pain. While she rebandaged and taped as necessary, he stepped back and gave me a long, critical assessment. "You know," he said, "there's no shame in stopping now."

"But I won the last round," I protested.

"Exactly. You've been fighting all day, and I'm concerned for your safety." He hesitated, then asked, "Do you want to talk to your grandfather about this? I don't think he'd be upset if you bowed out."

I shook my head and rolled down my sleeves as Ms. Veracruz finished. "*He* wouldn't quit."

Magus Lowe was careful in his reply, considering his audience. "I think he'd be sensible enough not to run headlong into a fight with the odds heavily against him."

"But they're not," Kitty piped up, and held out her notebook. "See? Maria's odds are down to five to one."

"What are you…" He peered at the notebook, scowling. "What the heck is *that*?"

"Current odds. Tom set me up," she offered.

"Did he?" Magus Lowe muttered. "Charming." He glanced at the door, but the shade was still down, blocking our view of the corridor. "Listen, Maria," he said, sliding closer. "The Crowes are an old family."

"I know, I know," I replied impatiently, "he works for Kitty's mother."

"Not just that. Hunter's dad is one of the Arc 1 magi as well. The boy's very talented, and this is supposed to be his big victory. Should he start losing to a new-blooded first-year…"

"I'll be careful," I assured him.

"All I'm saying is that there's no shame in walking away now."

I made no reply, and Magus Lowe sighed. "All right," he said softly. "Try not to break anything else out there."

The ninth- and tenth-years were distinct from each other and from the eight classes before them. Those of us still in school had something to prove, and many of us had signed up to participate on the slim chance of success. By their first year past graduation, some of the ninth-years had gone on to university, while others remained in the installations, furthering their magical studies. Most, though not all, returned for the Games, and while some had obviously been practicing, many had been enjoying post-school life a bit too much to be true contenders. I'd lucked into facing off against a few of the slackers, and it quickly became obvious how out of practice they were.

Far fewer of the tenth-years returned, as those on mundane study tracks had learned their lesson the previous year. The ones who showed up were at their top of their class, in at least decent form, and ready to go. There was no wand below maple among them.

I survived my first round by the skin of my teeth, having jumped to the ground to avoid a strong bolt and taken the opportunity to entangle my opponent's ankles with a sneak attack from the floor. Before he could break the spell binding him, I'd smashed through his shield with a continual barrage of missiles, and he conceded. The next round was a bit easier—the girl I fought had been working in the library for the last two years, and though she knew all manner of techniques, she was relatively slow. My opponent in the quarterfinals clipped my wand arm, forcing me to fight left-handed until I regained feeling in my shoulder, and she went down only through a stroke of luck: when I tossed her toward the ceiling, she dropped her wand in surprise, and she didn't trust herself to make the descent unarmed. In the semifinals, my adversary tried the same trick on me, but I overloaded his levitation spell to break it, controlled my drop with my free hand, and kept my shield up with my wand until I was back on the floor and ready to go. It took us ten long, aching minutes to reach a resolution, and in the end, ours proved to be a contest of shields, both of us firing through our defenses until his cracked.

The crowd chanted my name louder than ever as Magus Lowe set up for the final round—not just the bulk of the first-years, as I'd come to expect, or Arc 2, cheering for the home team, but a wide swath of the spectator bleachers. Their shouts and claps rang around the room, and I looked up at them, too exhausted to truly process the moment.

Kitty, mistaking my expression for awe, dabbed a streak of blood from my arm and said, "Everyone likes a good Cinderella story, you know? No one expected combat to be so interesting this year."

"And the bookies?" I muttered.

She consulted her notebook. "Two to one on you."

I wiped my face on my sleeve and looked down the bleachers, where Hunter sat in a knot of Arc 1 competitors. "Have you noticed his wand? He's on pine."

"No, he isn't."

I turned back to Kitty, confused, but she shook her head. "Mom has a pine wand. It's *ornate*. Those things are carved up, some have crystals stuck on them—all sorts of decoration. Daddy always said it was silly. Hunter's isn't pine—it's too plain."

"Maybe he didn't decorate," I posited.

Kitty's eyebrow rose. "A Council aide not showing that off? You think?"

I shrugged. "Don't know too many Council aides."

"I met him last summer. He was nice enough to me, but he snapped at the other aides. If he had a pine wand, I bet it would be fancy." She watched him give it a few warmup flicks. "Probably a composite like Natalie's. It might be closer to pine than yours, but I can't tell from here."

"Thanks anyway," I replied, and stood as Magus Lowe quieted the crowd. "Wish me luck."

She raised both thumbs, and I was on my way.

As I took my place opposite Hunter, I tried not to panic. He was big, easily two heads taller than me and far broader across the chest. While I was a sweaty, bloody mess, he appeared almost fresh, as if the last four rounds had been no more tiring than a game of checkers. His blond hair still seemed perfectly gelled, and he made a show of cracking his knuckles as we stared each other down.

When Magus Lowe was satisfied, he stepped between us and lowered his voice. "Fair fight. I mean it." We nodded, and he stepped back and raised his hand.

The instant it fell, I was on the defensive, pouring everything I had into my shield as Hunter threw a savage volley of bolts at me. The barrage sent me to one knee, and I yelped as the force of his blows drove me backward across the mat, ripping a fresh hole in my leggings with the friction. Finally, he dealt me a massive hit, and my wand flew from my grasp as I rolled into the padded part of the wall.

I staggered upright as quickly as I could, only to see my wand in Hunter's hand. He smiled almost pleasantly, then cracked it over his knee and tossed the pieces aside.

As the crowd began to shout in protest, Magus Lowe ran behind Hunter to get in my line of sight, then moved his arms into an X as if he thought I'd forgotten how to end the bout. I ignored his gesticulations. I was sore, tired, and now unarmed, but the look of smirking satisfaction on Hunter's face fueled my anger, and I let my inhibitions fall aside.

Spreading my arms, I whispered my will into the ether, and fire bloomed around me in a perfect circle that rose to my chest. With a touch of concentration, tendrils of flame coalesced into waiting missiles, and it was my turn to smile as Hunter's eyes widened. "Yield?" I asked.

In response, he redoubled his shield, and I let the fireballs fly.

I forced him back, one hard-fought step at a time, until

Hunter transferred his shield to his empty hand and started casting lightning with his wand. Distantly, I was aware that Magus Lowe was trying to call the bout, but Hunter and I kept him busy as he and the other referees took on the more pressing task of shielding the crowd from our ricocheting spells. For a moment, Hunter and I reached a stalemate, fighting furiously but unable to break through each other's defenses—and then I had an idea.

Screaming as I channeled more power into my craft without a wand to focus it, I called upon my dwindling reserves, then flung *all* of the fire around me toward Hunter. The sudden shift forced him into immediate defense, and his shield formed almost a sphere around him. He managed to hold the flames at bay for a moment...but then I began to squeeze. Picturing the fire as a ball, I held out my palm and curled my fingers inward, trembling at the resistance of Hunter's shield. Quickly, before he could stabilize enough to fight me back, I flung him into the air, surrounding him in a sphere of swirling flame that grew smaller...*smaller*...

With a soft *thud*, Hunter's wand fell through the fire and smoldered on the mat.

"*End bout!*" Magus Lowe bellowed, magically amplifying his voice about the deafening crowd. "*Cease casting!*"

I exhaled a single word, and the fire disappeared. Slowly, not quite trusting my failing strength, I returned Hunter to the floor, then sagged and bent over, panting and shaking with the exertion. When Magus Lowe touched my shoulder, I jerked and straightened, and he nodded once before raising my arm.

The spectators went to their feet. All I wanted at that moment was to be off mine—preferably somewhere with a hot tub and a *solid* piece of numbing magic—but I remained in the middle of the room after Magus Lowe stepped aside, smiling and dipping my head in acknowledgement of the applause. I doubted I'd be able to find Val in the press above, so I looked at the contestant bleachers and picked Kitty out of the crowd. Beaming in her place on the front row, she held her hands above her head and clapped…and then, without explanation, her expression changed. I saw her mouth my name—for all I knew, she was shouting it, but the room was far too loud.

Then I was flying, thrown from my feet by an unexpected blow and hurtling straight for the wall.

The competition room, like the practice rooms, was well padded on the floor and several meters up the walls. But the ceilings were high in that space, and the top half of the walls was nothing but naked stone.

Fortunately, I didn't collide head-first, but the force of the impact on my back knocked the air from my lungs, and my skull hit an instant later. Breathless and too tired to save myself, I bounced off the wall and slammed to the floor in a heap. My ears rang, and my stomach spasmed as if it wanted to turn itself inside out, but I finally managed to draw a sputtering breath and opened my eyes.

I wished I hadn't. The world wasn't spinning, exactly, but nothing was standing still, which only made my queasiness worse. As I tried to focus, I made out Hunter's shape as he ran across the mats toward me, wand outstretched…

And something streaked from the bleachers.

I recognized the blur as Kitty just before she took a flying leap onto Hunter's back, yelling her best soprano war cry. She wrapped one of her skinny arms around his neck and held on while he thrashed, but she lasted only a few seconds before he shook her off. Ignoring her, he turned his attention back to me and raised his wand.

Whatever he was planning, I missed it. A solid form materialized in front of me, and with a feral roar, Val flung Hunter halfway across the room. He landed poorly, breaking a leg on impact, but he had enough sense to try to recover his footing—and when that failed, to crabwalk away.

Even from behind, I could tell that Val had let the glamour drop. Glowing white in his fury, he advanced on Hunter, not running but not wasting time. Hunter still attempted to scramble back, but with only one functional leg, he wasn't going anywhere in a hurry. I couldn't tell if he tried to plead for mercy—the noise of the crowd had turned to screams, no less deafening and far less pleasant than the cheering had been—but before Val could reach him, Toula appeared between them.

"*Don't*," she ordered, holding out both hands to stay Val's progress.

I couldn't tell what he said in turn, but her expression was firm, and she didn't budge. Suddenly, Magus Lowe was crouching at my side, and he carefully rolled me onto my back. "Maria? Are you with us?" he asked, bending low to be heard over the ruckus. I grunted in reply, and the tip of his finger began to glow. "Follow the light, there's a good girl," he said, passing it around my field of vision, and I did my best to track it. Satisfied, he began to mutter, and I twitched as I felt a sensation like thick bands around me. "I'm stabilizing you. Be still, now," he soothed. "We're going straight to the infirmary."

I noticed another magus working on Kitty, who winced as she was helped to her feet. When I looked back toward the standoff, I saw that it had just broken, and as a pair of magi ran to tend to Hunter, Val appeared at my side.

"Might be concussed," Magus Lowe told him before he could ask. "I'm taking her to the infirmary."

"She needs to go home," he protested, but Magus Lowe shook his head.

"Bee knows how to treat a concussion. How about letting an actual doctor have a look, eh?"

"Arnold—"

"There is a *pro* two towers over," the magus snapped. "Don't be stupid."

And Val, worried but chastened, replied with a frustrated huff, then helped him float me on my way.

CHAPTER 9

My head pounded as if a company of miners had found a gold seam between my ears, but Dr. Powell was merciless. "Back off, both of you," she said, shooing Magus Lowe and Val away from my infirmary bed. "I need her as focused as possible, so no numbing until we know what's wrong."

"She was thrown into a wall, that's what's wrong," Val protested. "Let me—"

"*No*," she insisted. "I'm sorry, but if I need to get her in for a CT tonight, the last thing I want to worry about is interference with my machines."

His forehead furrowed. "CT?"

"Computerized tomography. Old but reliable. If there's a chance of internal hemorrhage, I'll want a backup check."

Far out of his league, Val stepped aside and let the doctor work. She checked my vision, which was beginning to return to normal, then gave me a physical examination with the help of an imaging spell. "Bruised to hell and back," she decreed, rubbing her chin as she considered the bluish me-shaped construction hovering over my body. Beneath the translucent outer layer, I could see my bones displayed. Dark red patches pulsed in dozens of places, and lighter threads circled my limbs and torso. "Two broken ribs. Vertebrae seem to be intact, thank goodness"—she moved up the bed and squinted at my projected head—"and cranium has no visible fractures. Congratulations," she told me, "you're hard-headed."

"Need to run the CT?" asked Magus Lowe.

"Not as long as she checks out this way. I'll keep an eye on the projection for the next few hours, see if anything worsens, but for now, we can start treatment. *Carefully*, if you please," she added, turning to Val. "That imaging spell takes a fair bit of doing, so don't wreck it."

He worked quickly, even under Dr. Powell's watch, and I closed my eyes as the pain began to dissipate.

"Nope," she said, and patted my cheeks until I looked up at her again. "No sleep for you, little miss. You're under observation."

I groaned and glanced to my left, where one of the nurses was prodding Kitty for injuries on the next bed. "I'm fine, really," she said as the nurse flashed a penlight into her eyes. "I hit the mats, that's all."

"We're taking no chances," Dr. Powell interrupted. "I heard you got thrown."

"Like five feet down."

"Don't be difficult, dear." She pulled off her gloves and slipped a fresh pair from the box on the counter. "Right, I'm going next door to look after the Crowe kid. If you try to kill him, Val, I will be *cross*."

As the two-way swinging door flapped behind her, Kitty muttered, "Dang, she's bossy."

"She and Ros have been close since they were your age," Val quietly replied, "and if I were to antagonize her, I can imagine what sort of reception I'd have at home."

The nurse, realizing he was now down to Magus Lowe for protection against Val, quickly wrapped up his examination and escaped the room.

Once we were alone, Val turned his attention to Kitty. "What were you *thinking*, child?" he asked as he pulled together another healing enchantment. "You had no chance of disabling that boy. Running at him unarmed..."

Kitty shrugged. "Maria would have done it for me."

"Maria also might have won that fight," he countered.

"I had to *try*," she protested, and wiggled her fingers

while the enchantment shrank around her until it was hidden deep within her aura. "Daddy said you're supposed to do the right thing, even if it's probably not going to work. It's more important than winning."

Val considered that for a long moment, then squeezed her shoulder. "You bring honor to him," he murmured. "Now be still." As Kitty stretched out, he added, "By the way, your chokehold is terrible. Who taught you that?"

"I saw it on TV. If you hold on tight enough, the other guy passes out—"

"Yes, I know." He waited until Arnold stepped into the hall, then leaned closer to her and whispered, "We'll see about your form another day."

The door quickly opened again as Arnold ducked back into the room. "I heard Toula and Eva down the hall. Sounds like *someone's* displeased."

"I can't imagine why," Val muttered, and waved a gate open. "Call me when they've left—I don't think my continued presence here would help matters." Seeing me struggle to sit up, he hurried back to my side and pressed me flat. "Do as your doctor said, carissima filia. I'll return in a few minutes," he promised, and took his leave.

The gate vanished just as Magus Stanhope stormed into the room, and I feigned sleep before she noticed me. With my eyes barely slit open, I could see a shape of approximately Toula's size enter behind her and close the door.

"Mom!" Kitty cried. Her bed creaked as she slid off, and she started across the room to meet them. "I'm okay, I just hit the mats—"

"What the *hell* do you think you're doing?" Magus Stanhope snapped.

Kitty stopped in her tracks. "I'm not on bed rest, it's all right—"

"Consorting with *that?*" Her mother's finger jabbed toward me. "What are you doing? Are you *trying* to embarrass me?"

She seemed to shrink as her mother berated her. "Hunter was going to hurt her," she protested. "I had to do something."

"*He* is my aide," the magus retorted, "*she* is a damn mongrel, and you—"

"Eva, *Eva*," Magus Lowe interjected, taking Kitty by the shoulder. "Please, not now, this isn't a private space. Unless you'd like this conversation to be overheard by the entire infirmary?" When she said nothing, he steered Kitty toward the door. "Come on, love, let the grownups talk. Your bags are in the dorm, yes?"

They weren't—Kitty had left her things locked in Magus Lowe's office when we crossed that morning—but she was clever enough not to correct him. "Yes, sir."

"I'll walk you over, then," he offered. "Just in case you get dizzy."

When the door closed, Toula and Magus Stanhope waited for the length of a long ten-count until either spoke again. "Not even going to fake it, Eva?" Toula murmured once Kitty was well out of earshot. "I'm pretty sure kids aren't supposed to bounce."

"You set this up to humiliate me," said Magus Stanhope, stepping into Toula's personal space. "My daughter and a goddamned mongrel—"

"*Your* daughter?" Toula laughed. "Finally, she claims her! I was beginning to wonder if Orson found her out in a cabbage patch."

"Yes, she is my daughter," she said stiffly, "and I don't need your critique of my parenting."

"What parenting? Shit, that kid got *shot* at, and you still couldn't pop over to check on her. I mean, her dad drops dead, her mom doesn't visit—it's been a real banner year for Kitty, you know?"

"You have no—"

"What? I don't have kids, so I can't possibly understand?" Toula retorted. "Maybe not, but I *do* know a thing or two about parental abandonment, and let me tell you, sweetheart, it leaves scars." It was her turn to close the distance between them, and Magus Stanhope took a step in retreat. "I don't know what sort of game you're playing," she continued. "I suppose I could break through that block of yours, but that would be rude, wouldn't it?"

"Stay the fuck out of my head," she warned.

"*Gladly*. I get enough headaches already from you and your little Conclave friends—and that's not me poking around, that's just observation," she said before Magus Stanhope could protest. "Your alliances haven't gone unnoticed."

"Is that a threat?"

"No. That's me wondering what the hell you're doing dropping Kitty over here. Are you hoping she'll discover some untapped talent, or are you just keeping her out of your sight? I mean, a witch in the family—that's got to smart."

"The decisions I make for her education are none of your concern."

"They *become* my concern when they endanger her! Jesus," she muttered, pacing across the room while one hand ran through her short hair. "What do you expect me to do, look the other way when I see her get the stuffing beaten out of her?"

"It's not your place—"

"Did you even read the reports I sent you?" Toula interrupted, wheeling on her. "Were you at all concerned? That shit with Francine's kid—"

"*It's not your place*," Magus Stanhope repeated. "These matters work themselves out if you leave them alone."

"These *matters*?" she echoed. "You mean the witch in the family?"

"Stop saying that," the magus muttered.

"What? She's a witch, accept it!" Toula leaned against the counter and folded her arms. "If you were hoping she'd run away and join the circus if the harassment got bad enough, then I'm sorry to disappoint you. She's a good kid, Eva. Top marks in everything but practical work, and Arnold says she does her best. You did know she won her year yesterday, right?"

"Academic?" Magus Stanhope replied, staking a spot against the wall opposite Toula. "Big damn deal."

I wanted to jump off the bed and yell at her, but Toula beat me to the opening. "It *is* a big deal. She's working harder than the others—she's trying her damnedest to make the best of the talent she has, and you should applaud her for that."

The magus remained unmoved. Instead, her attention shifted to my bed, and I lay perfectly still under her gaze. "I want *that* out of here. You have no right to bring another mongrel into this facility, much less the school—"

"Okay, first," said Toula, straightening, "there's no rule against it. Second, Maria is barely witch-blooded."

"That's like being barely pregnant."

"Not even a remotely fair comparison. Want to see her lattice? You have to squint to find the trace, and the rest of it is classic magus material. You saw her today, you know she was casting."

"*Right*, until she went full inferno—"

"Still casting." Toula hesitated, then pushed on. "The kid's had a knack for fire as long as I've known her. Carver's been working with her since she was five."

Magus Stanhope twitched at the name. "*Helen* Carver?"

"Sure as hell not Aiden," Toula retorted. "And Badger Parsons has been working with Kitty since Christmas. She's making progress."

"The Fringer?" she asked, perplexed. "I thought she ran off to Faerie."

"Oh, she did." Toula crossed to the foot of my bed, the better to stare Magus Stanhope down at close range. "When those Conclave idiots went after Kitty, my brother got concerned. Kitty's been sleeping over with Maria for…oh, most of the year."

Even watching through my barely opened eyes, I could

see that the news hit Magus Stanhope like a punch in the stomach. "*What?*" she yelped. "You let her—"

"You are aware of what 'in loco parentis' means, aren't you?" said Toula, calm in the middle of Magus Stanhope's sputtering. "I'm ultimately responsible for the safety of this installation's occupants, including the boarding students. If you weren't going to protect the child, then someone had to."

She paused, but the magus was unable to produce more than a strangled grunt in her fury.

"From everything I've heard and seen, it's been good for her," she continued, examining her nails. "Arnold said she's shown a marked uptick in her skills since Badger started tutoring her. And it's not as if Val's letting her run around unsupervised—she's at least as safe there as she was in the dorm. *Safer*, judging by her medical records."

Finally, Magus Stanhope began to recover her voice. "I forbid—"

"Oh, good luck with that. The girls are *very* close, and Maria can make gates. But hey, look at it like this: at least someone's taken an interest in your daughter's welfare, since you obviously don't give a damn." She stepped closer to the magus and lowered her voice. "Here's the deal. Either you take Kitty home and do right by her, or I'll look after her as I see fit. Your call. And if you don't like my terms, I'd be happy to take the matter to the full Council. Your relationship with your elder daughter hasn't gone unnoticed."

"My family is none of the Council's business," said Magus Stanhope. "And there is *nothing* wrong with sending a child to boarding school."

"I wouldn't have opened the dorm here if there were," Toula replied. "But the other boarders at least visit home. Their parents call, send packages. Hell, I know damn well that if anyone else in the dorm had a term like Kitty's first, I'd have parents in my office demanding to know what was going on. You never seemed bothered. *Val* has been a better advocate for that child than you have, and that says a lot. So yes, I think your particular strain of neglect would be of interest to the Council. Reflects somewhat poorly on your character and fitness for the office, doesn't it?" As the magus sought a response, Toula murmured, "You know what really struck me? When Kitty begged me not to step into the Old Guard situation because she was afraid you'd be angry. That child was down to the clothes on her back, hiding in the library, and she didn't want help because she was afraid it would upset her *mother*. Come on, Eva, that's not right. Sure as hell isn't normal."

"Let's not sidestep the larger issue," she pivoted, gesturing again toward my bed. "The mongrel—"

"Stays. This is the best place for her to learn to be responsible with her talent."

"*Talent?*" Magus Stanhope repeated incredulously. "Did you see what that little monster did today?"

Toula didn't rise to the bait. "Sure, I watched. I saw a well-trained student cast her way through several dozen bouts. She got lucky in a few places, but her training's solid. And she *was* casting."

"Tell that to poor Hunter."

"He threw Maria into an unpadded wall! And the broken leg is Val's fault, not hers."

"Which is something I think the Council would be far more interested in discussing than my family dynamics," said Magus Stanhope. "Your blood's offensive enough, but allowing *that* to enter the installation, unrestrained? He could have killed my aide!"

"Who could have killed his granddaughter. They're both at fault."

"But you still let it into the castle," she insisted.

Toula folded her arms and stared down the magus until the silence between them grew uncomfortable. "Yes, I allowed him to watch today," she finally replied. "He defended Maria, and when I told him not to kill Hunter, he backed down. Even if he doesn't always like it, he respects my authority here, and I afford him the same courtesy on his turf. But you know something?" she said, cocking her head. "It wasn't just Val who went after Hunter. I think Kitty got there first."

"Because you've brainwashed her," Magus Stanhope spat.

"Or because she thought a guy twice her age was trying to kill her friend. Who's to say, really? Children's motives are so difficult to understand."

"Your sarcasm is unnecessary."

Toula shrugged. "You still haven't told me what you're going to do. Why don't you take her home for the summer holiday, see how it goes, let me know in a few weeks whether she'll be back in the fall, huh?"

But Magus Stanhope brushed past her, heading for the door. "This isn't a convenient time. The dorm remains open, yes?"

"Well, yes," Toula admitted, "but—"

"Kitty has a bed here, I trust."

"*Eva.*"

The magus looked back over her shoulder. "You think you can raise her better than I can? Go right ahead, Toula. But I won't allow you to use her to humiliate me like this again."

"She tried to protect her friend, that's all," Toula replied, almost pleading. "It wasn't about you. Don't punish her, she's a good kid."

"Who's made me a laughingstock among my colleagues. No, she's where she belongs. Let me know if she starts showing any actual talent, won't you?" she added as she opened the door.

Toula began to move toward her, then stopped and let out a soft sigh. "I know she's not what you hoped she'd be, but you don't have to push her away. There'll be a place for her in the Arcanum when she's grown."

"Or you could do this organization a favor and give that place to someone who deserves it," said Magus

Stanhope. "Witches happen. We cut our losses. By the time she graduates, she'll see that her place is elsewhere."

The door closed behind her, and Toula stood in silence until the magus's footsteps faded. "I know you're awake," she murmured once the coast was clear.

I opened my eyes and met her gaze. "What gave it away?"

"Intuition and eyelid fluttering." She reached through the projection floating over me and smoothed my hair from my face. "Not a word of that to Kitty, understood?"

"Yes," I replied, then glanced toward the door at the sound of nearing feet and the thump of wheels over stone.

When the door opened, it was Magus Lowe and Kitty, now with her luggage. She looked around the room and bit her lip. "Where did Mom go?"

"She's very busy, honey," said Toula, moving away from my bed. "I'm afraid that she was called back to Montana in a hurry. She, uh…she said she loves you, but right now, with your sister getting into everything…"

Kitty's grip on her suitcase loosened, and her jaw began to quiver. "I…I'm not going home?"

"I'm sorry. She wants you to stay in the dorm over the holiday." Toula rolled her eyes to the ceiling in mock contemplation. "Of course, there won't be much supervision in the dorm until the term starts, and you might get into less trouble if you went with Maria…"

Kitty nodded and stared at her shoes, and my heart ached for her.

When Magus Lowe recalled Val, Toula filled him in on the change of Kitty's summer plans. From the looks they exchanged, I knew she was telling him more than she let on, but Val remained outwardly upbeat. "Her loss," he told Kitty, and nudged her toward the gate he'd left open. "Go on, dinner's waiting. I'll have Maria home as soon as Bee decides she's not in imminent peril."

Kitty started to leave, but she took a long last look at the closed door before pulling her things back into Faerie.

When I showed no sign of serious damage, the doctor allowed me to leave shortly before midnight, and I fell into a deep, enchantment-aided sleep that might have lasted the weekend had Kitty not shaken me awake on Saturday morning. "Awards brunch, remember?" she said when I mumbled in complaint. "You should probably shower."

It took me a minute to push myself up from horizontal—though I wasn't feeling much pain, courtesy of Val's handiwork, I was stiff and sluggish from over-exerting myself at combat. "Maybe I shouldn't go," I told her. "After yesterday—"

"You *won*, you are *going*, and I'm not leaving without you, so get to it," she ordered, and pointed to the bathroom.

I slid out of bed and padded across the room on unsteady legs, grumping, "You're bossy today."

"I don't get a Belgian waffle until you get some clothes on," she retorted.

As I finished drying my hair, Bonnie stopped by to check on us. "Good," she said. "You need to be out in a half hour, tops."

I ran a brush through my hair and decided the damp bits would see to themselves. "Val *wants* me to go?" I asked her.

"Absolutely." She stepped behind me and willed my hair into a French braid. "With a little prodding from Toula, I believe."

My eyebrow quirked in the mirror. "A little?"

"A lot. But I didn't tell you that." She glanced at the door as Kitty came in, then gave her a quick inspection, fixed a loose hem on her polo shirt, and nodded her satisfaction. "That'll do. Have fun, girls."

As usual, my gate dropped us near Magus Lowe's office, and Kitty and I made the familiar walk to the castle's dining hall. She'd brought her wand—I could see its outline under her shirt—and I felt somewhat naked without mine. I'd asked about repairing it, but Toula told me it was a total loss. Sure, I didn't exactly *need* one, but my empty fingers twitched and my palms began to sweat as the din of the brunch crowd crescendoed.

With so many people around, I planned to use the crowd to my advantage: slip in unnoticed, hurry through the line, and hide out at a back-corner table. But that plan fell apart before I'd taken ten steps into the room.

"*Corelli!*" came the shout, and I almost screamed when Tom threw his arms around me and squeezed. "Best fifty quid I've ever spent. Five hundred to one, and you *nailed* it!"

"Ribs," I gasped, squirming to break free.

"Oh, *crap*, sorry." He released me and stepped back while I prodded my taped side. The enchantment had done good work overnight, but I'd been a battered mess, and the bones were still soft beneath the healing bruises. "Little sore?" he asked.

"A bit. And you wagered *how* much on me?"

He grinned. "Money well spent. Maybe I can't cast for shit, but I'm pretty sure I'm the biggest winner this year."

Before I could counter that, Gwinn and Natalie ran up, eyes wide. "About time," said Gwinn, and pulled me away from Tom toward the long table where most of our class had landed. "Thought you might not make it."

She pushed me toward an empty seat, and I suddenly found myself the focal point of the table's stares.

"Right," said Natalie as she took the chair opposite mine. "So, there's about a million rumors going around."

"Great," I muttered, propping my head in my hands.

"But what I really want to know—and I think I speak for everyone—is how the heck you did half the stuff you did yesterday, and when you're going to show us how to do it, too."

Surprised, I looked up again, but Natalie seemed serious enough. "I, um…I mean, it was all casting…"

"Someone said you've got a private tutor," said Gwinn.

I nodded. "Grand Magus Carver."

Her jaw dropped. "Are you *serious*? She showed you how to do all of that?"

"Most of it. I started improvising at the end—"

"Okay, before we go any further," Morty interrupted, "exactly how fae are you, anyway?"

The table watched me expectantly, and I plucked Natalie's unused steel knife from her tray as a demonstrative. "Barely. I can't enchant."

"But yesterday, when you hit the wall, that *was*—"

"Val takes care of me. We're distantly related," I explained. "Directly, but distantly."

"Uh-huh. So all this time, your mundane grandfather in Rome…"

"*You* assumed he was mundane. *I* said he wasn't a wizard."

Conceding the point, Morty nodded. "But *you're* a wizard, yes? Or, ehm…mostly?"

"Had a wand until last night, didn't I?"

"But you live in—"

"Never mind that," Colleen interrupted, leaning across the table. "When do we get the crash course in casting fireballs, eh?"

"They're not going to let us do that," Quentin scoffed. "Not here, anyway."

"Why not? Maria knows the grand magus, doesn't she? She could ask."

The rest of my classmates perked as they came to the same realization. "You *do* know her, right?" said Natalie. "She's, like, your…grandaunt?"

"Add in a few dozen greats and yeah," I replied. "But Quentin's right, Toula's not going to want me throwing fire—"

A hand landed on my shoulder, and I turned to find Magus Lowe behind me. "We can talk extracurricular casting when you're back from holiday," he told the table. "And there will be *no* unsupervised fireballs, Lady Maria, is that *crystal* clear?"

"Yes, Magus," I mumbled, and he moved on to join the other teachers.

My classmates were quiet for a moment, and then Gwinn said, "You're a lady, then?"

"Kind of, I guess," I replied, and pointed to the food line. "Look, I'll answer questions, but can't I get some French toast first?"

They waved me on, but when I came around the table, I found Natalie, Gwinn, and Kitty waiting. "I'm thinking I could eat seconds," Natalie said, and the four of us set off.

"You didn't finish your first round," I murmured.

"There's still plenty of folks from the silo here, and you don't need to be wandering by yourself until they're gone. Safety in numbers, right?"

I glanced around and noted the other diners' reactions as we passed: whispers, pointing, glowers. "Aren't you going back to Montana today? You think it's a good idea to be seen with me?"

"Who said I'm from Montana?" Seeing my bemusement, she grinned. "Chicago. My parents got the heck out of the silo. Probably a good thing, since my oldest sister's a dud."

"Oh." I grabbed a tray, unsure of the appropriate response to that information. "I'm, uh...sorry."

Natalie snorted. "Don't be. She's been on a school trip to New Zealand all summer, and Mom and Dad are getting her a car for her birthday." Sliding closer to me as we entered the line, she added, "And I don't care what Magus Lowe says, we're going to need to see some fireballs."

"I'll do what I can," I replied, picking out silverware. "Honestly, I'm just surprised everyone isn't freaked out by my family situation."

"Oh, we are," said Natalie with a quick laugh. "*Believe* me. There was an impromptu class meeting in the dorm yesterday before dinner and everything. I mean, I'd be lying if I said your granddad didn't scare the crap out of me, but at the end of the day..." She shrugged. "You're one of us. You've *been* one of us all year." She glanced behind her, but the rest of our foursome had headed for the waffle station. "And everyone knows you've gone to bat for Kitty," she said quietly. "If you've been looking out for the weakest person in our class, you can't be all bad."

"Thanks...I think."

"Sure." She pulled an apple from the basket, inspected it, and plopped it onto her plate. "Besides, if Hunter had thrown me into a wall like that, I'm pretty sure my folks would have gone after him, too. That was such a jerk move."

"Is he here? Hunter?" I asked, eschewing the fruit for the deep pan of sugar-dusted French toast.

"Nope." Natalie walked around me to hit up the bacon. "The Arc 1 magus delegation left last night. *All* of them. Sore losers, huh?"

I nodded, grateful for their protest. Hunter Crowe was among the last people I ever wanted to see again, and I didn't trust myself not to make a scene in the dining room if he'd been there to taunt me.

Toula and Magus Lowe presided over the mid-brunch awards ceremony, making brief remarks and thanking everyone for participating before handing out trophies to each year's winners. Our table applauded for Amina and Masaji, then cheered and stomped when Kitty went up to the magi's table to claim her prize. The first-year trophies were smallest—every year's prize was larger than the one before—but a win was a win, and we celebrated our own.

With the other three contests fully awarded, Toula cleared her throat and glanced my way. "That leaves only combat. I realize there was some unintended controversy at the end of the day yesterday"—a few of the magi nodded at the far end of the table—"but the referees agree that the wins were fairly made. *The referees also agree*"—it was Magus Lowe's turn to emphatically nod—"that in the interest of student safety, this year's winner will be moved into individual practical training."

With that, Magus Lowe reached under the table and pulled out a cardboard box loaded with trophies. He plunked it onto the table, and Toula beckoned me up, saying, "Maria, sweetie, I believe these are yours."

There were a few boos and hisses from around the room, but my classmates did a fair job of drowning them out. When I reached the table, I realized that lugging the box back to my seat was going to be tricky—not only was I sore, but the top trophy was almost as tall as I was—and with a whispered word, I floated it into the air. My friends clapped and laughed, and Tom cleared a landing spot for my prizes.

When the ceremony ended, I got up to refill my tea. Before I reached the kitchen, however, someone gripped my shoulder, and I turned and found myself looking up into Magus Wold's thick glasses. "Nice work yesterday, Ms. Corelli," he said, releasing me. "Sorry, did I startle you?"

"It's nothing. Uh...thank you, Magus," I replied, flustered but pleased.

"I was surprised to hear the truth of the situation from Toula," he continued, brushing a speck of lint off the sleeve of his navy robe. "The idea that a witch-blood could cast like that..."

"Toula's witch-blooded," I pointed out.

"And a rarity. Your kind seldom exhibits talent at all, let alone talent at that level."

I wasn't sure whether I was being praised or insulted, but I tried to be polite. "I'm barely witch-blooded, Magus," I explained. "It's probably not fair to compare me to Toula."

He cocked his head and peered at me through his half-moon lenses. "No...I suppose it isn't," he replied, then slipped past me without another word.

Toula joined us for dinner at home that night, grateful for a meal at which she wasn't required to dress up and make polite conversation with prickly magi. "By the way," she said, passing me the bowl of green beans, "I'm sorry to have sprung the whole 'individual training' thing on you this morning. It was decided last night, and I needed to set a few minds at ease."

Val frowned. "What individual training?"

"I can't, in good conscience, let her continue to do wandwork with her classmates," Toula explained. "She's way too strong, and if something were to go wrong, there would be too many kids running around."

"Well, since I don't have a wand…" I muttered.

Toula reached into her bag and passed a brown wand box across the table. "Pine. You're ready. It's a plain model," she cautioned as I opened the box for a look, "but you can trick one out when you're older. And that's a Levey wand—I made sure of it. None finer."

But Val wasn't satisfied. "The purpose of sending her to Glastonbury was for her to be around her peers, wasn't it?"

"And she will be, except for this one class. Look, Maria's hardly the first to go into private training—there are two others in Arc 2 and one in Arc 5. High-talent wizards usually get separated from the pack as they grow up, and if you don't believe me, ask Helen. Granted, it's rare to pull someone as young as Maria," she admitted, "but after yesterday's performance, we don't have a choice."

"But what about Kitty?" I asked, glancing down the table at my friend. "Magus Lowe normally pairs us."

"He's well aware of the situation," she replied, meeting Kitty's eyes. "Arnold's not going to let anything happen to you, kiddo. And in the meantime, if you keep working with Badger, who knows? You might be signing up for combat in a few years, huh?"

"I doubt that," said Kitty, but she grinned.

"Be patient," Val told her. "You won't learn overnight, but remember that you also won't get any *worse*." He sipped his wine. "And speaking of training, you and I have work to do after dinner."

Kitty put down her fork and seemed to blanch. "We...do?"

"Oh, yes." A smile flickered across his face. "That chokehold of yours is ineffective. Go ahead, eat up. You'll want your strength."

The summer holiday was brief at Arc 2, barely a month, but Kitty and I made the most of it. We packed our hours outside of extracurricular training with trips to the beach and into the settlement, where we could sit in a coffee shop and feel grown up. But the holiday ended all too quickly, and soon enough, we were back with our class as second-years, somewhat rested and slightly tanner than when we'd left. To our surprise, however, our numbers had shrunk—we'd left as thirty but returned as twenty-seven—and the situation was similar in the other classes.

"Maybe they transferred to Arc 1 or something," Kitty said that night as we sat out in the garden, stargazing before bed. "Maybe you spooked their parents."

"Maybe," I allowed, dangling my feet in the fountain. One day in, and I was already sore from my private lesson with Magus Popova, the upper-level practical magic instructor. Though she was encouraging, she took no prisoners.

A light flared behind us, and I looked over my shoulder to see Ros approaching. "That's part of it. I mean, you didn't exactly help matters—or I guess *Val* didn't help matters. Talk about blowing your cover in grand fashion." As she plopped down beside us, her leggings rolled up of their own accord, and her shoes vanished. "How's the water?"

"Warm-ish," I replied, kicking my feet.

Confused, the mosaic fish peeked out from hiding as Ros's glowing legs plunged into the pool. "You want the real scoop?" she asked.

Kitty nodded and slid closer. It had taken her a little time to adjust to the idea of Ros always being into everything, but she'd soon realized that the realm was happy to pass along the juicy bits—the information that the adults tended to speak about in euphemisms and code around us. Ros was also forthcoming about the miserable time she'd had in her one year of Arcanum education, and she was more than willing to lend a sympathetic ear.

"Here's the situation," she said, leaning toward us and keeping her voice low. "Your missing classmates have gone off to join the Conclave."

"Seriously?" Kitty asked, taken aback.

"I'm sure their parents were the ones who made the decision, but yeah, they're gone. Toula's pretty confident, and the intel she's getting shows increased activity at their camp."

"Where's that?" I asked.

"Northern Alaskan backcountry, roughly the middle of nowhere. The nearest road is twenty miles away, as the crow flies, and that's over a sizeable mountain. But they've made themselves a little base camp, barracks and other communal buildings and such. They need the people, that's for sure."

Kitty nibbled on her lip. "Are they going to attack us?"

"Right now? Doubt it. They've got a bigger problem," Ros explained, and gestured at the water. A glass-like three-dimensional map of what I assumed was the Conclave's facility rose from the surface, lit from below by Ros's feet. Between the buildings and the mountain was a swirling vortex. "A gate into the Gray Lands recently opened near their site," she said. "Within the last two months, I'd say. Toula's retained a team from the Dark Company to do recon, and their pictures are *interesting*."

"Interesting how?"

"Well, it's the *series* of pictures that's actually interesting. The Company folks send Toula pictures almost daily. Sometimes, the gate's patched, but within a few days, it's always open again." She smirked to herself and let the model splash back into the fountain. "Looks like the Conclave can't keep it closed. Maybe they'd be able to if this were a manufactured gate, but all indications suggest this one opened naturally, and those are a beast to manipulate." Seeing my confusion, she said, "Natural gates form at weak points in the skin between the realms. To close a Gray Lands gate, you have to build a patch and set up pockets of magic within the patch itself, or else the dark magic flow on the other side makes the whole thing unravel. Tough enough when the gate's opened in an otherwise normal part of the border, but if you've got a gate in a thin place, it takes more support to mend the hole. Mom said it's always a multi-magus job when the Arcanum gets involved. That's not to say a talented magus can't do it alone," she added. "Mom's done it, and so have Arnold and Toula. But if the circumstances are just right, and your pool of available talent is kind of shallow…"

"I thought the Conclave was mostly old-blooded," said Kitty.

"Sure. And the number of wizards up your family tree has absolutely jack all to do with actual talent. The only magus in the group is Francine Leighton, and most of the reason she got a chain was her family clout. I think Toula said she actually still had a maple wand."

"But they *could* attack us," I pressed. "Even with the gate—"

"They could do any number of things, but I'm looking at probabilities, here," she replied. "The Conclave's made up of wizards who haven't fared well under Toula's regime—folks like your Old Guard buddies who consider her an affront to their pure, undiluted, grade-A Arcanum blood—and people who were put on probation after Mulligan was taken out and didn't get involved when his dumbass son tried to stage a coup of his own. Toula executed all the conspirators, you see. The probationers left alive behaved themselves for a while, then ran off and started the Conclave."

I cut my eyes to Kitty, unsure if I wanted to press for details about Toula's idea of punishment.

"Their problem now is their wand situation," said Ros, filling the silence. "The magi and assassins who were involved with Mulligan and allowed to live were bound and stripped of their wands. Even assuming that the Conclave members have managed to get themselves unbound, they're still wandless—and unless you're very, *very* good, sealing gates requires the kind of complicated spellcraft for which a wand is almost necessary."

"So, they'll…steal wands from us?" I ventured.

"Not unless they decide to kill people for them, and that's been tried—not a great strategy. Since there isn't a trained crafter left in that realm, they'll have to make wands for themselves, and that doesn't end well. There are still some wizard-made wands in the Minor Arcanum, and I've seen them," she said, shaking her head. "*Vastly* inferior to a properly crafted wand. But unless they get a source for wands, the Conclave isn't sustainable as a magical organization—and given the typical old-blood feelings toward witch-bloods, I doubt they'll ever find a crafter. A bunch of wizards like that sure as heck doesn't have a witch-blood among them, so unless they kidnap a crafter, they're out of luck." Ros raised her toes from the fountain, and glowing droplets splashed back into the pool. "The Three offered to patch the gate—I mean, a Gray Lands gate is a Gray Lands gate, you know?—but Toula's declined for now. She's hoping the Conclave comes to its senses and asks for help."

"But…you don't think they're coming after us, do you?" Kitty asked.

"Nah. And certainly not you—they need high-end wands. Nothing to worry about.' Ros stood, instantly dry and dressed. "Anyway, that's what's going on with the missing kids. Keep it quiet, and with any luck, they'll be back in a few months."

She vanished, and as the mosaic fish returned to their vegetation, Kitty and I went to bed, somewhat reassured but still concerned about the Conclave and the gate they couldn't close.

Ros proved to be too optimistic. We never heard a word from our missing classmates that year or the next—nothing but rumors. Still, with nothing to immediately alarm us, we focused on the more pressing matters of our classes and exams.

By the end of our third year, Kitty had resigned herself to the fact that she was never going to get an invitation to Montana. Winter or summer, Magus Stanhope was always far too busy to host her, and after a time, Kitty stopped asking. Her suitcase remained in her closet, and she didn't mention it when her mother failed to show up for the Games. I cheered my classmates on—I'd been banned from competition—and then Kitty and I went back to Faerie to enjoy our short holiday, neither of us pretending there was any likelihood of a trip to Arc 1.

Having lived in the villa for almost three years full-time by then, Kitty had become a fixture, and she'd grown comfortable around Val, if still a little quiet. Bonnie gave her the same rough fussing that she gave me, lengthening her cuffs as needed and chiding her to eat her vegetables, and Kitty never wanted for anything. Still, I knew the rejection hurt, and I pretended not to notice when Toula pulled her aside during her third Christmas with us and said, "Some people are just assholes, kiddo. That doesn't mean you've done anything wrong."

But even if Kitty quietly dealt with her mother's abandonment, she refused to give up on her little sister. Every month, beginning in August of our fourth year,

Kitty typed a letter to Beth. She kept her words small and drew pictures in the margins, and sometimes, she included flowers from the garden or bird feathers she'd found, anything she thought a preschool-aged girl would like. Once a month, she put Beth's letter into the inter-installation mail drop and crossed her fingers.

There was never a response, and Kitty knew that any calls to her mother would go straight to voicemail. But she kept writing, just the same.

CHAPTER 10

To the mundane world, I suppose the idea of "magic school" must seem rather exotic. In truth, the years pass much as they would at any school, full of reports and essays and projects, a long march from autumn toward summer punctuated by midterms and finals. I gave book reports on increasingly longer novels, graduated from algebra to geometry to precalculus, learned to dissect an earthworm and safely titrate chemicals, suffered through a term of music theory and made a few subpar oil paintings. Of course, I studied the magical subjects as well as the mundane, with my schedule incorporating more complicated focusing techniques and technical crafting, introductory theoretical thaumaturgy, and Arcanum history and governance. The annual constant was our class in practical magic, Arc 2's answer to physical education and the source of many a trip to the infirmary. While the rest of my year zapped each other, I continued my private study with Magus Popova, whose idea of mercy was permitting me a water break every half hour.

Slowly, my classmates and I began to grow up. Wizard puberty is no less awful than the mundane variety—there's no spell that hurries the process along—and with so many teenagers living in the close quarters of the dorm, drama was a given. The cliques tightened; the girls fired off gossip like bullets, while the boys often settled their differences by more hands-on means. Everyone learned of the spots around the castle that were best for an unauthorized bout, the spots where a teacher was least likely to snoop.

And then, starting around our fourth year, my classmates began to take notice of each other not merely as peers or friends, but as potential partners and rivals. Spurred on by the flood tide of hormones, we began pairing off, experimenting with each other as crushes came and went.

Well, I say "we"—several of us weren't lucky in love. Kitty never found a boyfriend in our year, which I chalked up to her intimidating combination of looks and brains. Morty, delightfully awkward as he could be, never made it past friendship with any of the objects of his fancy. As for me, I had my eye on Tom for three years, but it wasn't to be. Tom was kind, but he made no move, and my quiet enquiries suggested that he wouldn't jump at the chance if I suggested a date.

Toula tried to console me after I came to her in tears upon learning that Tom was accompanying Natalie to a dance. "It's going to take someone special," she told me as I sniffled in her office. "Someone who's not scared off by your talent and...you know, *us*," she said with a grimace. "Give it time, honey. Once you're a little older and hanging around with people outside of your class, you'll see."

I didn't know whether I believed her—I'd never known anyone thrilled by the notion of dating a witch-blood—but as Kitty was almost always up to be my platonic date, I made the best of it. The only alternative was to run home to Faerie and bury my head beneath the covers, and the older I grew, the less appealing that possibility seemed. Oh, I loved home, but the longer I spent in Arc 2, the more the castle began to seem curiously like home as well.

Seventh year—"unlucky seven," as the upperclassmen dubbed it—felt like a string of meetings and information sessions interspersed with occasional classes.

Interested in uni? Now was the time to start making

preparations, especially as a proper transcript needed to be created, references arranged, and examinations sat.

Interested in postgraduate work within the Arcanum? Now was the time to begin exploring your options, whittling your interests, and working whatever connections your family had to score the best placement…oh, and you would also need a transcript, references, and the results of an entirely different set of examinations.

Want to live or work within a different installation? Sure, you could apply for an entry-level post and accommodations, but unless you liked bunkers in the middle of nowhere, you'd best hope there was an acceptable opening at Arc 3.

Keeping your options open? Well, hope you don't miss sleep too badly.

The eldest in our class, myself included, were less than a year from our eighteenth birthdays, but by the Arcanum's rules, we were still minors, nearing the liminal period between graduation and full membership. How we spent our time after eighth year would set up our trajectories for at least our first career within the Arcanum, if not the rest of our lives.

Honestly, it was a lot to put on our teenage shoulders, but those who knew assured us that mundane students had it just as badly.

I'd dutifully attended all of the sessions during the year, often at Kitty's insistence. Even though she planned to apply for university, she still wanted to see what might be available, and she prodded me into accompanying her. Unlike most of my classmates, I had a solid fallback plan—go home to Faerie until I figured myself out—but that option had grown less attractive. As much as I loved Val, and as beautiful as the villa was, I was still sleeping under someone else's roof and rules (few as there might be), and I itched to test the waters of independent living. For months, I'd been scheming of ways to convince Val to let me travel during the summer holiday, either alone or with Kitty. Not much had come of that, however—I could well imagine the look on his face if I'd suggested allowing me to traipse off across Europe with a backpack—and so, when the meeting for summer internships was announced at the beginning of March, I put aside my dreams of hostel hopping and followed the herd to the Council's meeting room.

Most of our information sessions were held in our usual classrooms. With fewer than thirty students and only a smattering of parents in attendance, we didn't need much space. But Toula was hosting this meeting, and she wanted the Council's long, oval table. We took our seats in the swiveling leather chairs, testing out their range of reclining until Toula walked in and the furniture quickly returned to its upright position.

"Well," she began, taking her place at the head of the table, "it's that time of year again, and I'm here to encourage you to apply for a summer internship within the Arcanum." She nodded, and one of the Council aides began to pass out packets of forms. "Will it make you wealthy? Not in the short term. Will it leave you much time for sunbathing? Not if you're serious about your job. But what it *will* do is give you a chance to work with one of the many groups within this installation. Now," she continued over the rustling of paper, "I can't guarantee that you'll be placed in your dream job, but if you buckle down and do well, you'll at least have solid references— and if you plan to stay in *this* installation, then you'll want people in your corner." She waited while we riffled through our packets, then said, "The application deadline is two weeks from today. Any questions?"

After a few general enquiries, Toula released us, but Kitty hung back while the rest of our class headed to dinner. "Excuse me, Grand Magus?" she asked softly.

Toula nodded acknowledgement but held up a finger to stay her question until the door closed, leaving the three of us alone in the meeting room. "What's up, Kitty?"

"I, um…I just wanted to know if there's any point in applying."

"You in particular?" She pondered the matter, then nodded again. "I should think so. Can't hurt to throw your name in the hat."

Kitty flashed a brief smile. "Just my pride, right?"

"You might be surprised," she said, and turned to me. "I've told Val that if you don't get your packet in, I'll be very disappointed. We don't want that, do we?"

"I'll do it, I'll do it!" I protested. "Not like he was going to let me hang out in Prague, anyway."

"*Prague*?" Toula echoed. "How long have you known Val?"

"You could tell him it's perfectly safe for me to go traveling," I hinted.

"And he'd see right through that. Forget it, babe. Aunt Toula works magic, not miracles."

The placement results were delivered to us on the last Friday of June in thick, cream-colored envelopes marked only with our names. As soon as class was over, Kitty, Gwinn, and I piled into Natalie's dorm room to learn how we'd fared.

"Here goes nothing," said Natalie, smiling nervously, and ripped open the flap. After a quick scan of the first page, she beamed. "Holy *crap*, I got Magus Lowe!" she crowed, holding up the letter as proof. "Baby Council aide!"

We enviously congratulated her, and Gwinn took her turn. "Svetlana Lahti? Oh, installation coordination—okay, this has definite potential for summer travel," she said, warming to the assignment. "You're up, Maria."

I unsealed the flap and mentally crossed my fingers. The introductory note on top of the packet was typed and perfunctory:

I have selected you to assist me this summer. Kindly report to my office on 29 July at 8:00. Bring a computer and notepad.

B. Wold

"Is this who I think it is?" I asked the others, showing them the note.

Natalie's eyebrows rose. "That's got to be Magus Wold. I don't know of anyone else in here who would qualify."

"Nice of him to assume you know where to find his office," Kitty added.

"But...Magus *Wold?*" I said, peering again at the letter. "Why would he want me? I heard he has a thing against witch-bloods."

"Maybe, but considering his boss..." said Gwinn.

She had a point—I could imagine the pariah magus trying to curry favor with Touk by taking me on as a summer project. "Well, could be a lot worse," I replied, putting the letter away. "Okay, Kitty, hit it."

She took a deep breath, grimaced, then opened her envelope and read the first page. A little wrinkle formed between her eyebrows as she did

"So...?" Natalie prompted.

Kitty flipped the page around to the group and shrugged. "Y'all tell me."

The letter, blue ink on unlined paper, was handwritten in block capitals that leaned to the right as if they'd been caught in a gale:

Salutations!

I'm Ted Girard. Glad you're coming aboard this summer!

You will need the following:
— *Long trousers*
— *Long-sleeved shirts (pref. wicking)*
— *Hiking boots (not new—break them in now)*

- *Good socks (and plenty of them)*
- *Waterproof jacket*
- *Waterproof camping backpack*
- *Toiletries suitable for camping (we recommend dry shampoo)*
- *First-aid kit (Plasters. Can't have too many!)*
- *Solar charger for computer, phone, etc.*
- *A personal copy of Maravillas de los Incas (digital is fine, translation is okay, but if you can read the original, all the better)*
- *Hunting knife (not a dinky multi-tool—something with a decent blade)*
- *Sunscreen*
- *Deep-woods insect repellant*
- *Sidearm (opt.)*
- *Tropical vaccine schedule (see infirmary)*

Looking forward to meeting you!

"What the *hell?*" Natalie muttered as she read the list. "What *is* this?"

"Sounds like you're going camping," said Gwinn. "Somewhere, ehm…not Somerset."

Kitty reread the letter—more of a packing list than an introductory letter, really—then put it away. "I mean, I'd like to travel," she said, regarding her envelope with a worried frown, "but I'd always thought I'd start somewhere with, you know…plumbing."

I stopped by Val's office after school to share my news, but his reaction was far from what I'd expected. "*Wold?*" he said, dropping his pen. "Absolutely not."

"But…I…I was selected…" I stammered, taken aback by his abrupt rejection.

"I don't care. The man's untrustworthy."

"It's only for the summer holiday," I tried. True, I hadn't been thrilled with my assignment, but the thought of the embarrassment that would come with declining it loomed over me. "And it's a good connection. Toula says it's important for our future—"

"Perhaps the others, but not you." When I regarded him questioningly, he said, "You only have one more year of school, and then you'll be free to come home."

Suddenly, the expansive office seemed to be closing in on me. "But...I mean, I thought I might stay in Glastonbury for a bit."

"A *bit?*"

"Study more. Maybe travel."

He sighed and rubbed his forehead. "Maria, your place is here. You needn't worry about cultivating Arcanum connections, especially not with *Wold.*"

Something new and hot within me struggled to break forth as Val dismissed my plans. "I want to do this. It's important, and I'm taking the internship."

One eyebrow slowly arched at the challenge, but I didn't look away. "Not if I say you aren't," he murmured. "I'm looking out for your best interest. You don't need to be associating with him, and someday, when you've accrued the first traces of wisdom, you'll understand why."

Before I could say something sharp and foolish, Toula rapped on the door and breezed in, all smiles. "Hey! Congratulations, you," she said, patting my back. "I know Bert's not the most *thrilling* magus, but he'll give you a good experience. You were his top pick, but I didn't tell you that."

"Yeah, well, Val said I can't do it," I told her, pointing across the desk in accusation. "So I guess I get to explain that to—"

"*Why?*" she cut in over me, turning to her brother. "The guy's brilliant. Maria could do with more research and less punching."

"With *him?*" Val snapped.

Toula kept her temper in check. "If I thought this was a bad placement for Maria, I would never have allowed it to be assigned. Assuming she does well, she could get a solid recommendation from Bert, which could help her career prospects."

"She's coming home."

It was Toula's turn to inch an eyebrow skyward. "Oh, really? You've made this decision unilaterally, have you? Finally decided to spring it on us all?"

"I—"

"You don't get to make that choice. *Ever*." She squeezed my shoulder so hard that I flinched. "If you care about Maria, and I think you do, then you'll back the hell off and let her do this. Don't foreclose her Arcanum options before she gets a chance to decide what she wants to make of herself."

"But—"

"But nothing. We have *talked* about this, Val. Let her live."

Val spared a glance for me, then locked eyes with his sister. For the next minute, the two of them stared each other down, their faces barely twitching as they engaged in silent argument, leaving me to watch and try to make sense of their shifting expressions.

When the standoff broke, Val sighed softly, picked up his pen, and resumed his work. "If he hurts her, I will kill him."

"Understood. Come on, honey," said Toula, steering me out of the room. "See you for dinner," she called over her shoulder, and we left him in peace.

I'd expected that Val would be in a foul mood that night, but he seemed to have cooled off, even if he and Toula kept trading quick looks, testament to their continued private conversation. As far as I was concerned, they could snipe at each other all they liked—Toula had assured me that my internship would begin as scheduled. "He's working through his own hang-ups," she'd confided once we were well clear of Val's office. "Most of them have to do with the fact that you're almost grown. Try to be patient with him, and if that doesn't work, call me."

Kitty had been privy to none of this, however, and so she immediately dragged the dinner conversation to the subject of our placements. I was grateful when she recounted the substance of her strange letter—better to put the spotlight on her internship than continue to needle Val with reminders of mine.

"That sounds like Ted," said Toula as Kitty concluded. "He can be eccentric, but he's harmless." She swirled her Bordeaux and puckered slightly as she drank. As a peace offering, she'd slipped back to Glastonbury to retrieve a bottle for dinner, one that an aide had recommended, but the tannins were unpleasantly prominent, and Val had replaced my glass with a sweeter white when Toula was distracted.

"Nice guy. Smarter than he looks," she continued, pushing her glass aside. "He really wanted you, Kitty. We had a selection meeting last week after we'd all had time to look over the applications, and Ted walked in, said he wanted you, and offered to fight anyone to get you."

"That's, uh…nice of him," she said.

"You don't quite get the picture. Ted capped out at an ash wand, and he challenged a group of wizards that was fairly stacked with magi. I don't think he anticipated a fight, but still…ballsy." Her hand automatically reached for her glass, but she stayed it and called forth a water goblet instead. "Ted doesn't just take people on, summer interns or not. He's excited about you."

"But what does he *do*?" Kitty asked. "The letter was vague about that."

Toula sighed. "And that would be typical Ted. The Away Team isn't discussed much on purpose, but since you're going to be working with them, I suppose I could fill you in."

I put down my fork and started to rise. "Should I—"

"No, no, sit. This involves you, too, whether Bert likes it or not."

Val grunted at the mention of my upcoming boss, but he let Toula speak uninterrupted.

"So…the Away Team," she said, leaning back and steepling her fingers. "Ted's not much of a wizard, but he's a decent archaeologist. Right after I took office, he asked me about putting together a group to hunt down missing magical items—books, jewelry, ensorcelled lamps, what have you. Since we'd almost lost Faerie *and* the Arcanum thanks to Simon Magus's damn diary, I didn't mind if Ted wanted to try to recover possibly made-up items. If they existed, I didn't want them in the wrong hands, and if they didn't, I wanted fewer things to worry about. Anyway, I gave him my blessing, he put together an *interesting* assortment of people, and they got to work. My understanding is they spend about half their time in the Archives and the rest in the field, so God only knows what they've planned for the summer."

"Have they ever found anything?" asked Kitty.

"Actually, yes. Don't look so surprised. The Arcanum's a thousand years old, built on the bones of older organizations, and spread out around the world. Of *course* we misplace things. Now, they've hit plenty of dead ends, too," she continued, "and they've concluded with fair certainty that quite a few items on Ted's initial list either never existed or have been destroyed." Toula chuckled to herself. "Poor guy has a few favorites he just won't give up on. Every couple of years, I get a proposal across my desk for his latest quest for the Holy Grail."

Kitty frowned. "Wait…literally?"

"Yup. He's working on the theory that it's not a relic, just a terribly ensorcelled chalice of some sort. No luck yet, but I'm not going to tell him no." She turned to Val and grinned. "Might try to convince Percival to go along sometime. Be good to get him out of the house, don't you think?"

"I think Helen might object," Val replied, but I saw mirth in the slight crinkling of his eyes. "You're never going to let Joey live that name down, are you?"

"You two be nice to Dad," said Ros, manifesting at the far end of the table with her arms folded. "He can't help it."

Toula held up her hands in surrender, and Ros, shaking her head, pulled out a chair. "Ted's good people," she said, pointing to Kitty. "Frank's been working with him for almost fifteen years, and if Frank trusts him, he's all right. Might walk into walls, but he'll take care of you."

Toula's mouth curled into a little smirk. "Frank still gives you the gossip, eh?"

"Enough." She looked over the remnants of dinner, then took a roll from the breadbasket and broke it in half. "And thanks," she said as the butter floated toward her.

Technically, Ros had no need of food, but I'd seen her crash enough meals to know there would be no leftover rolls. "So, it's Ted and Frank, then?" I asked.

"Not just them," said Toula. "There's Lakshmi Gupta, who does logistics—she got her start at Arc 4—"

"Daphne Hopkins," Ros interjected, buttering her dinner. "Only halfway decent wizard on the Team."

"She's good," Toula agreed. "Wrote a couple of well-received papers on theoretical spellcraft when she was in her twenties. Ted snapped her up as soon as she showed interest."

"Then there's Antony and Bob..."

"Antony Copeland's a former librarian, Bob Norge is a former archivist," Toula explained. "Bob knows what we have, and Antony's better on the technical side."

"He's one of my old classmates, incidentally," Ros told Kitty, "so if he gives you a hard time, let me know. And Mal."

"*Mal*," Toula said, nodding. "I still can't believe he's

old enough to be working."

Ros bit into her roll and spoke around her food. "Malcom Stowe. He's Rufus and Poppy's kid," she told me. "Smart, fit, almost useless with magic." Noticing Kitty's confusion, she explained, "His parents have run the settlement school since its founding. Rufus is half fae, Poppy's former *Company*, so you can see why Mal's never going to win any prizes for enchantment."

Val cleared his throat. "You could change that…"

"I offered. He's declined thus far. If he's still aging, it's at glacial speed, and I honestly think he likes shifting too much to give it up."

"Shifting?" Kitty echoed, raising an eyebrow.

"Lupine shifter. Gets it from his mom." She finished her first roll and groaned happily, then reached for another. "Anyway, Kitty, it'll be good for you."

But Val seemed uncertain. "If they're hunting magical items, and they have one proper wizard among them…that seems unsafe."

"Which is why they have a magus on call," said Toula. "Anything even vaguely affiliated with my office or the Council has a contact magus in case of emergency. Bert just gets called more often than most."

Ros snickered as she doctored her bread, and Toula glanced her way. "What?"

"I still can't believe you foisted them onto *Bert*," she said, grinning wickedly.

"It's good experience for him," Toula protested.

"*Right*. The guy who grew up in the library must so appreciate those midnight calls to Timbuktu. Frank says he's surly half the time when they drag him out."

"I said it was good for him, not fun."

"But why should they need a magus at all?" Kitty asked.

"Well," said Toula, "most of the items they're searching for weren't just forgotten—they were hidden away and protected. Magical tripwires and such, see."

But she frowned and shook her head. "The 2013 closure should have knocked any wards out—"

"*Most* wards. I mean, it would have taken out the silo's set had Greg not been powering them with Simon Magus's toys. Arc 2's were older and better constructed for emergencies, and they survived. Arcs 4, 6, and 7 went down, now. We had a nasty few months after Faerie opened again."

"How did any of them survive without magic?" Kitty pressed. "They should have disintegrated."

"Backup power supply." Toula grinned at our confusion. "The wards that lasted were built by the magical community's equivalent of doomsday preppers. They worked large pockets of raw magic into the matrices—not enough to keep them running indefinitely, but a sufficient supply to hold them together until we fixed the problem. *Gorgeous* construction, but a bear to build and replenish. It took teams weeks to fix them. The Council considered redoing the wards on the other installations to bring them up to code, if you will, but it was so much work that it went by the wayside." She gestured a lukewarm cup of tea into being as she spoke. "Anyway, sometimes the old ways are the best ways, and Ted's come across his share of old wards that are running *just* fine— hence the need for Bert." Looking at her watch, she asked, "Ros, would you do me a favor and let him know I'm on my way?"

I knew Toula well enough to know that the last request had nothing to do with the magus.

Ros never stopped eating. "Done," she mumbled through a mouthful of food.

"Movie night," Toula told Val. "My pick. Coileán's less than thrilled, but he's being a good sport." She slugged her tea back, winced at the slight burn, and collected her overnight bag from its place against the wall. "Thanks for dinner," she said, giving Val a one-armed hug, and opened a gate. Before it closed behind her, I saw on the other side a windowless room set up with a couch and a wide-screen television—and Coileán, who bore a look of deep resignation. Kitty seemed unfazed by the notion of the grand magus having her date night with a king, proof that my friend had spent *far* too long around my family.

Val smiled to himself for the first time that evening, then shook his head. "Poor boy," he murmured, and refilled his wine while Ros and the remaining half-dozen rolls disappeared.

Two minutes before eight on the appointed day, I stood on the thick hallway runner outside of Magus Wold's office and collected myself. My interaction with the man had been minimal until then, and now, I was expected to work closely with him for the duration of my short summer holiday. In truth, I envied Kitty—God only knew what her boss had in store for her, but at least she was going to see a bit of the world beyond Glastonbury. Given the little I knew of Magus Wold from Toula and Ros, I could readily envision myself enjoying the August sunshine from a library carrel.

With a last deep breath, I rapped on the heavy wooden door and waited. A few seconds later, it unlatched and swung slightly open, and a voice on the other side called, "Come in."

My new supervisor didn't rise when I let myself inside, but he did close his laptop. "Good morning, Ms. Corelli," he said, watching me over his thick glasses. "Thank you for your punctuality. I'll expect nothing less this summer, understood?"

I nodded, clutching my computer bag's strap as if the nylon could offer moral support. "Yes, Grand Magus."

"That won't be necessary. 'Magus' is quite sufficient," he replied, but his rigidity seemed to fractionally soften as he gestured to one of the brown leather chairs before his desk. "Have a seat."

I did as I was told and waited with my bag in my lap.

He pulled off his glasses and gave the lenses a brief buffing on his robe's sleeve. "Do you know why I selected you?"

"No, sir," I told him, assuming that a comment about sucking up to Toula wouldn't have been appreciated.

"My research interests lie in the fields generally lumped together as 'theoretical spellcraft,'" he said, raising his glasses to the light to look for smudges. "I'm conducting research for a treatise. Your marks in history and English have been satisfactory, and I trust you understand how the library works, yes?"

I nodded.

"Good. Beyond that, if my work progresses as intended, I may call upon you to assist me in practical testing of my theories. I believe that you, out of your year, are uniquely positioned to be of use in this regard. Is that acceptable to you, Ms. Corelli?"

"Yes, Magus."

"Very well." He pointed to a four-seat wooden table on the other side of the office. "You may set up over there. Here's the first book I'd like you to pull and read—I want a detailed summary as soon as practicable." He lifted a scrap of paper from his blotter, and I rose to take it from him. "Where possible, please secure electronic copies from the library. I can't very well make notations in the originals, can I?"

I smiled at the weak joke and plugged in my computer. As I unpacked the rest of my gear—notepad, pen, water bottle, headphones—Magus Wold opened his computer again and resumed working. "One little matter," he said.

"Sir?"

He didn't look up from his screen. "You *can* read modern Italian, correct?"

"Some, sir," I admitted. I seldom had cause to speak it at home, and I doubted that my vocabulary would be sufficient to parse the sort of texts the magus had in mind.

He grunted and sipped his tea. "Well, then, I suggest you borrow a dictionary while you're in the system."

Val had picked up enough Italian during his more recent trips to improve my fluency that night, but even with the boost, my assigned book was a half-comprehended slog. Toula came through the next day, chatting with a native Florentine in security just long enough to acquire her language, then meeting me for lunch and a rapid transfer of the tongue. "Better?" she asked sympathetically as I skimmed the book in her office.

"Some." The subject matter remained dense and abstract, even with an augmented vocabulary, and I made a face as I closed the book. "This is *awful*."

"It's good for you," she replied, then sent me on my way before the end of my allotted one-hour break.

The job might have been better if I'd had Kitty around to complain with at night, but she was already in the field—Ecuador, she'd told me in a message on the first day, but that was the last I'd heard from her. I'd have given anything to be trekking through the jungle with her instead of going cross-eyed in Magus Wold's office, but I kept my thoughts to myself and did my best to not go insane—and to not let on to Val that the internship wasn't all I'd hoped it'd be.

Every day was more of the same: show up at eight, read with my headphones for company until lunch, then eat with whomever I could find before returning to the office for a long afternoon. Few of my classmates' schedules synched with mine, and my friends were often absent from the castle's dining hall. I got the sense that lunch at Glastonbury's better restaurants was the understood compensation for the rising eighth-years' otherwise unpaid labor, but it seemed that Magus Wold either never got the memo or ignored it. He tended to eat at his desk, and when he did venture into the dining hall, he never asked me to join him. On occasion, I saw Magus Lowe stop and speak to him, but to everyone else in the room, Magus Wold might as well have been furniture.

I didn't blame his peers. Though only in his late thirties, Magus Wold seemed older, quiet and curt in his speech and fastidious in his dress. He seldom smiled, and when he let one slip, it quickly faded. If he had any interests beyond his work, he didn't share them with me. But more importantly, it was no secret that Magus Wold had been caught with the traitors during the last attempt at a coup. He'd ended his term as grand magus under arrest, and he'd been allowed to become an ordinary magus as a consolation prize—while Magus Wold hadn't exactly been conspiring with the traitors, he'd been unable to stop them when they threatened the future of magic itself. So while he wasn't convicted of treason, he also wasn't high on anyone's list of party invitees.

On the Monday of my second week, I returned to the castle dreading the day, but at least I had the assigned summary printed, bound, and tabbed. My boss gave me a brief nod of acknowledgement when I passed it across his desk, then said, "The next book I need you to read is in Latin, and Toula assures me that you're fluent, so I'd like this by the end of the week. Here's the citation—"

He closed his eyes and groaned as his phone began to chirp. "Damn it, *already*?" he muttered, then tapped the phone on in speaker mode and sighed. "Yes?"

"Bert? That you?" came an unfamiliar male voice. By then, I'd had enough exposure to peg the accent as North American, but I couldn't be more specific than that.

Magus Wold propped his head on two fingertips and began massaging small circles on his forehead. "Yes, Ted."

"Hey! Good morning! Man, you should see the sky out here, it's *gorgeous*. We're camped up in the canopy, and it's absolutely incredible. Clear night. I didn't wake you, did I?"

Magus Wold glanced over his shoulder at the morning

sunlight coming through the window. "It's just past eight here."

"Oh, good. My watch died two days ago, and my phone's been a little funky of late, but that happens out in the Amazon, eh? Speaking of which, we've got a situation."

"Yes?" he mumbled.

"Yeah. So, we found the necklace discussed in *Maravillas*—"

He straightened at the news. "You *have*?"

"We think so. There's an Incan temple about a kilometer from our camp, and we poked around yesterday. Sealed room at the heart of the complex, active wards all around. Something big's in there."

The magus sighed again. "Can Daphne not dismantle them?"

"She says she can," said Ted, "but see, this place is in ruins, and it's settled heavily over the years. I think some of the wards are actually support spells for the temple itself. If Daph cuts the wrong wire, we might be looking at a cave-in situation, and that would be a damn shame. Could you—"

"Right, yes. But it's, what, two in the morning there? Why don't we postpone this until daylight?"

Ted sucked his teeth. "See, that's the other problem. We've got a village of locals in the vicinity who do *not* like us poking around, so if we could do this under cover of darkness and get the hell out of here, that might be best for everyone's safety."

"You're afraid of jungle natives?" Magus Wold snapped. "What do they have, little dart guns? Bows and arrows?"

"Semi-automatics, actually. The kind of weapon I don't want to use to test my shielding capabilities."

"Oh." He scowled at the phone, but he sounded mildly chastened. "I see."

"Can you come, then? We'd like to be out by dawn.

Lakshmi has photos and coordinates, so you won't have to go through Arc 6."

"On my way," Magus Wold mumbled, and cut the connection. Standing, he tucked his phone into his robe pocket and gave me a weary stare. "Did Toula mention the Away Team to you?"

"Yes, Magus," I replied from my table workstation.

"Bloody nuisance is what they are. Magically inept treasure hunters without the sense to recruit any proper wizards to their ranks, and I'm stuck as their minder. At least they didn't call in the middle of *my* night this time." He shook his head and started for the door. "Let's hope this is simple. Carry on."

Only once Magus Wold had left the floor did I realize he'd forgotten to give me my next assignment. He had, however, left his computer unlocked, and I assumed I could figure it out if I sneaked a peek. Though I was disinclined to rummage through a magus's computer, I decided that Magus Wold would be even less pleased if he returned to find me twiddling my thumbs, so I hurried behind his desk and took a look at the document on top— a spreadsheet of books, authors, and library information. A few entries had an X in the *Acquired* column, but most were still in the queue.

On a lark, I printed a copy of the spreadsheet, then went to the library and cornered one of the reference staff. "This is all for Magus Wold," I explained, showing her the printout. "He prefers digital copies."

She perused the list, making notations in pencil down one margin. "Some of these have been digitized, and I can send you the batch. Some haven't yet been scanned, but we can put them in the pipeline."

"Fantastic."

She pointed to half a dozen books marked with stars. "These are in the Archives. I'm fairly confident that they've been digitized, but I can't tell you with full certainty. And I'm afraid I can't even pull them for you on student credentials," she explained apologetically. "But what I *can* do is prepare the batch and send a code to Magus Wold, and whenever he's ready for the scans, all he'll need do is enter that for delivery."

"That's great, thank you," I told her.

The librarian began to put my request into her computer. "Do remind him that the scans will lock after the due date if he doesn't ask for an extension. You wouldn't *believe* the moaning I hear from people who can't be bothered to mind their books."

I frowned. "He doesn't get to keep them?"

"Heavens, no. We don't make special provision for magi, much as they'd like it—and besides, some of the books in the Archives don't need to be in wide circulation." She paused a moment later and gave the list a second look. "Interesting selections. What's he up to this time?"

"I'm not sure," I said, and shrugged. "Far too many languages, if you ask me."

"Indeed," she muttered. "Well, you'll have your library files in half an hour, and the others will be digitized by the end of the week. Enjoy your reading," she said dryly, and made a face.

Magus Wold didn't return until the late afternoon, and his robe still had mud on the hem when he dragged himself into his office. He unbuttoned it and tossed it onto the couch, revealing deep sweat stains across his dress shirt and dirt caked onto his loafers, which he kicked into the corner. Settling in at his desk, he plucked a leaf from his curls, then startled as he noticed me at the table. "Oh! Maria. Sorry," he said, clutching his chest. "Forgot you were here today..."

"Everything all right?" I asked.

He sighed. "They did find the necklace they were after. Archives will take it from here. Half the fucking temple collapsed, so we had to rebuild that, because heaven forbid we destroy a site of historical significance," he said, rolling his eyes. "And the bloody natives came round to investigate until Frank pulled out the flamethrower. Maybe the Team should have thought of that before ringing me." He looked at his computer, which was as he'd left it, then at me. "Have you got an assignment?"

"I think this is the correct one," I replied. "You left without telling me, so I asked the library to pull all of your list, and this was the only one in Latin that wasn't in the Archives—"

"My list?"

My plan seemed less brilliant under his myopic stare. "You left your computer open, and I didn't want to waste our time, so I had the books pulled. They're digitizing a few for you, and you should have a message with a code to download the ones from the Archives. They wouldn't check those straight out to me. But here," I said, rising and offering him one of my portable drives. "All the books I have now, copied for you."

"What are you talking about? You can't make copies of library books, they're protected."

I realized my error and felt a flush creep up the back of my neck. "Uh...*well*, not generally, but if you have the proper software..."

Magus Wold regarded me strangely, then plugged the drive into his machine and opened the folder. He tested a file, and as I'd promised, the book appeared on his screen. "How...what did you..."

"I'm sworn to secrecy."

Quentin, courtesy of his sister and her miscreant comrades, had undertaken the solemn duty of passing down the trick to removing library copy protection in third year, once we started doing term papers and realized that renewing our books meant losing all of the notes we'd made in them. In general, the Arcanum's software was at least a generation behind the current standards. Getting our own digital copies was as easy as running a borrowed file through a small program—disguised as a scientific calculator in case of spies—and checking in the original on time before it locked.

The magus scrolled through the books I'd given him, then looked up at me with a rare, genuine smile. "This is brilliant. Good work. You've kept your own copies, I trust?"

"Yes, Magus."

"Excellent. Stay there."

I waited beside his desk as he retrieved the Archives code and received the restricted books. "If I were to put these in your hands, would you be able to work your plainly forbidden devilry on them as well?"

"Possibly. I've never tried an Archives file."

"Well, then, it's your lucky day. Give me your computer."

I did as he bid, and Magus Wold signed in to the reader under his credentials. The books from the Archives sat at the top of his list, and he passed the computer back to me. "See what you can do, won't you? I need a shower."

By the time he returned from his apartment, I had added copies of the new books to the portable drive and logged him off my machine. "All present and accounted for," I said as he skimmed over my work. "And, uh…you're not going to tell Toula about this, are you?"

"Why ruin a good thing?" He closed the folder and grinned. "Tell you what, Maria, I'm going to let you save me some time. The list you pulled today is only the start of what I'll need for my work, and I don't have endless hours to deal with the library. I'll get you your own credentials— limited to the time you work for me, naturally—and make you my official library gofer."

"*Archives* credentials?" I asked incredulously.

"While you work for me. Now, I won't be able to control what you pull, but I warn you that Archives requests are logged. If you start looking into materials you really shouldn't be reading, you'll be questioned, and I won't cover for you. Understood?"

"Yes, Magus."

"Splendid." He glanced at his watch. "Take what's left of the afternoon. I'll put in the request for you tonight."

As I gathered my things to leave, he added, "Maria...excellent work today. I appreciate it."

"Thank you, sir," I replied, and hurried on my way, basking in my good fortune.

CHAPTER 11

Library excursions didn't get me out of the castle, but at least I had an excuse to stretch my legs. As promised, Magus Wold had my credentials waiting the next morning, and I'd barely dropped my things at the table before he'd handed me a five-page typed list of books to pull. "This is only the beginning," he'd said, and shooed me out the door.

I waited at a table in the library's main room while the poor research librarian ran through my list, marking off what was available and what she would have to have scanned. "He's a rare one, Wold is," she told me once she finished. "Most magi don't trust anything they can't hold—offer them a digital copy if a book's checked out, and they look at you like you've tried to give them a loaded nappy. I'm glad to see at least one of our illustrious leaders has joined the twenty-first century," she muttered, and slid the marked-up list across the desk. "Available library books are waiting in your queue, scans should be in there by next Monday, and Archives materials will be to you by the end of the day." She paused, then asked, "Was the magus planning to log in under your name as well, or does he mean for you to read all of this before the term starts?"

"We're sharing," I explained, which was true in a manner of sorts.

The librarian looked relieved. "Oh, good. Well, just keep an eye on your account. I wouldn't want you getting a stack of love notes from us if he keeps anything past the due date."

There was no question of that happening. "Your copies," I told Magus Wold that afternoon, passing him another portable drive full of books. "And there's more to come."

"Thank you." Again, he favored me with a smile as he uploaded the books to his computer. "I suppose you can return these now, yes?"

"Next week." He peered at me bemusedly, and I said, "If I checked out and returned all of these on the same day, the library would think that's odd. Keep them out for a few days, then return them piecemeal."

"You kids really do think of everything," he replied, shaking his head, and bent back to his work. "Right, do it your way. And how's the reading coming?"

I glanced back at my computer, where my quarter-read assignment waited for me. "It's...challenging."

"Oh?"

"Yes, sir. Medieval Latin is weird."

One corner of his mouth began to twitch. "Classicist snob, are we?"

"I wouldn't go that far," I protested, but I could see his amusement. "But yes, the text is...*irregular*, and the subject—"

"Is dense, yes. Do the best you can," he told me, and I reluctantly went back to work.

By Friday, I'd pulled as much useful information from the book as I could, and I presented my report to Magus Wold electronically that time, which he seemed to appreciate. "I'll give you a break for the next one," he told me. "Have a look at Sneed and Parsons—it's only a hundred years old, and it's in English."

"Thank you, Magus," I said with a relieved sigh, turning to head back to my table.

But he stayed me. "Before you begin, I have another job for you. Go down to Ted Girard's office and fetch his monthly report, please. It's more than a week overdue, and he knows it, which I can only assume is why he hasn't answered my messages on the subject. If you have to stand over him and watch him type it up, do it."

"Sure," I said, but paused after two steps. "Um...Magus? Where is—"

"Go to the Archives. They'll direct you from there," he replied, and I was dismissed.

The Archives, repository of the Arcanum's most prized—and often dangerous—possessions, was housed one tower over from the library. As a student, I had no real concept of its size. The entrance was on the second floor of the tower, but the extent of the Archives' sprawl was a mystery.

My shiny new student credentials allowed me access to digitized Archives materials, but not access to the facility itself. I stood outside the electronic gate until the archivist on duty at the desk understood my purpose for being there, and then he buzzed me in and pointed to a door in the wall. "Staircase is over there," he said. "Five floors down, subbasement."

"*Five?*"

"They're below the original dungeon. All the floors with windows are occupied," he explained with a shrug.

Arcanum installations, aside from Arcs 1 and 7, had few elevators. In buildings with a large concentration of active magic, mechanical equipment had to be carefully spell-wrapped to prevent frequent malfunctions, and elevators were no exception. As a result, the inhabitants tended to develop muscular legs and a loathing for spiral staircases like the ones that had proliferated all over the Glastonbury facility. Those who couldn't manage stairs either lived elsewhere or tried to learn the rudiments of intra-realm gates, but as gates took work, most of us got our exercise instead.

Venturing down into the subbasement, I was slightly dizzy after three floors, and by the time I reached the bottom, I stopped and collected myself before opening the door.

I'd been expecting stone, of course, probably something damp and dripping, but the Away Team's office suite seemed as welcoming as anything in the castle. The staircase door opened onto a small vestibule with a pair of wingback chairs, a loveseat, and a selection of mahogany end tables holding brass lamps and haphazard stacks of ancient issues of *National Geographic*. A glass wall divided the vestibule from the suite itself. What little I could see of the suite looked decent enough: whiteboards and corkboards hanging at regular intervals along the stone wall of the interior corridor, interspersed with occasional landscapes in modest frames, and a nondescript runner. I assumed the actual offices were down the hallway, but I couldn't see far enough to tell.

To my surprise, the door in the glass wall was unlocked, and I let myself in. The corridor stretched in both directions before turning out of sight, and as I had no floorplan, I went left on a lark and hoped I'd run into someone friendly.

Just around the first corner, I came across a blond man about Magus Wold's age, who had pressed himself against the wall as he cradled a Nerf gun. "Excuse me," I murmured, trying not to startle him, "could you point me—"

He whipped around and pinned me to the stone with his free arm. "*Shh*," he whispered. "Absolute silence, okay?" I nodded, and he released me. "I'll help you, but give me a minute."

The man slowly padded down the carpet, and I followed at a safe distance, trying not to breathe too loudly. As we neared the next bend, he paused, then cautiously pointed the muzzle of the gun around the corner and shot.

A jet of fire exploded down the hallway, incinerating the ball the man had just released, and he dropped his gun and swore. "*Goddamn* it, how did you—"

"Know?" finished a familiar basso, and I peered past the shooter to find Frank standing in the middle of the hall, smirking—and for once, without his dark glasses. "You're getting quieter, but I can still smell you coming…and your new shadow isn't even trying to block her thoughts," he added, pointing to me. "Hello, Maria. What brings you—"

Before he could finish, Kitty darted out of the office behind him and shot the back of his shirt with a water pistol. Shocked, Frank whipped around, and Kitty grinned in triumph. "*Teamwork*, baby," she said, and noticed me. "Maria, hey! Are you lost or something?"

"Confused, I think," I replied, trying to make sense of the tableau.

Frank shook his head and grunted. "It's a slow Friday. Antony likes to play with his little toys when he's not busy, and *this* one"—he turned to Kitty—"needs to choose her allies more carefully. Really, Kitty? I'm wounded," he said, pressing a hand to his chest. "Absolutely gutted."

She smiled impishly and loosed a short squirt.

He pulled the gun from her hands, then melted the plastic barrel with a quick burst of flame and passed the runny hunk back to her. "Nice try, kid."

As Kitty binned her ruined gun, Frank turned his attention to me. "Looking for Kitty, or are we on official business?"

"Um…well, Magus Wold sent me to…"

"Official, then." He rolled his eyes—red-irised, I noticed, which explained his upstairs eyewear. "Let me guess, monthly report?"

"Is it ready?"

"Hell, no. Come with me, I'll take you to Ted. Maria is Bert's summer intern," he explained to Antony, who grimaced at the news and patted my shoulder.

"It's not *that* bad," I protested.

"Don't worry, you're among friends," Antony replied,

and disappeared into his office.

"I'm in town this weekend. See you at dinner? We've got to catch up," Kitty told me with a sympathetic smile before heading back to work.

As I followed Frank down the corridor, I tried to defend my boss. "He's only prickly because his research keeps getting interrupted," I said, hurrying to keep up with Frank's long strides.

"Mm. What's he working on now?"

"Well, um…I'm not entirely clear, actually. I've spent the last two weeks taking notes for him and pulling books, but I'm guessing the topic's kind of technical."

"Sounds about right." Frank looked down at me with a knowing expression. "I don't bother asking him anymore because he's never forthcoming with details. Since he keeps his thoughts blocked off, I have no real clue as to how he spends his time."

That took me by surprise. "He can block you?"

"Many of the magi have the knack, and Bert's better at it than most." He paused outside a wooden door and rapped twice, then cracked it open. "Ted? Bert's sent a victim. Do we sacrifice her, or do we allow her to escape with the monthly numbers?"

"Oh, *shit*, that's due, isn't it?" said Ted, a chubby man with a gray ponytail, khakis, and a silk shirt with a stylized flaming phoenix across the chest. "Ack. Sorry, come on in," he told me, and pointed to his couch. "Have a seat. This is going to take me a few minutes. Help yourself to the *Nat Geos*," he added, then gestured to the minifridge in the corner. "Pop's in there. Don't be shy. It's Maria, right?"

"Yes, sir," I said, settling onto the couch. "Sorry to interrupt…"

"Not your fault," he replied with a tired smile. "His Nibs will have his paperwork in triplicate if it kills us."

Kitty came home with me, fairly bursting to talk about her trip to Ecuador, including the impromptu excursion they'd taken out to the Galápagos. "Best summer job *ever*," she declared over dessert while Val scrolled through her photos. "The Team's fantastic. Lakshmi and Bob don't travel much, but everyone else is great at camping. And Frank has stories," she added, pointedly raising her voice and glancing at the ceiling.

Ros manifested in the seat across from her, and Kitty yelped in surprise. "Bet he does," she said, folding her arms on the tabletop. "Spill 'em, babe. Whatever he's told you, I can top it."

I had nothing to compete with Kitty's travels—no Incan ruins, no giant tortoises, no accounts of Frank and Mal arguing over which of them should attack the jaguars roaring in the trees around them. But I had Archives credentials, and for the first time, I was able to do some careful exploration of the Arcanum's offerings. Sure, it wasn't as thrilling as a field trip, but I appreciated having that much restricted knowledge at my fingertips—and no one batted an eye when I stated that the purpose of my loans was work for Magus Wold. Moreover, thanks to the Team whisking Kitty off to Cambodia, then Tasmania, I had plenty of time to myself to explore. It wasn't the most exciting summer holiday I'd ever had, but at least Magus Wold seemed to be pleased with my progress.

In mid-August, after I'd settled into an almost comfortable rhythm, Val asked me over dinner one Thursday night whether I had weekend plans. When I answered in the negative, he grinned and summoned forth cups of coffee for us both as an aide brought out a fruit trifle. "Firola's ball is Saturday night," he said, smiling at me over his cup. "I think it's time for you to make an appearance, carissima filia."

I almost squealed. Though not of Mab's blood, Lady

Firola was a legend among the court's social circles, well connected by networks of old favors and famous for her beauty. Her annual soiree marked a high point on the calendar, and only those in the court with sufficient clout—or sufficiently good looks—made it onto the guest list. The party lasted from dusk until dawn, a night of dancing, feasting, and *other* activities taken into private corners of her legendarily baroque mansion, a home that I had glimpsed only from a distance. Some of the whispered stories I'd heard through the villa's gossip network almost beggared belief, but given what I knew about the hostess, I couldn't discount them as fiction.

"Really? She invited me?" I asked Val, beaming with excitement.

"Not directly," he admitted, putting a slight damper on my joy. "But I will bring you as my guest." He hesitated, then put his coffee aside and took my hand. "As Toula keeps pointing out, you're growing up. It's time that you begin to learn the court's nuances, and that means introducing you to society."

I didn't care what reason Val had for taking me along—I was just thrilled to go. I spent half the night planning, creating, and discarding dresses, sustained myself with caffeine and a library nap the next day, and returned to the drawing board on Friday evening until I'd come up with an acceptable frock, a deep green, off-the-shoulder gown that brought out the coordinating tones in my hazel eyes. I'd started to fill out by then, and careful alterations gave me the illusion of a more curvaceous figure. On Saturday morning, I turned my attention to my hair and makeup, trying and rejecting one look after another until Bonnie stepped in and saved me from myself. "You're going to a party, not a pageant," she said as she twirled and pinned my brown waves into a complex, half-braided chignon. "You don't need quite so much volume, and you're overdoing your face. Don't worry, I'll fix it."

As Bonnie experimented with cosmetics, I let my mind

wander to the party and forced down the first butterflies that threatened to flutter up from my stomach. "Not nervous, are you?" she teased, shaping my unruly eyebrows.

I supposed my facial twitching had given me away. "Just thinking of whether I'm going to know anyone there," I replied, trying to keep my head still.

"Mm. Probably not." She squinted at me, then made yet another minor adjustment to even out my brows.

"What about Seamus and Badger? They'll be there, right?"

"Negative."

"But Seamus is—"

"Oh, I'm sure he's on the guest list—wouldn't do to snub one of the blood, you know," she explained. "He just won't come. The way I heard it, he and Badger attended once, years ago, and the comments about her were so nasty that he said to hell with them all."

"Nasty?" I echoed as the butterflies flapped harder. "How so?"

"Look up." Bonnie raised my chin, considered her handiwork, then nodded and began hunting through my makeup kit for brow powder. "I can't tell you exactly what was said, but the impression I got was that people were just *tacky*."

There was no exact Fae equivalent for the English term, one Bonnie had adopted in Texas and brought back with her, but she'd employed it enough around me over the years to make her meaning perfectly clear.

"But you'll have Val there, hon, so I wouldn't worry. Ooh, gracious, *no*, why do you have blue eyeshadow?" She mimed a horrified shudder and put the compact aside. "And a few of the guards will attend. Kiet, certainly, but I don't know who else."

I closed my eyes as she resumed working on my face. "Val's worried about security? At a ball?"

"No, I imagine this is his captain's doing, and he knows

better than to object. Besides, if anyone gets hurt feelings, he'll have guards on hand to separate them. That place is going to be crawling with full-blooded faeries, you see. Get a few drinks in everyone, and...*yikes*. Thank you, no, I'll be over here where things are sane."

Bonnie's assessment was hardly reassuring, but by evening, having removed half my eyeliner and whipped up an emerald necklace and earrings to complement the dress, she decided that I passed muster. Val was more favorable in his assessment when I presented myself. "Beautiful," he decreed, and kissed my cheek. "And far too old." Opening a gate to the festivities, he murmured, "I'm very proud of you, Maria. Stay close, now, and let me make the introductions."

I followed Val through, flanked by Kiet and three other guards, and found myself in a foyer large enough to house elephants. The room was beautifully appointed—a marble floor that swirled in black and white, ten-meter-tall windows overlooking manicured lantern-lit gardens, slim tables topped with golden candelabra and sprays of blooming roses, and a massive crystal chandelier hanging stories above our heads, twinkling in the candlelight.

"Wow," I whispered, craning my neck to take it all in. "This is *gorgeous*."

Val chuckled and wrapped his arm around my back. "Come. There are far more extravagant sights within."

Still, he let me linger as I watched the other guests arrive, some singly, some in groups, all dressed magnificently. For a moment, I worried that my ensemble was too plain, but before I had time to deeply fret, a statuesque blonde in a form-fitting black gown swept into the room.

"Ah," said Val, catching sight of her as she sped our way on spike heels. "Firola. A pleasure to see you again."

"My lord," she replied with a slight smile that didn't touch her vivid green eyes. "This is...unexpected."

"My apologies, but I assumed one more guest would

cause no hardship." His grip on me tightened as he spoke. "Maria, this is Lady Firola. Firola, have you met my—"

"A guest would have been no trouble," she interrupted, "but may I ask why you brought your *pet*, my lord?"

Val stiffened beside me. "I beg your pardon?"

"The girl," she said, her smile edging toward frosty. "Why is she here?"

"Because she is coming of age," he told her, keeping his voice level, "and as my heir, she needs to meet the right people, such as—"

Firola interrupted his explanation with incredulous laughter. "You—you're joking, surely," she tittered. "The mortal—"

"Lady Maria *is* my heir," he said in a tone that brooked no argument. "And as such—"

"*How*? Be reasonable, my lord," she said, folding her arms over her generous bosom. "She's barely fae, isn't she? She couldn't possibly be the heir."

He cocked his head. "You think? Well, I suppose we can settle this question easily enough. Ros?"

A few seconds later, Ros materialized, severely underdressed for the event in a T-shirt and yoga pants. "What?" she asked, catching Firola's look of disapproval. "I'm entitled to a night in with my boyfriend. Not getting dolled up for *you*."

"Settle this, please, and I'll leave you and Sam alone," said Val.

Ros rubbed the back of her neck and grimaced. "Can we, uh…talk about this another time? This really isn't the best—"

"I know you're still with him," Val interjected. "He's not missing you. Just answer the question, yes? So we can all get on with the evening?"

"Val…"

"*Please*?"

Ros scowled at him, then cut her eyes my way, and I saw a flicker of guilt in the look she shot me. "She's right," she muttered. "Maria can't inherit."

"What? *Why*?" Val protested. "It's hers by birthright, she's my blood—"

"Way too distantly. Toula's your next heir, followed by Mab's remaining grandchildren. I could give you the exact order, if you want, but that's really neither here nor there right now."

"But—"

"*No*, Val. I'm sorry, but no. Can't happen. And it's not your call," she said, cutting him off as his mouth opened once more. "If your child were still here, then yeah, I could work with a quarter blood. An eighth, maybe. A sixteenth would be pushing it. But *Maria*? Forget it." She glanced at me again and added, "Kid's a wizard in almost every sense of the word, and a pretty damn good one, but I have to agree with Firola here. I'm sorry."

Val looked stricken, and as Ros disappeared, Firola daintily cleared her throat. "My lord...really, having her here, it would be such a...a *scandal*. I'm sure you wouldn't want to insult the court...would you?"

I glanced past Firola through the open doors into the next room, from whence drifted the strains of a string quartet, the smell of roast beef, and voices raised in conversation and laughter, and I wanted nothing more than to melt into the marble below my feet. A few of the recently arrived guests whispered behind their hands as they passed us, and I wondered how quickly word of Ros's pronouncement would spread. At least one of the foyer loiterers was looking at me as if I were no more than a dog turd in the middle of the floor, and I cringed under the weight of the stares.

Val, who had kept his arm around me since the moment we walked in, slowly removed it. "Kiet," he murmured, barely disguising his anger, "would you please escort Maria home? I won't be long."

"He forced my hand. I'm sorry, honey, I feel terrible." Ros sat beside me on the edge of the fountain channel, waiting as I tried to stop my tears of humiliation. "You look really nice, by the way. Here, tissue?"

Blindly, I groped at the air until she pressed the wad into my hand.

"I should have said something sooner," she muttered. "Didn't think it would come to this tonight, but...shit." She awkwardly patted my back as I sobbed. "It's nothing personal, Maria, please understand that. You can't be Val's heir because there's no way I could make you a queen. There's a power surge that goes with the throne, and I couldn't give that to you. It's not a matter of wanting—I *can't* do it. Hell," she said, sighing, "I can't even make you fae for practical purposes. Not if you'd like to keep breathing. Minor issue, that."

Ros meant well, I knew, but my mind was barreling down a million dead-end alleys, looking for the way forward. Ever since I'd come to live with him, Val had insisted that this was home, that I belonged here...

And Val was wrong.

I didn't belong, I would *never* belong, and at the end of the day, no matter how much time I spent on my makeup, I was still nothing more than his little pet.

Pet. The word raked across my soul. Not fae enough, certainly not a lady, just...a pet. A thing. No better than a dog...

No wonder they called us mongrels.

"Firola has absolutely no regard for anyone else's feelings," said Ros, interrupting my circling thoughts. "Never has, never will. Typical faerie. Don't take it to heart, okay?"

I looked up at her, still sniffling, and rubbed my nose dry. "What am I supposed to do?"

"Well," she replied, taking my hand, "if I were you, I'd keep on doing just what you're doing. I meant what I said back there—you're growing into an excellent wizard. If

Glastonbury makes you happy…you know, go for it."

Eventually, Ros was able to coax me off the ground, out of my dress, and into bed. She pulled the pins from my hair before leaving me, and I rolled onto my side to stare at the garden, freed from my finery but feeling no better. I was still awake when Val cracked the door open to check on me, but I closed my eyes and feigned sleep, and he let me be.

I didn't want to hear apologies or tirades about Firola or promises that nothing had changed—that, at least, wasn't true.

All I wanted was to forget and move on.

That night, for the first time in years, I dreamed of Zio Luca again—the heat of the fire, the acrid smoke in my nose, accenting the smells of cheap liquor and roasting meat, his animalistic screams as the flames consumed him…

Suddenly, the fire was gone and I was alone in the burned-out shell of our flat, now nothing more than scorched walls and hanging plastic sheeting. Disoriented, I ran from room to room, looking for a way out, but the flat went on forever, and I was alone, so very alone. My dream self cried in panic, and I caught myself calling for Val as I bolted awake in bed.

Panting, I lay on my sweat-soaked sheets and stared up at the softly pulsing lights of my old canopy until my pounding heart slowed. The child I had been yearned to leap from bed and run through the villa to Val's suite, but I pushed that urge aside. I was almost a woman, after all, and I had no need of such comfort, no matter how much I craved it.

Still, sleep was a long time in returning. After a wearying night, I rose early Sunday morning, threw on sweats, and returned to Glastonbury, where I alternated between completing my assignment for Magus Wold and catching naps in a carrel. I stayed late, eating dinner in a solitary corner of the dining hall, and slipped back across the border long after nightfall. When Val found me in my room, he asked how my work was progressing, but that was all—no admonishment for leaving without a word, and no attempt to bring up the previous night, for which I was grateful. I wasn't ready to talk about it, and neither, it seemed, was he.

In retrospect, we should have done just that. Wanda would have been happy to have us both in, had it come to that point. But I didn't want to relive that night ever again—and besides, a new concern had begun to infect my ruminations.

Val had taken me in because, however distantly, I was the closest thing he had to the child he'd never known. I'd done well in my studies, mostly minded my manners, and by all metrics, he appeared to be proud to have me around. Now, I'd failed him—publicly, dramatically, and without hope of redemption. He could treat me however well he liked, but in the end, I would never be more than the all-too-mortal mongrel living in his house. Maybe I could find a niche in the Fringe settlement someday—Seamus and Badger and the Stowe clan certainly had—but I would never be able to fill the role for which Val had taken me.

I wasn't enough. I would never be enough, no matter how many trophies I brought home.

When I was in Glastonbury, far from his mental prying, I allowed myself to wonder if Val regretted the choice he'd made. But I never gave voice to those thoughts, and if Val knew of them, he didn't let on. He kept his distance for the rest of the month—perhaps neither of us knew how to begin the conversation we should have had—and knowing that my star had forever been dimmed, I retreated into my work. There, at least, I was pleasing *someone*, and Magus Wold seemed willing to look past my mongrel status.

Just before the holiday ended, when the other summer interns were having their last lunches in town and the Away Team was finalizing plans to take Kitty out that night with a fake ID, Magus Wold accepted my final book report with a nod. "You've done good work this month, Maria," he said as he saved the file.

I stood beside his desk with my hands clasped, waiting to be instructed or dismissed. "Thank you, Magus."

"Better than I'd hoped." He looked up over his computer and smiled. "Would you be interested in continuing as my research assistant during the term? I can't offer you more than pocket money, but you'd keep your credentials."

Maybe it was the satisfaction of validation after that disastrous party, or maybe it was the lure of the Archives, but I felt myself grinning for the first time in days. "I'd love to," I told him. "It'd be an honor."

"Splendid. Report after your last period Monday," he replied, and resumed typing.

Freed early from my work, I went home and straight to Val's office, though I paused outside the door, replaying what I'd said to my supervisor. Hoping I wasn't about to step on a mine, I knocked and let myself in. "I've been offered a term position with Magus Wold," I told Val, who regarded me silently from the far side of his desk. "More research and such. I'm taking it...I mean, unless you think..."

He hesitated, then nodded faintly. "Good. That...that's very good, Maria."

"So I, uh...I may not be home for dinner as much this year. May need to stay late."

"I understand."

He called my name when I was halfway out the door, but when I turned back, he seemed to be at a loss for words. "Toula will be pleased," he finally managed, and I saw myself out.

CHAPTER 12

Of our original class of thirty-two, only twenty-four made it to graduation. The ones we lost along the way cut off all contact—it was as if they'd run to the moon and thrown out their phones after leaving orbit. Toula seemed disinclined to discuss the matter, so I did a little Archives snooping on my own before the big day, which revealed a startling trend. Although there had always been a bit of attrition in each class at Glastonbury, the rate had spiked only once—after my first year—but it hadn't returned to its pre-spike level. The younger classes were losing people more rapidly than mine had, and their starting numbers were lower. A deeper delve into the population records showed clusters of families seemingly disappearing month to month, never noted in another installation or at a non-Arcanum address.

One week after I began my personal research, Toula asked me to swing by her office, where she greeted me with a printout of my Archives history and a pointed, "Did Bert ask you to pull these records?"

There was no sense in lying. Magus Wold had been teaching me how to improve my mental defenses in his spare moments, but I knew my budding skill wouldn't be enough to keep Toula out of my head if she was determined to break though. "No."

"This is a lot of personal information, and you don't have any business with it. Cut it out," she ordered, and dismissed me.

But I paused at the door. "Toula..."

"Yes?" she asked, settling in behind her desk.

"The missing—have they all joined the Conclave?"

Her expression barely shifted, but she seemed older in that moment, burdened by an unseen load. "Presumably. Why?"

"Just...curious."

"I see." She folded her hands and regarded me with a carefully blank expression. "Whatever findings you think you've made, Maria, I'm confident that I'm well aware of them."

I hesitated, my hand on the doorknob, then blurted, "If I left, would it help? If I stopped coming around—"

"I thought you were going to keep working with Bert after graduation."

"I *was*, but the numbers went up after my Games sweep, and I thought maybe—"

"No, honey." Her face softened a degree. "You have as much right to be here as anyone in your class. Kicking you to the curb would only be a concession to the separationists, and I seriously doubt that it would be enough to bring them back into the fold." She paused, choosing her words carefully. "Your continued presence here is...*symptomatic*...of a larger perceived problem. That would be me. Treating a runny nose won't make a cold go away any faster...or so I've been told," she added with a small, wry smile. "Never had one. I'm tempted to fake one someday just to build rapport, you know?"

"I don't think anyone would believe you."

"Yeah, you're right." She glanced at the clock. "Go on home, it's getting late. And I don't want to get another call from the Archives about you, okay?"

That ended my investigation. Having pinged on the Archives' radar once, I couldn't risk losing my credentials—not if I was going to come on as Magus Wold's aide.

The decision had been an easy one for me. After nearly a year of reading, reporting, and assisting the magus with the occasional bit of experimental casting, I'd found that I almost understood what he was doing—and more concerningly, I was enjoying the work. Sure, the reading was still dry, but when Magus Wold's translation requests went far beyond my knowledge, Helen took me into the settlement, paired me up with appropriate native speakers, and taught me to extract what I needed. Doing so by spell instead of enchantment was a less elegant process and gave me a headache, but I was pleased to have the trick in my repertoire. By the end of the year, I could have crossed Europe and a good portion of Asia without a translator, an unexpected perk to my continued internship.

Toula was pleased that I had a job offer, let alone a position as a Council aide, and my friends were happy for me, if relieved that they'd secured spots doing work for someone other than Magus Wold. Only Val seemed uncertain about my career choice.

"Are you *sure* this is what you want?" he pressed over dinner one night when it was just the two of us. Kitty—who, like me, had kept up her internship during our eighth year—was with the Away Team in London, celebrating after acquiring a box of magical treatises for a steal at an estate sale. "Working with him full-time…"

"He grows on you," I replied. "And he likes my work. Besides, he lets me go out sometimes when the Team has an issue—"

"Yes, in his stead," Val retorted. "His sense of responsibility is staggering."

"I can handle myself," I said, bristling at his tone.

"I never said otherwise. But I get the impression that your presence makes his life more *convenient*, and I…only wonder if you could put your skills to better use in another capacity."

"Such as?"

Val shrugged. "You could continue your studies, decide what you want to do. If you went with Kitty—"

I laughed at the absurdity of the suggestion. "To

Oxford?"

"Toula offered to provide appropriate paperwork—"

"Yeah, last summer. Kitty got her letter in January. That ship has sailed."

"Oh." Stymied, he scowled at his plate. "What if you came home instead for now? Applied to join her next year?"

"Val—"

"I don't trust him."

"What, because of the coup?" I asked incredulously. "Magus Lowe was just as much at fault for that, and you don't seem to have any problem with him."

"Because I saw what Arnold did during the Mulligan years. Bert abandoned his post and went with Moyna—"

"They had his parents! What was he supposed to do?"

"Is that what he told you?"

"Well, didn't they?" I pressed.

"Yes," Val reluctantly allowed, "but that shouldn't have mattered."

I stared at him. "That's his *family.*"

"And I appreciate that. But the future of magic was at stake, Maria. Coileán was ready to die to protect that future, and Bert…" He snorted. "Bert tucked his tail and went along like a beaten dog."

"He was *twenty-three*! That's only five years older than me, Val. *Five.*"

"Which is why it's a terrible idea to make a child grand magus."

If Val had been hoping to goad me, the night was a smashing success. "I'm not a *child,*" I snapped.

His eyebrow arched ever so slightly. "The Arcanum disagrees."

"I'm just not a full adult by their rules. That doesn't make me an idiot."

"Of course not. I didn't say you were anything of the sort."

I pushed back from the table and stood, the better to

glare at him. "Then stop second-guessing me. I'm going to work for Magus Wold, it's going to be fine, and it's what I want."

Val took a sip of wine, unruffled by my indignation. "It's your decision, but I have always looked out for your best interest—"

"And I can handle it from here," I interrupted, and stormed out.

He might not have liked my choice, but Val held his tongue. Nothing more was said on the matter until mid-July, when I came home to tell him I'd been offered a flat in the castle. "It'll be convenient in case I need to go out after the Team in the middle of the night," I explained, hearing how weak that sounded even as the words came forth. "My schedule's going to get weirder, I think. It's better for me to be on hand in Glastonbury."

Val started to protest—I could see it in his eyes—but he surrendered before the first syllable could escape, his shoulders slumping ever so slightly in defeat. "If that's what you want, Maria."

I nodded and turned to leave his office, but he called me back: "Carissima filia?"

"Yes?"

The emotion he was trying to disguise was a complicated thing, but I thought I picked worry and a little sadness from the mix. "You will always have a place here. Know that."

Perhaps Val meant it, but I knew that he was wrong once again. I smiled tightly, suddenly fighting not to cry, and hurried on my way.

Two weeks later, we graduated in a flurry of speeches and applause, all of us sporting formal robes for the first time—and for many, probably the last time for another two years until our cohort had its coming-of-age ceremony. The graduates' families and close friends gathered at the front of the hall chosen for the occasion, the better to take pictures, with two exceptions. Val slipped in late and loitered near the back, keeping a healthy distance between himself and the room full of wizards. When I finally picked him out of the shadows, he thought, *I can see from here. No need to spook the herd.*

It helped that Toula had a prominent spot in the platform party and a camera she wasn't shy about employing.

The other exception was Magus Stanhope. Though Kitty and I scanned the front rows and the reserved magi seating, looking for a glimpse of her, she was nowhere to be found in the audience. But Kitty kept a stiff upper lip, gave a heartfelt address, and graciously accepted the many academic prizes Magus Lowe conferred upon her—a load of plaques and trinkets so cumbersome that I had to help her carry the lot once we were released to our well-wishers.

As we headed toward the rear to meet Val, one of the Arc 1 magi caught Kitty's sleeve. "Lovely speech, dear, really lovely," she said, smiling. "And Oxford is such an accomplishment. I'm sure you'll wow them."

"Thank you," she replied, shifting her burden of awards. "Um…Magus Johansson, do you know if my mom—"

The magus's warm smile chilled and hardened into a brittle thing on the verge of crumbling. "I believe she had a prior conflict with your sister."

"Oh? What's going on?"

She hesitated before speaking again. "Beth's been at softball camp this month. If I recall, today was one of her games." The magus patted Kitty's shoulder, giving her a little squeeze before she slipped away.

Kitty watched her go, and I finally managed to steer her through the crowd. "It's okay," I whispered, pulling her close with my unencumbered arm. "You knew she was going to be awful."

"Softball," she muttered, then sniffed and ducked into

an empty row of chairs. Dropping her prizes on a seat, she dabbed at her eyes with her new robe's sleeve, then took a deep breath, plastered on a smile, and picked up her things again. "Damn her. Reception?"

The hardest part of postgraduate life was the scattering. While I moved into the castle, some of my friends—or at least the people with whom I'd spent the better part of my life for the last eight years—were moving out. Natalie took a job at Arc 1 as a general assistant to the magi stationed there, Gwinn went home to Dublin to start at Trinity College, and Tom left on a solo trip of undetermined duration, reportedly financing his world travels through subtle manipulations at the roulette wheel and craps table. There wasn't much he could do without a wand, but then again, it took hardly any effort to flick over a die.

At least I had Kitty for a while. Ted had promised her a permanent place on the Team after graduation, and so she hung out in the Team's subbasement hole between trips to Cambodia while she waited out her last months before undergraduate life. When she was around, she crashed in my new flat, and when she wasn't, we called or messaged almost daily. Even when she went into the field, I knew it was only a matter of time before Ted called Magus Wold with a request for assistance, and sure enough, I would be dispatched to handle the difficulty while the magus worked in peace.

The Team was prone to ribbing—after I pulled off a particularly complex spell that counteracted the three protective layers around the Team's targeted amulet without setting off the booby traps some overzealous wizard had left behind, Ted started calling me "Lady Maria," and the moniker followed me for months. But overall, I fit better with the Team than Magus Wold ever had. In fairness to him, they were a strange lot. Ted was the visionary, prone to big-picture thinking and bouts of ramping himself up about the next great idea for fieldwork before Lakshmi dragged him back down with questions about logistics. I'd made the mistake of walking in on one such planning meeting just as she stood, planted her hands on her ample hips, and shouted, "You are *not* going to the bottom of the Atlantic, I *don't* care what's down there, and if you think you can shield against that much pressure and cold, I'm taking you to the infirmary to have your head examined!"

Lakshmi was the den mother to them all, especially Ted. A short woman with a booming voice and a taste for hot-pink saris, she'd started in inter-installation logistics at Arc 4 after university, forced back into the Arcanum fold by Mulligan's edict. While she'd resented her new position, she'd struck up a friendship with one of her counterparts at Arc 2, Rodney Featherstonhaugh, via text chat. She'd surprised him in Glastonbury one day, and Rodney, a thin, retiring fellow prone to sweater vests, had taken one look at his pen pal and fallen head over heels. Lakshmi kept a recent family picture in her office: her smiling in voluminous rose silks, flanked by their two grown boys, each a head taller than her, and Rodney, bald but beaming. Though she wasn't a magus-level wizard, she had a talent for gates, and so she seldom did fieldwork. Instead, she managed the office and did what was necessary to meet the others' needs, whether that meant sending aerial photographs and extra batteries to drop spots at midnight or dragging Magus Wold from bed when he refused to answer his phone.

Below Lakshmi in the Team's unofficial chain of command was Bob, the former archivist. Though Ted's age, Bob seemed older, or at least more measured in his reactions. He favored tweed jackets and bowties, even if the rest of the Team was slumming, though the picture of the aged English academic was ruined by his thick shock of white hair, which always locked as wild as if he'd touched a power line. He was soft-spoken and deferential during meetings, polite to a fault—or so I thought until I caught him muttering incomprehensibly when confronted with a sloppy report. Apparently, thanks to his Dubliner mother, Bob could swear like a sailor in Irish. He didn't travel due to a bad hip, and I'd begun to suspect that he never left his office until the morning I met his husband, Sylvester, who stopped by with currant scones from a recipe he'd tried.

The closest the Team could get to cloning Bob for fieldwork was Antony, an American witch who had the technical skills and functional joints his elder lacked, even if he was still working to match Bob's knowledge of arcane artifacts. Kitty confided that Antony looked after her—witches had to stick together, after all. His wife, Madison, who worked as a librarian in the castle, would have preferred that he stay home, but Antony enjoyed poking his nose into places it had no business being. Occasionally, I'd catch him in his office with his precocious six-year-old daughter, Allie, who seemed to think of her father's colleagues as her extended family of aunts and uncles.

A few years Antony's senior, Daphne was the most talented wizard on the Team, though even she barely merited a maple wand. Her research interests were as many and esoteric as Magus Wold's, and I seldom escaped the basement without having a chat about my latest reading. Her love of books aside, Daphne was happy to go into the field, even if she looked flimsy enough to fly away in a stiff breeze, a gawky flagpole of British Jamaican descent who wore her hair in purple-tipped box braids and had a fondness for trench coats. Her office was decorated with pictures of her cantankerous Siamese cat, Lothario, but she'd stopped bringing him to work when Frank and Mal made one too many jokes about eating him.

Knowing Ros and having previously met Frank, his peculiarities didn't surprise me. Aside from his size and pseudo-albinism, he seemed unremarkable, a solid researcher and a true asset in rough terrain. But Frank didn't hesitate to peer into other people's thoughts, and as he'd mastered the ability to breathe fire, he used it to full advantage, for which his comrades were grateful when confronted with wet logs on a cold night of camping. Frank wasn't shy about the fact that beneath the Arcanum trappings, he was a dragon ensorcelled into a more convenient form, but by the time I met the Team, they seemed unfazed by his moments of inhuman behavior.

The newest member of the Team was Malcolm Stowe, who coupled his mother's athleticism with his father's love of research. I'd seen him occasionally in Faerie—the first and only grandchild of the large Stowe clan was heavily doted upon—but Mal was ten years my senior, and I'd never had a chance to know him there. Initially, having found him surrounded by a fortress of books and happily devouring them, I thought he favored Dr. Stowe, the principal of the settlement school. He was certainly as easy-going as his father. But then I came into the basement one day in search of a missing section of the monthly report, rapped on his office door, and caught him in his shifted form, a monstrously large brown wolf. He lay on the rug two meters away from Allie, batting a blue rubber ball back and forth with his nose and paws. "He's a big puppy," she told me as I gawked and stammered out the reason for my visit. Mal snorted at my awkwardness, then turned his furry head and glanced at his desk. A sheet of paper flew into my hands—the report, I realized, staring all the more. With a sound suspiciously like a sigh, Mal rose and nudged Allie and me into the hall, shut the door, and emerged a moment later in his usual form.

"How…" I began, at a loss for more.

He smirked. "What, you've never seen a wolf enchant? Here, let me show you something on that page," he continued as if nothing at all were unusual about the previous five minutes. "Bert's going to have questions about this graph."

"Forget the graph," I interrupted. "You can enchant

like…*that*?"

"What little I can. What you saw is about the extent of it, but hey, at least I've got a party trick."

He looked down when Allie tugged on his shirt and asked, "Puppy?"

"In a minute, sweetheart," he replied, ruffling her hair. "Let me talk to Maria, okay?"

She scowled her displeasure, but she obliged.

As I grew to know the Team, ostensibly an organization for wizards, I began to understand Frank's and Mal's presence in it. Ted honestly didn't give a damn about his people's magical credentials—if they could do the research, maybe understand an extra language or two, and didn't mind packing for the desert or the tundra at a moment's notice, then that was enough for him. Sure, it helped that Daphne was a competent caster, but Ted prided himself on choosing colleagues with varying skillsets. Regarding Mal, the fact that he was a terrible excuse for a lesser blood in terms of talent was of no concern to his boss, who appreciated his willingness to shift and growl at things—and sometimes people—lurking outside their campsites. In my dealings with the Team to that point, I'd never seen him in action, but Kitty swore she'd watched him bring down a bear during a weekend trip into the Rockies. "Poor Frank looked so jealous," she confided. "He stays bound unless they need a weapon of last resort, since no one on the Team is talented enough to put the spell back together. Anyway, Mal was ripping into the bear for a snack, and Frank sort of sidled up and asked if he was going to finish it, and he ended up charring steaks and viscera for them both." She shuddered at the mental image. "Ted made them bathe after that. God knows they needed it."

Kitty had eagerly accepted Ted's offer of a spot in the pack, though both agreed that she should get her degree first. The Arcanum was paying her tuition and fees out of Toula's discretionary fund, after all, and that was too good an opportunity for her to pass up. Kitty had decided to study Classical archaeology, a three-year program, as so many of their searches led them back to the proto-arcana of the Mediterranean—the members of which, judging by the sheer quantity of long-lost artifacts the Team had recovered, had the collective memory of a senile squirrel concerning where they'd stashed their ensorcelled valuables. It helped that Kitty was starting her course with fluency in Latin. Val had caught her puzzling over our textbook one night during first year, realized the problem, and quickly gave her what she needed to avoid ever studying for a Latin test again—that is, once she learned the differences between his version of the language and the later Classical variety. When she'd explained her university course to him and mentioned that she'd be studying Greek, he'd taken her to Eleanor's estate and cornered the captain of her guard, Nico, to ask what he still remembered of the tongue. Nico had shared with Kitty what he knew, but he hadn't been able to completely save her from language classes—he was born in the late sixth century, and Greek had evolved beyond its Classical form by that point. But Kitty could make sense of the Greek alphabet before the first day of class, and that was gift enough.

Though I missed her terribly when she left for Oxford that autumn, I was thrilled for her. We talked almost daily, either by phone or message, and while I seldom had exciting news to share—the reading I was doing for Magus Wold that season was boring even by Daphne's elevated standards—Kitty was happy to tell me about her college, her lectures, and the other freshers on her floor, particularly the ones with whom she shared a kitchen. She mock-sighed about the fact that despite her long reprieve, she was finally back in a dorm, sharing facilities.

Not until November, well into her first term, did I begin to hear frustration in Kitty's voice during our talks. "It's my visa," she complained one night. "Getting a job on a student visa is tricky, even when you're not working around classes. I've been doing a little private tutoring for some hallmates in intro Latin, but I feel bad charging them more than a pittance."

"You've got a job waiting here," I told her. "There's no need to find another one while you're studying, silly."

"You say that, but I enjoy eating."

I frowned at the books spread out across my kitchen table. "Are you not?"

"A lot of ramen," she admitted after a moment's hesitation. "The college meals aren't expensive, but several quid a pop, three times a day...it adds up."

"I thought the Arcanum was paying—"

"Tuition and fees, and my room. Toula gave me a stipend, but it's not lasting as long as I'd hoped."

"There's an easy way to fix that," I replied. "Call Toula. She'll take care of it."

"No way."

"Why? Want me to call her?"

"*No*," she insisted. "Please. It's fine, it's just a little tight, things will be better after the holidays."

"Kitty, instant ramen isn't real food. You're going to get scurvy or something. I promise you, Toula will fix this if you tell—"

"Toula's done *everything* to get me here," she quietly interrupted. "I'm not going to her with my hand out for more."

"Fine, then Val—"

"Put a roof over my head for eight years. I can't just keep running to someone else to make my problems go away." She quietly sighed on the other end. "I'm going to be fine. A job will come through eventually, and until then, I'm not starving. Please don't say anything to them. Okay, Maria?"

I understood Kitty's push for independence—having my own place was still a thrill—but as a resident and employee of Arc 2, my meals were covered. Still, I promised Kitty that I'd respect her wishes and say nothing to Toula or Val.

I made no such promise about *Bonnie*, however.

Late the next evening, I got an earful from Kitty when she called, but she sounded more annoyed than angry. As it turned out, Bonnie had relayed the situation to Val, who had informed Toula in the morning, who had quickly made the arrangements. Kitty had been reading in her room when she heard a knock at the door, and she did a double-take when she found Val waiting in the corridor. He took the brief tour, wandered back to the kitchen, and told Kitty to show him which of the cabinets was hers. A box of corn flakes, a tin of tea, packs of sweetener pilfered from the college, and twenty-four bricks of chicken-flavored ramen hardly constituted a proper pantry, but Kitty dutifully opened the door and showed him.

"He looked hurt," she recounted. "Aghast, but more wounded than anything. I told him what I told you, and he said I hadn't been sent away to go hungry. Anyway, Toula had given him a prepaid card, and Val went with me to Tesco to make sure I bought more than just ramen, and he said that Toula said there'd be money in my account in the morning."

"So...are you cross with me?"

She answered with an exasperated huff. "By 'don't tell Toula and Val,' I meant anyone likely to immediately blab to them as well."

"You weren't specific."

"*You're* sneaky."

"I'm your friend," I countered. "Did you at least get a decent dinner tonight?"

"More than decent. And now I'm sitting here with a pack of Jaffa Cakes, and I'm *not* sharing them, so there."

When I got off the phone, I went home for the first time in weeks and found Val in his office, reading petitions as usual. He looked up as I slipped in past the guard, then beamed. "Maria! You didn't tell me—"

"Spur of the moment." I flopped into a chair and suppressed a yawn; Glastonbury was currently several hours ahead of Faerie, and my bed was calling me. "Thanks for taking care of Kitty."

"Of course." He rose and joined me in the other chair. "I wish she had said something sooner. Toula feels terrible about the situation."

"Kitty told me she doesn't want to be greedy."

Val looked at me incredulously. "The Arcanum has a substantial fortune, and this"—he twitched a finger, and a mug of strong coffee appeared on the table for me—"is nothing. I told her to call the next time she needs anything." A second cup appeared for him, and he frowned as he drank. "Be honest—what else is she lacking? Has she mentioned anything? I haven't…"

"Haven't what?" I asked when he paused.

Val seemed almost sheepish when he resumed. "Before your graduation, I might have conveyed my misgivings about your immediate career choices to Wanda, who might in turn have informed me that unless you're about to throw yourself into a volcano, I need to back off and stop checking to see what you aren't telling me. Treat you as an adult, as it were."

"Stay out of my head, you mean."

He nodded.

"Thank you." I drank and tucked one foot beneath me. "And unless Ted has plans he hasn't told Magus Wold yet, there are no volcanoes in my immediate future."

"*Good.*" Val wrapped his hands around his mug and stared into its depths. "You're growing up."

"That's what I keep hearing."

He smiled briefly at that. "Your life is your own, carissima filia, but…"

I waited through the silence, letting him struggle with his words.

"Please understand," he finally said, "that this is difficult. For me."

Sipping, watching him as he frowned at his own thoughts, I was suddenly struck by how young he seemed. From that angle, had I not known better, I'd have thought him no older than Frank or Mal, certainly younger than Antony and Daphne. I knew Council aides in their thirties who would have seemed senior to him. But then Val looked up at me again, and the illusion shattered as the truth flickered in his eyes.

"You'll be twenty in a year," he murmured. "*Official.* And by Toula's account, you're working well and eating regularly, so I shouldn't complain. But…"

"Still isn't enough?" I asked, inwardly flinching as I recalled the look of guilt in Ros's eyes and the disdain in Firola's. *Mongrel. Pet.*

He hesitated. "I have always tried to do the best thing for you. And yes, I realize you are no longer such a child, but…to me…"

"No, I get it. I'll be fifty, and you'll still think of me as a kid."

"A hundred. Five hundred, perhaps. There are days when I wonder about Eleanor and Coileán, you know." He held my gaze as I drank. "I like to imagine that I've acquired at least the beginning of wisdom in my years, Maria. And I see you doing what anyone your age might, and I…" Val sighed. "I want to protect you. You don't want that, I'm well aware, but—"

I reached across the gap between our chairs and grasped his hand. "I appreciate it."

"But to use Wanda's delicate phrasing, I need to butt out?"

"Just a little."

"Very well. As much sleep as I'll lose…"

I snorted into my coffee. "Drama queen."

"We'll revisit this conversation when you have children," he retorted. "If something happened to you, and I could have prevented it…"

"I can't live in a bubble, Val." *Or stay in Faerie forever,* I began to say, but swallowed the words at the last moment.

"No," he replied. "And I promise I'll do my best to treat you a competent adult. But that doesn't mean I have to like it—"

"Obviously," I teased.

"And it doesn't mean I'm going to sit here and let either of you girls starve. That much I insist upon." He finished his drink, and the mug vanished. "When I was your age, do you know what I did? *Whatever my father wished.*"

"Times change, don't they?"

"Indeed," he muttered. "But there's something to be said for taking counsel from your elders, little one." Catching me in a yawn, he patted my shoulder and rose. "For example, I would suggest you go to bed. That coffee was decaffeinated, by the way."

"Aren't we clever?" I said, and pushed myself from my chair. Before I left, I hugged him and murmured, "I'm happy, really. You don't have to worry." I stepped back but held my grip on his shoulder. "So, you promise you'll stay out of my head? Let me do this for myself?"

"You have my word," he replied, and shooed me on my way.

CHAPTER 13

Over the next two years, life fell into a comfortable rhythm—never quite predictable with the Away Team to consider, but comfortable. Magus Wold began writing his treatise ahead of schedule, allowing me more time to conduct research into my own interests. As much as I'd hated the old books when I'd begun, I'd slowly grown to appreciate them, and Toula continued to suggest titles I'd find useful, either from the Arcanum library or from Coileán's considerable stash. True, the texts were usually dull, but the techniques and theories in the old manuscripts went far beyond the material we'd been taught, and I often found myself stopping mid-page to test what I'd read.

But if I performed well as Magus Wold's research assistant, I was an utter failure in my more personal endeavors. I'd hoped that socializing with the older teens who'd come to Arc 2 for their first jobs would lead to romance, but the best response I had from anyone I fancied was polite collegiality. I didn't try my luck in Faerie—who would have wanted a known mongrel, anyway?—and though I encountered several handsome strangers on my outings to Glastonbury, I couldn't see myself pursuing a relationship with a mundane. I had enough baggage without having to introduce a partner to the concept of magic. So I carried on in my singlehood, throwing myself into my work to avoid the uncomfortable feeling that I was missing out on all the fun.

Kitty, on the other hand, managed to snag nights on

the town with mundane male companions, even the occasional one-night stand. To no one's surprise, she excelled in her classes, though she never managed to find a student job to cover all of her incidentals. This chafed as a source of embarrassment, but her benefactors failed to see the problem. "You're there to learn," Toula told her over her first winter break. "If you'd moved to Oxford to wait tables, I'd be concerned if you didn't have a job by now, but as it is, you're doing what you're meant to be doing. Call me once you have an idea of what you'll need for fieldwork this summer—I don't want you doing without."

As for Val, he continued to drop by every few weeks and check on her. This presented no real problem; the university was a fairly international place, and few looked askance at a fresher and a passable postgrad in conversation. After one such trip, Val expressed to me his continued befuddlement at Kitty's reluctance to ask for help. "Her mother is useless. She has no one," he muttered over dinner. "If she thinks I'm leaving her to fend for herself, she will be disappointed."

That first spring, once the weather began to turn from cold and wet to merely cool and wet, Kitty found other visitors at her door: Eleanor and Dr. Stowe, who took her out to talk shop at a quiet pub. Dr. Stowe knew the town only from academic conferences in his former life, but Eleanor, who had passed several decades of the eighteenth century there as a don, had more than her share of stories, which she was only too happy to relate after a glass of wine. Both enquired about Kitty's studies and her college, made jokes about academic dress, and insisted that she order the steak and chips. "Some graduate students sat in the booth behind us and started going over their research and what they'd recently done at the Bod," she told me over the phone. "You should have seen the looks on their faces. *So* happy to be eavesdropping. And then they ended the night bickering about George III. Honestly, those two are *nerds*."

Nerds or not, that had good taste in pubs, and they arranged to meet Kitty about once a week for dinner for the rest of her time in Oxford. Whether the purpose of their visits was to check up on the undergrad or just to provide an excuse for them to hang out in town for a few hours and pretend to still be academicians was immaterial.

Although graduation dates varied among the installation schools, which had all done their own thing after the Mulligan years, some traditions remained untouched. The first of May was the official date on which a given year's students were recognized as adults—despite the fact that many of us had been of age for months by that point—and Kitty returned to Glastonbury with the rest of our class and our peers across the Arcanum for the ceremony. "At least I get a full-length robe for a change," she joked as we took our seats. "A scholar's gown doesn't even have proper sleeves."

After the usual speeches and exhortations to make something of ourselves, we retired to a lovely reception for our friends and family. Val had opted not to attend, for which Toula had been grateful, and Magus Stanhope was nowhere to be found, but Kitty and I hopped around the room, chatting with the friends we hadn't seen since graduation and our acquaintances from the other installations, making plans to come back for the Games that summer. Though I was still barred from competition, I enjoyed the spectacle, and Magus Wold had suggested that I might be allowed to help referee the younger students' rounds.

As I made a third pass of the crudité, Magus Lowe appeared at my elbow and cleared his throat. "Maria, might I have a word with you?"

"Certainly, Magus," I said, and followed him through the reception room's adjoining kitchenette and out into the hall. He gave me no clue as to what was on his mind until his office door was closed behind us, and I took the proffered chair with concern.

Magus Lowe sat beside me, smoothed his robe over his knees, and smiled. "Ms. Corelli, I've been authorized to offer you a job."

"A job?" I repeated, taken aback. "That's, uh...that's very nice of you, but Magus Wold—"

"Your loyalty is commendable, but will you at least hear me out?"

"Sorry, Magus," I mumbled, clasping my hands.

"Thank you." He shifted in his chair and crossed his legs. "My dear, I'd like to offer you a position on the Council."

I jerked and stared at him, and he chuckled softly to himself. "Bert has been pushing your name forward for months. We couldn't make an offer until you came of age, naturally, but now that the ink's dry, and with Don Forester's retirement, there's no reason to delay any longer. So, any interest?"

Slowly, I coaxed my voice into action. "I'm sorry...did you say—"

"There is a position for you on the Council, should you so desire. Not the Inner Council, mind you—that will still be some time in coming, I should think—but you—"

"A *magus*?"

"You're surprised?" he asked, white eyebrows rising.

"Well...I mean, I'm witch-blooded..."

"As is the Grand Magus, far more so than you. Yours is an incredible talent—I doubt that Helen was any stronger at your age."

"She can still beat me," I countered.

"Yes, and she's what, sixty?" Magus Lowe leaned closer, his eyes crinkling behind his glasses. "Believe me, you've been on the Council's radar for quite some time. We knew you had the talent, and you've developed the practical skills of a young magus. My concern was whether you had the temperament for this sort of position, but Bert has been most complimentary of your work, both as a researcher and with the Away Team. If you can impress *him*, then I'm satisfied. Now, you would be teaching, you understand," he explained. "Given your skills, I would probably assign you to a practical class, probably with the younger students—and don't worry, I can show you what you need to know. You would have time to continue your research or work with Bert, or both…and Toula would assign you to a group for supervisory purposes." He paused and smiled again. "In light of Bert's well-documented disfavor for his current assignment, I suspect you might be given the Team. So, what do we think?"

I took a moment to compose myself, trying to calm my racing heart, then managed, "This…isn't just Toula's doing, is it?"

"Worried about nepotism?" said Magus Lowe with a smile. "Don't be. She's certainly in favor of it, but your biggest cheerleader for the last two years has been Bert. Trust me, Maria, he is *very* pleased with your work." The magus studied me for a moment, then stood and shook the wrinkles from his robe. "Why don't you sleep on it? Take a day or two, then tell us your decision."

Numb from shock, I let him escort me from his office, but I didn't return to the reception. Instead, I took myself home and ran straight to Val's office, but I found it empty.

"They're meeting," said Ros appearing in the middle of the room. "Over at Coileán's. Go on."

"I don't want to bother—"

"*Go on*, Magus Corelli."

I scowled, and Ros shrugged as she grinned. "Val may be staying out of your head, but I don't have that option. Talk to him."

She vanished, and with a moment's concentration, I opened a gate onto Coileán's massive, immaculate lawn. A pair of his guards kept watch at the palace's main door, but they allowed me to pass—most of them had served under Val, some for centuries, and the older ones found excuses to visit the villa when they were off duty. For form's sake, one escorted me to Coileán's office and passed me off to her fellow, who rapped on the door and announced me.

The Three were indeed meeting, but judging by the glassware and the items on the coffee table between Coileán's couches, they weren't in the middle of anything crucial. "Is that...Settlers of Catan?" I asked.

The kings looked somewhat abashed, but Eleanor perked. "Oh, do you play, dear?"

"Uh...not exactly. Val, could I, um..."

"Of course," he said, rising from the game, and followed me into the hall. With a nod to the guard, he led me into an empty sitting room and closed the door. "How was the ceremony?"

"Fine, uh..." I took a deep breath, conscious that my legs were turning jittery. "I've been offered a spot on the Council," I told him in a rush. "Magushood."

I'd anticipated that he'd be surprised by the news, but Val seemed calm—resigned, almost, his smile slightly strained. "Congratulations."

"Did you know?"

"Toula hinted," he admitted, then folded his arms and frowned into space for a moment. "Maria...you don't have to do this."

"It's a pretty big honor," I began, taken aback. "Why wouldn't I?"

"You don't need the Arcanum. Come home."

Caught off guard, I floundered as I replayed Val's suggestion. Return to Faerie full-time? For *what*? To be his pet wizard, living in his metaphorical basement for the rest of my life? I would never truly belong in that realm—never be anything more than the mortal foundling he'd deigned to take off the street. Firola had made that crystal clear three years before.

The Council, on the other hand, was willing to overlook the taint on me. Magus Wold believed in me. If Toula could do it...well, so could I.

"I *want* this," I told Val. "Maybe it'll be boring and I'll regret it someday, but for now..."

He reached out to cup my cheek. "Please, carissima filia."

"Val...we both know I'm not your heir," I forced myself to reply.

"That has nothing to do with—"

"It *does*. You need to let me go. Please be happy for me."

I could tell from the look on his face that there was more he wanted to say, but instead, he sighed softly and released me, and nodded his silent acceptance.

Once the memory of Firola's miserable ball had been dredged from my subconscious, my mind refused to let it go that night. What could possibly be waiting for me in Faerie? I would always be *less than*—nothing I could do would ever make me respectable in the court's estimation. Sure, Val's staff still addressed me as a lady, but the gesture stung. I knew they did so only out of respect for his wishes, not because I merited the title. So what if there was the teensiest bit of enchantment in my work? I was a wizard through and through, and that was my lot.

I had no cause to wish for more than I'd received. Who *was* I, anyway? An orphan brought home like a malnourished kitten out of pity nothing more. A partial substitute for the child Val had abandoned, the beneficiary of his guilt and sense of duty. We could pretend until the end of time, but I wasn't a lady, much less the high lady he'd once believed me to be before Ros had popped *that* bubble in grand fashion.

But I could be a magus. And that was okay.

There was nothing for me in Faerie, not anymore. My place—my *true* place—was in the realm of my birth, defending it against threats from all sides. Nothing Val could do would change that. I would never be anything more than the lucky recipient of the benevolence born of the shadow on his conscience, and the constant reminder of his disappointment that I couldn't be the child he'd wanted.

Sometimes, I thought, rolling over to face the wall as my throat constricted, love wasn't enough to transform the people around us into what we wished they were.

The news of my appointment wasn't universally celebrated—some of the Arc 1 magi were my most vociferous opponents on the Council—but the majority was sufficiently large, and Toula made it official that June. Val stayed well away from my ceremony, but Kitty camped in my flat for the weekend, fussing over my robe and hair while I just tried to remember my planned remarks and not throw up with nerves. Late that night, after the festivities, I flopped onto my couch—robe, chain, and all—and Kitty joined me with ice cream and spoons. I wished she could stay longer, but she still had a week to go in the term, and then she was heading down to a site outside of Athens with one of her professors for the rest of the month. As for the remainder of her summer holiday, Ted had *plans*, and I doubted I'd see her much around the castle. But that Saturday night, still dressed in our finery, watching stand-up reruns, and gorging ourselves on chocolate chip straight from the carton, I thought the moment was quite possibly perfect.

Kitty caught an early train on Sunday, and shortly after lunch, Toula stopped by in her customary weekend T-shirt and leggings. "Didn't have too much fun last night, did you?" she asked when she found me still in my pajamas and bathrobe. "Have you eaten?"

I yawned and shook my head, and a plate of pancakes materialized at the table. While I tucked in, she pulled out a chair and sat beside me with a cup of strong coffee. "So, now that the hoopla's taken care of, let's get down to business. I'm rotating you in as the Away Team's contact magus. Sound good?"

Mouth full, I settled for giving her a thumbs-up.

"Thought so. Bert will still be on standby for now in case you get in over your head, but Ted says you've been able to handle yourself thus far. He's pleased," she added, passing me a napkin as maple syrup dripped onto the tabletop. "They're going back to South America this summer, God knows where." She shook her head and sipped her drink. "If you want to go along for the trip and see how these things work in the field instead of waiting by the phone, get your shots and be my guest. Once school starts, now, I'll need you in residence, but August is mostly yours."

I nodded and reluctantly dropped my fork—Toula's pancakes were divine but detrimental to conversation. "Magus Lowe said I'd be teaching, yes?"

"That's right. And I think, at least for this first year, that it'd be best if you worked directly with *Arnold*," she said, emphasizing his name while mussing my hair. "You're Council now, honey, you can be a little less formal. Same goes for Bert and everyone else."

"But not you," I teased.

"I demand nothing less than 'Aunt Toula,'" she replied, grinning. "Look, I know it's going to feel weird at first, but get used to considering the Council your colleagues. They'll treat you like you don't know anything for a while—let's be honest, you don't—but keep your eyes and ears open, and you'll catch on soon enough." She paused to drain another inch from her mug, and I gave in to the temptation of my cooling breakfast. "So," said Toula once I'd sneaked another bite, "how's Bert's research going? He said you've been a big help."

"Going well," I mumbled as best I could, and forced my food down. "He's writing, but he's still working out a few kinks in the theory as he goes."

"Still trying to push past the Ertz Limit?"

I nodded. Working around the Ertz Limit was the bane of every theoretical thaumaturgist who tried to test his theories. Any channel of spellcraft—even the best stack—had a limit. Run too much power down a channel, and it broke apart. For wizards, whose most complex crafting was composed of networks of carefully balanced channels, exceeding the Ertz Limit had ruined many a spell.

"He's trying to work out a way in which it can be surpassed purely with spellcraft," I explained. "He picked apart all the records from—"

"Moyna and Russell Mulligan's attack on Faerie, yeah." Her coffee mug, which had become dangerously depleted, refilled itself. "Which was accomplished through a combination of spellcraft and enchantment. Believe me," she said, chuckling, "I got an earful from the Archives when you pulled those records."

I bristled in defense. "That was authorized. I only requested the records he asked for—"

"You're not in trouble, and he'd pulled enough related sources to show me why you were digging in there. It's just…" She made a face as she chose her words. "You know, there are resources in the Archives that are restricted for a reason, and when certain individuals access them, the archivists let me know. It's a security thing, that's all. I don't mind if you look over those reports—hell," she added with a little laugh, "Ros probably knows the spell's contours as well as anyone, if you want to talk to her about it."

But something Toula had said pricked at me. "You're monitoring *certain* individuals?"

Again, she struggled to find the right phrasing. "I realize Bert's gotten a bad rap that he doesn't deserve…mostly…but given his family connections and his…well…"

"Well *what?*"

She regarded me with frustration—but then again, I was asking her to give voice to an unpleasant reality. "Bert's loyalties have been the subject of speculation ever since he was caught with the Mulligan crew in their little flotilla. I doubt there's any truth to the rumors, but I can't just ignore them. I've seen what happens when inconsequential matters are ignored around here," she muttered.

"He hasn't done anything wrong," I protested, bristling. "All he does is do research and take care of the Team."

"I'm aware."

"Then why are you *spying* on him?"

Toula sighed. "Because it's one of the conditions for his continued presence on the Council."

"Come again?"

"Eat your breakfast, Maria, it's getting cold." She waited until I started chewing—probably hoping to stop my interruptions with pancakes—then said, "I know damn well that Bert didn't collude with Russell. He was as surprised as the rest of us, and he was just a scared kid. Ros brought him to Faerie for a few days when everything went to hell. He kept in touch with Arnold, who was covering for him back here, but he thought his place was in Glastonbury, never mind the danger. And right about the time he came home, Russell's crew kidnapped his parents. He panicked." She shrugged and sipped her coffee. "Sure, Bert should have been more observant, but the same could be said for Arnold and everyone else on the Inner Council. Bert just happened to be the one sitting at the head of the table at the time."

"So if he didn't collude—" I began through a mouthful of food.

"He cooperated. At least in part. Enough to fall under suspicion, but not so much as to be convicted of treason." Seeing my confusion, she leaned toward me and lowered her voice. "The Council was fighting itself, and Bert was a bargaining chip for a while. You've got to understand, the Council almost fell apart in the year after I took office. I had a core of supporters who thought I might actually do a decent job, there was a larger group that just wanted stability, and then there was a faction who might have hacked me to bits if it wouldn't have meant bringing Val and Coileán's vengeance on the Arcanum. Hell, Ellie probably would have joined in, too," she mused. "But there weren't as many hard-core haters as I'd feared coming in."

"The ones who don't like witch-bloods?"

"Oh, it's more than that. When we took James Mulligan out, we removed the entire Council with him, see. It was just Helen and Arnold at first, and Helen stepped down almost immediately, so Arnold had to build a Council from scratch. He brought in some promising unconnected wizards, but for continuity's sake, he also tapped quite a few of the Mulligan-era aides. Some were great, got right with the program. Some were…questionable. Most of them had been kids when Mulligan took power, and they'd done well under him, and then suddenly, he's out, and there's faeries in the silo. Some of them internalized the previous regime's attitudes toward just about everyone who wasn't Arcanum. Arnold did what he could to make the magi work together, but he could only do so much.

"Anyway," she continued, swirling her coffee, "there was still tension between the former aides and Arnold's handpicked crew when Bert took office. The aides had been the ones who'd trained him, so I think they had hope of regaining power within the Council. But Bert was out in less than two months, and everyone realized how close we'd come to another Mulligan coup—or worse, a hostile takeover from Moyna's band. So yeah, there were some magi who hated me on principle, but more than I'd anticipated were willing to give me a chance if it meant peace. And while the Council factions bickered behind closed doors, there was the question of what to do with Bert. Keeping him on was a concession to the old aides, but the only way we got to that point was if I agreed that he should be monitored for the duration of his magushood, just in case he'd been more than an unwilling cooperator."

"But that's been, like…eighteen years," I said.

"I know, and Bert hasn't put a toe out of line. There are plenty of folks on the Council I'd worry about sooner than I'd worry about him, but that was the agreement. Someday," she said, pushing back from the table, "you'll learn there are certain hornet nests it's best not to poke."

"But if he's been great all this time—"

"It's not fair, I get it," Toula interrupted. "Politics is seldom about fairness, honey. I'm more concerned with keeping the Arcanum intact. By the way, your first Council meeting will be tomorrow at ten. Robes are optional but encouraged."

Hoping to avoid being the lone person at the table, I slipped into the Council's main room shortly before the meeting with the arriving Arc 7 magi. The windowless space would have been a decently large chamber, had it not been filled with a table that seated seventy. Tight wards of spellcraft around the perimeter prevented eavesdropping, and as the magi took their seats, a pair of Toula's aides checked the fixtures for bugs both magical and mundane.

I hung back in the corner, afraid of taking someone's assigned chair, but Magus Wold lifted a hand and smiled. The seat beside his was empty, and I gratefully snagged it. "Don't be nervous," he murmured. "Watch and learn. And have you got plans this afternoon, or can we talk about chapter three?"

The mention of the familiar in the middle of the foreign helped ground me, and by the time Toula called the meeting to order, I no longer felt quite so anxious. The proceedings were unremarkable, monopolized by a discussion of teacher placements for the next term before turning briefly to the question of constructing an eighth installation. "Arc 4's pet project," Magus Wold whispered in my ear. "The subcontinent desperately wants an alternative to Mongolia. Arc 5 wants to split as well, and"—he discreetly pointed down the table to one of the local magi I didn't know—"Jack there has been proposing a location in Scotland for the last five years. Why this island should require two installations when there's only one on the entire African *continent* is a mystery to me, but that's the Scots for you."

I nodded but said nothing, instead watching as the speakers took their turns—and sometimes talked over each other—with the aid of voice-amplifying spells. Few in the room had brought wands, but the simple magic necessary to be heard seemed to be a matter of second nature to the assembled. Most sat with their peers from their installations. Some of the magi around the table caught my eye and smiled in reassurance during the meeting—even Magus Johansson from Arc 1, who had been so complimentary of Kitty—but Magus Stanhope, two chairs down from her, looked at her notepad and little else for the duration.

She wasn't an outlier. Casually studying the room, I caught several magi scowling whenever Toula spoke, then several others rolling their eyes when one of the first camp made a proposal. Some around the table seemed bored, judging by their doodles, but others were heavy-lidded, victims of the time difference.

Near the end of the hour, Toula announced that I'd be rotating onto the Away Team, and Magus Wold would be rotating off. "Bert has requested more time for his current research," she said, "and I'm putting him on a six-month sabbatical, with the proviso that he can be called out if anyone else needs quick assistance."

The looks he received were a mixed bag. A few magi nodded in agreement, but the majority regarded him coldly, if not with anger. A moment later, Toula ended the session, and Magus Wold quickly rose. "See you at half one," he told me, and slipped away.

That afternoon, I met him in his office with my computer bag, just as always, and set up at my usual table. For the next half hour, we discussed chapter outlines and sources still to consult, and then I opened my notes and started to put my thoughts in order. But as I worked, I found my thoughts circling back to Toula and to the morning's meeting.

After a time, I cleared my throat. "Magus?"

He looked up from his computer with a little smile. "Yes, Magus?" My face flushed, and he chuckled. "It's all right. I'm called Bert, you know."

"*Bert*, then," I replied, feeling almost naughty. "Uh…this morning…" His expression remained a mask of polite curiosity, and I forced myself to press on. "Some of the Council, they…uh…"

"Hate my guts?"

I nodded, growing more embarrassed by the second.

But Bert just shrugged. "Nothing new there, my dear. Don't let it bother you," he said, and resumed typing.

I hesitated, gathering my resolve, then blurted, "Toula monitors you."

That time, Bert didn't look up. "Again, nothing new."

"Doesn't that upset you?"

He sighed softly, then closed his computer and folded his hands in his lap. "Honestly? It's infuriating, insulting…a scarlet letter I don't deserve. But it is what it is. What, did she mention something?"

"How are you so *calm* about it?"

His mouth curled into a slight smirk. "There's no sense in railing. Why are you so upset?"

"Because it's not right," I said, indignant. "Because you haven't done anything wrong, but they treat you like you're going to…to…I don't know—"

"Let faeries into the castle? No, that's been done." He

smiled as my expression soured. "Only teasing, Maria. But you understand, don't you? You've never worked against the Arcanum, but mark my words, you'll be watched with suspicion until the day you die. Some of the Council will *never* trust you, and there's not a damn thing you can do about it."

"It's not fair," I muttered.

"Life seldom is. Toula does her best, but her hands are tied. I'm not bothered."

"She could stop checking on your reading list."

"Toula doesn't care about my reading list. She trusts me." Bert paused, drumming his fingers on the arm of his chair, then beckoned me closer.

Puzzled, I rose and perched on the edge of his desk.

When he spoke again, his voice was barely above a whisper. "Toula trusts me, and I trust you, which is why I'm going to let you in on a secret. This is hidden from the rest of the Council—I doubt even Arnold knows of it, and he's practically her right hand. But before I tell you..."

I sensed the force of his attempted mental invasion in the instant before he hit, and I threw up my defenses as he'd taught me, picturing an endless stone wall against the onslaught. Bert's attacks were brute things, a sledgehammer beside the needlelike precision and delicacy of Val's riffling, but they were no less effective, as I'd learned in my time in his employ—particularly when I tried to bluff my way through a conversation about a book I was supposed to have read.

"Good," said Bert as he retreated. "Very good. This information *cannot* be shared—is that clear?" I nodded, and he nudged his chair closer to me. "For some years now, I've served as an ambassador of sorts. To the Conclave."

My eyes flew open wide. "The *Conclave*?"

"Shh," he whispered, and I mumbled a quick apology. "Yes, the Conclave. I'm sure you understand that a significant portion of the Council would be opposed to any dealings with them, hence the secrecy."

"But...*why*?"

"Why what? Why open a line of communication? Why send me?"

My thoughts whirled, so I settled for nodding.

Bert chuckled to himself at my reaction. "Start with the latter. I have a fair number of connections to the Conclave—friends, cousins, and the like. Probably more connections than most. That, coupled with my, shall we say *unusual*, history with the Council, puts me in a unique position. I can speak for the Grand Magus, and they know me well enough to trust that my word is good."

"But why send anyone at all?"

"Because the alternative is war, and neither side wants that."

"You think they're strong enough to beat—"

"No, of course not," he said, cutting my question short. "In a fair fight, the Arcanum would trample the Conclave before tea. The goal, however, is to avoid outright conflict."

"I don't understand."

"Neither did I." He gave me one of his small, indecipherable smiles. "Not at first. Fortunately, Toula came to her position with an understanding of power dynamics that I lacked during my tenure. You know of the Minor Arcanum, I take it?"

"I've heard of it."

"They're decentralized, but they're a larger group than I'd first imagined. They also established communication with the Conclave—ideologically, they're somewhat different, but they share that commonality of being splinter groups. If we attacked the Conclave and tried to forcibly reintegrate them, the Minor Arcanum wouldn't take it kindly. Even the Company might protest at this point."

I frowned. "The plan is to just let them go, then?"

"No. The plan is to preserve the status quo until they have no choice but to come back. The Council doesn't want bloodshed if it can be avoided. And there are children in that camp to consider—yet another reason why no one wants to authorize a strike." He shifted in his chair and folded his arms. "As I said, we could crush them, particularly because no one is currently crafting for them. They don't have enough wands to go around. Toula's holding back, partly out of respect for the Minor Arcanum, partly because that's what the Council desires, but mostly because she knows the Conclave will fall apart in a matter of years. There's this gate into the Gray Lands—"

"It *still* isn't closed?"

"You've heard of it?"

"Yeah, but years ago. I thought they'd have fixed it by now."

"Not for lack of trying," said Bert. "They keep patching it, but it's only grown. Rather stable by this point, I'd imagine," he muttered. "Anyway, Toula is allowing the Conclave to exist unharmed, but only as long as they stay at their camp in Alaska."

"Next door to a Gray Lands gate."

"Precisely. And my job is to relay messages between the two parties." Bert shook his head. "Honestly, it's always more of the same. They want autonomy and access to a crafter, Toula wants them back in the fold and promises a fight if they expand their territory, and meanwhile, the Minor Arcanum wonders why everyone can't get along."

"But if they've lasted this long beside a gate, then why would Toula think—"

"It's not the gate you have to worry about. It's what comes *through*. And as I said, they don't have enough wands to arm everyone."

I could picture the unfortunate situation in my mind's eye. The long Alaskan winter nights, an insufficiently protected security force, and something *big* crawling out of the darkness, crunching across the snow...

"That's horrible," I murmured.

"It's the proverbial rock and hard place for the Conclave," said Bert. "But anyway, Toula sends me because no one tries to kill me on sight and because I'm proficient with mental blocks." He smiled tightly. "I doubt there's anyone with a particular mental talent in the Conclave, but if there is, no one's going to be picking my brain for the Arcanum's secrets."

"I thought most magi could block."

"Sure, but to different degrees," he explained. "It's like any other talent. I'm rubbish at advanced healing craft, but I can defend myself."

"Same," I admitted.

"Exactly. And since Toula knows how well I can keep intruders out of my thoughts, she tasked me with Conclave negotiations." He leaned back and rested his hands on his stomach. "I'm glad you're able to block as well as you can, Maria. It saved my life during the coup." I cocked my head, and Bert nodded. "I spent time with Russell Mulligan and Moyna and their people. Russell wasn't a particular threat to me, but I'm sure you know how talented faeries can be at mental manipulation."

I nodded vehemently.

"If I was going to stay alive, I had to make them think I was cooperating, and that meant blocking all attempts to pry. It was exhausting, but I made it out intact." He paused, then regarded me strangely. "Your grandfather— how comfortable is Toula with allowing you to be around him, now that you're Council?"

The question took me aback. "She's never said anything. And Val respects my privacy, he doesn't snoop anymore..."

"But he could," Bert murmured. "Maria...I don't mean to cross a line, but if I were you, I would limit my time in Faerie until I was absolutely positive that I could keep the Arcanum's secrets protected. You know now what Toula and I have been doing with the Conclave. Does *he*? And if not, would Toula wish for him to know?" Bert sat up and clasped my hand. "You're a magus now. That means you defend the Arcanum against all threats—including the courts."

"Val understands the situation," I told him with more confidence than I felt. "He wouldn't go into my head without permission."

He nodded and released me, then opened his computer again. "I understand. But for your sake, remember that *wouldn't* and *couldn't* are very different things."

CHAPTER 14

As Toula wished, I began working as Magus Lowe's classroom assistant that autumn. Once again, he was the teacher and I the student, but this time, I was focused not on the subject matter of his lessons, but rather on the mechanics of their presentation. Producing a shield was almost instinctual to me; helping two dozen ten-year-olds craft one was a different matter entirely. But Magus Lowe—well, *Arnold* now—was patient with me, and once our students realized that I was the infamous first-year who'd swept combat, they were far more eager to listen when I demonstrated techniques.

When not in the classroom, I spent most of my time with Bert. The editing was going well, and he anticipated finishing before the holidays, a new volume for the library to print and put on the shelf for the next poor theorist to come along. We made plans to celebrate with champagne whenever he was through with it, considering that the final draft was the end result of an almost four-year project— assuming, of course, that I was in the castle. Ted and the Away Team had three expeditions planned before the end of the year, and I took a more active role with the Team than Bert ever had, sitting in on meetings and even doing a bit of side research to lighten their load. Kitty would pick up that slack in the summer, once she graduated, but with Kitty working on her final year at Oxford, I didn't mind pitching in. As the days grew short and dreary, I found that my office's windows made little difference in terms of seeing daylight, and so I often took my work into the

Team's subbasement suite, where at least there were people and a bottomless pot of hot coffee.

I made the trek downstairs early one Thursday morning in December, planning to continue proofreading part of Bert's manuscript ahead of my afternoon classes. Before I'd had time to do more than plug in my computer, however, Ted found me in my conference-room hideout and shut the door. "I need you to go with Frank, right now," he murmured, crouching beside my chair. "Grab a coat and gloves, you'll want them. Boots, too."

"Sure," I said, puzzled, and started packing my things. "Where are we going?"

"Tell you once you're dressed. Hurry, kid."

I didn't bother with the stairs. Returning to my flat via gate, I threw on more substantial attire and hastily opened another gate into Ted's office, where Frank was already waiting. His lone concession to winter was a windbreaker, but due to his internal combustion, he didn't need much. Standing close to him was like snuggling up to a radiator.

Ted locked his office door before giving us the assignment. "There's been an attack of some sort," he told Frank. "Bert's going over ASAP. Boss wants us to scout and report as per usual."

Frank nodded, then pointed to me. "She's been briefed?"

"Not yet." Turning my way, Ted quietly explained, "Toula assigned Frank and me a little side gig. You know about the Conclave?"

"Yes..." I replied, liking this conversation less by the second.

If Ted saw my unease, he gave no sign. "Bert's been the off-the-books go-between for years. Frank goes after him to keep an eye on things."

"Without his knowledge," Frank added.

My eyebrows rose. "Spying?"

"Monitoring," said Ted. "As a security measure. Anyway, Toula normally handles the gate situation, but since you're here now, she said you could take over for her. I've got some landmark photos." He handed me a stack of printouts, all depicting a compound of single-story buildings in various seasonal conditions, and a set of binoculars. "Frank knows what to do on the ground. Your job is to get him there and back—and don't get caught, eh?" he said, only half in jest.

Feeling slightly queasy, I concentrated on the pictures until I had a clear destination in mind, then opened a small gate and braced myself against the shock of the bitter midnight wind in northern Alaska. "Don't worry, your face goes numb," said Frank, and shouldered past me through the rift as blowing snow melted on Ted's rug.

I followed him and found myself in a thick stand of pines, an ineffective buffer against the icy air. With his long legs, Frank was already several paces ahead of me by the time I closed the gate, and I hurried to shiver beside him as he surveyed the land.

Ted's pictures had been accurate once. The compound of low buildings they depicted was still ringed with a chain-link fence within the partly active ward bubble, but sections of the fence had been melted and refrozen on the ground. Three of the buildings were blackened husks, and a fourth was smoldering. "What hap—" I began, and then my adjusting eyes picked out the bodies in the snow.

The largest, rimed and disappearing, was so massive that I'd mistaken it for a hillock at first glance. But as I looked closer, I picked out darker flashes beneath the white layer, and then a glimpse of leathery wing.

"Is that…a dragon?" I whispered.

Frank grunted beside me. "Juvenile. Maybe a year old. I suppose he—she—got disoriented and came through. Or maybe the hunting here looked promising." His mouth opened slightly as he took a deep sniff, and the tip of his tongue flicked at the frigid air. "Cooking smells beneath the smoke."

My nose was already running with the cold, and all I

could smell on the wind was the charred buildings and the sickly familiar scent of roasted meat. Near the dragon's corpse, someone had laid out six bodies, which, though half-buried by the falling snow, still showed me enough to understand that they'd met their end in flames.

"Moon and stars," I mumbled, and covered my mouth and nose with my mitten, trying to block the smell of burning death. It seemed to linger in my nostrils, however, growing more pronounced as my mind began to race...

Frank pinched my shoulder hard enough to make me whimper with the pain, but at least it dragged me back from the edge of the cliff toward which I'd been running. "Focus," he muttered.

"I'm trying—"

"And I'm trying to ignore the fact that *that* looks like my sister," he said, jabbing one finger toward the dead dragon. "Stay with me, Maria."

I swallowed my rising bile and looked away from the bodies, doing my best to push Luca's screaming face from my mind.

The Gray Lands gate was huge, easily three stories tall and almost equally wide. Its edges crackled with energy, just like the gates I knew, but the magic that flowed through it was *wrong*, puddles of shadow instead of the familiar rainbow-hued swirls. The ward, I realized, was fully activated after all—the bits nearest the gate glowed faintly, but the outflow of dark magic was wearing them down like an acid bath.

"I've never seen a gate that large," I said to Frank.

"It's grown. Get down."

He pushed me to my knees, and we peered out from behind a drift as an intra-realm gate opened with a flash like lightning. Out stepped an indistinct figure, more an ambulatory pile of clothing than a man. A less swaddled woman met the newcomer at the fence, and the two passed into the compound together.

"Bert," said Frank, pointing to the departing pair. "He's

never been fond of the winters here."

I concurred—even hiding close to Frank, my face ached, and my fingers and toes were losing feeling. "Are we supposed to follow them?"

"No. Perimeter's guarded." He gestured toward the sentries walking the fence. "We're to report on the gate and on how long Bert stays. I never know what they talk about—it's difficult to pick up on anyone's thoughts from this distance, and Bert keeps his defenses up at all times," he added, sounding peeved. "Toula usually sees this for herself—I'm here in case the situation goes sideways."

"What do you mean?"

"Plan of last resort: get close enough to the gate that my bind breaks, then go to town."

I glanced again at the young dragon in the snow. The ones I'd seen in Faerie were easily twice as large, jet-sized airborne lizards with nightmarishly big teeth and claws…and in the presence of sufficient dark magic, able to rain fire from above.

I kept my thoughts walled off, but even still, Frank seemed to intuit their direction. "Which is why we're not going any closer to the gate," he said, nudging me in the side. "Toula's always handled that spell, and I don't want to return to Glastonbury at full size. *That's* an awkward phone call."

"Does it…break often?"

"Nah," he said absently, keeping his eyes on the camp. "Twice in the field thus far, intentionally both times. Once to deal with a tiger, and once because we were deep in cartel territory and accidentally discovered *all* the cocaine. I had to eat a guy before the rest of them ran."

"Wait, you *ate*—"

"It was self-defense. Okay, looks like they're walking toward the burned buildings…"

For the next half hour, I shivered and froze as Bert toured the destruction. My eyes kept drifting from the gaping hole between the realms—the *growing*, gaping hole—to the fresh corpses being buried beneath their snow blankets.

We could seal that hole. If not Toula, then surely the Three could do the job. No one needed to die because of curious, hungry Gray Landers.

I must have inadvertently lowered my defenses while I contemplated the scene, as I barely felt Frank's mind poke at mine. "Politics, kid," he murmured, watching Bert take his leave. "Or so I've been informed. You're strange creatures, you know that?"

The memory of the snow-covered bodies haunted my dreams for a week, but I could speak to no one of how the sight had shaken me. Certainly not Toula—I tried to avoid her at first. Val would have heard me out, but confiding in him would have meant telling him about a confidential Arcanum matter, and I knew that option was foreclosed. I couldn't very well go to Kitty, who wouldn't have been able to keep our conversation in confidence, had anyone taken a glance at her thoughts.

By the following Wednesday morning, having slept poorly and still too disturbed to say more than necessary to Toula, I cornered Bert in his office and locked the door. "Your edits are good," he said in greeting. "I think we can put this to bed by next week—"

"I saw the dragon in Alaska."

He paused, then closed his computer and motioned me toward one of the chairs across from his desk. I sank into the nearer of the pair and folded my arms, and he waited while I collected my thoughts.

"You're being followed," I finally mumbled. "Toula's been trailing you when you visit the Conclave's compound. She sent me in her place last week. Guess she doesn't trust you as much as you thought."

"I see." His voice seemed as neutral as if I were discussing the morning fog.

"I saw the gate, and the dragon, and the bodies…" I paused to take a deep breath and push the encroaching image from my thoughts. "*Why*, Bert?"

"Why?" he echoed. "They think the dragon was hungry and getting desperate."

"Not that. Why leave that gate open? If something like *that* could come through…"

He sat in silence for a moment, then murmured, "That's not the first time. They've had raiding riders. A troll or two. Hungry yeti. That was their first dragon, but hardly their first casualties."

"There are *children* in that camp."

"Yes. Thirty-seven underage, several born in the compound."

"And they're trapped there, next to that giant gate…"

He smirked faintly as my voice faded. "You've heard the story of Scylla and Charybdis, yes?"

"Yeah, but—"

"That's our plan exactly. Force them to choose between fighting monsters and returning to the Arcanum's control."

"But people are *dying*."

He shrugged. "If memory serves, Odysseus chose to lose a handful of his men fighting Scylla than risk the entire ship against the whirlpool of Charybdis. When the Conclave loses too many—or, God forbid, when Nath gets an urge to expand her territory—they'll come crawling back. Given their lack of a crafter, we're probably a little closer to that point every day."

"That's brutal," I muttered.

"That's the way of the world, my dear." He sipped his tea and regarded me over his glasses. "Why tell me this? I'm hardly surprised that Toula's been watching, but why let me in on it?"

"Because you trusted me. And I trust you. It should go both ways."

He stared at me, surprised. "That's…kind of you. I

appreciate that, Maria." He smiled briefly, then cleared his throat and drank, hiding the twitching I'd noticed in his face. When he put the mug aside, he was placid once more. "None of this will get back to Toula, I assure you. And I thank you for your confidence."

"Of course," I said, but chose my next words carefully. "Bert...do you agree? With the plan, I mean."

He gazed into the corner, raking his teeth over a chapped spot on his lip. "No, I don't. I think it's inhumane. But mine is not a popular voice on the Council, and so I do as I'm told and convey my reports to Toula as directed." After a brief hesitation, he asked, "Did she tell you why they called me last week?"

"No."

"The bodies outside the compound weren't the only casualties. I'm not a great healer, you know, but I was able to help the healers on the premises. It's the dark magic outflow, you see—unless you really shore up your spells, they fall apart, and the burn victims needed immediate attention. Officially, I'm not supposed to render aid, but surely there's room in this world for a little mercy." Bert opened his computer and beckoned for me to join him. "But enough of that. You and I aren't going to change the world today, and in the meanwhile, I have a proposal for you. The situation in Alaska has piqued my more academic interests."

"How so?" I asked, coming around the desk.

"One of the problems in the Conclave is the lack of a crafter, right? We all know the best crafters are witch-bloods. *Why*? What makes them so uniquely capable of producing fine instruments?"

I could only shrug. "Booker said—"

"Booker had theories, that's all. I want to explore this, really get to the meat of it. Would you be interested?"

"Absolutely, but if you're looking for someone to test your theories on, you should know that I'm no crafter."

"Oh yes, understood—I'm more interested in your

research assistance. Are you in?"

He stuck out his hand and smiled as I shook it.

"Where do we begin?" I asked. "You haven't found that long-lost book by Erik Niger, have you?"

Bert snorted and rolled his eyes as he released me. "I write theoretical works, Maria, not *fantasy*. Erik Niger, indeed," he muttered, but smirked at my teasing grin. "Why don't we stick to sources that have actually existed? But library assignments are for later—this is in *very* early days, and I'd prefer not to engage in public discussion until I have at least a grounding in the present scholarship. Do me a favor and don't mention it yet, hmm?"

"Mum's the word," I told him, excited by the project and honored by his trust.

As the long British winter began to thaw and the days lengthened toward spring, I heard little from Kitty, who was desperately trying to finish with good marks. She had no reason to worry about flunking out, but Kitty having always been the sort of student who considered a B to be tantamount to failure, she fretted and lost sleep over her final papers. But when the last assignments were in and graded, she passed with top honors, and she and I went out on the town for a lavish dinner at one of the restaurants she'd only been able to afford when Eleanor and Dr. Stowe picked up the tab.

Kitty had decided to graduate in absentia. Most of her peers had signed up for one of the degree ceremonies and were finding appropriate robes, but she told me she was ready to get back to Glastonbury and move her things into the flat Toula had assigned her as a graduation present. I suspected that I knew the real reason why she'd chosen to forgo the pomp, however. Graduation was a time for family celebration, and Kitty hadn't heard a word from her mother in years. She called Montana every few months and wrote occasional messages, but the calls went unanswered, the messages ignored. Still, despite the silence, she dutifully kept up her monthly ritual of sending a note to Beth—sometimes a long letter filled with stories about her classmates and her program, sometimes just a postcard of the university with a quick greeting on the back. One month, she sent Beth a box of her favorite tea. When she did a stint of fieldwork, she mailed her sister a stack of photographs and a shard of pottery that shouldn't have gone missing. There was never a reply, but Kitty remained hopeful, despite it all.

On what would have been her graduation weekend, I helped her move her belongings into the castle, create the furniture she lacked, and choose paint colors for the place. We were both sweaty by the end of the afternoon—even with the aid of spellcraft, moving was seldom fun, and Kitty and I kept shifting the furniture to test out configurations—and we called a halt to the affair late in the day so that we could clean up for a welcome-back dinner with the Away Team that night. But before I could head to my flat for a shower, there came a knock at the door, and Kitty found Toula and Val on the other side, the latter dropping his glamour as she let them in. "He didn't know the way here, and I couldn't let him wander around alone until he found you," Toula explained, and Val rolled his eyes.

"I won't detain you long," he told Kitty, then pulled a silk pouch from his pocket. "A token. Congratulations."

Kitty smiled bemusedly, then poured the contents of the pouch into her hand and whispered, "*Oh.*"

Looking over her shoulder, I saw a pendant in her palm, a cluster of long yellow and tiny dark-brown diamonds arranged in the form of a sunflower, the sort of intricate setting made possible only though magic. The crystalline petals curved and curled far too realistically to have been cut that way.

She stared at the gift without speaking, and Val's brows drew together in concern. "Is it…all right?"

He staggered back when she unexpectedly threw her arms around him and chuckled as he recovered his balance. "Oh, good. I thought I'd offended."

"It's *perfect*," she told him, releasing her hold to clasp the gold chain around her neck. "And far too nice. You shouldn't have."

"Maria received her own jewelry last year," he replied. "And since I assume you won't be applying for the Council any time soon…"

Kitty's fingers brushed against the pendant, and she grinned. "You can keep your chain," she told me. "And your Council meetings. I'm *pretty* sure my job's more fun."

Ted wasted no time in putting Kitty to work, and for the next few weeks, I saw her only with her nose in a book or staring at her computer in her subbasement office. The plan, I was told, was for the Team to poke around in a series of Siberian caves that August—they had a lead on three long-missing books, but the clues they'd found to that point had been cryptic as to exactly *which* cave was hiding them. Even with all of the prep work, however, Ted declared an unofficial three-day holiday during the Games.

Though I would have liked to watch with the Team, who made it a point to bring snacks, I spent most of the first day on the floor, rotating in and out as a referee and judge for the rapid casting competition. I'd paid particular notice to the roster for the first-years, but there was no sign of Kitty's little sister, and I saw no one who looked anything like her among the Arc 1 contestants. Nor did she appear among the technical casters. I knew Kitty was disappointed—she had hoped to see Beth for the first time in a decade, cheer her on, and at least ask about her unanswered letters—but I couldn't help her, and Magus Stanhope was nowhere to be found.

The situation was unchanged the next day for the academic competition, but Kitty remained undaunted.

"Come on, you remember how impressed Mom *wasn't* by my win," she told me over dinner, once I'd been able to slip away. "Beth will be there for combat, I'm sure of it."

Early the next morning, I looked over the roster before the contestants filed in and finally found her: Elizabeth Stanhope, Arc 1.

Stanhope.

Kitty had never told me that Beth had a different surname. Had Magus Stanhope changed her daughter's name after her husband's death? Did Kitty know about that? I wanted to talk to her, but with the tight schedule, there was no time for me to find her before the first rounds began.

Combat was always a little anarchic on the floor, no matter how well the referees worked. Missiles had a tendency to fly in odd directions, especially in the younger classes, and my job was as much about scoring the bout in front of me as it was protecting the other competitors and spectators from inexpert wizards. I barely took a break for the first two rounds, and it was with surprise that I realized my first match in the third round included Beth.

Though blonde, Beth's hair was darker than her sister's pale locks, closer to their mother's honey tones, and fell straight to her shoulders. She was tall for her age and slender, her eyes chestnut brown and slightly squinting as she sized up her opponent. She carried an ash wand, I noticed—far better than Kitty's wand, but nowhere near a magus's. Still, Beth was quick on her feet and controlled in her casting, and she easily won her round. I was too busy with my duties on the floor to pick Kitty out of the crowd, but I imagined she cheered as loudly as any of the Montana crew when I called the bout.

Beth didn't win her year's contest—that honor went to a girl from Arc 5—but she made it into the quarterfinals, a respectable showing for a magus's daughter. Assuming Kitty would need a moment to make it through the press, I headed for the contestant bleachers as soon as the event ended, intending to keep Beth back on some pretense. But there was no need—Kitty had raced down the spectator bleachers before the end of the final bout, and she was on the floor by the time I zeroed in on the target.

"Beth!" she cried, beaming, and jogged past the mats to greet her. "You were *fantastic* out there! It's so good to finally see you again!" She reached for her in an attempted embrace, but her sister recoiled and regarded her with confusion and a touch of alarm. "It's me, Kitty," she said as Beth withdrew. "It's okay, sorry, didn't mean to scare you…"

On learning the stranger's identity, Beth's young face hardened. "What do you want?"

Kitty seemed stung by her tone, but she recovered quickly and pressed on. "To see you, silly! Gosh, last time I saw you, you were, what…five months old? Look at you now! Wow, guess we know which one of us took after Mom, huh?"

Her effusiveness did nothing to thaw the ice in Beth's stare. "Yeah. Excuse me." Brushing past her sister, she began to follow her classmates, but Kitty caught her arm to stay her.

"Can't we talk a little?" Kitty asked. "Come on, there's probably snacks in the dining hall or I've got cookies in my office—"

"Let go of me!"

Surprised and visibly hurt, Kitty released her hold and stepped back. "I…I'm sorry, did I do something wrong?"

"What, you mean besides disowning us, running off to England, and never even calling? And now you want to *chat?*" Beth snapped. "About what? I've got nothing to say to you."

"Disown—no, that's not what happened!" Kitty protested. "Mom sent me here, *she's* the one who never let me come back to the silo. I…I mean, yeah, I went to uni here, and I'm working here now, but I never disowned anyone! I've called for years! Did you never hear my messages?" She moved closer, and Beth, despite her tough façade, took a step back. "My letters—didn't you get my *letters*?"

"What letters?"

By that point, Kitty was almost in tears. "I've been writing you for years. Tell her, Maria," she begged, turning to me. "You know I've been writing her."

"She has, I swear it," I told Beth. "She used to send me letters for you from Oxford, and I'd put them in the inter-installation drop. Every month, no matter what."

Briefly, I considered the pair—Beth still defiant but confused, Kitty pleading—and saw the answer to the puzzle even as their mother hurried our way. Of course Beth hadn't received her mail—if Magus Stanhope wouldn't even take her elder daughter's calls, then surely she wouldn't give the baby unvetted correspondence.

"Eva," I said, raising my voice to be heard over the crowd around us, "congratulations. Beth did well out there."

She had no time for me or pleasantries. Snatching Beth by the shoulder and pushing her toward the pack of departing students, she wheeled on Kitty, blocking her view of Beth's escape. "Stay the hell away from her," she muttered, her voice low but sharp with warning.

For once, however, Kitty didn't back down to her long-absent mother. "That's my *sister*. Did you steal her mail? Seriously? I can't even write a damn postcard to my own sister?"

"You're a disgrace," her mother replied. "And if you have a shred of decency about you, you'll stay away from Beth. Think about someone else for once in your life, Katherine. She has a chance of success—she doesn't need *you* around to ruin it."

Kitty's face went scarlet, but it was anger I saw in her eyes, not embarrassment. "A *disgrace*? Mom, I just earned a first at Oxford, and I had a position waiting for me with the Away Team. How the hell is *that* a disgrace?"

"You know damn well what I'm talking about."

Kitty smirked. "Of course, yes, how stupid of me to associate with people who are bothered when I'm *attacked*. Or *hungry*. Or in need of *clothing*. What did you think I wore through school, potato sacks? Not that you ever cared." Her shoulders trembled with her fury. "You know what a disgrace is, Mom? It's sending your child away when it's not convenient to have her around. It's doing everything you can to let her know she's not wanted because she's not good enough. And it's stealing a little kid's mail so she grows up thinking her sister doesn't give a damn." Kitty laughed once, incredulously. "And here I was, wondering why Beth never wrote me back. You hateful *bitch*."

I saw Eva's hand twitch and shielded Kitty, and her mother's slap hit the wall of spellcraft instead of her daughter's face. She turned to me, almost as crimson as Kitty, and snarled, "This is none of your business, mongrel."

Blinking away my sudden mental flash of Firola's smirk, I slid between them and stood nose to nose with Eva. "Call me that again," I murmured, "and I'll show you why I'm on the Council. Right here, in front of everyone. This *is* combat day, isn't it?"

If she could have killed with a look, I'd have dropped dead, but fortunately for me, Eva was just a wizard, and she glanced away first. "You stay away from her," she told Kitty once more, then marched off after the crowd.

I turned around to Kitty and reached for her. "Come on, let's get out of—"

"No." She slid from my grasp, blinked hard, then shook her head. "No, thanks. I've got work to do."

"Kitty…"

"I'll see you later, Maria," she said, and hurried away—but not before I saw her first tears spill.

I checked on Kitty during my breaks throughout the day,

then brought in Chinese takeaway for dinner that night, which we ate in the privacy of her kitchen. Withdrawn and quiet, she picked at her lo mein, blamed her lack of appetite on a big lunch I knew she hadn't eaten, then feigned weariness and begged off for the evening. I cleaned up the leftovers while she brushed her teeth, and I saw myself out.

A few minutes later, I found Val in one of the gardens, enjoying the twilight breeze and a glass of wine. "Any casualties?" he asked in greeting, motioning a second chair into existence.

"Just bruises and scrapes," I replied as I settled in. "Kitty saw her sister today."

I could tell Val was smiling, even in the low twilight. "A good reunion, I hope."

"Not exactly."

His smile faltered, then disappeared as I recounted the morning's events. By the time I finished, he had put his drink aside and was glaring into the shadows of the bushes. "She had no right."

I shrugged. "That's Eva for you. When has she ever cut Kitty a break?"

"Yes, but..." He sighed in frustration. "I wish I knew why she hates that girl. It's unnatural."

"Not every mother is maternal..."

"Yes, mine included, but Mab had little use for any of her children. Eva loathes the one and loves the other, and it's...puzzling."

"Kitty's dad raised her, so maybe that's why Eva is so distant."

"I could understand distant, but this is something more."

"Well...yeah," I said. "There's Eva—this magus, right, looking to prove herself—and she has a kid, and that kid is barely even a witch. You've heard Aiden's stories."

"More of them than you have, I'm sure," said Val. "I just have a difficult time imagining what drives her hatred.

Treating the girl as disabled would make sense, but she cut her off. It's unnecessarily cruel." He mulled it over a moment more, then asked, "Does Kitty need anything?"

"Not that I know of," I replied, and rose to go. "Sorry to ruin your evening—I thought you'd want to know."

"Yes, thank you. Get some rest, I'm sure you're exhausted," he said, giving my hand a squeeze, and released me to leave.

I'd opened a gate and was about to return to Glastonbury when I felt it: a quick, familiar sensation like the fluttering of a moth's wings deep within my mind. On instinct, I threw up my defenses, then whirled around to find Val staring at me. "What are you doing?"

Faerie had almost lost the last of the sunset, but I could see his features in the warm glow spilling from my den, and his expression rapidly shifted from surprise to guilt. "I...um..."

"You *promised*, Val. No more spying. You swore to me."

My voice sounded sharper than usual, but then I felt as if I'd been slapped. At the very least, I'd been betrayed.

"I'm sorry," he said in a rush, holding up his hands in surrender. "I thought perhaps you hadn't told me everything about today—"

"And if I didn't, it's none of your business!"

He took on a placating tone. "I worry about you, Maria. Both of you. That's all. I shouldn't have—"

"You're damn right you shouldn't have." I glared back at him, flushing with my flaring temper. "You promised."

"Maria—"

"I *defended* you," I continued over him. "Bert warned me, but I said you wouldn't try to pry. Probably a good thing he taught me blocking, isn't it?"

"Maria, I'm sorry. It won't happen again, I swear—"

"*Don't.* Just...don't." I stepped back toward the gate, angry but afraid I'd say too much. "I'll talk to you later, Val."

I had one foot in the other realm when he asked, "How much longer are you going to stay there?"

"Where? Glastonbury?" I asked, glancing over my shoulder at him. "Until Toula sends me elsewhere, I suppose."

"You know what I mean."

At that, I pulled my leg back into Faerie and turned to face him again. "I am a *magus*. I'm happy. You expect me to give it up *now*? A year in?"

"I'm not suggesting you quit tonight, but eventually…soon…"

"I'm *happy*," I snapped.

"And I worry for your safety," he retorted.

"What could you possibly be worried about?"

"The Conclave," he said, counting off on his fingers. "People like Eva. Your beloved *Bert*. Nath, when next she tries to invade—"

"Bert? Seriously? He reads books and writes at least twelve hours a day. What's he going to do, throw a codex at my head?"

"You underestimate him."

"And you suspect him for no reason! He's my mentor, not my nemesis! Hell, he's the one who worked to get me onto the Council!"

That reminder did nothing to convince Val. "I worry about you in that place," he murmured. "Toula as well, but she can protect herself. You're young yet, you're inexperienced in actual combat—"

"I'll manage," I muttered, and slipped away.

CHAPTER 15

Val and I didn't speak about that night. In the year and a half that followed, I never sensed him attempt to circumvent my mental defenses—and I made a point of keeping them engaged. The spell that protected me from intrusions went up as soon as I crossed the border between the realms, and it remained active for the duration, a silent reminder of my responsibility to the Arcanum. If it offended Val that I didn't trust him enough to let down my guard, he never showed me. He treated me as well as ever, gladly hosting me whenever I returned, and extended an open invitation to Kitty, my frequent companion on those trips. Her job wasn't as classified as mine, and she enlivened dinners with stories of the Team's travels and near-misses. Val learned not to ask me more about my work than generalities, and he gradually accepted that the only answer he would receive was some variant of, "It's fine."

I loved him, and he had been wonderful to me, but there were areas of my life of which he simply could not be a part. I think it hurt him to be shut out, but he never complained to me.

I suspect, however, that he mentioned the matter to Toula, who hinted that I could relax—just by entering the realm, my thoughts were open to Ros, and there wasn't a damn thing I could do to prevent that. But even if Ros eventually decided to pass on information to the Three—and as nosy as she could be, she *could* keep a secret—the principle of the thing made me take precautions.

It wasn't as if I dropped my guard around Toula, either. Those magi with the skill tended to keep themselves protected from prying minds, and so no one seemed surprised when I followed suit. By then, of course, I had my own secrets to keep, and I didn't want Toula to know how I truly felt about her Conclave policy.

At least Bert's research was no longer a total secret. He had mentioned the subject to Toula and Arnold, neither of whom held out much hope for his project, and the research librarians I consulted surely suspected the nature of our work. As Bert followed rabbit trails through the literature, I did my part by tracking down the works cited in margins and footnotes, gleaning what I could from the library and Archives, and delivering digital copies to him, already annotated with my cross-references and findings. Even with the both of us working, however—and Bert, whose sabbatical had been extended, was working on the project full time—progress was slow.

Naturally, the problem was the topic. Bert wanted to pinpoint the factor that gave witch-bloods the ability to craft highly complex magical implements. The combined research of centuries had generated precious little on the subject. We knew that mundanes couldn't craft—a mundane could shove dragonscale or dried phoenix blood into a wand shaft all day long, and the end result would be no more useful than a stick pulled from a dead tree. Wizards *could* craft, albeit poorly. A wizard-made wand might work, but never as well as a crafter-made product, and it would be prone to breakage in periods of stress—exactly when it was needed the most. Whether faeries could craft was anyone's guess; Val said he'd never seen the point, as a wand in a faerie's hands was as useful as if it had been passed to a mundane. What was it, then, that gave those with mixed wizard and fae blood—particularly in equal portions—the unique ability to produce items of power that they themselves would almost certainly be unable to use? And, on a more practical bent, was there a way for the average wizard to work around his limitations?

The answer to that question over the years had been a resounding *no*. No one in the available literature had discovered the secret, though not for lack of trying. Pushing beyond the books, I asked Arnold to put me in touch with his Minor Arcanum contacts and soon found myself out in a pasture in New Mexico, experiencing firsthand just how useless wizard-made wands could be. My elderly hosts, the Joneses, had saved their old wands as last-ditch backups, though both worked exclusively with crafter-made models—Levey wands, I surmised, judging by the fine work. The Minor Arcanum's homemade models were thick and unwieldy, studded with quartz bits along boosting pathways carved into the wood. While they could channel magic, they did so poorly—perhaps effective for shooting bolts, but not the sort of tool one wanted for technical work like warding.

At a loss, I went to the Fringe settlement and sat in while Amy Levey herself, the notorious product of two witch-blooded parents, experimented with new composite cores. She couldn't tell me why the art of wandmaking came so easily to her, but having been a crafter for forty years by then, she had a knack for combining her materials in the perfect balance to suit individual wizards' needs. As she assembled her wands, I watched her hands and the flow of barely energized magic around them. She beckoned me closer to the bench and allowed me to try, but when I began to pack a wand, the magic near me glowed with activation, the wand shaft warmed in my hand, and the tiny scoop of dried phoenix blood sparked in warning. Hurriedly, I passed the implements back to Amy before I could ruin them, and she smiled in understanding. "There's a good reason that magi don't craft," she said. "It why that story of Simon Magus making his golden magic-storing balls makes no sense—someone like him wouldn't have been able to pull it off without a good crafter doing the heavy lifting." Seeing my frustration, she jutted her thumb toward the wall that separated her carefully controlled workshop from that of her husband. A shielded monitor in lieu of a window showed him hunched over the guts of a computer with a soldering iron. "If you think you make a poor crafter, hon, go talk to Kip."

Gray Landers were well outside the scope of our research, but I made a note and mentioned it to Bert on my return. "Of course he can't craft," he replied. "Kadalin can't even work with dark magic, I believe. Then again," he added, shrugging, "they're basically mundanes spliced to horses, so no real surprise there." He paused, then grimaced and resumed typing. "Never really saw how Kip and Amy got together, to be honest with you. Not my cup of tea."

"Kip stays transformed," I told him.

"So does *Frank*, but even if I fancied men, I wouldn't pursue him."

After a moment, I murmured, "You wouldn't pursue Amy, either."

At that, Bert stopped again and lowered his computer screen to find me staring at him from my chair. "No," he admitted, "I wouldn't."

"She's perfectly nice."

"That's not the point."

I drummed my fingers on the armrest as I mulled that over. "What about me?"

Taken aback, he jerked in his seat, and his eyes flew open wide behind his thick glasses. "*You?*"

"Not *me* me," I rushed before he could get the wrong impression. "Someone like me. Ninety-nine-point-nine percent wizard."

Bert's relief at the clarification was palpable, but he struggled nonetheless to answer me. "It's, ehm…it's not that there's anything *wrong* with you, Maria, but—"

"But what? I'm seventy-six generations removed from a fully fae ancestor. *Seventy-six*, Bert. The only indication that Val and I are related is the aural signature...well, and this," I added, pointing to my crooked eye tooth. "Could be chance, might be genetic. So, given all of that distance, all of that dilution..."

At least he had the grace to look slightly abashed.

"I just think it's in everyone's best interest that we not mix the bloodlines," he mumbled. "It's nothing personal."

"Easy for *you* to say. And if we never mixed, what would we do for crafters, hmm?"

"Fair point, but they should be the exception to the rule. You end up with someone magically inept who may or may not have any actual skill with crafting—"

"Or then there's someone like me. Hypothetically, if I had a kid with a wizard, do you think that kid wouldn't be able to cast? Seventy-seven generations removed?"

"I...assume that child would be much like you, barring a dud situation," he grudgingly replied.

"So it's the *tainted* blood you can't get past, yes? Not any actual risk of magically inept children."

By then, Bert had flushed to his hairline with the awkwardness of the situation. "It's a personal preference, that's all. I respect you as a colleague, and I'm fond of you as a friend, but...*that*..."

"I get it," I said, giving his explanation a quick and merciful death, and rose. "Anyway, I'll be in my office."

"Maria," he called when I was halfway across the room, and I turned to find him watching me with a furrowed brow and worried eyes. "Are you cross with me? I don't mean to be offensive, I assumed you'd prefer honesty—"

"You didn't tell me anything I didn't already know," I replied, smiling slightly, and took my leave.

Nothing new, I mused on my way back to the quiet of my sanctum. Of course Bert wouldn't be any different from his old-blooded peers, but still, I'd had hope—not for a romantic relationship with him, but for a situation in which he could contemplate having a tainted partner. It was silly of me to have expected a different outcome.

By twenty-three, I'd accepted that my chances of finding love in the Arcanum were slim to nonexistent. I hadn't discovered my soulmate while in school, but then few of us had; with our small classes, the rest of our year eventually became more like cousins than potential partners, and only two pairs came through graduation together. Several years beyond that enforced companionship, I heard occasional news of my peers partnering off, usually with people from other years or installations, and I celebrated their engagements and the first births with as much enthusiasm as anyone. Kitty had certainly tested the dating waters at Oxford, even if she had married herself to her work since her return. But as for me, there had been no overt flirtation, let alone an offer of a drink or dinner. The potential suitors my age would have approached with caution already due to my position, but the rest of my baggage made me, quite frankly, undateable.

Not that things were any more promising in Faerie. Of Val's court, the full-blooded treated me with disdain, and though the others were more polite, they stayed away. I knew many of the Fringe by face, if not by name, and while my eye had lingered on several during my trips to the settlement, I'd realized that they, too, gave me a wide berth. Most of the Fringe had little use for the Arcanum—with good reason—and magi even less. As a magus with a connection to Val, whose power and talent made most Fringers uneasy, I was a double threat.

There was, of course, a vast world of unattached mundanes to explore, but that did nothing to soothe the sting of institution-wide rejection.

Bert was right—I would always be different, regarded with suspicion even if I did nothing wrong. I was lucky, I decided, to have a mentor who understood the place I was coming from, even if he, too, saw me as something *other*. Perhaps someday, given enough time and acclimatization, he'd come around. Perhaps not.

In either case, I thought as I opened my latest digitized tome, I had work to do. Our questions weren't going to answer themselves, and so I pushed my hurt to the darkest corner of my mind.

With the new year, Ted produced his customary virginal white board, pre-marked into a calendar, and hung it on the wall with a tongue-trilled drumroll. I studied it once he'd marked up the first quarter—long research blocks until March, and then simultaneous projects noted in three different colors. Perplexed, I visited his office to ask how and why the Team was fracturing.

"Everyone else's schedules have left our spring calendar FUBAR," he griped, showing me the scribbled notes in his battered leather planner. "The biggest issue is Arc 5's availability. There's a ring, quite possibly ensorcelled to shoot fireballs, and it just so happens to be located *here*," he explained, poking the world map on his wall. "We think. The trail goes cold right about here, anyway."

I squinted at the territorial designations around his finger. "I'm not trying to tell you how to do your job, Ted, but don't you think it would be better to wait until—"

"It's *just* an Ebola outbreak, and we're taking all necessary precautions," he interrupted, sighing dramatically. "You sound like Lakshmi. Anyway, Arc 5 is offering muscle and a couple of medics, but our scheduling stars align for only a brief window, and we'd already put trips in the pipeline. So I'm leading the Congo trip with Frank and Daphne, Mal and Antony are making a last trek into Siberia before the weather gets too warm, and Kitty's heading to your old stomping grounds for a little Mediterranean fun."

I frowned. "Rome?"

"Yep. Got a decent lead on an old wand, said in two of the commentaries to rival a dragonscale, but I kind of doubt it's survived. She's going to poke around for a few days and see if she can't prove me wrong. Maybe get a good pizza or two down her," he said, and chuckled to himself. "Kid hasn't taken a vacation yet, and this is the closest thing I can offer right now."

"Nice. Tell her I know of a few quality gelaterie if she gets desperate," I replied.

Cornering Kitty at dinner that night, I leaned across the table and raised my eyebrows. "You're going to go play in *my* hometown, and you didn't invite me? I'm wounded. *Deeply.*"

She smirked and waggled her spoon at me. "Someone has to keep the kiddies from killing each other."

"Arnold's a big boy, he can handle class without me. Come on, I'll hold your map."

"Thanks, but I'm set," she said, grinning. "Tell you what, once I get settled in, I'll shoot you a message, and we'll go play tourist. Sound good?"

"Acceptable, I suppose," I said, and dropped my things on the table. "What's the soup?"

"Disappointing," she called as I headed for the queue.

On the second Saturday of March, I saw three of the Team off to meet their Arc 5 reinforcements, then made a gate for Antony and Mal onto the tundra the next day. Antony looked less than pleased by the assignment, but Mal, who'd shifted for the occasion, seemed quite content to run around in the freezing air, tail wagging and tongue lolling. "Try not to let him get shot," I said, and closed the gate behind them.

That left only Kitty, who took her leave on Monday morning before dawn, armed with a backpack, books, computer, and a few special tools Amy had whipped up at the Team's request. She showed me a picture of her hotel, promised she'd call with dinner plans, then stepped through the gate I'd made into a darkened alley with a whispered, "Ciao, bella!"

With the field teams sorted, I went about my week, refereeing beginners' bouts for the first-years and marking up books in my spare time. Kitty sent word that night that she'd made it safely to her hotel, and I began searching online for promising restaurant options.

The Siberia team checked in on Tuesday—Mal called, as Antony was too busy clutching hand warmers to deal with a phone—and Daphne sent Lakshmi and me a brief note on Wednesday morning to say that they were on schedule and in good shape. Tired from a late Council meeting and going cross-eyed with my reading, I put my things away early that night and called it a day.

When my phone rang around ten, I was sound asleep, and I cried out as I woke to its blaring chime. Fumbling on the nightstand, I silenced the alarm, glared blearily at the hour, and held the phone to my ear. "If this is about dinner, can we do it tomorrow night?"

"Not dinner," said Kitty. "I've got a situation."

"Need me now?"

"*Yeah*. Hang up, I'll send a pic."

By the time the location picture came through, I'd thrown on a dark sweatshirt and jeans, the better to sneak around. I didn't recognize Kitty's surroundings, but then again, Rome and its metropolitan area were lousy with ruins, and in the darkness, one fallen temple looked much like any other. Concentrating, I opened a gate and hurried through to find Kitty waiting beside a section of limestone wall, phone in hand. "What's wrong?" I asked, taking a quick look about me as I closed the gate. We seemed to be outside the city proper, in the middle of an ancient complex, and something told me that the authorities would have more than mere questions if we were caught at that time of night.

I couldn't see Kitty well in the darkness, but her voice was strained. "Thought I found the wand. Got a subtle spike on this," she said, pulling one of Amy's toys from her pocket. "But it's not a wand signature. Something's drawing on the background magic."

The cold air, such a departure from my warm bed, sent prickles up my back and arms. "Ward system?"

"Can't tell. Whatever it is, it's in the wall." She patted the nearest block for emphasis. "Want to make a hole?"

What remained of the wall—the foundation of the building, more properly—was thick and still solid, which lessened the chances of a cave-in. "Sure," I told Kitty. "Where would you like it?"

She walked up and down the wall for a moment with her detector, then stopped in front of an innocuous block and nudged it with the toe of her sneaker. "Here."

A few seconds of thought and a whispered word later, the mortar around the chosen block and the ones above it cracked and disintegrated as I slid the stones from their resting place. I could see nothing beyond them—the night was overcast, and I was too busy magically shoring up the wall to conjure a light—but Kitty held her phone's torch high and slipped into the hole.

A moment later, I heard her voice, quiet but agitated: "Holy *shit*. Maria, get in here."

Confident that we weren't in imminent danger of falling stones, I followed Kitty into the foundation—which, curiously, contained a small void, just large enough for the two of us to stand shoulder to shoulder. Once inside, I didn't need Kitty's light to see the source of the magic spike. A stone in the interior of the foundation practically glowed to our eyes with the strength of the ward network around it.

"I think you may have found more than a wand," I whispered. "There are pockets of magic in that matrix. Must have survived the '13 closure."

Kitty grunted, too busy deciphering the words carved in the stone to give me a proper answer. And so I waited, breathing the stale air and dust of centuries, until she whistled softly and pressed her palm against the writing.

"Ordo Lucis."

"You think?"

"That's their mark," she said, pointing to a symbol at the top of the stone—three intersecting lines forming a crude star, cut through midway down their rays by a circle. "I don't believe this. They're all over the books, but we thought the last of their hidey-holes had been uncovered by now."

I knew little beyond a rough sketch of Ordo Lucis, an ancient Roman organization of wizards that had eventually been subsumed into the eastward-spreading Arcanum. "What do you suppose is in there?"

"Not what," Kitty muttered. "*Who.*"

"Come again?"

"See for yourself." She squished to the side, giving me a better view of the inscription. "It's a warning," she said as I scanned it by the light of her phone. "Dangerous monster, do not release, et cetera, et cetera."

"They don't give much detail..."

"'Monster in the wall' would probably be sufficient for most people, don't you think?"

I shrugged. "We're not most people."

"Bingo. Can you get that block out without bringing down the wall?"

"Give me room."

Kitty stepped out of the foundation, and I adjusted the spell while I pried the block loose and floated it into the grass. When I saw it properly, I almost put it back.

The block in question wasn't a solid block at all. It was a stone box—a coffin, perhaps—held closed by spells and rusting chains. The warnings carved at its foot continued on the lid, all of them promising grave danger to the one stupid enough to open the box. The responsible part of me hinted that it might be a good idea to put the box back in the wall and wait for daylight and reinforcements before ignoring my predecessors' instructions, but as I began to think that option over, Kitty reached into her backpack and produced a small rod. "If I blast the chains off, can you get past the wards?" she asked.

Throwing caution to the wind—I was a magus, after all—I stayed her until I was sure the foundation was stable, then stepped back while the preloaded spells shattered the brittle iron links. It took considerably more effort to overload the wards and break them, but soon enough, the box was unprotected, and Kitty hoisted her phone's torch for a look. "Want to slide the lid off, or should I?"

"That probably weighs a ton," I replied, and moved it aside with a flicker of spellcraft.

I don't know what I expected to see in the box—bones, maybe, or some sort of early writing. Maybe nothing but dust or a note telling us a previous treasure hunter had beaten us to the prize.

I did *not* expect to find an intact body.

The man in the box lay with his eyes closed, his arms by his sides. He wore a blue, short-sleeved, knee-length tunic, sandals, and an emerald ring, but nothing more—not a typical burial, I surmised. It was difficult to see much detail with the sole torch, but I could tell he was young, probably close to our age.

"Moon and stars," I whispered. "What could he have done to end up like that?"

"No idea," Kitty began, then hesitated for an instant before reaching in to feel his face. "He's warm," she said, withdrawing her hand as quickly as if she'd touched a hot stove. "Oh, shit, Maria, he's *alive*."

"*What?*" I yelped, and leaned closer to the supposed corpse. He was indeed warm to the touch, but beyond that, I could just make out the binding spell hiding deep within his aura—again, a spell reinforced with pockets of raw magic against catastrophe. Whoever had bound him wanted to be certain that the bind would *last*.

"What do we do?" asked Kitty.

I straightened, tried to calm my racing mind, and settled on a course of action. "We patch that wall and get him the hell out of here, that's what we do. Get your things—I'll take you back to your hotel tomorrow."

There's no set protocol for waking someone who's been unconscious for centuries.

Ordo Lucis hasn't bothered to date the box, but judging by his dress alone, the man was almost certainly Roman—though whether he'd been born in the Republic or Imperial period was impossible for me to tell. Not wanting to frighten him more than necessary, I stretched him out on my guest bed, drew the curtains, lit a pair of candles on the dresser, and closed the door, leaving Kitty in the den to pull everything she could find on his captors. My plan was to bring him up slowly from sleep, and I began by gently breaking through the bind crafted around him, praying that whoever had buried him alive had knocked him out beforehand. I'd only been to the Fringe's recovery home once, but the screams of the insane, the ones who'd lost their minds after being immobilized in the darkness for more than a decade, had haunted my dreams.

Bit by bit, I removed the spell around him, then stepped back from the bed and waited. After a moment, his chest began to visibly rise and fall, slowly at first, then more rapidly as he drew deep breaths until finally, with a gasp, his eyes flew open.

"Hic salvus es," I said, hurrying to his side as he strained to sit up. "You're safe here." He struggled against my arm, and I insisted, "Ne quoquam exsurgatis."

Panting, he surrendered and flopped back onto the duvet. "Úbi sum?"

"Uh…Britannia," I murmured.

"*Britannia!*"

Again, I pinned him to the bed when he started to thrash. "It's a long story, and I hope you can fill in some of the missing details, but right now, you need to be still. You're weak. Please don't fight me."

"Britannia," he repeated, dazed, but stopped pushing against me. "How…how did I get to Britannia?" A fresh wave of panic crossed his face. "A messenger, is there anyone? My grandfather—"

"Calm down," I soothed, "it's all right."

"I must send a message," he insisted, staring me in the eyes. "My wife, my cousin, they've faked my death, my son…" He grabbed my wrist with surprising strength. "My son is only days old. Please help me. Send a messenger. Whatever the price, my grandfather will pay him well."

Seeing his desperation, my heart broke for him, but there was nothing I could do to ease the inevitable blow. "I'm very sorry to tell you this, but you've been sleeping for a long time."

"Of course," he said, nodding, "yes, if I was taken all the way to Britannia… How long? Is it yet midsummer?" When I hesitated, his brows drew together. "Past midsummer? Autumn?" He paused, searching my face for a hint. "Later than that?"

"By my best guess," I said slowly, "and this is a rough approximation…you slept for about, um…two thousand years."

His dark eyes widened, and he laughed nervously. "A joke, yes? Please tell me how long—"

"I'm trying to tell you. I could be off by a few centuries, but unless I'm gravely mistaken…"

My voice trailed away, and I let him struggle upright. He rolled off the bed and staggered to the window, then pulled back the curtain.

There wasn't much to be seen of Glastonbury from my guestroom, especially not at night, but the electric lights of the roadways and the distant city center glowed from the gloom. Anyone sensitive to magic would have also seen the faint lattice of the camouflaging ward around the castle, which seemed a deep purple to my eyes—visible, but not so bright as to blot out the town and the few stars that popped from the patchy clouds. As I joined the man, he pressed his hand against the cold glass and looked up at the flashing lights of an airplane passing low overhead.

And then, without another word, he fainted.

By the time he came around, I had floated him back onto the bed. "I told you you're weak right now," I said as he blinked at me in his stupor. 'You haven't moved for ages. Give your body a chance to recover."

His eyes began to focus again, and as he remembered where he was, they started to fill. "This is impossible," he croaked. "I'm dreaming, you're a dream, this is impossible…"

While he was busy denying his senses, I opened the door, bent as if reaching for something in the corridor, then whispered a bottle of wine into existence and carried it to the bed. "Here, *slowly*, try to sit up," I said, and helped him maneuver against the headboard with the aid of the decorative pillows. "Drink this."

He was strong enough to hold on to the bottle, and he gulped straight from the neck until he had to come up for air. After contemplating the glass bottle in his hands—a typical wine bottle, thin-walled and green, but different from any glass vessels he would have known—he stared into space for a long moment, then looked at me again. "Tell me this is a dream."

"I wish I could," I replied, perching on the edge of the bed beside him. "And I'm so sorry."

He turned away and sniffled, then murmured, "Publius."

"Hmm?"

"My son. He was ten days old when I left him…and you're telling me he's dead?"

"I'm so sorry," I repeated, at a loss for a better sentiment.

As I considered stepping out to give him a moment alone, Kitty knocked and opened the door without waiting for an invitation. "Got what I was looking for," she told me, squinting into the near darkness. "Is he…*oh*.

Uh…salve," she said, switching tongues and lifting a hand. "Sorry, I thought you would still be asleep…"

"Come in," I said, waving her into the room, then looked at the man. "This is Kitty. She found you."

"Kind of dark in here, huh?" she said, and flipped the switch to the overhead light.

The man cried out and tried to push himself into the pillows as the light came on, shielding his eyes with his arm, and Kitty realized her mistake. "Oh, *shit*, sorry, didn't think," she mumbled, reaching for the switch again. "Want it off?"

"Leave it," I told her, and gripped his shoulder to calm him. "It's not going to hurt you," I murmured. "It's only a lamp."

Slowly, he pulled his protective arm from his face and peered at the ceiling. "*That* is no lamp."

"Now it is," said Kitty, blowing out the candles before they could drip wax onto the dresser. "Yeah, sorry, should have warned you. Hello again. Nice to, uh…see you."

For the first time, I got a proper look at our guest, but nothing about my previous assessment changed. He was approximately our age, with a mussed head of dark, wavy hair, wary brown eyes, an aquiline nose, and an olive complexion—and he was staring at Kitty as if seeing a ghost.

In fairness, she cut an interesting figure that night, her face dirt-streaked and her pale hair pulled into a high, messy ponytail. It didn't help that she was carrying a tablet in one hand, and the glow of its screen only augmented her strangeness. She still wore her field clothes, a black T-shirt over loose-fitting khakis and hiking boots, surely not the sort of ensemble the man had ever seen.

Kitty stared back at him, shifting under his gaze, then tucked her computer against her chest and approached. "I'm not even going to ask you if you're all right because that would be a stupid question," she said, taking a seat at the foot of the bed. "You look like hell, my friend."

In reply, he took another swig from the wine bottle, which he clutched like a teddy bear.

"Now," she continued while he drank, "would you mind telling me what, exactly, you did to piss off Ordo Lucis?"

His face screwed up in puzzlement. "What's Ordo Lucis?"

"Short answer, the people who stuck you in a wall. Slightly longer answer, magi."

"*Magi?*" he echoed. "I know no magi, I have nothing to do with them."

"Well, someone obviously knew you." She put the computer aside—face-down, I noticed, hiding the glowing screen—and tucked her foot beneath her other leg. "What happened? What do you remember?"

The man drank again, then wiped the traces on his hand. "Does it matter?" he asked and gestured toward me with the bottle. "*She* says I've slept for millennia."

"More or less," Kitty agreed. "But satisfy my curiosity anyway. You were locked in a stone box covered in warnings, the lid was chained shut, and you were hidden inside a foundation. That's not the sort of thing Ordo Lucis would have done on a whim. Did you have enemies?"

"No," he protested, then paused. "Yes. *Two*, it seems."

"Magi?"

"Not to my knowledge. My cousin and my wife." After another long gulp, he leaned back into the pillows and closed his eyes. "Last night, Titus, my cousin, woke me. He said his sister was delivering her child, but the birth was difficult, and I needed to come."

"You're...a doctor?" Kitty guessed.

"No." He hesitated, then said, "The gods gave me a gift for healing. Not always, but often, broken limbs and such injuries...I can help. Valeria is sickly, so I went. Fabia came, too, in case another woman was needed."

"Fabia?"

"My wife. She should have been resting, our son is so young, but she and Valeria are as sisters."

Kitty, it seemed, had reached the same conclusion I had about the wisdom of correcting his tenses at that moment. "So you, Fabia, and Titus go out to help his sister..."

"Her husband's family lives a long distance away, especially in the dark," he continued, his eyes moving behind their lids as if he were watching the scene play out. "We hadn't gone far before something hit me. I went limp, I couldn't stop myself from falling." He chased his shudder with more wine. "I was facing the ground, but I heard other voices. Men, perhaps three. They had a cart, and they covered me with a blanket, and..." He scowled, then muttered, "I don't know where we went, exactly. I couldn't see anything."

"Don't worry about it," said Kitty. "These men left your wife and cousin alone?"

He opened his eyes and snorted. "They were conspirators. I couldn't see, but I heard everything they said on the journey." Agitated, he rubbed his free hand over his face, then through his hair. "They needed me to die."

"Why?"

Even if centuries had passed, the hurt on his face was fresh and deep. "Titus has always loved Fabia. I knew she favored him to me, but I'm older, and my grandfather made arrangements with her father. If we had divorced, I doubt that she would have been allowed to marry Titus in my stead. She and I only married two years ago. I...I thought she had put aside her feelings for him, that she was growing fonder of me, especially with our son, but..." He sighed and stared past Kitty at the wall. "I heard them plotting. The men with them—you think they were magi?" he asked.

Kitty nodded. "If I had to guess, I'd say one of them hit you with a partial bind. It's designed to stop voluntary movement while still keeping your target breathing and pumping blood."

His eyebrows rose. "You know something of magic?"

"I'm a much better scholar than practitioner," she replied with a self-deprecating smile. "But I do have a good understanding of the theory. So, uh…this is going to sound terrible, but why didn't they just kill you? Why go to the trouble with the box?"

"I don't know," he mumbled. "One of the men said he would give them something that would look like me— their story was going to be that we were set upon by robbers, and Titus took Fabia to safety while I fought them." He huffed a sound that seemed almost like laughter. "I suppose even Titus feared the gods enough to save my life. Twice, he asked the men for reassurance that they wouldn't kill me. They promised." Again, the wine bottle rose. "It might have been kinder."

"You're having a bad night," said Kitty. "And alcohol's a depressant, so maybe we should switch to something else," she added in English, cutting her eyes to me.

"This is better than full-blown panic," I murmured, and she acquiesced with a roll of her eyes.

"What?" he asked, looking back and forth between us for an explanation.

"Never mind," she told him, slipping back into her oddly accented Latin. "What happened next?"

He took a moment to collect his thoughts. "We reached our destination—a temple being constructed in another part of the city. I could see it by their lamps when they lifted the blanket. There was a long stone on the ground, and they removed the top…and then I was floating away from the cart and into the box. Titus looked in once and asked if I could hear anything, and the men said I probably could. He told me…" Pausing, he swallowed hard. "He apologized but said it was the only way for them to be together. He said he would raise Publius as his own son. And then…and then I heard them leave. Fabia never said goodbye."

"Shit," Kitty whispered.

"I heard chains. One of the men lowered a chain onto my leg, then pulled it out again. He…he seemed concerned," he said, frowning at the memory. "'Nothing happened,' I remember him saying that. And then another told him it didn't matter, they knew what I was capable of doing, and monsters had to be destroyed."

"So they *were* going to kill you," she pressed.

"Apparently. But the man with the chain argued with the others. He said they couldn't be certain. I believe they compromised in the end. That first man held a stick over me and started muttering, and…"

"And?"

"And then I was here," he finished, and swigged. "And you tell me my newborn son is dead."

I didn't know how to help him, but Kitty, despite her mother's reservation, had grown up with a father and friends who expressed their feelings through touch. She slid past her tablet, crawled up the bed, and surprised him with a tight hug—and he, despite his initial shock, quickly returned it.

"It's going to be all right," I heard her murmur. "Not tonight, not tomorrow, but someday, it's going to be all right. And in the meanwhile, there's no shame in mourning them." Pulling back slightly, she released him, then pried the half-emptied wine bottle from him and set it on the nightstand. "You know, I've been rude—I didn't even introduce myself. Kitty Connolly. This is Maria Corelli," she said, gesturing to me. "And you are called…Publius?"

He started to reach for the wine, then realized the direction of his hand's drift and stayed it. "No. Marcus Valerius Maximus. Publius is my grandfather," he explained. "He treated me as a son, and I wanted to honor him with mine."

Kitty glanced my way again and muttered in English, "Isn't that Val's name?"

I shrugged. "They didn't have that many options."

"Still." She looked at Marcus, who watched us blankly, then back at me. "Why don't you go tell him what we've been up to? I'd feel *loads* better."

CHAPTER 16

It was midmorning in Faerie when I walked into Val's office, and though he seemed pleased to see me, he glanced at the desk clock he kept set to Glastonbury time and cocked an eyebrow. "Can't sleep, carissima filia?"

"Oh, it's more than that." I helped myself to a generous splash of the wine on the side table before approaching his desk, and Val's other eyebrow joined its fellow in surprise. As I sat and tried to calm my jagged nerves, he approached and gripped my wrist.

"You're shaking," he said.

I couldn't deny it—the wine was sloshing up the sides of the glass—but I concentrated until I managed to get a long sip down. Sitting in familiar surroundings in full daylight, the night's events finally hit me, and I struggled to keep my legs from joining my trembling arms. "Kitty found someone."

Val leaned against the desk and folded his arms. "I don't follow…"

"Buried alive. I don't know exactly how long, but he was bound."

"Sane?"

"Seems to be. Really upset. Maybe edging close to tipsy, but he needed it. Hell, *I* need it," I muttered, drinking again. "Would you come talk to him, please?"

"Me?" he replied bemusedly. "If you like, but Helen would have greater insight into his condition—"

"He's Roman."

Val's jaw sagged for a few seconds as he processed that.

"You're certain?"

"All signs point to yes. I didn't even try to get a time reference out of him, but Kitty and I pulled a guy in a tunic out of the ruins of a temple foundation, and he called himself Marcus Valerius Maximus, and now he's in my spare bedroom, freaking out at electric lights, so you tell me."

"Moon and stars," he whispered, and ripped open a gate. I barely had time to knock the rest of my drink back before running after him.

Catching Val by the shoulder in my foyer, I steered him to the kitchen table before he could charge in on the newcomer. "Let me bring you up to speed, at least," I insisted.

He listened impatiently as I recounted what Marcus had told us, shaking his head. "Poor boy," he said as I concluded. "But he seems lucid to you?"

"He was when I left. Kitty's with him."

"Good." As he stood, his clothing shifted into a rough copy of Marcus's, albeit in yellow. "Something familiar," he told me, shrugging, then hurried across the flat and let me open the door.

The relief on Marcus's face on seeing Val was immediate. "Salve," Val began, closing the door behind us. "You are called Marcus Valerius?"

He nodded.

"As am I. Maria told me what happened to you. Are you hurt?"

"Weak," he replied, lifting one arm and letting it flop onto the duvet. "I tried to stand, but…"

"You'll recover. A few meals, re-acclimatization…and I may be able to speed the process," he offered, approaching the bed. "Maria said you have a gift for healing. I do as well, but probably more effective than yours."

"You haven't seen mine," said Marcus.

"No," he agreed, "but I've had time to practice…"

Having moved closer to the head of the bed, I caught a

glimpse of Val's face as its color drained.

"Your ring," he murmured, pointing to Marcus's hand. "May I see it?"

Troubled by Val's reaction, Marcus held it up for inspection. "My father's, and his father's before him," he said as Val stared at the emerald.

"Your father gave it to you?"

"My grandfather. My father died before I was born." He paused, frowning. "Do you recognize it? Do you know my grandfather?"

"Please, may I…"

Marcus pulled the ring off and passed it to him, and Val turned it to see the interior of the thick gold band. There was an inscription inside, but I was too far away to make out the characters.

"Your grandfather," Val began, barely speaking above a whisper. "A senator called Publius Valerius, married to Aemilia?"

The stranger grinned with excitement. "Yes! You know him?"

"Three sons?" Val pressed. "Publius, Gaius—"

"And Marcus, my father. Your hand is shaking," he noticed, suddenly concerned. "Are you well?"

But Val ignored the enquiry. "How did your father die?"

"In battle in Celtiberia. My mother was so distressed when she learned that she bore me too soon, and she died at my birth. But my father left that ring with her for safekeeping, and my grandfather gave it to me when I came of age."

As Marcus studied Val's face, looking for an explanation, I finally saw it. Val's eyes were his most notable feature because, like the eyes of any faerie of considerable years, they didn't seem to fit the rest of him. But seeing the two men in profile, freed from the sometimes unnerving sensation I got when confronted by the full force of Val's stare, I realized just how similar they appeared.

"You look ill," said Marcus, taking the ring back from Val. "Is something wrong?"

He said nothing for a moment as he stared at Marcus, and then I heard him murmur, "Maria, wake Toula."

Ten minutes and one rushed recitation later, I escorted Toula into the room. Kitty still sat on the bed beside Marcus, but Val had stepped to the window and was gazing out at the night. He turned as we came in, still as pale as when I'd left. She took one look at him, then at Marcus, and muttered, "*Shit.*"

"Told you," I said.

Toula's Latin was even more strangely accented than Kitty's, but still, Marcus seemed to understand her as she drew near. "Hi, I'm Toula. I need to see something, this will not hurt, but it may feel strange. And yes, it's magic, don't panic."

The look on his face suggested he was prepared to do just that, but before he could protest, she whispered the spell into action and held out her hand as a misty white sphere coalesced into an aural lattice. A twitch of her finger split the lattice—one half blue, one half equally blue and red—and she tapped her ring and moved her finger until a mate to the mixed half hovered in the air beside it. She looked to Val and nodded, then broke the spell and shoved her hands into her bathrobe pockets. "Whatever binds Ordo Lucis put on him must have blocked my trace attempts. I'll leave you to it," she said, and slipped out of the room.

Marcus looked at the three of us in confusion. "What was that? Who was she?"

I turned to Kitty, but neither of us wanted to make the first move.

After a long, awkward moment Val quietly said, "Your father didn't die in Celtiberia."

"Yes, he did," said Marcus, "the other men told our family, they buried him abroad—"

"That gift you have for healing isn't natural," he interrupted, sounding dazed. "It's magical talent, however weak. Maria said you weren't hurt by iron, but then again, you're quarter-blooded."

"I don't understand—"

"I'm sorry. Gods forgive me, I'm so sorry," he said, and rushed from the room.

Leaving Kitty to calm Marcus, I found Val at the kitchen table with his head in his hands. He gave no indication that he noticed me, and I waited for a minute before trying to draw his attention. "Tell him," I said. "He's just lost his entire family, give him something."

When Val raised his face, I saw he'd been silently crying. "He was trapped in there, and I did nothing. Two thousand years, and I did *nothing*."

"You didn't know he existed. And you heard Toula— they blocked him from being traced. Val," I said, squeezing his shoulder, "this isn't your fault—"

"If I'd gone home, if I'd taken Caecilia and fled...maybe she would have lived. And he...*he*..."

I barely noticed when the guestroom door creaked open, but I looked up at the sound of shuffling and found Kitty and Marcus crossing the den. Unsteady on his feet, he leaned heavily on Kitty, but she was only half a head shorter and strengthened by months of fieldwork with the Team and free weights in the castle's gym.

By the time they'd reached the edge of the room, I'd pulled out a chair for him to land on, but he stopped and looked Val square in the face, then softly, incredulously, whispered, "*Pater?*"

To say that Val had a lot of explaining to do would be a gross understatement, but Kitty had the sense to get him and Marcus out of my kitchen before Val could launch into anything complicated. "Take him over and get a healing enchantment going," she ordered. "It'll work better there, anyway. And until he gets vaccinated, he *cannot* hang out around here." They gave her twin looks of confusion, and she sighed deeply and rubbed her forehead. "Pathogens, Val. He's probably mortal, and the germs have had what, twenty-one hundred years and change to evolve? We'll call Dr. Powell and explain the situation."

"Pathogens?" Marcus echoed, feeling out the unfamiliar word.

"Uh…damn it. Look, this is going to sound insane, but there are things too small to see that get in you and make you sick. You've heard of the humors?"

He nodded warily.

"Complete nonsense. Topic for another time. For now, you're at risk if you stay here, so why don't you go with Val?"

Marcus's brow furrowed. "Val?"

"Me," he cut in, and hoisted Marcus from his chair. "Come—I'll tell you everything."

In retrospect, we probably should have warned Marcus before Val opened a gate, but he calmed quickly enough, and with a little persuasion, he was through. I sealed the hole behind them, then sank onto the couch, closed my eyes, and groaned.

The squealing of springs told me that Kitty had taken the recliner. Neither of us spoke for several minutes, and then Kitty mumbled, "Well, that was fun. What the hell do we tell Ted?"

"I'd leave it to Toula. You want to go back and look for that wand?"

"*Fuck*, no."

"Plan to sleep tonight?"

"Doesn't seem to be in the cards. Hand me the remote."

I floated it to her, pulled the couch afghan over me, and rolled over to watch as she scrolled through the disappointing late-night options.

Even with my roiling thoughts, however, I caught

myself in a nap shortly before dawn, then made a pot of strong coffee while Kitty washed her face. With those essentials covered, and feeling slightly closer to human after an infusion of caffeine, I sneaked her back into her hotel room, courtesy of the photos on Kitty's phone—taken just in case of such a need. She gathered her few belongings and checked out, and we grabbed breakfast at a nearby café in lieu of the promised girls' dinner. Ted called to check in during the meal, and I let it go to voicemail. While waiting for the bill, I sent messages to Bert and Arnold saying I was feeling ill and quarantining myself for the good of the installation, and then I turned my attention back to Kitty, who was knocking back espresso as if she'd discovered the fountain of youth. "Is it working?"

"Not quite. I'm at that weird place between wired and exhausted," she said. "Like, I wouldn't trust myself to operate heavy machinery, and I think I might be hearing colors."

"Want to go back to my place and try to sleep?"

She pushed the tiny cup aside. "Yeah, okay."

Kitty crashed on the couch—neither of us was eager to return to my spare bedroom—and I fell onto my abandoned bed, trying to make up for the miserable night. But sleep came only in short spurts, and by eleven, I knew the effort was futile. I opened the door to find Kitty awake again, watching antiques be appraised on TV while eating my bag of frozen strawberries, and grunted a greeting. "I'm going over. Want to come?"

"Probably best if I don't," she replied, sucking the red stains off her fingertips. "This is a family matter. Unless you need moral support…"

"I'll manage," I said through a yawn, then made myself more presentable and headed for the villa.

Night had long since fallen in Faerie, which did nothing to help my tired brain, but the smells of the garden outside my suite provided a touchstone of familiarity. I stood for a moment in the courtyard and stared up at the star-strewn sky, just breathing. And then, as it penetrated my constant mental barriers like they were nothing but wet paper, I heard Ros's voice: *Two doors down.*

The villa was pocked with little gardens—every bedroom opened onto at least one—and a low privacy wall separated the one that Kitty's and my rooms had shared from the next garden over. Following Ros's hint, I wandered back through my room, down the breezeway past Kitty's, and found the door to the next suite open. The room itself was dark, but I picked out what appeared to be a small lamp in the garden beyond, and I let myself in.

Marcus was sitting on the ground with his feet in the fountain, staring into the gently stirring water, and I cleared my throat so as not to scare him. It didn't work— he jerked and looked up in surprise—and I raised a hand. "Sorry. It's me."

He watched as I took a seat on the tile beside him. "I didn't hear you—"

"Fountains hide a lot of background noise." I kicked off my shoes and slipped my feet into the channel. "How are you?"

He paused, and I thought perhaps he hadn't heard me until he said, in accented Fae, "Numb. It's better than feeling too much, I suppose."

"Val gave you the language, huh?"

Marcus nodded. "He said it was necessary in order to be understood here. A useful trick, I'll grant him that."

I tried to tread carefully. "Are you two, uh…okay?"

"He's treated me with nothing but kindness," he replied, his voice nearly monotonic. "Told me much." He lifted the lamp and peered at the water. "Have you seen the fish in here? It's too dark now, but there are fish in the mosaic, and they *move.*"

"Oh, yeah," I said, chuckling. "First time I saw them, I went swimming for a closer look."

"In the fountain?"

"I was five." I leaned back to look at the sky again. "I mean, it had been a rough few days. I'd been eating out of rubbish bins because I ran away from home after accidentally burning my guardian to death, so you know, why not? They were pretty."

"He spoke often of you," said Marcus.

"Yeah, well, knowing him, he's going to kick himself until the end of time for what happened to you."

"That was the impression I got."

We sat in silence, listening to the fountain splash.

"You were orphaned, too?" he asked.

"My parents died when I was a few months old. Once Val realized the connection, he raised me."

"Do you ever wonder what they were like?"

"Sometimes," I admitted. "I look like my mom, I know that, but all I have are a few pictures. I've never even heard their voices—which isn't as weird a thing to say in this day and age as it must sound to you."

"How so?"

"Recordings. Audio, video…home movies…" I shrugged. "I've searched everywhere, but all I can find of them are pictures. And I can't track down their old friends or distant relatives and ask them because officially, I'm still missing and probably presumed dead."

"I'm sorry."

"Me, too."

Marcus was quiet again, then murmured, "I believed my father was a war hero. That was what they said—he had fallen in battle while defending a comrade. All my life, I've believed that, and now…"

"Have you met Coileán?" I interrupted.

"Briefly. Why?"

"If you want to know what Val's done in combat, go talk to Coileán's guard. He trained almost all of them."

"He didn't mention that."

"Maybe not, but I don't think there's anyone in this realm who would call him a coward. And I *know* he feels guilty about leaving you. He thought he was doing the right thing."

"I realize that, but—"

"But the world you know is gone, everyone you've ever known is dead, and now your father shows up out of nowhere. I get it."

"Do you?" Marcus muttered. "Yesterday—*my* yesterday," he amended—"life was good. I had a family, friends, a son...I was always my grandfather's favorite, so that didn't hurt the situation. Today?" He raised his hands and let them fall into his lap. "Gone. Everything is dust." He glowered into space, and I let him stew. "Do you know what makes it worse? Those magi, or whatever they were—I'm sure they kept their bargain. My family probably thought me dead, Titus and Fabia probably married, and I bet they were happy together. They took *everything* from me, and there's nothing I can do. Unless you know of some way to send me back?"

"No. If there's a way to use magic to travel through time, we've yet to discover it—and since no one gets visitors from the future with, I don't know, winning lottery numbers, it looks doubtful that it's even possible."

"So that's it? I'm stuck here?"

"There *are* worse places to be stuck." When that garnered no reaction, I slid closer and said, "Look...I know it must be overwhelming. And I'm terribly sorry about Publius. If it's any consolation, you know he lived to manhood. Hell, I'm proof of that—seventy-odd generations removed, but he was definitely my ancestor. Guess it doesn't make it any easier, but at least your cousin didn't get rid of him."

"You're right," he murmured. "But he...he was a beautiful boy. I had so many hopes for him, and they *stole* him from me, and I'll never see him again..."

It took Marcus a minute to re-solidify his shell of apparent numbness.

"Hey. *Hey*," I said, patting his back once his shaking

subsided. "you're not going to fix everything tonight. Why don't you get some sleep? The beds here are great, trust me, and if Val didn't tidy the room up, I'd be happy to make changes."

"I can't sleep," he whispered.

"Not tired yet?"

Even in the low light of the lamp, I saw the fear in his eyes when Marcus faced me. "I tried in the afternoon, but when I lay there, my heart started pounding, and…"

"*Ah*. Panic attack," I told him. "You've just been through a traumatic situation. This isn't unusual."

"This…*feeling* came over me that if I closed my eyes, I wouldn't open them again, or I'd be back in that box…" He took a steadying breath. "Foolish, isn't it? Nothing but weakness."

"Stop it."

"It *is* foolish!"

"And that's trauma for you." I thought briefly, then stood enough to pull my phone from my pocket. "Okay, here's the plan. I have a lovely therapist here, but it's too late to visit her tonight. Instead, what do you say we go to town and drink until it doesn't hurt quite so badly? You, me, Kitty," I said, holding up the phone. "I know a place. It's either that or sit here and wait for the fish to come out again, and they seem to sleep once the sun goes down."

Marcus hesitated. "I don't want to trouble you—"

"It's no trouble. I'm taking a sick day from work, and I mean, you *are* family. Come on, one drink. Maybe several."

He nodded, and I dialed Glastonbury. "Need you here," I told Kitty. "We're going to go get plastered, and someone has to be the responsible adult." Without further ado, I opened a gate to my apartment, then gave Marcus a careful examination in the sudden flood of daylight. "And we're going to have to do something about your clothes."

"What's wrong with them?"

"For starters, lack of trousers."

The Tavern was the only bar in the Fringe settlement, but it was all anyone needed.

What had begun as a modest drinking establishment had grown until it encompassed a full block. First came the beer garden, and then the main room was expanded (and soundproofed) to make space for a stage and dance floor, and then someone with a memory of actual taverns mentioned the idea of serving food and adding a few rooms on the new second floor in case anyone was too inebriated to stagger home. By the time I was old enough to drink—the unofficial age in the settlement was sixteen—The Tavern was the evening venue of choice for those with a thirst, and Kitty and I had sneaked over on occasion.

In general, faeries avoided the settlement, as they made the locals nervous. The Stowe clan got a pass, partly because their youngest sibling was a Fringe coordinator with barely a shred of talent, and the rest of the bunch didn't mind pitching in as needed to keep the town running. Rufus ran the school, Robbie had built most of the place, but one of the favorite Stowe sons turned out to be Adam, the right-hand man behind the main bar. With an encyclopedic knowledge of cocktails, a connoisseur's taste for whiskies, and a willingness to combine just about anything in a shaker or light it on fire, Adam had earned a spot in the Fringe's collective good graces, and slowly, others of the half fae had begun stopping by.

The proprietor—Slim to nearly everyone but his aged mother, who always spoke of him as Ricky—didn't care who walked through the door, just as long as no one started trouble. A former crafter and coordinator, Slim had retired from all duties but the bar, but that alone was enough to keep anyone busy. He was a wiry man, bald as an egg and seemingly middle-aged, but I'd seen him manhandle unruly patrons out the door without assistance. Besides Adam, Slim had one other full-time bartender—Lilian, one of Val's court—and a rotating crew of teens and twenty-somethings looking for a fun job. The three older adults could keep the rest of the staff in line—Slim was, by far, the youngest of the trio—and the bar ran like a well-wound watch. As a bonus, The Tavern had gained a reputation as a safe place for cross-court chats, and it wasn't uncommon to spot members of all three courts sitting in the shadows.

There was never a quiet night at the joint, but Thursday was only the precursor to the weekend, and Slim waved from behind the calmer front-room bar when I led our party in. "What's up?" he called, polishing a pint glass. "What are we drink—*oh*, hello, long time no see," he said, spotting Marcus, then put the glass aside and frowned. "Wait...who—"

"Slim, this is Marcus," I said, pushing him toward the bar. "Marcus, Slim. We're going to need something strong."

"Sorry," said Slim, chuckling, "I thought you were someone else. Arcanum?"

"Just a minute," I told the others, then beckoned Slim to the corner and whispered the pertinent details.

When we returned, he leaned on the bar and gave Marcus a more careful study. "*Damn*, you look like your old man," he said. "And Maria says you've had one hell of a day. What's your poison, kid?"

Marcus stared at him blankly, and Kitty stepped in to assist. "He wants to know what you're drinking."

"Oh," Marcus mumbled, "um...wine?"

Slim considered that, then shook his head. "Not effective enough. How old are you?"

"Twenty-four...uh...that is..."

"No, that's fine. You're old enough to handle this," he said, pulling a decanter and a glass from the wall behind him. "This," he said, pouring two fingers of the amber liquid, "is aged tequila. The good stuff. One hundred percent agave, several years in oak. I'll be happy to explain what that means later, but for now, you just need to know that if you don't respect it, it'll kick your ass." He pushed the glass across the bar and nodded. "All right, slug that back."

After a brief hesitation, Marcus did as ordered, draining it in a long shot. He slammed the empty glass onto the bar, breathing heavily, and winced.

"Smooth, isn't it?" said Slim.

"Exceedingly."

He poured a refill and pointed to an empty table. "You three go take a seat and work on that. Girls, I'll have the Cosmos out momentarily."

As we settled in, I leaned close to Marcus, who had grudgingly agreed to don jeans and a polo but insisted on keeping his sandals. "Slim knows everyone in town and at least half of the courts. He's a good guy. And folks tend to stay on a first-name basis around here, so if you'd rather use a name other than Marcus, tell me now."

He knocked back half of the second drink, then shook his head. "That will do. But, uh…"

Marcus jerked when I slipped into his thoughts, but I was out before he could protest. "Fae isn't a particularly cased language. Names aren't declined, so no one beyond Val would think to address you as Marce."

"I see." He sipped, swished the tequila around his mouth, and swallowed. "That sounds strange."

Kitty clapped him on the shoulder. "We haven't even gotten to English. You haven't seen strange yet, bud."

When Slim brought the rest of our drinks, he carried with him one of the five-slot pieces of wood he used for tasting flights, but I could tell by the color of the drinks that he wasn't serving beer. "Tonight's about trial and error," he told Marcus as he set the plank in front of him. "Rum, vodka, a fairly inoffensive whisky, one of my favorite bourbons, and this"—he pointed to the glass on the far right, which held a distinctive green liquid—"is absinthe. You'll need these," he added, putting a small plate with a slotted spoon, sugar cube, and glass of water beside him, "and I'm *confident* that these two ladies can get you sorted."

"I have no idea what you're talking about, Slim," said Kitty, grinning.

"Uh-huh. You're in good hands," he said to Marcus, and left him to his sampler.

Marcus was no lightweight, but Slim had given him the tools to take off the edge and then some, and he methodically worked his way down the plank. By the time Kitty showed him how to prepare absinthe, he was almost in a good mood—far more talkative than he had been, and even laughing at Kitty's bad jokes. We ordered frites and a round of beers to go with them, and as the evening progressed, Marcus slumped back in his chair with a dazed look on his face, watching the crowd ebb and flow through the bar.

I caught Slim's eye when a group walked in with instrument cases, and he came over to explain. "Thursday late-night cèilidh. They're setting up in the main room, if you want to head that way."

Kitty was excited to go, and Marcus was too buzzed to protest, so we took what was left of our food and drinks next door and scouted out an empty table away from the stage. As I returned with a fresh round of beers, the caller took the microphone, and Kitty waggled her eyebrows. "Who's coming with me?"

"What, to dance?" I asked.

"No, to start a mosh pit. *Yes*, to dance. It's not that hard."

"I don't dance," Marcus slurred.

"We'll keep your seat warm," I told her, and shook my head as she wove through the tables toward the front.

To my surprise, Kitty was *good*—maybe not the most talented dancer on the floor, but more than competent with the steps. She twirled and wove and clapped in the rows and rings, flushed with alcohol and exertion, and only took a break when the band stopped for a drink. When she returned to our table, Marcus took her hand and mumbled, "Beautiful."

"You're drunk," she countered.

"You're sweaty. And see?" he said to me, pointing to the door as some of the late-coming dancers entered in kilts. "No trousers. Why is it not a problem for them?"

"Because they're Scots," I replied.

"Huh?"

"Caledonii, I mean."

"So? Why are they special?"

"Best to just accept it," said Kitty, and slipped away again.

She was drenched by the start of the fourth and final set of the night, but by then, Marcus had retreated far enough from the edge of full inebriation to be mellow without all of the sloppiness, and he followed her onto the floor. True, his form left much to be desired, and he and Kitty ended most of the dances off to the side, holding on to each other and laughing at some misstep that had almost been catastrophic, but he was smiling—actually smiling—and I congratulated myself as I nursed another beer.

How much he would regret in the morning was another matter, but I pushed that nagging thought away and watched the dancers whirl.

"Maria."

As I rose from sleep, I realized first that I'd developed a crick in my neck, and second that I'd slept with my head on the bar table. Someone had cleared away the glasses since the time I'd promised myself that I'd just rest my eyes for a bit, and one of the staff was pushing a broom across the floor, tidying up after the night's revels.

The skylight above us showed that morning had come with a vengeance, and my eyes smarted as I glanced toward the sound of the voice and found Val standing over me.

"Crap," I mumbled, my tongue thick and dry.

Val rolled his eyes, then touched my head, and the dull ache faded to nothing. "Had fun?"

"Yeah, I…" Suddenly remembering my companions, I sat up and scanned the room.

"There," he said, pointing to another table. Kitty had fallen asleep with her head against the wall, while Marcus dozed on her shoulder. "All accounted for."

"I'm sorry, I didn't mean to keep him out this long…"

"Ros told me. Don't apologize." He slid a tall glass of water in front of me and added, "Drink this, you need it. I'll wake them."

I watched as Val shook them awake and fixed their hangovers, and then he opened a gate back to the villa and nudged Marcus through. "Come with us or go back to Glastonbury," he told Kitty and me, "but whatever you choose, girls, get some rest. *Please*."

When they'd gone, Kitty checked her phone. "It's a little after eight p.m. You want to—"

"Yeah." I opened a gate into my flat, and Kitty, barefoot and blistered, limped after me.

She soon stumbled into unconsciousness, but I've never slept well after a night out, and going back and forth between the realms had messed up my internal clock. Resigning myself to the inevitable, I restarted the coffeemaker and opened my computer, deciding that if I was going to be a wreck in the morning, at least I'd have been productive.

But even with a couple of cups down me and one of the easier books pulled up for annotation, I struggled to focus. I had no idea of how things were going with Val and Marcus, or whether dragging Marcus out for the night had been a wise move in the end. He was traumatized and mourning, I chided myself, so clearly, the smart thing to do was get him drunk enough to momentarily forget. Responsible adulthood at its finest, that.

And Toula tasked me with teaching *children*.

The shifting numbers on my computer's clock served as an indictment for my ineffectiveness, and I tried to push the mess in Faerie aside. I shoved on my headphones, pulled up a playlist of familiar reading music, and forced myself to make sense of the words on the screen.

And it worked—for a few hours, at least. By two in the morning, I'd finished the book but was no closer to sleep, and my curiosity hadn't abated. Checking that Kitty was still drooling on the couch pillow, I headed back across the border and immediately regretted forgetting sunglasses. I felt a pair manifest on my face, then opened my sensitive eyes to see Ros's smirk.

"Had fun, did we?" she asked.

"What do you think?" I grumped.

"That water would be a more sensible beverage choice for you right now than coffee, but hey, that's on you." She winked and vanished, and I looked around the central courtyard for signs of life.

The villa was quiet—I could hear the guards training out in the field beyond the walls, but everyone else seemed to have settled in for midday. Taking my best guess, I went to my wing but found Marcus's door closed. I heard footsteps inside at my knock, however, and stepped back as he answered. He was still wearing his clothes from the night before and smelled faintly of beer and sweat, but he smiled when he saw me.

"I thought you'd gone to bed," he said.

"Didn't work. How're you feeling?"

He had to mull that over. "Not as bad as I thought I would feel. Thirsty more than anything."

"*Marcus.*"

"Less numb," he admitted, and retreated into the room. "Come in. Where's Kitty?"

"Back at my place. The dancing queen is sleeping it off."

His brow wrinkled as he closed the door. "She's a *queen?*"

"No, no, it's from an old song. Kitty's just Kitty."

It might have been my imagination, but he seemed momentarily disappointed that I'd come alone.

"How are you settling in?" I asked, changing the subject. "Are you and Val, uh...getting along?"

Marcus smiled again, though it was tinged with sadness. "Yes. He was with me all morning, but he had business this afternoon. It's interesting," he added, sinking into a chair, "how much familiarity one can find in a stranger. There is much of my grandfather in Pater."

"Considering his mother, that's probably a good thing," I replied, taking the other chair. "Has he mentioned her and—"

"In detail. And what he forgot, Toula supplied."

"I didn't know she'd been over."

"Briefly, this morning. Pater said she would have a less...*biased*...view of the Arcanum."

I smirked at that and crossed my legs. "Honestly, we're not all like your friends in Ordo Lucis. Some, maybe, but I like to think I take a more diplomatic approach."

"They were not my friends," he muttered.

Briefly, I tried to read him, then took the plunge. "How are you holding up? I'm sure everything's still fresh and weird, but—"

"What can I do? I have no choice but to make the best of it. And there are worse alternatives," he added, leaning toward me. "I could still be in that wall. They could have left me conscious all this time."

That notion was enough to send a chill up my spine. "You've spoken to Helen, I take it."

"She told me what happened to the ones kept underground, and she said it's wisest not to discuss the matter with your friend Slim."

"*Definitely*. And yeah, it could be worse," I said, grasping his hand, "but that doesn't mean you have to be fine today."

"That was what Pater said...and I'm to meet someone

called Wanda shortly?"

"My therapist. She's as nice as they come, and you can tell her anything—Val knows damn well that he's not supposed to pry. If she has an assortment of cookies, chocolate chunk are the best."

A look of confusion creased his features again. "Chocolate?"

"Oh, uh…it's sweet, it's good, trust me."

Marcus considered that, then sighed. "I'm going to be asking stupid questions for a while, aren't I?"

"They're not *stupid*, you missed the last two thousand years—"

"Two thousand, two hundred, and eleven, by Pater's calculation, but who's counting? I can barely comprehend that much time, and he…"

"He got here the long way," I supplied.

"Immortality," he murmured, then fell silent for a long moment before clearing his throat. "Maria…I met a woman called Ros this morning."

I could guess from his pensive expression what Ros had stopped by to chat about. "She made you an offer?"

"Yes. As I am, apparently, Pater's heir. You know about the process? Augmentation?"

That development cut me like a knife to the heart, but I tried not to let on. "All I've heard is that it can be excruciating. Talk to Helen's brother or her husband—both went through it."

"And you chose not to do so?"

I could feel my shoulders tensing. "It's not an option. My blood's too diluted to do it with any modicum of safety. But then again, I'm not a complete lost cause," I joked. "I *did* make magus."

The corner of his mouth ticked upward. "Maga, you mean?"

"You would think, but somewhere along the way, the Arcanum decided to use the masculine for everyone. Just give up and embrace the multitude of ways in which we butcher Latin."

Marcus rolled his eyes, then sobered. "Would you accept her offer? Were you me, would you do it?"

"I can't make that decision for you—"

"I've been here *one day*. You've had, what, twenty years in this place?"

"Eighteen."

"Eighteen, then. What would you do?"

I sat back and steepled my fingers. "On the plus side, you'd have a massive boost to whatever talent you have now, you'd stop aging, you wouldn't need a score of immunizations, and you could live indefinitely. On the minus, you'd need a good pair of gloves if you ever wanted to handle anything iron- or silver-based again."

"That sounds manageable…"

"And animals would run away from you, at least anything from the mortal realm. There's a good reason why Val didn't give me a pet."

He thought that over, then said, "I've never wanted to take up farming."

"Then maybe you should consider accepting. There are worse career choices than 'high lord.' But as I said, I can't make that decision for you." I stood and opened a gate into my den, where Kitty still slept. "And in the meantime, some of us have class to teach in a few hours, so Magus Corelli's out of here."

"*Maga*," he teased.

"Don't be pedantic."

"I'm not pedantic, I'm *correct*. And you still owe me an explanation for the Caledonii."

I crossed through the gate and looked back. "You're now the heir to one of the faerie courts. Believe me, you have bigger things to worry about than kilts."

"You're saying I should accept the offer, then?"

"Yeah," I replied after a short pause, and pulled the gate closed. "I would."

CHAPTER 17

I wasn't there when Ros did her work, amplifying the effect of Marcus's fae blood until he was functionally like his father. He told me later that he'd sooner hack off a limb with a dull knife than go through that torture again, but he came through with no ill effects—well, except for one nasty surprise.

For wizards and faeries alike, magical talent grows over time, which is part of what makes the more senior faeries so terrifying to the average wizard. No one had ever considered what effect a stasis bind would have on that process. Logically, a subject properly bound should awaken just as he went under, unchanged in form or talent. The only real data available to that point came from Helen, who had been bound for eleven years and apparently looked no older when she was freed than she'd been when she was kidnapped. But Helen was an exceptionally talented wizard to begin with, and so no one officially remarked on any surge in her abilities.

Marcus was definite proof that those binds had no effect on talent. Though mentally twenty-four, he suddenly found himself in possession of an enormous talent—if Val hadn't enjoyed a boost from the realm, the two would have been nearly equal in terms of raw power. But since Marcus had little understanding of his limits or best practices, he was a walking disaster in the making.

"He's not to go anywhere without my express permission until I'm satisfied with his progress," Val told me over the phone during my lunch break, as I slugged back my tenth cup of coffee of the day. "It's far too dangerous."

"You're going to train him, then?" I asked, casting my mug full again with a two-fingered wave.

"No," he said, sounding frustrated. "It's been suggested that I might go easy on him, which would serve no one's best interest in the long run. Mina will be overseeing his education."

I frowned and stirred in cream. "Coileán's captain?"

"I trust her judgment. She'll be able to handle him."

"And, uh…does *Coileán* know about this?"

Val snorted. "I trained Aiden when the realm made him Coileán's equal. He owes me this much."

Despite his concerns about Marcus, Val insisted that I could come over, but I declined, citing my frequent excuse, work. But in truth, my work was no worse than usual. For the first time, I felt like my presence in the villa would have been an intrusion.

Val suddenly had his son, the unknown person he'd spent most of my life mourning in silence. Marcus, who'd always thought himself orphaned, suddenly had a father who was prepared to do quite literally anything to make the absence up to him. I knew they needed time, both to get acquainted and to wrestle with their emotions—Val's guilt and unexpected joy, Marcus's deep loss and trepidation about an unfamiliar future. There was nothing I could do to ease that process for either of them.

On a more personal level, I was hit by a wave of insecurity. Yes, Val had doted on and fretted over me, but as Ros had made perfectly, painfully clear, I was nothing more than his fortunate fosterling. Now, Val had his true child—a grown son, a man who looked and spoke as he did, who knew the same people and places. Next to that, what was I but the also-ran? I couldn't compete with someone who bore Val's name.

Marcus had taken the deal, passed through the fire, and would eventually no longer be a threat to random strangers. In time, he'd learn the ins and outs of Faerie, the deep-seated feuds and petty grievances and the other myriad disputes Val managed, and he'd acclimate. He'd be a son of whom Val could be proud. An heir.

And I...

Well, my magus portrait hung with the others in the hall outside Toula's office. And someday, it would still hang in the Archives' storage room, protected by magic and climate control from the ravages of the years, even once I was no longer around to see it.

The mortal realm was my birthplace and my birthright. My parents had lived and died there. My future was in Glastonbury.

The part of me that clung to the fantasy of being someone's child needed to grow up and face reality.

"They're trying to keep it under wraps, but I hear Ted's people found something big."

Startled, I looked up from my work to find Bert standing in the open doorway of my office. He rapped twice on the frame, too late, and smiled. "Sorry, didn't mean to startle you. May I come in?"

"Sure. Close the door."

He did as I bid and took one of the chairs in front of my desk—junior magus furnishings, pulled from storage on my appointment, which I'd since converted into plush armchairs. My young students were nervous enough coming to my office without having to withstand rickety furniture.

"Not something," I told Bert in a low voice. "Some*one*."

He stared at me over his glasses, blinking in surprise. "Dare I ask?"

"It won't leave this room?"

Bert mimed buttoning his lips. "Mum's the word. What on earth did they find?"

"Val's son. He's alive."

"*How*? Isn't he quarter-blooded? Quarters are mortal, yes?"

"He was locked in a stasis bind," I explained. "Kitty finally got a good look at the warnings on the box they buried him in. It was dark when we actually got to him, and then we found, you know, a *body*, so we didn't stick around for full analysis." I paused to pull up the notes she'd sent me. "Quarter fae with a talent for healing who lacked the sense to keep it a secret. I don't know whether Ordo Lucis figured that out on their own or got information from his wife and cousin, who needed him out of the way so they could hook up, but the warnings are the sort of thing the Ordo used to write about faeries in general. From everything Marcus said, they would have killed him if he'd reacted when they tested iron on him. Couldn't be sure, so they buried him alive instead."

"Good God," Bert muttered. "And he's...intact? Mentally?"

"Seems to be. Val's monitoring him." I pushed my computer away and folded my arms on the desk. "But yeah, that's the big find of the month. I'm serious, not a word."

"Of course," he replied, and sat back in the chair, absently rubbing his chin stubble. "Not to pry, and tell me to shove it if I'm crossing a line, but what does this mean for you?"

I started to tense but tried not to let on. "Nothing. Val's thrilled, and I'm sure they have a lot to catch up on."

"What about you?"

"What *about* me?"

"Well, ehm...speaking as your mentor and friend, Maria, that's one hell of an adjustment. Just found yourself a brother, eh?"

"He's not my brother," I said testily.

"Not technically, but in light of your family situation—"

"Can we talk about something else?"

"Sure," said Bert, gentle even as I snapped. "But may I make one suggestion? You have a therapist, do you not? Someone in Faerie, if I remember correctly?"

I nodded. "Yeah, she's over there."

"Make an appointment. This isn't the sort of situation you should work through alone."

I knew he meant well, but that was easy for Bert to say. As much as I could have used a session or two with Wanda, I couldn't take the risk. No matter what Val had promised about letting Wanda keep my confidence, I knew the temptation was strong for him to sneak a peek—and unlike me, Wanda had no defenses. The tangle of emotions I was trying to unknot was mine alone, and I didn't want Val to know. I was ashamed for my feelings— they marked me as an ingrate, at the very least—and I saw no reason to mar his happiness with my problems.

So I stayed away.

All through the rainy British spring, I kept myself busy in Glastonbury, tutoring my lagging first-years before their term exams and delving deeper into my research. Without any trips to Faerie to take up my time, my Archives queue became almost manageable, and Bert thanked me for picking up the pace on my end of the project. I knew he was hoping to find the silver bullet somewhere in the literature, but with no firm leads, all we could do was keep reading and experimenting, and hope for a miracle in the marginalia.

Finally, in June, my absence caught up with me. I was working one night at my kitchen table when my phone rang—an unknown number. Preparing to turn down a solicitor, I answered with a curt, "Yes?"

"*Maria?*" someone shouted on the other end in accented Fae. "*Can you hear me?*"

I held the squawking phone away from my ear, recognized the voice, and gingerly eased the phone back into place. "You don't have to shout," I told Marcus. "I'm speaking normally. Drop it down, you're going to rupture my eardrum."

"Oh, sorry," he mumbled, chastised. "Better?"

"Much. When did you get a phone?"

"Today. Pater showed me how to talk to you...are you busy?"

He sounded so eager that I closed my book and lied. "No. What's up?"

"I, um...I was hoping to see you again. Someday. My control is much better now, I haven't set any accidental fires of late..."

"*Good.* How's Mina treating you?"

"She...well...I think she enjoys inflicting pain, honestly, but Pater approves, so...it is what it is," he said, sighing. "He's never made you fight her?"

"No, Helen threw me into walls instead."

"Ah, then you understand. But, uh...it's a lovely night here, and if you aren't busy..."

The ramifications of Marcus's insertion into my life still nagged at me like a sensitive tooth, but I couldn't blame him—he hadn't asked to be in that situation—and I knew I couldn't avoid the other realm forever. "Sure, why not?" I said. "Want me to invite Kitty? She's in town for a few days."

"Yes, certainly," he replied, sounding thrilled at the notion. "And I'll be very careful, I promise—"

"Relax—you're talking to a magus, here. Be over in a few minutes."

"Maga," he whispered.

"Seriously, this again?" I hung up as he chuckled at my frustration.

For a sub-average witch, Kitty exhibited no sense of self-preservation and eagerly agreed to hang out with Marcus and me. She brought along her computer with its layer of protective enchantment and announced that it was movie night. Marcus had no idea what she was talking about, and he stared raptly at the screen as she scrolled through her catalogue of titles, most of which she'd imported from the Arcanum's extensive collection. "Any thoughts?" she asked us.

Marcus gestured toward me and said, with a little smirk, "I'll defer to the maga."

Kitty raised a questioning eyebrow, and I took a closer look at her offerings. "You've got some classics in here, haven't you? We could do *Spartacus.*'

"That's *cruel,*" she chided. "And you've lost selection privileges, missy. Let's see...okay, here's a classic we can all enjoy: archaeology and Nazi punching, part the first."

"I'm sorry, what?" said Marcus.

"Just sit back and enjoy," she ordered, projecting the film onto the screen I'd conjured on the garden wall. "I'll explain as we go."

Thirty seconds into the movie, however, we realized our mistake, and Kitty paused it while I put my fingers on Marcus's temples and said, "I'm not as good at this as Val is, so I'm sorry for the discomfort you're about to feel."

"What—*ouch!*" he cried, jerking away, and rubbed his head. "A little warning, please!"

"Oh, good, it took," said Kitty, switching into English. "Right, shh, watch. This is *totally* what I do for a living."

The movie took twice its run time to finish, as Kitty had to keep stopping it to give condensed lectures on two thousand years of European and Middle Eastern history, politics, and religion. But despite the lag, both she and Marcus were game for the sequel. Having promised Kitty that I'd convince Ted that she was due a day of vacation, I begged off and went down the hall to my old room for the night. When I awoke and checked on the others, I found them still out in the other garden, huddled under blankets against the chill and watching their fourth movie. "We raided the kitchen a few hours ago," said Kitty, holding up an almost empty bowl of popcorn. "You want some?"

I declined the unpopped leavings. "Marcus, don't you have training today?"

"I did," he replied, "but we're taking…what was it?" he asked Kitty.

"A mental health day."

He grinned. "Yes, that."

"Uh-huh," I said, folding my arms. "Well, I'll let you two explain that to Val. Good luck."

To my surprise, he acquiesced. By lunch, Kitty and Marcus had finished their *Indiana Jones* marathon, and as he had more questions than she could field, she called Aiden for tech support. "He worked up a computer that's pretty much idiot-proof," she told me later. "There's a bunch of protective blocks on it until Marcus figures out how not to kill his machine. But he can get online now."

Back at the villa, she showed him a few of her favorite informational sites, explained how to navigate, then headed for her old room next door and a nap while he began the long process of catching up. By the time Kitty called me for a gate home, she'd put her number in Marcus's phone as well, just in case.

That small gesture led to almost nightly calls for the rest of the month. While Marcus spent his days being taught and pummeled by Mina, he was obviously lonely by nightfall. Val had a court to run, after all, and there was no one in the villa even close to Marcus's mental age. Kitty and I were the only connection he had to other twenty-somethings, and so we made a point of visiting after work, either singly or together.

By early July, Val deemed Marcus competent enough to be allowed back across the border. One Monday, I'd taken my class of first-years into the competition hall to acclimate them to the larger space ahead of the Games. Arnold was away on a long weekend, but the students gave me no trouble, and I'd already received word from Toula that I'd be teaching them solo as second-years in the autumn term. As I paired them off for combat practice, I glanced into the balcony bleachers and spotted two observers near the front, one familiar and the other with a sweatshirt hood obscuring his face. Telling the first pair to get into place but hold their fire, I jogged across the mats and called, "Do you need me, Grand Magus?"

"Just wanted to see how this bunch is coming along," she said, waving to the kids as they stopped and stared, then continued in Fae: "And someone needed to get out of the house. Do you mind an audience?"

On closer inspection, I recognized Marcus beside her. "No, that's fine," I told her in kind, then turned back to the room and switched tongues. "The Games are held before an audience," I told the uneasy first-years. "Congratulations, you now have spectators. Don't let them throw you off."

For the next two hours, I ignored the balcony and focused on my young charges, alternately refereeing and coaching them on their form. One or two had promise, but I didn't expect a decisive victory from Arc 2 that year, and half of them had already opted out of the combat contest. Still, I wanted them to make a good showing in front of Toula, and they didn't disappoint. At the end of the period, she applauded as they went on their way, and I dragged myself into the upper balcony for a debriefing.

"That's what you *do*?" Marcus asked as soon as the room was clear.

"Part of it." I tucked my wand away—I used it only for demonstrative purposes—and massaged my wrist. "And much of the rest is research and Council meetings."

"You're telling me," Toula muttered.

But I noticed the glint in Marcus's eye. "You want to rumble?" I asked.

He smiled. "Is that a challenge?"

"Guys, hold on," said Toula, "this isn't smart…"

We ignored her. "Right, meet you down there," I said, sloughing off my robe. "I'll go easy on you."

"Thank you," said Marcus, "but that won't be necessary."

"Ooh, poor choice. Cockiness gets you smacked

around here."

"*Guys*," Toula moaned. "Seriously—"

"You're refereeing!" I called to her, and took up my spot on the floor.

Grudgingly, she descended to join us, and Marcus faced me, hood down and fists raised in expectation. "You're both idiots," said Toula. "Fair fight, nothing lethal, try to avoid head shots. Ready?"

She lifted her hand, and as she dropped it, I threw up a shield and started firing.

All else being equal, Marcus could have steamrolled me, and I knew it. Despite his strength, though, I had experience and combat reflexes on my side. He blocked well and hit hard, but my shield was a complex thing, maximizing the power I was able to feed into it with amplification channels, and it didn't break under the barrage. Though sweating and sore with his blows, I slowly drove him across the room, then called forth a spell I'd worked out and held in reserve: a whip-like rope of responsive flame that shot from my fingertips at my whispered command and snaked behind him. Surprised, Marcus let down his guard as he tried to avoid the fire coming for his ankles, and I took the opening and tossed him into the padded wall.

He groaned as he recovered his feet. "I yield," he said, waving his arms in surrender. "What was *that?*"

"That was me attacking your flank," I replied, letting my shield dissolve. "Hasn't Mina mentioned the importance of protecting against that?"

"Maybe," he admitted, and rubbed his shoulder.

"Are you hurt?"

"Not badly. My pride, more than anything." He grimaced as he rejoined us. "I'm already tossed about by a damn woman on a daily basis. It's humiliating."

Toula and I traded glances, and she snorted her disapproval. "Come on, bud," she said, steering Marcus toward the exit. "We're going to have a nice long talk about not pissing off half the population."

"What did I say?" he asked, perplexed.

"While you're at it, might want to mention current attitudes toward slavery, too," I called after them.

"Oh, *God*," she muttered, and picked up her pace. "Yeah, you, me, office, pronto. Aunt Toula needs to save you from yourself."

I couldn't really fault Marcus, who had much to take in, and all at once, but with the end of the term at hand, I also couldn't be there to tutor him. Fortunately, Kitty was in a research phase at work, and she was usually available for a chat—and by the middle of July, she wasn't even bothering to look at her caller ID before picking up. I overheard snippets of their conversations through her closed office door when I visited the subbasement, and she always seemed to laugh.

At least she had a distraction. The year before, she had been morose in the leadup to the Games, and she'd hidden in her office with coffee and homemade Chex mix throughout most of the festivities. I'd tried to coax her out—Eva's sentiments aside, there was no reason for Kitty to miss the fun—but she'd refused to emerge from her hole. The source of her self-imposed isolation had been, I assumed, Beth. I knew Kitty had stopped writing to her since her brushoff the summer before—there was no point in sending letters just to be intercepted, anyway, and Beth had made no attempt to pull answers from Kitty over the long year. I'd suggested that perhaps Beth had questions for her that their mother hadn't allowed her to ask—maybe she was hoping to snag a minute with Kitty in secret—but Kitty had remained unconvinced and unmoved. "I'm sure she'll tell you if she wants to see me," she'd said, and that had been the end of the discussion. And it seemed Kitty had been correct: though I'd made myself available to the Arc 1 second-years throughout the games, Beth had avoided me.

But Kitty was in better spirits that year, and I had a plan to bring her back to the Games, using Marcus as bait. Surely, I reasoned, she wouldn't mind babysitting him while I was busy on the floor.

Early on the Tuesday morning before the Games' commencement, I was puttering around my kitchen, making breakfast at home to avoid the press of the overflowing dining hall, when Kitty rang. "Coffee's almost up," I said in greeting, tucking the phone against my shoulder as I dealt with the toaster. "And I've got *news*. A bunch of the Arc 7 kids got smashed in town last night and wandered back in the dark, and some slept in the fields. One actually fell asleep straddling the camouflage ward—"

She cackled. "Oh, *no*. Headless torso effect?"

"No, just a pair of legs. Toula sent a group of them home this morning for being so irresponsible—I mean, can you imagine what the police report would have looked like? Anyway," I said, chuckling as I poured my extra-strong brew, "chaos reigns in the dorms, at least two of the Arc 3 kids are throwing up with an alleged stomach virus, so *that's* going to be a delight, and my schedule for the rest of the week is a solid-gold disaster, so can I tempt you with food and relative quiet?"

"That sounds great," said Kitty, "but—"

"No, no buts. Eat food, get gossip, this is the morning's itinerary."

"Unfortunately, I've already left town."

"What? *Why*?" I put my undoctored mug aside and scowled at the refrigerator. "There's nothing on the schedule until Peru."

"Right. I'm taking a few days as my impromptu summer holiday."

"Does Ted know about this?"

"Not exactly…"

Listening more closely, I could make out the rush and

hum of road noises in the background. "What should I tell him, then? You're on a bus to…"

"It's, uh…not a bus. I…*kind* of borrowed one of the cars."

"Kitty!" I exclaimed, laughing incredulously. "Let me guess, Toula doesn't know about this, either?"

"I mean, she gave the Team the access codes to the garage…"

"For emergencies."

"Not like anyone's leaving the castle for the rest of the week. She won't miss it. So, the plan is to head north, drive around the Highlands for a day or two, then come back south, hit London, and be home in the middle of next week. We'll keep you posted—"

"What *we*? You've got an accomplice in this?"

"Well, you know, I figured it's about time for Marcus to get out, and—"

"Wait, *wait*. You've got Marcus? Have you lost your *mind*?"

"He's going a little stir-crazy," she protested. "And he really likes the sunroof, so I can't just turn back now."

"Seriously, Kitty—"

"Good luck with the Games. And I'm going to want all the dirt when we get back. Ta."

She hung up, and I stared at my phone in disbelief for a moment before taking a bracing drink of coffee and calling Val. "Kitty and Marcus are apparently driving toward Scotland on holiday in a liberated Arcanum car," I told him. "Do you want to handle this, or should I?"

"*Liberated*?" He chuckled on the other end. "If Toula doesn't care, what's the problem?"

"She doesn't know. If he loses control—"

"He won't, especially not with Kitty. I have confidence."

"You trust him to hold it together for a week, in a small car, with a witch?"

"With the one person in the world willing to field his

midnight questions, you mean? Yes. He won't do anything to jeopardize that. Really, he has improved," he added. "Mina's satisfied with his progress. He's still working to master it, naturally, but that will be years in coming. For now, I wouldn't think him an immediate threat."

"I get it, but…"

While I struggled to produce a proper reply, Val said, "Kitty's a clever girl, and I'm sure they'll be fine. As for you, carissima filia, come for dinner tonight, before the rest of your week's insanity. It's been far too long."

I mumbled a promise to be there and hung up, listening to my coffeemaker drip its last drops and trying to process the notion that Kitty and Marcus were playing tourist together.

I sincerely hoped that she steered him away from the kilt shops. Beyond the obvious, any ensemble that included a steel dagger in his sock would only end in disaster.

I was surprised when Toula called me at home shortly before noon. She, the installation heads, and their aides had been in a meeting all morning, and I'd only just escaped from a practice run with the other referees ahead of the next day's contests. Honestly, I was hoping for a moment's peace before the afternoon's slew of last-minute list checking and safety drills, but one did not blow off the grand magus.

"What's up?" I asked, continuing to scan my inbox as I took the call.

Toula's tone was unusually icy. "Maria, I need you to come to my office, please. Now."

As I jogged up the tower staircase to her suite, I tried to concoct an excuse for Kitty that wouldn't end in an official reprimand, but nothing came to mind during the quick trip. Advocate for mercy, then? Or maybe I could plant a seed with Toula suggesting that Kitty was doing her own research—I'd just have to call Kitty and make sure our stories aligned. Bracing myself, I rapped on the door and waited for it to unlatch, then walked in, prepared to face Toula.

I hadn't expected her to have company.

A man and a woman sat on one of the office's leather couches, both regarding me solemnly. The woman I recognized—Carey Jones, the Minor Arcanum contact who had let me play with her wizard-made wand—but the man was an enigma, an elderly stranger of Carey's age with a full head of curly white hair and dark eyes that followed me intently.

"You...wanted to see me?" I said to Toula, ignoring his stare.

"Maria. Join us." She pointed to the facing couch, and I took a seat beside her. Once she'd settled in, Toula put a manila folder on the coffee table and looked me in the eye. "I'm going to ask you a question and I expect a truthful answer," she said, her tone low and tightly controlled.

I nodded, trying not to imagine all of the unpleasantness awaiting Kitty on her return.

"Have you sent digitized library or Archives material to anyone outside of the Arcanum?"

The unanticipated question threw me, and I couldn't hide my surprise. "What, uh.. *no*, of course not," I managed, recovering. "Why would you think—"

"Anyone at all. Someone in the Fringe, perhaps? Val?"

"No."

"How about contacts at other installations?"

"No," I repeated, puzzled. "Nor would I. Everyone I know at the other installations has credentials."

"You're not loaning restricted materials to an old classmate, say? Pulling something the average person couldn't request?"

"*No*, and may I ask what you're getting at?"

She sighed softly, then nodded to the others. "Maria, I believe you've met Dr. Jones, and this is Tanner Adler from the Dark Company."

"Oh. Uh…good morning," I said, still perplexed by Toula's line of interrogation.

Tanner nodded and cleared his throat. "Wish the circumstances were better."

Toula opened the folder and handed me a printout. "Do you recognize these titles?"

I scanned the list, frowning. "Yes. You pulled my library history?"

"That's not you."

"*That*," Tanner interrupted, "is a list of files we recovered from a Conclave machine. We finally got an agent into the compound long enough to copy a hard drive."

I stared at Toula, aghast. "You think I've been sending files to the *Conclave*?"

"No. Not intentionally, at least." She put the list back in the folder and crossed her arms. "I'm well aware of the existence of Gutenbook. Or is that still what it's called? Your little protection-removing app?" Seeing me flounder, she smiled grimly. "Kids think they're *so* sneaky. We do have an IT department, you realize. They offered to write a patch for the library system to plug the hole that app exploits, but I hate to think of the wailing and gnashing of student teeth that would follow."

"All right, yes, I've used it for years," I said, picking up speed, "but I would never send Arcanum materials outside! Ask the IT people, check my messages—"

"They did."

That hit like a punch in the stomach, but I tried not to show it. "So why drag me in?"

"Because I also had them cross-reference that list with the logs, and you're the only person whose checkouts match. One hundred percent of the Conclave's books have been on your account."

"They're for research!" I protested. "And I've pulled far more than those!"

"I know, honey, calm down. No one's accusing you of treason."

"But it *is* worrying," said Carey. "Do you know much about the Conclave's situation?"

More than I liked, thanks to the espionage field trips on which Toula continued to send me. "The gate's large and stable. They've lost at least ten people this year."

"It's been a bad season," Tanner agreed. "*We* almost lost an operative."

"Of late, they've been amping up the pressure for us to sell them wands," Carey continued. "With their recent losses, they may be getting desperate."

"We've seen scouting parties come through from the Gray Lands," said Tanner. "Raiders. The Conclave has held them off for now, but we could be looking at a siege situation if the numbers shift too drastically. If they were smart, they'd abandon ship, but they're stubborn." He shrugged. "The sentiment in camp is that they can beat back the Gray Landers and close the gate once they get the right tools. Optimistic fools, but foolish nonetheless."

Carey regarded him pensively. "If I may ask how foolish?"

"Let's just say my folks are getting combat pay," he replied, cutting his eyes to Toula.

"What concerns us," said Carey, turning back to me, "is the potential for attacks on our people. The Minor Arcanum was targeted the last time a rogue group of wizards needed equipment, and we don't have a nice little castle like this one to hole up in. We haven't had reported deaths yet, but my side is scared."

Toula opened her folder again and riffled through its contents. "Your research concerns witch-bloods and the nature of crafting, right?"

"More or less," I replied as she pulled out a copy of Bert's sabbatical paperwork, which included a prospectus on the project. "The stolen books—"

"Are related to your work. Every one of them."

"I swear, I don't even keep my copies in a network folder, they're all stored on my computer—"

"Yeah, IT checked that, too. For both of you."

I stiffened as I realized what she was saying. "You don't think *Bert* would—"

"I don't know. His network drive has copies of most of the books you've checked out since you *interned* with him. Guy's a library hoarder."

"I gave him copies, but Bert wouldn't share them with the Conclave!"

She merely shrugged.

"Toula," I insisted, "Bert's not a traitor. You watch him like a hawk. Has he ever sent books to anyone?"

"Not that we can see, no."

"So why are you accusing him? What has he ever done to you?"

"Lower your voice," she murmured.

I realized I'd crescendoed almost to a shout and backed off. "Bert's a good man. I know him, I work closely with him, and I spy on him for you. He's not working with the Conclave."

"I never said that he was. The current hypothesis is that there's a leak somewhere in the network, and the person on the other end stumbled onto Bert's collection. That folder was locked this morning, and IT will move the contents offline for him this afternoon."

My boiling blood began to cool at the news. "Okay. Good."

"Which leaves you. I don't doubt your sincerity, but in case the leak is coming from your end, we need to take some preventative measures. Your library and Archives credentials are revoked as of now."

"But...but you can't..." I sputtered.

"I can, and I am," she said firmly. "I'm sorry, Maria, but this is the best option."

"We're going to sneak back into the compound in a few weeks and run a scan again," Tanner explained. "If there's a new book in there, you'll have another lead."

"Just until we figure this out," said Toula as I gaped at her. "Think of it as, uh…an unplanned vacation."

Bert, at least, shared my indignation. "This is an outrage," he said, slamming his computer closed. "Staff poking through my files, reading my mail, reading *your* mail—and why? Because *they* can't keep their own network secure?"

"The best estimate they could give me was 'a few weeks,'" I muttered as he scowled at his desk. "I can't even run a catalogue search. And IT put a block on my machine, too, so I can't read any new books. I'm sorry, Bert, I tried to change her mind, but Toula wouldn't listen."

He came around his desk and stooped to grip my shoulders, pinning me to my chair "This is *not* your fault, dear," he murmured. "It's a bloody outrage, but it's not your fault. I'll get by until your credentials are restored."

"I know, but I'm really sorry.. '

"Maria." He held my stare while I tried to keep my embarrassed tears at bay. "You're a magus. You deserve better than this. *I* deserve better than this. And someday, once this mess is sorted, you and I are going to have a talk with Toula about easy scapegoats."

I nodded, grateful for his support, and silently accepted the handkerchief he offered.

"You aren't hungry?"

I looked up from my largely untouched plate and found Val watching me with a little wrinkle between his eyebrows. My lack of appetite was a pity—his kitchen staff made a roast chicken that rivaled the best of anything I'd eaten elsewhere, and I usually left nothing but bones. But after the day I'd had, the knot in my gut left little room for food.

"Tired," I replied, only a partial lie.

I didn't feel an attempted intrusion, but Val knew me well enough to see through my façade. "You're troubled."

"A little."

"I assure you, Kitty will be safe. Marcus called shortly before you arrived—they're in Glasgow for the night. Spent a few hours taking pictures in the Lake District, I believe," he said, reaching for his phone.

"It's not about that."

He stayed his hand. "No? Work, then? Complication with the Games?"

"No…Toula's making my life hell, that's all."

"Explain."

I knew that tone well enough to surrender. For the next few minutes, Val listened without interruption as I recounted the morning's summons and my unjust punishment. "Now, it's just a matter of time until one of the research librarians finds out and starts spreading rumors," I griped, resting my head on my arms beside my plate. "And since I'm caught up on my end of the reading, I can barely do anything to help Bert."

"Good." He sipped his wine, unflinching as I glared at him. "He's obviously the source of the leak. Now that you're cut off, either he'll get desperate and give himself away, or the Conclave will get desperate and do something stupid like attack the Minor Arcanum."

"You have no proof," I snapped. "*Zero*. Bert's not like that. Didn't you hear me say they think it might be a network security issue?"

"Because they're being conservative before attacking a magus head-on. Be logical, girl. He's the simplest explanation."

"That doesn't make it the *correct* explanation!"

He gave me a long, doubtful look over his glass. "Tell yourself what you like, but listen to experience, won't you?"

"Not when experience jumps to baseless conclusions."

"Beyond that." Val reached out and took my hand. "Maria...it's time."

The non-sequitur threw me. "Time for what?"

"The Conclave is a stirring volcano, and Toula knows it. That she was meeting with Tanner and Carey is testament to the scope of the problem. This will only worsen. It's time to come home. For your own safety, for *my* peace of mind—"

I yanked my hand away from his grasp. "Did you forget that part about how I'm a magus?"

"So is Helen."

"She's different. I swore to protect the Arcanum and the mortal realm, and I'm not going to break my oath just because you're jumping at shadows."

"Shadows?" he said with an incredulous laugh. "Open your eyes! Bert's using you!"

"Bert is my *friend*," I barked, going to my feet. "He trusts me, and I trust him. He respects me."

"He respects what you can do for him. Ask Ros if you'd like to know his true sentiments about witch-bloods."

My face burned with my sudden anger. "You don't even know him! You don't know anything about him! And you don't get to decide how I live my life!"

Val remained placid, regarding me with the sort of expression one might use on a tantruming toddler. "Be reasonable. You can't stay there forever, and with this Conclave matter on the horizon—"

"*Watch me.*"

"Excuse me?" he said, taken aback.

"You think I can't stay? Watch me. I'm a magus, it's my life, and I'll fix my own messes."

"Maria, you're being ridiculous—"

"*My. Life,*" I snarled. "You don't have to like it, but maybe someday you'll respect my choices."

Val began to speak, caught himself, then rubbed his face while he chose his words. "I am only looking out for your best interest—"

"You don't know what my best interest is! Ever think of that? And you've certainly been wrong about me before." I felt the warning pricking of tears and tried to blink them away. "This is my life, messes and all. When are you going to stop trying to make me something I'm not?"

"What are you talking about?"

What rushed forth surprised me with its rawness. "I've always been the stand-in. Well, now you've got Marcus, haven't you? And he's actually fae. We both know I'll never tick *that* box."

"*Maria…*"

I glared down at Val, distantly conscious that my fists had begun to shake. "Look me in the eye and tell me that you'd have kept me if Marcus had never existed."

He seemed stricken. "Maria, please—"

"*Tell me.* Tell me you'd have wanted me just for *me*. That I was enough without his ghost."

He held my furious gaze for a moment, his eyes as dark and unnerving as always, and I readied myself for a rebuke, a denial, an admonition to stop being foolish.

Instead, quite unexpectedly, he looked away.

Holding my breath so as not to cry, I ripped a gate open, stormed back to Glastonbury, and slammed it in his face.

CHAPTER 18

In the days that followed, I made no attempt to speak to Val, nor he to me. If he sent word to Marcus of my blow-up, Kitty didn't let on. Her calls were brief and breezy, quick updates as to location and itinerary. From the sound of it, they were having a lovely time, planning their stops as they went and enjoying the relative warmth and short nights of late July, and I didn't want to ruin the mood.

Several times a day, I received photos from one or both of them, visual proof that they were still alive and sightseeing. Kitty had taught Marcus to use the phone on his camera, and while his composition still needed work, he had proven to be an enthusiastic novice. His only disappointment, she reported in one call, was the universal lack of garum, a fermented fish sauce, at the table. "He thought it might just be a Scottish thing. Poor guy looked like I'd put his dog to sleep when I told him no one makes it anymore," she confided. "He spent half the night last night experimenting at reproducing it, and I woke up with, like, fifty clay jugs around the room, and he was pulling his hair out, trying to get it *just* right."

"Has he considered soy sauce?" I asked.

"Didn't work for him. He really wants it for chips."

"Tell him there's a stash in the villa, and dare I ask what you did with fifty jugs of quasi-garum?"

"I told him to make them disappear. There's no way in hell that I'm leaving that much fish sauce in the car."

The two of them might have been content to extend their travels for the rest of the summer had Ted not called me the following Tuesday afternoon. "Tell Bonnie and Clyde it's time to get their butts back here," he said. "We've got a problem. Team meeting at seven tomorrow morning."

I relayed the summons, and the travelers, who already had evening plans, pulled into the Arcanum's garage shortly after dawn on Wednesday. While Marcus collapsed in my spare room to nap, I made more coffee for Kitty and hurried into the subbasement for the update.

We arrived just as Mal brought in a tray of pastries pilfered from the dining hall's buffet. "Good man," said Ted, snatching up a cruller, and dimmed the lights while the rest of us ringing the conference room table raided the breakfast offerings. Once his computer was projecting onto the wall screen, Ted called up a picture of an overgrown complex of stone buildings surrounding a low step pyramid. "Behold, Brigadoon."

"Uh...*that* ain't Scotland," said Antony.

"Unofficial nickname," Daphne piped up, already making notes on her pad. "I don't know what the Inca called it, but the Spanish designation was 'Ciudad de los Demonios.'"

"'City of Demons,'" Ted offered. "Someone dubbed it Brigadoon a while back because of the camouflaging—" He paused as the conference room phone rang, then flipped on the speaker and smiled. "Right on time. Thanks for calling in."

"Sure thing," said the voice on the other end—female, possibly American.

"Folks," said Ted, "this is Yolanda Ford, our contact in Peru—"

Before he could finish, Mal lunged across the table toward the phone. "Lonnie? Is that you? It's Mal."

"*Hey!*" she cried, breaking into Fae, and I realized that what I was hearing in her accent was traces of the settlement patois. "The hell are you doing in Glastonbury, man? They let you out?"

"Got a job, didn't I?"

"An *Arcanum* job?"

"Eh"—he glanced around the table at the rest of the Team—"it's kind of a mixed bag. How're you doing?"

"Well, I'm up on a mountain in the dark, trying to finagle a sat phone, so…great, really. You?"

"Hungry," he replied, biting into his breakfast. "How've you—"

Ted pointedly cleared his throat, and Mal slipped back into his chair with a mumbled apology. "Classmate," he explained, reverting to English. "Haven't seen her in ages."

"Okay, settle down," Ted told him. "Everyone else, Dr. Ford is a returned Fringer, and since she's down in Peru right now, she's been nice enough to keep me apprised of the Brigadoon situation."

"Which is…" Antony prompted.

Yolanda's voice crackled with the rough connection and the breeze on the mountaintop. "Imminent catastrophic illusion failure, more or less. Brigadoon started as an Incan site, we *think*, but it's never been studied because the last inhabitants left protective measures in place. It's been camouflaged for centuries, and officially, it's undiscovered. Hang on, let me get out of the wind," she muttered.

"And the spells are failing?" asked Bob. "Why not send a magus or two out to patch them?"

"Because they don't run on magic," said Daphne. "They're powered by *dark* magic. That's what makes Brigadoon so weird."

"Yeah, we don't know who lived there last," Yolanda continued, "but we know they weren't human. There's two layers of wards in play. The camouflaging ward is easy enough to see through with the right equipment, but the barrier ward has been impenetrable until now."

"What changed?" asked Antony.

"Arc 6 got off its collective ass and shut down the nearby Gray Lands gate. It's too remote to have been a real concern, but it's kept the Brigadoon wards going strong. Now that *that* gate's closed, and with a gate into Faerie opening a few miles away, the wards are finally failing. The site isn't quite visible to the naked eye—it's like looking through a thick fog—but the barrier can be breached."

"And we're on a tight schedule," said Ted.

"Bingo. My best guess is that the wards will fail completely by this time next week. There's a mundane group doing some aerial surveying out here, and once the wards drop, those folks will almost certainly find the site from above. Before they do, I plan to 'discover' the place—or what's left of it."

"You think we're dealing with support wards?" Kitty asked.

"Presumably. The site looks far too good for its age. So now's your chance to get in and poke around before the mundies descend. I can give you a few days' cover."

"We'll be down tonight—your night, I mean," said Ted. "Give us a few hours to pack and plan, and we'll hit it."

As Yolanda signed off, Ted went around the table. "Lakshmi, has she sent you site—"

"Photos? Yes." She showed him her tablet as proof. "I'm working out a safe landing spot. We do this without support from Arc 6?"

"It's a solo hop," he said, nodding. "Bob—"

"Already on it," he interrupted, not looking up from his laptop. "Arcview's being slow this morning, but I'll pull whatever we have on the place."

"And I'll help," said Antony.

"Good." Ted pointed to Daphne, Mal, and Frank. "Pack and get some rest—it's going to be a fast trip. As for you," he said to Kitty, "maybe rest first. You look like shit, kid."

"Long night," she mumbled.

"Yeah, well, welcome back. Maria, what else do you

need from me?"

"Nothing," I replied. "I'll handle the paperwork and Toula. Call me if it gets hairy," I added, and escorted Kitty upstairs to bed.

She didn't sleep long. By midmorning, Marcus was awake again, blinking blearily in my kitchen as I worked on my end-of-term marking at the table. I called Kitty to join us and relayed to him why their trip had come to such an abrupt end. Marcus listened, silently frowning, then asked, "*Where* are you going?"

Kitty sighed. "Maria…"

I cast a projection of a globe into the air, and Kitty steered it closer to him. "We're here, yeah?" she said, pointing to the southwestern part of England. "And Peru is over here." She rotated the globe and tapped the western coast of South America. "New World, see? We shouldn't be gone long."

"To look at ruined buildings that may still be standing only because they're being held up by dark magic, which will fail within a few days?" he pressed.

Kitty shrugged. "More or less. That's the job."

"That's dangerous! And Maria *isn't* going with you?"

They looked at me and my stack of class notes. "I'm on deadline," I said, "but they'll let me know if there's a problem."

Marcus was unmoved by this information. "What if there's an emergency and you need immediate help? What then?"

"Well," said Kitty, "Daphne's competent, Ted's not bad, and if worst comes to worst, there's always Frank."

"He has talent?"

"No, but he's not above roasting our problems."

Unconvinced, he ran a hand through his short hair in agitated thought, and something within me flinched at how much he resembled his father. "Let me go with you," he told Kitty. "I know I still have much to learn, but—"

"Marcus—"

"*Please.* I won't get in the way, I could carry your things—"

"That's sweet of you, but it's not my decision," she said gently. "You'd have to convince Ted."

"Fine. Where is he?"

Seeing that Marcus was not to be dissuaded, I opened a gate into the subbasement. Ted, who was busily transferring files onto his field computer, looked up and smiled at my knock, then noticed my companions. "Hi, there!" he said, brightening. "Clyde emerges!"

"Clyde?" Marcus muttered.

"Tell you later," said Kitty. "Ted, he wants to tag along to Peru. Pretty please?"

Ted leaned back in his chair and folded his arms as he gave Marcus a once-over. "Well, now, this isn't a sightseeing jaunt. Anyone who goes is going to be working in one capacity or another, so, uh...what do you bring to the table?"

"I can carry my share," he replied. "Stand watch." Glancing at Kitty, he mumbled, "What was that—"

"Schlepp," she offered.

"*Yes.* I can schlepp."

"And throw fireballs," Kitty added.

They waited with eager, hopeful expressions, and Ted and I exchanged a look. "Schlepping is an underrated skill," he finally said. "And since we'll be dealing with altitude, it probably wouldn't hurt to have extra hands. So yeah, I guess you could do a trial run..."

"*Thanks*, Ted," Kitty began, "I'll help him pack—"

"*Ah*," he said, punctuating the interruption with an upraised finger, then pointed to Marcus. "On one condition: you clear it with your dad, and I do mean clear it. Full disclosure. That's a conversation I do *not* want to have."

In reply, Marcus pulled his phone from his pocket and stepped into the hall.

Ted shook his head as the three of us overheard

snatches of rapid Latin. "You two following that?" he asked, getting back to work.

"Oh, yeah," I said, and plopped onto the couch.

"And?"

"He's trying to explain how running around a site protected with dark magic is a good and necessary thing."

"Mm. Succeeding?"

I listened for a moment. "Maybe."

It took him several minutes to convince Val, but Marcus eventually returned triumphant, and Ted slid a printout across his desk. "Standard regional packing list, ignore it at your peril. No alcohol from this point on—it'll only make your altitude sickness worse. Drink plenty of water today. Bring pain medication with you."

Marcus looked to Kitty for an explanation, and she patted his shoulder. "I'll handle it," she assured Ted, and I sent them back to her flat via gate.

When they had gone, I said, "He's been training, but I wouldn't ask for anything complex in terms of magic."

"Oh, I'm not so concerned about that," Ted replied with a sly smile. "I finally get a few days with the craziest thing this group's ever dug up. Honestly, I don't care if he just sits there and files his nails as long as he'll take questions."

I saw the Team and their eager plus-one off at four the next morning, dropping them at the site under cover of darkness. Despite the early hour, Lakshmi and Bob were on hand for last-minute instructions. Lakshmi stood by the gate, already wearing the earpiece she sported constantly during excursions, and double-checked bags and lights as the others passed through. As usual, she chided Frank for underdressing for the weather—"You're going into the Andes, not to the beach," she said, taking over his T-shirt—and as usual, Frank patted her head and insisted he was fine. Meanwhile, Bob handed out plastic baggies of currant scones, an offering from Sylvester's kitchen, and took custody of Lothario to give Daphne peace of mind. The cat was vocally unhappy—he hissed whenever Marcus got within a few meters of his carrying case—but that couldn't be helped.

As for Marcus, he was nothing short of psyched. Kitty and I had worked up appropriate attire and gear for him, and I'd gone into town to procure a pair of good gardening gloves to protect him from the bits of steel in the Team's usual gear. Regardless of the iron-based danger—not to mention an unmapped site surrounded by dark magic wards—Marcus was almost ebullient as Lakshmi double-checked his backpack and Bob stowed a baggie of snacks inside.

"You listen to me, now," she said, standing between Marcus and the gate. "Don't be stupid out there. Do what Ted tells you. We've been at this for twenty years, and we haven't lost anyone yet. Don't break our streak."

Not even Lakshmi's warnings could dampen his spirits, however, and off he went into the darkness, trailing Kitty with a solar-charged torch in hand.

Transport accomplished, I returned to my flat to sleep. There was no rush to get to the office. I was on schedule for my final reports on the first-years, and beyond that, I had nothing to do. Cut off from the library, I couldn't continue my research for Bert. I supposed I could take books from the stacks and read them on the premises, but most of the items I requested were kept away from the public's grubby hands, and I doubted the librarians would be allowed to pull them for me. The situation was humiliating enough without spreading the news that I'd had my credentials suspended, so I decided it was safer to avoid the library entirely until Toula saw sense and ended my punishment.

I wanted to escape the castle—maybe do as Kitty had done, slip off in a "borrowed" car and drive until the road ran out—but with the Team in the field, that wasn't an option. I was on call around the clock until they returned. A jaunt into Faerie might have done me good—it would have been a welcome change when the walls of my flat started closing in—but I'd made up my mind that I wasn't going back until...well, I wasn't sure of exactly what would have to happen before I crossed over again, but there would have to be something definite. The continued silence from Val told me that moment had yet to arrive.

I missed him. There was no point in lying to myself about that. And, I reasoned, it wasn't fair for me to expect an apology from him when he had, technically speaking, done nothing wrong. So what if he'd only taken me off the street because of Marcus? He owed me nothing, much less the immediate, unquestioning love to which some part of me insisted I'd been entitled by virtue of...what? He hadn't known me—I was just an overly talented kid with a kill under my belt and a wagon full of baggage. And he'd done his best with me, I *knew* he had, but...

Val had never cried for me. He'd wept for his son, someone he'd never met.

Restless, I rolled over to the nightstand, where I kept the old photo of my parents and me in a polished wooden frame. At least Val and Marcus had memories of the ones they'd lost. I couldn't remember my parents' voices, the way they'd smelled, my mother's smile, my father's laughter. Had my mother teared up when she held me for the first time? Had my father been misty-eyed when a nurse put me in his arms? Had they sworn then—maybe not in words, but in the deep, unspoken thoughts of their souls—that they would love me and protect me for no other reason than the fact that I was theirs?

I liked to imagine that they had.

But they were gone. Zia Giulia had kept me out of charity and duty, and Val had taken me to assuage his guilt. And yes, he'd treated me well, but only because of the Marcus-shaped stain on his conscience.

Pater. Marcus had adopted the name immediately,

accepted him—and from what I could tell, he seemed to have forgiven him for his absence. There was so much of the one in the other that watching Marcus was like seeing Val before the weight of two millennia pressed him into the man I knew.

Val had never been *Pater* to me. The notion had never been discussed. After all, I wasn't his real child—I was the changeling, gifted at magic but not in the way that mattered. He'd grown fond of me, but I would never be Marcus in his eyes.

So what did I expect from him? He'd been honest with me. It wasn't his fault that the truth broke my heart.

Lonely and depressed, I turned to Bert for company and wasn't disappointed.

We had dinner at a nearby pub, greasy fish and chips and subpar beer, and I filled him in on the Peru excursion. "I can't imagine taking Marcus on a trek like that," he said, shaking his head. "Has anyone bothered yet to tell him the Earth's round, or do you think he worries that he's getting dangerously close to the edge?"

"I think Kitty's working on him," I replied, picking at my peas. "She survived a week alone with him, so maybe she's covered the basics by now."

"The heliocentric solar system? Dinosaurs? The peril of putting diesel in the wrong sort of engine?"

"She can only work so quickly, Bert."

He chuckled and reached for the vinegar. "Any idea what they're meant to find in El Demon City, then?"

"Not a clue. I think Ted just wants to have a look around while the place is untouched."

"Figures. Well," he said, liberally dousing his chips, "should they find anything interesting, do let me know, won't you?"

I raised my beer in salute and drank. "Maybe they'll find something new for us to research," I said, wiping the foam from my mouth.

Bert's brow furrowed. "You don't like our current project?"

"Oh, no, it's fascinating," I assured him, "but we haven't exactly had success."

"Which is why we keep going. You'll never discover anything with that attitude, madam."

I grinned and speared a chip. "Here's to tilting at windmills."

"It's a time-honored tradition." He ate in thoughtful silence for a moment, then asked, "Any word from Toula on getting your credentials back?"

"Not a peep," I muttered.

"Just a thought, but have you considered asking your grandfather to work on her? Massage the situation, as it were?"

I shoved chips into my mouth to give me time to think of an answer. "It wouldn't work. They try not to step on each other's toes."

"But considering it's *you* in the middle of this—"

"He and I aren't speaking at the moment."

"Oh." Bert put down his fork and cocked his head. "I'm sorry to hear that. Are you okay?"

I drank deeply to wash down the rash things I wanted to say. "Getting there."

He grunted and picked at his fish. "This wouldn't have anything to do with Marcus, would it?"

The look I shot him wasn't kind, but Bert ignored my glare. "Did you take my suggestion and see your therapist?" he asked.

"I've been a little busy," I said, spearing peas with more force than was strictly necessary.

"Not so busy that you couldn't manage that if you wanted." He hesitated, then added, "I'm worried about you, dear."

"There's no need to worry—"

"There *is*. People like us...we don't have many sources

of support," he said, pushing his food around his plate. "I've always been able to lean on my parents, no matter what's happened in the Arcanum. If you're on the outs with your family…"

"It's fine."

"No, it isn't. Look at me, Maria."

Reluctantly, I raised my eyes to meet Bert's, dark and concerned behind his thick glasses.

"We have so few people we can count on, you and me," he murmured. "Don't burn your bridges."

I shrugged weakly. "I've still got you in my corner, haven't I?"

"Of course," he said with a weak smile, and reached across the table to pat my arm. "Misfit magi against the world, eh? Best finish your dinner, now. If our intrepid explorers call in the middle of the night, you should at least get a few hours of sleep. Take it from experience," he muttered, and bit a chip in half.

I was surprised but not overly concerned when the Team didn't call that night. They would need time to acclimate and make camp, I reasoned, plus put up whatever defenses they could manage against wandering mundanes. They would have spent that day examining the site, getting the lay of the land before making their entry, and if Yolanda was right, they wouldn't need my help to get through the barrier wards.

Either that, or they had all died horribly, but I chose to focus on the positive.

Friday came and went without a peep from Peru, though, and I began to become slightly antsy. I assumed that Lakshmi, at least, was in contact with the field team— surely, she would have alerted me if there were trouble— but the radio silence, plus the complication of the tagalong, left me uneasy.

The waiting ended at three o'clock Saturday morning,

when Ted yanked me from a running dream with the blaring jangle of my phone. "Hey, Maria," he said to my mumbled greeting. "Got a sitch. Want to pop over and help?"

Ten minutes later, having acquired clothes and shoes, I rubbed the sleep from my eyes and stumbled into the Team's campsite. They'd found a suitable valley for their needs, a wide spot between two jagged, tree-draped peaks large enough for a circle of seven tents around a central fire. Dinner appeared to be winding down as I took a seat by the fire pit, and Kitty passed me a forked branch. "S'mores?" she offered.

I took a deep breath—the sudden change in elevation made me lightheaded—then exploded into a coughing fit as I inhaled smoke. "Here," I heard Frank say, then let him pull me to my feet and steer me around the fire. "Don't sit downwind until you adjust," he suggested. "And drink this."

I found a warm tin cup pressed into my hands and did as he said, tasting an unfamiliar brew. "What is—"

"*Drink it.*"

As I drained the cup, I heard Frank's voice in my head: *Coca tea, fairly diluted. Don't tell Daphne, she'd be horrified. It does the trick, I understand.*

While I rested, my head started to clear, and my breathing began to feel less desperate. Maybe it was only a placebo, but I didn't mind the tea. *You haven't tried it?* I thought, lowering my defenses just enough to let him see.

Frank smirked and shook his head. *No need. Altitude this low doesn't bother me. But seeing as I'm the one member of the party who didn't have a rough twenty-four hours, I took on tea duty. Here.* He pulled the battered camp pot from the embers and refilled my mug. *Yolanda met us shortly after arrival with the leaves. Ted made the arrangements in advance. But really, don't tell Daph. She thinks this is green tea.*

I glanced to my left and found Daphne with a similar mug in her hands. *How much has she had?*

Oh, plenty.

As my eyes adjusted, I spotted Marcus lying in his tent with the door flap down. "Did you wear him out already?" I asked Ted, pointing across the fire.

"He earned a nap," he said, squatting beside Frank and me. "Kid stopped a cave-in today, at least until we got out. We might have had to call you to dig us free otherwise."

"Cave-in?"

Ted waved dismissively. "One of the buildings we were investigating collapsed. Yolanda was right—the wards are failing *fast*. The support just so happened to go once everyone was inside. Marcus kept the ceiling up while we got the hell out of there." He helped himself to the tea and rocked back on his heels. "Nice guy," he said quietly to me. "He hasn't been any trouble, and he's followed directions. If he keeps going the way he has, I wouldn't mind taking him out again." He snorted, then added, "Don't think Kitty would mind, either."

"They're still getting along?"

Ted looked at me like I was daft. "Little more than that, I'd say."

I wrote Ted's insinuation off as nonsense. Marcus's first four months out of the wall had surely been difficult, and Kitty was one of the few people around him who couldn't throw him across the room as a training exercise. It was only natural that he'd gravitate toward the friendliest of his tutors.

Still...

No, I decided. Marcus was passed out in his tent, and Kitty was sitting a fair distance away, flambeeing marshmallows with Antony and Mal. There was nothing to see there but camaraderie.

Frank quietly snorted beside me, and I shored up my mental defenses. I glanced at him sharply, and he smiled with far too many teeth.

"Right, so what's the problem?" I asked Ted. "You're worried about triggering more collapses?"

"In a word, *yeah*. Yolanda was too generous in her estimate. I think we need to finish our work here tonight—anything later is just asking for disaster. Here's the plan." He grunted and shifted until he could pull a notepad and golf pencil from his back pocket. Ted was still active, but he was also heading toward seventy, and his joints had seen better decades. "This is the complex," he said, flipping to a rough sketch. "Central pyramid, eight outbuildings. We've hit the perimeter already."

"You don't waste time."

"You wouldn't, either, if you knew the site. Nothing of use to us yet, but plenty of leavings for Yolanda's people to pick through. Charred bones."

"Human?"

"Some. The ones that clearly weren't have been destroyed." He turned the page, showing me a drawing of a heavy, one-eyed skull. "I'm no anthropologist, but something tells me that's not one of ours."

"Certainly not Incan."

"Nope. Ah, thanks," he said as Frank, who had slipped off while we were talking, returned with a tablet. "Photos do it far better justice."

I watched as he scrolled through the daylight shots of the outbuildings, trying to make sense of the blackened bones scattered on each floor. "Some sort of burial complex?"

"Not originally," said Ted. "I think we're looking at the aftermath of a battle." He pulled up an image of a skull with a knife melted into one eye socket. "Again, I'm no expert, but that isn't a natural death. There are signs of trauma on many of the skeletons—aside from the obvious burning, I mean. And they're piled in those buildings haphazardly, like they were shoved in and forgotten. This wasn't an organized cremation."

"What the hell happened, do you suppose?"

"No clear answers yet, but maybe the pyramid will give us some insight." He showed me a close-up photo of the structure. "Atypical for Incan architecture."

My knowledge of ancient Mesoamerican building techniques being roughly nil, I could only look at Ted blankly. "How so?"

"Check out the top."

The stone pyramid terminated in a flat base a few meters square. "It's, uh...missing a capstone?"

"Nope. You're thinking of Egyptian pyramids. The ones around here were often more like bases with temples on top, see?" Ted opened another folder and showed me reference pictures. "So ours"—he split the screen to emphasize the difference—"is too small to put a real temple on top, and there's no trace of one having been there. Plus, there's a door." He zoomed in on the side of the temple and pointed to an indentation in the stone. "That thing's hollow."

"Unusual?"

"*Highly.* Which makes me think this place was never Incan at all. Hiram Bingham, eat your heart out." He flipped back to the pictures of the sprawled skeletons, some of which still wore heat-warped steel armor or flaking scraps of leather. "Now, the natives were known for telling the invaders stories about giants and headless men and races of one-legged peoples and such, but those stories were mostly designed to make the invaders go explore elsewhere. So tell me, if you were a sixteenth-century Spaniard who came across a settlement of large, cyclopean humanoids you *weren't* expecting, what would you call them? 'Los demonios,' maybe?"

I stared at the pictures, trying to make sense of the puzzle. "What you're saying, then, is that we have a settlement built by Gray Landers, protected by dark magic, in the middle of Inca territory. At some point, the inhabitants clashed with the exploring Spaniards, and...what then? Who shoved the bodies into the outbuildings and started the fire?"

"No idea!" he said cheerily. "Let's give it another hour,

and we'll tackle the pyramid, eh?"

By the appointed time, I was feeling the full effects of the medicinal tea. Marcus had rested and recovered from his exertion—faerie or not, the sudden force it would have taken to hold up a building was extreme for any beginner—and he yawned a greeting as we made our way up the mountain with headlamps and torches. "Have you seen anything like this?" he asked, gesturing toward the magical net that surrounded the site like thinning smoke, a system of ropelike strands slightly darker than the night around them.

"Wards? Yes. The system around Arc 2 is more complex than this one," I replied, puffing up the path. "*Dark* magic wards? No. And you've been able to pass through without difficulty?"

His headlamp bobbed as he nodded. "It tingles, but there's no pain."

"Bad sign for structural integrity."

"But good for us, yes?"

"Unless that pyramid collapses while we're inside…"

My pupils contracted as Marcus's light swung my way, and he chuckled to himself. "What's funny about that?" I asked.

"Nothing. It's your expression—you look like Pater when you're disquieted."

"We don't look at all alike," I muttered.

"Feature for feature, no," he concurred, "but I've seen that face."

Even with the tea at work, I saved my breath and let it go.

Soon, we crested the path and entered the high valley, passing through the failing wards without impediment. I could feel them try to block me, but rather than deliver a painful shock, they gave me a brief sensation of gentle pins-and-needles that passed almost as soon as it began. Counting heads, Ted ascertained that no one had been left behind, then dropped his gear and started setting up lights outside the pyramid's sealed entrance. "All right, Magus," he called, waving me over. "Think you can move the slab?"

I examined the door by torchlight, noting the weak web of dark magic sealing the space between the rough-hewn stone and its casing, then stepped back and stretched out my hands. Whispering to center myself, I channeled my will through my fingertips, flinging forth cords of magic that anchored themselves in the rock. With a tug, the stone began to shift, grinding against its neighbors, then pulled free and fell into the grass.

"Nice," said Ted, patting my shoulder, and strode inside.

As the others filed after him, Marcus caught my elbow and murmured, "You made that look *easy*."

"Just practice," I replied.

"It's more than that."

He was regarding me with admiration, I realized, and brushed it off to hide my surprise. "They didn't make me a magus for my beauty and charm."

"Mm. Obviously not," he agreed solemnly, though the grin gave him away.

I started to protest, but Ted's shout from inside the pyramid cut me short: "Get in here, pronto! Holy *crap*, we've got bodies!"

Running inside, I found the others standing in a rough semicircle around at least a dozen skeletons. Unlike the ones in the ringing buildings, these hadn't been burned, and their clothing was more complete—full breastplates, tattered clothing, even a crested helmet.

"Spaniards," I said, holding my light high to see the scattered remains.

Antony, who had squatted beside the nearest of the bodies for a closer look, stood and scowled at the scene. "Not a proper burial. Even if they'd been rushed, wouldn't they have laid the corpses out in some sort of order? What did they do, just toss them in and—"

"Hey, guys?"

We turned to Mal, who had retreated to the opening for a better look at the stone I'd pulled away. "Check this out," he muttered.

It didn't take much imagination to see what was making Mal look so queasy. The inside surface of the stone, now face-up where I'd left it, was crisscrossed with grooves and cuts, particularly at the edges. A glance back at the skeletons showed swords lying with some of the bodies—*broken* swords, mostly. "The wards," I whispered.

Kitty ran her fingertip over some of the deeper defects in the stone. "They were buried alive," she mumbled. "*Oh*, the bodies—"

"Weren't bodies yet when they came in," Ted finished. "Damn it, that...that's a hell of a way to go."

As one, we turned to Marcus, who had blanched and stepped back from the door of the tomb we'd just opened. "It's okay," Ted told him gently, "you don't have to come any farther. Why don't you sit outside and keep watch, hmm?"

Relief flickered across his face, but it faded as he looked at Kitty, who was adjusting her headlamp to press on. "What if it collapses? If the wards fail, and you're still inside—"

"I'm going in," I said, cutting him off. "We've got it. If there's a problem, give us a shout or something."

I could that tell the notion sat uneasily with him, but Marcus remained outside the pyramid, watching as we made our way down the stone corridor into the heart of the structure.

Better safe than sorry, Frank thought. *If he started ruminating about this and had a panic attack...*

"Are you *trying* to give me nightmares?" I asked, stepping over a femur.

He chuckled, then stopped short and shone his light toward a skeleton a few meters ahead, which still sported the remains of what appeared to be a dark-colored habit.

"Look at that."

I crouched beside the body and gingerly extracted a leather-bound book from the skeleton's embrace. The rest of the party gathered around, and I passed the find off to Antony, who among us had the best training in the preservation of delicate codices. He cradled it in the crook of his arm, barely cracking the spine, and gave the first pages a cursory examination. "Spanish. The hand's pretty clear. And I see dates—this might be a diary."

Ted groaned and pointed to the exit. "Okay, folks, time out. If there are traps ahead, I want to know about them."

Rejoining Marcus, who seemed pleased but perplexed as to our early return, I explained the situation while Daphne pulled together a cushioning spell to protect the fragile book until the Archives could work on it. Ted sat on the pyramid and scanned the pages by headlamp, his lips moving as he worked out the words—his Spanish was rusty, but he could read it better than anyone else there that night, seeing as I'd only had to pick up Old Spanish in my research. Half an hour later, as I tried to surreptitiously move closer to Frank—even in late July, nights in the mountains were freezing—Ted finally looked up from the book with a grimace. "Well, the good news is there are probably no traps. The guys in there triggered whatever defenses the pyramid had, and with the wards as weak as they are, we shouldn't have problems."

"And the bad?" asked Mal.

"I'm going to have nightmares for a week." He closed the book and stood. "Our friend back in there was Arcanum, sent along as clergy on this expedition. Apparently, we had half a dozen or so plants in the group. They were carrying books for an outpost."

"Probably the Bolivian settlement," said Kitty.

"My thought exactly," Ted replied. "Maybe these books were why it vanished." Catching Marcus's expression, he explained, "When Europeans began exploring and colonizing over here—"

"Among other things," Antony muttered.

"—the Arcanum sent people as well. Some mixed in with the other settlers, but in a few cases, we tried to establish independent settlements hidden from mundanes—much like this place, I suppose. Anyway, all of them failed but for the one in Brazil. The Bolivian outpost is infamous for simply disappearing. It's the Arcanum version of the Roanoke Colony...well, except the Roanoke mystery was eventually solved. No one's ever provided a definitive answer as to what happened in Bolivia."

"Tell you later," Kitty whispered to Marcus.

"I mean, it's unsurprising that so many of our settlements failed," Ted continued. "There was virtually no support here, and since so much of the indigenous wizard population was killed off after the Great War, the settlers had no one to turn to in case of emergency."

"What about gates?" Marcus asked.

Ted shrugged. "That's a higher-level skill. If something happened to the ones who could make gates, the rest were stuck." He glanced back at the old book in his hand. "Assuming our diarist had his facts straight, their camp was set upon by things out of the Gray Lands in the middle of the night. They carried off most of the Spaniards' food and water, plus the bulk of their treasure—items they'd taken along the way, I suppose. The Arcanum's books were hidden in one of those chests."

"And they tried to retake them," Daphne murmured.

"Yeah—ostensibly for the gold and whatnot, but same result. They tracked the pillagers back here and saw them disappear, which was almost enough to make the men run. I mean, asking mundanes to fight oversized cyclopes was bad enough without throwing magic into the mix. But the wizards in the group realized they were dealing with a ward situation, and our priest here"—he tapped the diary for emphasis—"got a little long-winded and creative with his prayer while two of his compatriots sneaked away and blew a hole in the wards."

Antony's brow had furrowed as Ted recounted his findings. "Hang on, wait. I didn't think cyclopes were talented."

"They aren't," Frank cut in. "Not according to the Fringe, at least. They're more or less dumb muscle."

Ted nodded. "Right. But our brilliant forefathers didn't have that sort of intel, and so they were unprepared when a party of svartálfar came running out of the breach."

Most of us winced, and Kitty explained to Marcus, "Nickname for one type of Gray Lander. I'm not sure what they actually call themselves. A little smaller than us, allegedly purple, and at least as gifted with dark magic as we are with the regular stuff. But I thought they were subterranean," she said, glancing at Frank.

"Often," he replied. "Not always. And keeping bodyguards around sounds like par for the course for them."

"Long story short," Ted resumed, looking around our huddle, "the Gray Landers had taken the loot into this pyramid, where the svartálfar seemed to have been living. Some of the Spaniards chased them in to recover their stuff, and one of the svartálfar closed the door and engaged the wards behind them. The Spaniards killed them all, but then they couldn't get out."

"What about the wizards who got through the barrier wards?" Mal asked.

"Killed in battle, it seems. The few men left standing outside the pyramid burned all the corpses and told the men trapped inside that they'd come back with help. But there were no wizards left in their party, and I guess they weren't quick enough."

"And they wouldn't have been able to find their way back," Daphne added, looking unwell. "Once they got beyond the wards, their odds of finding the hole again couldn't have been good. The wards might have even healed themselves, depending on how the Gray Landers built them."

I looked again into the dark maw of the pyramid and quickly glanced away when my headlamp found bone.

"I think the priest knew," Ted murmured, giving the book to Antony for safekeeping. "It would have taken a strong wizard to find and free them. He said he wasn't powerful enough to move the door…and since the end of that diary discusses the Arcanum in detail, I'm guessing he suspected that no mundane would ever stumble onto it. Shit." He sighed and shook his head. "So, who's up for a spot of tomb robbing?"

We looked at each other in silence, no one rushing to make a decision, until Frank stood from his seat on the pyramid and brushed off his trousers. "We're wasting time, and no one in there is going to object. Come on."

"I don't know," said Daphne, "it just feels *wrong*…"

"The books were for the Bolivia camp, right? We're rerouting them to another installation. Think of this as delayed delivery."

"But…all of those people in there…"

He grunted as she wavered. "Okay, stay with Marcus. Anyone else with me?"

The rest of us followed him into the pyramid, moving quickly and saying little. At least we didn't have to hunt long—the men had piled their stolen treasure in a room just off the main passageway. It was telling, I thought, that there were no bodies near the gold and books, which must have seemed far less important than they previously had as the food and water ran out and the torches sputtered their last. With a quick spell, I levitated the mass toward the exit, stepping over the dead and cringing every time something—*someone*—crunched underfoot, then dropped it in a heap in the grass. "What now?" I asked Ted.

He took a long look around the site, arms folded and mouth tight. "Let's get the goods back to camp, and then I think it would be best if we wiped this place off the map."

"But Yolanda—" Mal began.

"Will understand," he said firmly.

I took my phone from my pocket. "Shouldn't we call this in first?"

Ted sighed but waited as I quickly explained the situation to Toula. When I returned to him, I reported, "She says to be careful. Do what you think is best."

"Great. I'm going to need your help."

Bypassing the mountain path, I opened a gate straight to the Team's base camp and floated our prize through, and Ted sent everyone but Marcus and me back to begin sorting it. Once the three of us were alone, Ted muttered, "This pains me, but can you scour the site? Just make it all disappear?"

"*All* of it?" asked Marcus. "I can try, but I've never attempted something so—"

"Stand back," I interrupted, and stepped into the complex. I could feel the weak pull of the wards around us, but there was nothing else actively impeding my work. I stretched out both arms, fingers splayed, and closed my eyes as I breathed and centered myself, focusing on the spell I needed to weave. Once I could picture it in my mind, I drew a stream of ambient magic into me and out through my fingertips, and I opened my eyes as brilliant ribbons wrapped around the outbuildings and the pyramid, covering each with a tight spell that only the magically attuned could see. When the spell solidified, I shot a final pulse through my work, a concussion that rendered the stones and bones inside the wrappings into no more than fine dust. The spell collapsed, and with a wave of my hand, I sent a blast of wind whipping around me, scattering the debris to the night.

Marcus gawked, but Ted nodded his thanks. "Okay, clean slate," he said. "How about we leave a little something for Yolanda?"

I frowned. "What did you have in mind?"

"*So* glad you asked." He pulled out his phone. "Let's look at some reference pics, and we'll plan it out."

It took another two hours before Ted was satisfied, but

the faux ruins we left would be sufficient to mollify our Fringer archaeologist. By the time I opened a fresh gate to the camp, I was bone-weary with the hour, the elevation, and the strain of my casting, and even Marcus, who had assembled a few buildings at Ted's direction, seemed to be dragging. As we shuffled through, I noticed lights in one of the tents, and then Kitty popped her head out of the door flap. "You need to see this," was all she said before ducking back inside.

We found the rest of the Team sitting in a tight circle around the pile of old books. "What do we have?" I asked, squatting to take a better look.

"A lot of duplicates," said Antony, gesturing toward the bulk of the volumes. "A few I'll want to review with Bob once we get them protected and stabilized. And then there's this." He held a thick book toward me, its brown leather cover rotted through in places to reveal the wood below.

I took it from him and gingerly opened to the first page, which was covered in a tight, neat hand—Latin, I saw after a quick scan, hardly unusual for a book of that age. "Any idea what this is?"

Kitty stood and pointed to the inside cover, where two letters had been carved into the wood: *E N*. "We've only just started reading it," she said, "but this may be something extraordinary." Her voice faintly shook with excitement. "I don't think Erik N ger was a myth after all."

CHAPTER 19

The members of the Team back in Glastonbury barely complained when Ted called to wake them early on Saturday morning. As the others dumped their hastily packed gear in their offices and the corridors, Bob took custody of the book, Lakshmi set up the projector, and Sylvester, having been in the middle of breakfast preparations when Bob was recalled to work, started tea and coffee in the Team's kitchenette while he worked on eggs and toast. By eight, we'd begun the caffeination process, and while Frank ate an entire package of bacon, Bob projected the first page onto the conference room screen.

"Right, then," he said, stepping back to look at the magnified characters. "No immediate signs of dating, but I've only looked through the first leaves. Vellum, obviously. The leather over the cover was a later addition, so for the moment, I'd be comfortable dating this to the proper period. Scribe has a clear hand—that's textbook Carolingian miniscule—but on first impression, this appears to be a personal book of some sort. Definitely not Church material. As you can see, we're dealing with Latin—"

"We are?" Marcus interrupted, scowling at the projection.

Bob nodded. "Medieval scribes tried to save space with their text blocks, and they employed a complex system of sigla—*systems*, actually," he amended. "What I'm seeing here suggests a British scribe."

"It just takes a little practice," Kitty whispered as Marcus rubbed his eyes in frustration.

Before Bob could resume his lecture, Mal raised his half-eaten toast to catch his attention. "Time out, please. For those of us who *don't* have an encyclopedic knowledge of the Arcanum's back catalogue, what's the big deal here?"

"Oh, ehm...Magus," he said, glancing my way, "I believe this is in your wheelhouse, yes?"

"Sure," I replied, grateful that I didn't need to consult my the locked-down books to recall the basics. "Erik Niger, *if* he existed, lived in Britain or southern Scandinavia sometime in the tenth century. He would have predated the Arcanum, but not by too much. We have none of his supposed writings or any firm biographical information on him—nothing but references to him in other people's work, and the last of those references was in the early sixteenth century."

"Close to the time that the Bolivian outpost was established," Kitty pointed out.

"I mean, we don't even know where the 'Niger' name came from," I continued. "Maybe he was dark-haired or something, who can say? But *supposedly*, he discovered the trick to producing wands without going to a witch-blood and wrote a book about it...which was never seen again."

"Okay," said Mal, propping his chin in his palm while he studied the screen. "So, assuming for the moment that the story's true, how would some random Scandinavian-Brit wizard's book end up on a trip to *Bolivia*?"

The table's eyes turned back to me again, and I quickly mulled over the variables. "Bert and I have discussed the possibility of an historical Erik Niger, and our conclusion was that if he existed and wrote a book, it would have been far too dangerous for public dissemination. Assume Simon Magus got wind of it in the early days of the Arcanum. If the records are accurate, he had a firm clamp on most of the crafters working in that period, which meant that he controlled the production and distribution of wands. He wouldn't have put a how-to book in circulation that could have undercut his control." I sipped my coffee as the mental picture coalesced. "Say the book existed. Say that it was packed off into the early Archives until it became no more than rumor. And then, centuries later, when a new outpost was struggling…maybe someone pulled it from storage for them."

"But why bother?" Daphne interjected. "The people back in Europe could have gone to them by gate whenever they liked, so why leave them to craft for themselves? For that matter, why put wizards in a mundane expedition?"

"Well, I can think of a reason," said Bob. "Consider the period—the Bolivian outpost was established around 1540 and disappeared by 1560. In the middle of that, you had the transition between the Spanish Century—"

"Five Spanish grand magi in a row," Kitty murmured to Marcus.

"—and the return to France with Grand Magus Roux in 1550. Like her mundane countrymen, she was more concerned with our North American prospects, and so several of the early Central– and South American outposts either consolidated or went home during her tenure."

Daphne nodded. "Right…"

"She probably wouldn't have sanctioned much support for a little settlement in Bolivia—it wouldn't have been a priority. Maybe they asked for assistance and were denied." Bob folded his arms and shrugged. "There was a suspicious loss of records during Roux's tenure, particularly pertaining to the early New World outposts. Probably a case of selective executive arson. The prevailing theory as to why the Bolivian group fell off the map is that anyone there with significant talent either moved to one of the other settlements or was killed. Maybe Roux refused to help, or maybe they didn't have anyone talented enough to open a gate, let alone get a message through. Perhaps those books you found weren't supposed to have left the

Archives—maybe those wizards were making a little off-the-record trip to help their countrymen in the wilderness." He paused, grimacing to himself. "It's entirely possible that the outpost had disappeared by then. Maybe they tried to get there by gate and found nothing left. Hiking through the mountains with a bunch of armed mundanes would have been a safer way to look for them."

"And if help wasn't coming from the top," said Daphne, "then a book about homemade wand production—"

"Would have been priceless," he finished. "With all of that in mind, I'd guess that whoever packed this book off to South America believed it to be the genuine article, which means…"

Ted sighed and rubbed his field stubble. "It means we're going to have a long day. Who wants to transcribe?"

Anyone with an Arcanum education had suffered through at least a taste of medieval paleography, and people like Bob and Antony, whose former jobs had involved far too many handwritten books, could decipher more quickly than most. Still, even with the fairly clear script, we spent all day working through the book, with Bob decoding the sigla aloud and Kitty typing it up, making corrections as she went. I pulled up a computer beside hers and worked from her transcript, translating it for the members of the Team who had endured only the bare minimum of Latin classes (or, in Mal's and Frank's cases, none). The others did what they could, taking shifts to make tea and bring food in between naps on the office couches. Marcus even offered to take over transcription, but Kitty turned him down. "You're two-fingered on a good day," she said, massaging her wrist. "Get some rest."

While it was difficult for me to do more than the mental processing needed to switch between languages, particularly as the work went on and my lack of sleep caught up with me, I couldn't suppress my mounting excitement. What I was reading was either lunacy or genius—perhaps a bit of both—and after two and a half years of fruitless research with Bert, I wanted nothing more than to test the techniques described on Kitty's screen. If our supposed Erik Niger was indeed the genuine article, and half of what he had written was accurate…well, the ramifications were huge.

And not all in a good way.

Suppose wizards could learn to craft at the level of a trained witch-blood, thereby destroying the monopoly witch-bloods had on the market of wands, rods, and other tools. What use would the Arcanum then have for its witch-blooded cousins? As it stood, even die-hard purists couldn't escape the fact that they needed associates with tainted blood—it was the single truth that shouted down any suggestion of finishing the good work Grand Magus Mulligan began. And *that* was a sobering thought. Mulligan had taken hundreds of Fringers hostage, partly as an incentive to make Slim craft for the Arcanum. What if he hadn't needed Slim? What reason would he have had then to let anyone in the Fringe live?

Wizards *could* craft, of course—the Minor Arcanum was proof of that—but the end result was seldom good. Maybe, even with the techniques spelled out in the old book, no wizard-made tool would quite equal of that of a witch-blood. But what if they were close?

When we called a halt for dinner—by then, Bob was losing his voice, and Kitty's fingers had begun to cramp—I pulled Ted into his office and locked the door. "You've been reading along?" I asked softly, standing close to him to keep my voice low.

He nodded. "Something else, isn't it?"

"Yeah. What are we to do with the book?"

"I was about to ask you the same question."

"Well, if it were up to me, I'd take it to Toula and keep it quiet until she decides," I replied. "Personally, I'd like to look it over with Bert."

"*Bert*?" Ted echoed, flabbergasted.

"This is groundbreaking for our research—"

"And he may very well have been leaking material to the Conclave for years. It's okay, I got the quick version," he added as I jerked in surprise. "A little warning from the boss, and an explanation as to why I shouldn't ask you to do any research for us right now. Don't worry, no one else knows…well, maybe Frank," he allowed, "but I haven't said a word."

My cheeks warmed even as Ted tried to reassure me. "Bert's not behind the leak. He wouldn't do that. I've *worked* with him, Ted, he's not double-agent material."

"That's above my pay grade. But for now, all things considered…don't you think it would be best if we didn't share the text with anyone until Toula clears it?"

"I suppose," I muttered, then had a nasty thought. "Do you have a spare computer down here?"

Frowning, he pulled an old laptop out of a filing cabinet. "Still runs, but I'm sure it wants upgrades. Why?"

"*My* books are the ones that were leaked. What if the weak point is my computer?"

His eyes widened. "Oh, shit," he said, and hurried after me as I jogged back to the conference room to scrub the translation from my machine.

Ted and I inhaled sandwiches, then left the rest of the Team at dinner to catch Toula in her office. From the looks of it, we'd only *just* caught her—she sported sweats and had slung an overnight bag over her shoulder, and she was packing her computer when we came in. "Hey, guys," she said, shoving the computer into its case. "How was Peru? Anything interesting?"

I glanced at Ted, then back at the grand magus. "Are you going anywhere with reservations, or can we talk now? It's important." And then, feeling Toula probing at the edges of my mental defenses, I dropped the walls and thought, *If you're just going to see Coileán, this is bigger.*

Even if I had yet to acquire the knack of projecting my thoughts, Toula was adept enough to pluck the message from my mind. "Of course. Have a seat," she offered, and pulled her phone from her pocket. "Just let me send a quick text…"

Dinner and a movie? I thought. *Something more exciting?*

The irked look she gave me over her phone spoke volumes.

Once we had Toula's attention, Ted and I reported on our findings. By the end of the condensed recap, her jaw sagged slightly, and she ignored her phone as its screen flashed with a reply message. "You really think it's genuine?" she asked us.

Ted could only shrug. "At this point, it's too early to tell. Bob seems optimistic, but we'd need time for analysis—"

"And someone to test the instructions, naturally," I added.

Toula ran a hand through her hair, then leaned back in her chair and stared at the ceiling in thought. "You'll have it transcribed by morning?" she finally asked.

"Odds are good," said Ted. "Can we keep it that long?"

"Protect it overnight. I need to think this through," she replied, and collected her bags. "That book does *not* leave the subbasement, understood?"

He saluted. "You got it, boss."

"And not a word about it to anyone outside the Team. *Anyone,*" she repeated with emphasis, locking eyes with me.

Toula had yet to acquire a gaze as disconcerting as Val's, but the warning in her stare was more than sufficient on its own. "Secret's safe," I said, and raised my mental walls once more.

Not until one the next morning did we finish our

transcription work, and by then, I was almost too exhausted to see straight. I stumbled up to my flat and collapsed onto my unmade bed, still dressed, and had just enough presence of mind to kick off my shoes before falling asleep.

Left to my own devices, I probably could have slept all day that Sunday, but Toula called to rouse me shortly after ten. "Sorry, honey," she said as I mumbled something vaguely akin to a greeting into the phone. "My office in half an hour, okay?"

"Not dressed," I slurred.

"Just pull your hair back and throw a robe on. That covers most fashion sins."

I knew better than to argue, and Toula had the decency to have coffee ready when I arrived. Ted was already waiting, looking slightly more chipper than me if still raccoon-eyed, and I sat beside him while Toula opened her computer.

"Thanks for the late-night work," she began, pulling up the transcription. "I know that was a beast, and please convey my thanks to Kitty and Bob if you see them before I do." She steepled her fingers beneath her chin. "I'm not going to lie—if this is more than a hoax, it's *major*. I'm going to assemble a team of archivists to examine the book itself, and if they have any reason to believe it might be genuine, then we'll need volunteers to read it and test his instructions. What's his supposed secret, anyway? I haven't gotten that far."

"Heavy meditation," I replied between sips. "He describes a technique where you bring yourself to the verge of a trance, and then you sort of...well...suppress yourself, I guess. I didn't exactly study it while I was typing."

"Mm. So basically, you put yourself into a hyper-focused state, and that fixes it?"

"He describes it like forcing your aura back and away— almost like stripping it from your hands. Says it's a difficult state to maintain, and it's quite painful, but if you do it properly, you mute your natural energies to the level of a witch-blood—at least around the parts of you doing the crafting."

"And you wonder why this never caught on," Ted muttered.

Toula grimaced in understanding. "I've never tried aural manipulation, but everything I've read about it says it hurts like the dickens. Probably a good thing that this method never made the rounds."

"If you're desperate enough…" I said, shrugging.

"Look, I understand desperation, but pain alone can kill you. If there's any truth to that book, then it's a manual for unintentional suicide. Still…" She paused, collecting her thoughts. "I can't risk releasing this book for general consumption until I'm convinced that it's harmless, but in the meantime, it might serve as excellent bait."

"The Conclave," I murmured.

"Bingo. Here's my proposal, and tell me if you hate this," she said, pushing her computer aside. "We pack the book off to Faerie for the time being. Safekeeping," she explained as Ted's mouth opened. "Coileán knows at least as much about old books as the folks in the Archives do. He won't let anything happen to it."

Ted's brow furrowed. "You're sure about that?"

"We're talking about a guy who has foam blocks scattered around his library," she replied, rolling her eyes. "And who complains *vociferously* if one should happen to bend certain spines too far—trust me, I ransacked the place during the Mulligan years. He'll keep this book safe if I ask nicely."

"And…you propose to send a team of archivists into *Faerie*?" I pressed.

"Ha. No, they won't touch it until I bring it back. What I want to do is leak the news and put a dummy copy in the Archives—explain that it's completely off-limits for now, throw up some tripwires, and see who comes snooping."

I frowned at that. "If the leak is an IT problem, then why would you expect someone from the Conclave to find a way into the Archives?"

"Because maybe it isn't just an IT problem," she said, and held up a finger as I started to protest. "I've got to cover all the bases, Maria. We put a lookalike in the Archives, somewhere protected but still accessible to the right people. We keep security cameras on it and alarm wards around it. If someone goes for the bait, the cameras will see all, the wards will alert security, and we'll find the source of the Conclave leak."

"You *honestly* think Bert's behind it," I snapped, still too tired to be properly cautious. "Unbelievable."

"I never said—"

"People are *dying* in Alaska, and you don't give a damn. But copies of a few books go missing, and it's, 'Oh, let's set up a sting operation!'"

Toula stared at me without speaking while I huffed my indignation. After a moment of icy silence, she asked, "Are you finished?"

I glared back at her but said nothing.

She folded her hands on her desk and held my gaze. "I give much more than a damn," she said softly. "Do you want to know how many in the Conclave have died as a result of that fucking gate? I can tell you name, age, and manner of death. I carry guilt for every one of them because yeah, we could have patched the gate years ago. But I'm trying to hold this organization together. If the Conclave successfully splinters off, then who's next? Maybe we end up with a few dozen arcana again. *That* worked so well. So what would you do, Maria? Would you close the gate and wait for the Conclave to become desperate enough for wands that they attack the Minor Arcanum or us? Or would you do nothing and watch them die because they're too damn stubborn to return to the fold? There's no threat of punishment if they return—I've made that abundantly clear. All they have to do is reaffirm their loyalty to the Arcanum and their willingness to abide by our rules." She cocked her head and slowly blinked. "Well? What would you do?"

"I don't know, but people are dying."

"Yes, thank you for alerting me. The Inner Council does a fine job of that already. But seeing as you have no better solution—"

"You could always storm the compound," Ted interrupted, holding up his hands in placation when we turned on him. "Just a thought, don't mind me."

"You're not the first to suggest that," said Toula, rubbing her shoulder. "We could probably do it without too much bloodshed—at least on our side—but it would push us into conflict with the Minor Arcanum. I want the Conclave to disband and come back to us, but they need to do it of their own volition. And we're also trying to avoid a Waco situation, you know? Go look it up, kid," she told me as my confusion registered.

Ted nodded. "I get it, but how big a concern is the Minor Arcanum, anyway? You think they'd try to attack us outright?"

"No, probably not. It's…well…it's the principle of the thing, see. This matters to them. If they had their way, we'd at least close the gate and let the Conclave fend for itself. Of course, now that the Conclave's trying to coax them to sell their wands, the sentiment in the Minor Arcanum is shifting more toward caution—they're worried about attacks," she explained. "Desperation is a *powerful* motivator. Which is why I suggest that we go forward with my plan to bait a trap with your book. If the Conclave has a friend on the inside here—if the leak is anything more than a network breach—then the book should prove irresistible." She looked my way and arched an eyebrow. "Unless Magus Corelli has a better idea?"

"No, Grand Magus," I forced myself to mutter. "Maybe this will finally set your mind at ease about Magus Wold."

"Let us hope," she replied, and pulled her computer into position again. "All right, I'll get the wheels in motion, and I'll let you know when I need you again. Play this close to the vest."

"Of course," said Ted. "Nothing but discretion here."

But Toula had eyes only for me. "I mean it, Maria. It's time to be a team player."

If Bert was surprised to get a last-minute brunch invitation from me, he proved to be game for the outing, even if I asked him to meet me at a pub far less popular than our usual watering hole. By the time he arrived, I'd already snagged a back booth with a clear line of sight to the door, and Bert, picking up on my unease, looked over his shoulder before he slid into his high-backed seat. "Are we expecting trouble?" he murmured.

I waited until our bored server took his food order and left him a lager in a nearly clean pint glass, and then, keeping my voice low and one eye on the front windows, I told him everything—the book, the trap, all of it. He listened in silence until I finished, then reached across the table and gave my hand a tight squeeze. "Thank you," he whispered. "You're a good friend, Maria."

"Don't let me down," I replied, only half in jest.

Bert nodded. "You obviously believe me. If you didn't, you just blew the grand magus's plan to hell."

"As I said, don't let me down."

"No fear. Now, as soon as it's released, I call dibs on that book. This might be just the thing we need to finish the damn paper before I'm ninety."

I drank and wiped the foam from my lip. "Bert...the people in Alaska..."

"Yes?"

"You think they're desperate enough to try the Erik Niger method?"

"Absolutely," he replied without hesitation. "Did Toula

send you after me on the last trip?"

"Yes."

"Then you saw what the raiders did before they were subdued."

I nodded. Frank and I had arrived before cleanup was complete, and the torn body of a teenage girl was still bleeding out into the grass just beyond our hiding place.

"Desperation makes people do stupid things," said Bert, wrinkling his nose at the sour smell of his beer. "Even clever people."

We drank quietly for a few minutes, waiting on our food. Finally, I said, "I don't want to sit around the Team's office all night, waiting for the alarms to go off. Want to join me for a late dinner? Somewhere that *isn't* the castle?"

Bert chuckled but shook his head. "Thanks for the offer, dear, but I'm due at my mum and dad's at half-five."

"You can't blow that off?" I asked hopefully.

"No. There reaches a point when you miss enough Sunday dinners that your mum pulls out a diary and pins you to a date and time. Or mine does, at least." He swirled his beer, perhaps hoping that aeration would improve the flavor. "Why don't you go see your grandfather? Get out of here for a bit, clear your head, avoid Toula before you talk yourself out of a position."

I grimaced at my drink. "We, um…we still aren't exactly speaking."

"*Still?* What on earth did you quarrel about?"

"I just confronted him with some unpleasant truths and told him to stop trying to change me." My fingernail found a scratch in the wooden tabletop, and I began to pick at it. "He never wanted me to be a magus in the first place, and with the Conclave situation now, he's trying to make me quit and run back to Faerie for the rest of my life."

"Which could be a long time, were you to do so," Bert pointed out.

"Well, *yeah*, but it's my life! He has no right to try to

force me into pretending to be something we both know I'm not just because *he* thinks it's a good idea!"

"Whoa, now, I'm not arguing with you," said Bert, raising a hand to ward off my sudden anger. "But I'm also not surprised. That's rather what parents do, you know? Tell you all the ways you're mucking up your life because they think they see you running off a cliff. Sometimes they're right, sometimes not, but good luck trying to convince them they're wrong. Mine have done the same sort of thing for years," he confided, leaning across the table. "They were perfectly happy while I was on track to be grand magus, and they were as pleased as Punch during most of my *illustrious* ten-week tenure, but since then?" He shrugged. "Nothing's been quite right. I didn't fight hard enough for my job. I should have tried to have Toula expelled. I haven't done enough for my kin and family friends in the Conclave. I have yet to bring home a new Mrs. Wold and give my parents grandchildren. And on, and on." He grunted and paused for a swig of beer. "They see me as having been robbed of my rightful position, stuck in a lesser job, and left to wallow in my sorrow as a middle-aged bachelor, and they're constantly suggesting ways that I might improve my lot."

"That's obnoxious."

"But hardly atypical. Parents want the best for their kids, no matter how old those kids might be. So I listen to Mum and Dad's self-improvement advice, nod in the appropriate places, and ignore ninety percent of it. Seems to work for me. But look, as obnoxious as it can be, I know my parents mean well. They have my best interest at heart, even if they don't exactly know what it is. And I'm fairly confident that the same's true for Val."

"He's not my parent," I mumbled.

"Bollocks he isn't."

"He only kept me around because he felt guilty about Marcus," I retorted. "And now that he has Marcus—"

"Forget *why* he took you in," Bert interrupted. "He *did*.

And if he's pushing you to move back there, he's obviously not washing his hands of you just because Marcus turned up. Come on, Maria," he said, lowering his voice, "do you honestly think he doesn't care for you?"

"He never wanted me, he wanted *Marcus*. He kept trying to mold me into a substitute, and then we found out I couldn't be, and…" I paused, forcing down the tears that arose from the toxic combination of my resentment and sleep deprivation. "You would think he'd be proud of me, wouldn't you? Think of how many people would be thrilled if their child became a magus, *particularly* at my age. That's a decent accomplishment, isn't it? I've done well, haven't I?"

"Certainly."

"Then why can't that be good enough for him? Why does he keep trying to change me?"

At that, Bert chuckled to himself and sat back in the booth. "Because there will *always* be something that isn't just right, my dear. Tell me, are you religious?"

I frowned at the enquiry. "Not exactly…"

"Neither am I, but I was raised Anglican. There's a story that's stuck with me as I've grown older. I can't tell you chapter and verse, but the gist is that Jesus's family thought he was mad at one point and tried to bundle him off home. Now, tell me, if good old Mary is second-guessing *her* kid's life choices, then what possible hope do the rest of us have?"

I mulled that over as I drank. "If he would only have a little confidence in me—"

"We *are* still talking about the two-thousand-year-old faerie, yes? The one who sees his all-too-mortal granddaughter run off to Glastonbury and get on with the Arcanum's least popular magus? I mean, if it were me, I'd be scared to death."

"He's never had a kind word for you."

"Not surprised. I did almost fuck us all over that one time—"

"That didn't begin on your watch!"

"No, but I was at the helm when it exploded. You take the job, you take the credit and blame alike." He paused as the server approached with our hamburgers and chips and waited until she was out of earshot once more. "Go home. Talk to Val. Don't let this fester." When I continued to glare at my burger, Bert said, "Let's put this into perspective, hmm? He's known Marcus all of what, four months? And he's known you for…twenty years?"

"Eighteen. And a half, I guess."

"Okay. You don't just throw away a child after eighteen and a half years, not if there's anything decent in the pair of you. Go hash it out with him.'

I bit into my burger, found a piece of gristle, and spat it into my napkin. "Maybe later. Once this nonsense with the book is over and we've both been exonerated…"

Bert raised his glass and clinked it against mine. "To getting your credentials back and finishing this damn project."

"Cheers," I muttered, and drank deeply.

Toula closed the Archives by edict that afternoon on a pretense—an emergency systems check, which, among other things, sucked oxygen from the area around the book and manuscript stacks in case of fire. With the place to ourselves, Antony, Bob, and I got to work in a quiet corner of the acquisitions room, putting our faked book on an empty shelf and cocooning it with cleaning and protective spells like any other damaged find. A sign by the shelf indicated that the book was not to be disturbed for the next week while the process was in motion. With that sorted, Antony turned his attention to the security cameras, checking that all were functional—seldom a guarantee in the Archives, a facility that relied far more on magic than technology to preserve its holdings—and I started designing the tripwires, wards hidden in the floor that would trigger an alarm with installation security if crossed. Toula had decided not to let them in on the full project, but she instructed them to alert Antony if anything arose. As for Antony, he had patched into the Archive's door and camera systems with Toula's blessing, and he set up a command center in his office for the long night's vigil.

"If no one makes a move tonight, someone else is going to have to take a turn," he told me as he tweaked his machine. "Madison's been doing the single-parent thing since Thursday, and I'm sure she'd like a break."

Leaving him to his preparations, I retreated to my flat, eager to work on my sleep deficit. I'd barely snuggled back into bed for a long afternoon nap, however, when someone knocked at the door. Groaning, I pulled a bathrobe on and stomped through the flat, hoping that whatever messenger awaited me would be quick about it.

To my surprise, I found Marcus on the other side of the door, disguised by a navy hoodie—perhaps inappropriate for late July, but moderately effective at preventing startled double-takes from those who knew Val's face. "Oh, good, I thought you might still be with Antony," he said, tucking his hands into the sweatshirt's pouch pocket. "Busy?"

I gestured to my robe. "Going to sleep off Peru and everything else. Need something?"

"No, no, just bringing an invitation. Pater asked that we come to dinner tonight."

I suppressed the sudden, irrational thought that Val and Bert had been scheming behind my back. "Thanks, but I need to be here now. Have fun."

But Marcus frowned. "He was hopeful that you might be free."

"Sorry. Antony needs me around for book-minding purposes."

"Antony could call you, couldn't he?"

I gave Marcus a long look, and he backed off. "Yes,

magus duties, I understand. But you know Pater will be disappointed."

"Won't be the first time. See you," I said, and closed the door before he could press me into a conversation I didn't want to have.

More exhausted than I'd realized I dozed all through the late afternoon and into the evening, waking only at nine once my stomach began to complain. I made a sandwich and ate it standing at the kitchen counter, checking my messages. The day had been quiet—Sundays often were—and aside from the chatter in the Council group about the ramifications of finding Erik Niger's magnum opus, I had little to read. Grabbing a bag of cheese puffs, I flopped onto the couch and turned on the television in search of mindless entertainment.

An hour into a movie I'd seen a dozen times before, my phone began to ring. I sat up and pulled it off the table, assuming I'd see Kitty's name. When the ID named Antony, however, my heart began to race. "What's up?" I asked.

"It may be nothing—"

I cut him off. "You wouldn't call at half-ten if it were nothing."

"Nothing *firm*, then." He let out a long breath. "Just got a blip on the door log. Bert's entered the Archives."

CHAPTER 20

My stomach lurched toward my throat. "Excuse me?" I said, hoping I'd misheard.

"It's Bert," said Antony. "About, uh…ninety seconds ago. Main doors. They record all after-hours entrances, you know, and—"

"I've got to go," I blurted, and slapped at my phone until I severed the connection.

Bert.

Bert.

I wanted to cry, and puke, and scream, but mostly, in that moment, I wanted to punch something. Bert, the one person I'd defended against all accusations, my mentor, my colleague, my *friend*…

He'd betrayed me.

Dinner at Mum and Dad's, indeed. Maybe he'd gone to give himself an alibi, and now, when most of the castle was turning in for the night, when there was no one on duty in the Archives to question his presence, he'd let himself in with his magus credentials to do a little browsing. The sick feeling in my gut told me exactly where I'd find him.

I lingered in my flat only long enough to pull on sweatpants and tennis shoes.

The Archives were protected by barrier wards, strong enough to keep out anyone who couldn't make excellent gates, which prevented the bulk of the Arcanum from wandering around without authorization. Those who merited after-hours access—magi, archivists, most librarians, and the Away Team—had old-fashioned magnetic cards, which were paired with a fingerprint scanner for added security. Toula might have revoked my borrowing privileges, but no one said anything about deactivating my card.

I ripped open a gate to the hallway outside the Archives' lobby, but before I could let myself in, Antony called again. "I've got him on security camera in there," he said without preamble. "Heading right for the book. But the cameras are snowy, there's a surge or something up there, and I can't get a good look at it. Hang on, let me get security—"

"I've got it," I said, and hung up on him again, too angry to wait for backup and too comfortable in my furious invulnerability. Silencing my phone so as not to announce myself, I scanned into the Archives and headed for the staircase.

Between the lobby on the second floor of the tower and the Team's lair in the subbasement five floors below were dozens of rooms—climate-controlled rooms for housing the collections, laboratories for cleaning and preservation, reading rooms, a lecture hall, and offices for the archivists. The acquisitions room where the fake book was being housed was only two stories belowground, but with my anxiety and mounting anger, the spiral staircase seemed to go on forever as my feet slapped against the worn stone steps. After a seeming eternity of running, I slammed open the door to the basement level and ran for the book. "Bert!" I yelled as I neared. "Damn it, Bert, I know you're in here! Face me! *Bert!*" Vaguely, I was aware that my fists had begun to spark, but I was too enraged to worry about maintaining control. "Come out!" I bellowed, and then I hit the push-bar into the acquisitions room with all of my weight.

The door flew toward the wall as I ran inside…and there, standing by the fake book with a look of surprise and guilt, was Bert. One hand still trailed along the shelf, reaching for the ensorcelled volume.

"*Bert*," I snarled, advancing on him as pale flames licked up and down my arms in the cold room. "You *bastard*."

"Maria," he said, far too calmly for the situation, "if you'll hold your temper for a moment, I'll explain everything."

"Like hell you will. You goddamn traitor, you *lied to me*!"

Suddenly, even as I bore down on him like a missile, Bert did something that stopped me in my tracks.

He *smiled*.

And then he waved one hand toward the nearest security cameras, Antony's eyes in the Archives. The hexed cameras exploded into flaming plastic and a shower of glass shards, and I instinctively ducked and covered my head as a pair of cameras on either side of the aisle popped and crackled. When I looked up again, Bert was still grinning triumphantly...or was he smirking? I rubbed my eyes as Bert seemed to blur...

...and in an instant, the illusion fell away.

"Well done," said Magus Stanhope, giving me a mocking golf clap. "Such *passion*. You sold it, I'll grant you that. It'll look fantastic in replay, I'm sure."

"*Eva*?" I cried, shocked to a halt.

"Mongrel."

I barely felt it when my shield rose between us, so instinctive was the spell. But I registered then what I'd only barely noticed a moment before: the temperature in the room was too low. The Archives were always cool, but there was a *breeze* blowing through the stacks. Turning, I found the source of the distortion on the security footage at the end of one of the cross-aisles: a gate leading onto the path into the Conclave's compound. It was still early afternoon in Alaska, but the day was cool and windy, and a litter of loose paper rustled on the floor with every gust through the gate.

"You're the—"

Leak, I'd meant to say, but I never had the chance.

What happened next was largely my fault. Tired, disoriented, keyed up to show Bert my righteous anger, and thrown at finding Eva in my crosshairs instead, I was off my game, and so I didn't properly approach the confrontation as a combat situation with unknown adversaries. As a result, I made a stupid beginner's mistake. I didn't guard my flank—and I never heard Eva's accomplice slide out of the shadows behind me.

Before I could finish my thought, my back and legs were awash with searing pain, a wave of heat and light that wrapped around me like an agonizing cocoon. Dimly, I realized that I was on fire, but not until I'd gasped with the shock and inhaled the flames, scorching my mouth and throat. I screamed and flailed as instinct shrieked at me to put out the fire, roll on the floor, *do something*, and by the time I'd recovered enough presence of mind to apply spellcraft to fight off the inferno, I was on the ground and wailing. Suddenly, something sharp and hard drove through my back, pinning me to the floor like a wriggling beetle.

With one lung rendered useless, I fought to breathe with its charred mate. I couldn't rise—any attempted vertical motion drove the barbs on the impaling rod deeper into my flesh. As the last of the flames flickered out, I tried to piece together the events of the previous minute. Before I could make much progress, however, footsteps neared, and I twisted my head just far enough to see a pair of hiking boots pause beside me. "Oh, that was too easy," said a vaguely familiar voice—British and female, but no one I immediately knew. "I was hoping for at least *some* challenge."

"It's just the little mongrel, what did you expect?" said Eva. "Come on, Francine, let's get out of here."

Magus Leighton. The name registered as the former magus squatted beside me, smiling as I sucked at the air. "Just a minute," she said. "I want to watch this."

"*Francine*," Eva warned, "enough. If she's in here, the cavalry probably isn't far behind."

"It's not *your* daughter's life she ruined," Leighton snapped. "I don't see Beth working in IT, do you?"

"And if Dahlia hadn't gone to college, we wouldn't be here now. I know how you feel, dear, but let's not get caught, okay? This is too important," she said, passing the book to her partner.

Leighton smiled at me again before she stood. "You're sure they'll pin this on Bert?"

"Positive. Remind Dahlia to switch our fingerprints back in the system, won't you?"

"Of course." She kicked me in the side, and though I tried to scream, all that emerged was a weak squeal like a leaky balloon. "Very well, if you insist," she said, and sighed.

I lay prone on the thin carpet, too weak to free myself, focusing on my breathing, and listened as their footsteps faded and the gate closed. The wind died in the room, the paper fell, and I fought to pull air into my lungs. Fire—she'd set me on fire. The pain wasn't as I'd imagined—it seemed sharp and bright in some places and almost nonexistent in others—and I took that to be a good sign. *Just another moment*, I told myself, just a few breaths more to gather my strength, and I'd wiggle my phone from my pocket...

It was funny, I thought. This was justice for Zio Luca, wasn't it?

I was still lying to myself that I was almost ready to attempt movement when I heard the door open and Toula shout, "Maria? Are you in here? Mari—*oh, my God.*"

She slid down beside me and reached for my neck, but paused, seemingly confused. I blinked at her and tried to speak, but nothing would come from my raw throat or breathless lung. "Hold on," she said instead, pulling out her phone. "Don't move, baby girl... Bee, I'm in the Archives, I need you *now*," she said into the phone, her voice shaking. "Where are...okay, here's the gate."

A few seconds after Toula's gate appeared, Dr. Powell hurried through, wand in hand and bathrobe flapping. She took one look at me and murmured, "*Christ*," which is seldom a comforting word to hear when uttered in that cadence by the person who's meant to keep one alive. Pushing Toula out of the way, she started muttering a spell. It took effect none too soon, and I felt the first twinge of relief as my breathing eased—not much, but to a noticeable degree. With the immediate problem of breathing lessened, though, I had more mental resources to devote to various patches of pain all around my body, and I almost wished the suffocating feeling would return as a distraction. More concerningly, I recalled the minor matter of the apparent stake through my chest.

"That's not going to last," Dr. Powell quickly told Toula. "Get him here."

"You need another healer?" Toula asked.

Dr. Powell paused, and in that silence, even through the pain, I understood what she wasn't saying. My heart, already beating overtime, seemed to freeze.

"No. Just get him here," she replied, and knelt beside me. "Maria, I need you to be absolutely still. This should help…"

While the doctor worked on the numbing spell, I heard Toula walk a few meters down one of the aisles. "Val?" she said, her voice still wobbly. "Maria's hurt. It's bad. Can you...yes, hold on."

By then, weakening, I had closed my eyes. I heard another gate open, then rapid footsteps and Val's voice: "*No*! No, no, Maria—"

And then, suddenly, the world went silent.

I opened my eyes to see undemarcated blackness in all directions, like I was floating in a pool of ink. No—not *floating*. There was something solid beneath my feet, a definite up and down. I wasn't hurting anymore, at least, and my breathing was unlabored again, but where—

My breath caught in my throat as I leapt to the logical conclusion...but then I heard Ros.

"Ack, sorry, new to this," she said, a formless voice from everywhere and nowhere. "Hang on, no one panic, nobody's *dead*."

I winced as light flared above me. There was the sun, the cloudless sky, the familiar brown peaks of the mountains ringing the villa's high mountain meadow, and standing near me with identical looks of befuddlement were Toula, Val, and Dr. Powell.

"Working out the kinks, you know?" said Ros, manifesting beside us. "Okay, that's better. Sorry."

Dr. Powell recovered her bearings first. "Ros, what the hell—"

"Gate's open, and you were close enough to work with. We're in a space between moments—I can't hold this together for long, but I thought this would help."

"*Right*," she mumbled, staring at our surroundings. "This is...what, a projection?"

"More or less. Like a visualization skin on reality. Sorry, Bee, I'll try to warn you next—"

"Never mind that." Dr. Powell turned to me and folded her arms. "I'm not going to sugar-coat this, Maria. You're in deep trouble."

I glanced down at my body, which seemed to have returned in the condition it had been in prior to running into the Archives, then back at the doctor. "I'm burned, aren't I?"

"That's part of it."

"How badly?"

She studied me briefly, and I could only imagine what version of me she was picturing. "At least ninety percent of you is burned, I'd estimate. Whatever hit you was *hot*."

"*Ninety*?" I echoed, aghast. "It doesn't hurt that badly—"

"Because a good portion of your burns are at least third degree. Some are worse. When the damage goes that deep, the nerves are destroyed. Whatever burn pain you're feeling comes from the second-degree spots. You're, ehm...the damage is extensive. And then there's the rod through you—looks like a piece of rebar with spikes on. Missed your heart, but one of your lungs has to be more than punctured. I might be able to get it out, but I'll have to pull it all the way through, and it seems to be melted to your back. Sorry, I know that's graphic—"

"I could disintegrate it," Toula offered.

"Which could worsen the internal bleeding," said Dr. Powell. "On top of the burns. You're bound to go into shock before long," she told me. "It's...not pretty."

"That fucking bastard," Toula muttered, shaking her head. "I'll kill—"

"It wasn't Bert," I insisted. 'Francine Leighton hit me from behind. Eva Stanhope disguised herself, and I think they messed with the system, they said something about Dahlia Leighton and computers—"

"*Eva?*" she interrupted, eyes wide. "You're sure it was Eva?"

"Positive. She fried the cameras once I started yelling at 'Bert,'" I muttered, kicking myself for my carelessness. "Eva's the leak, the Conclave has a way into our network, and Bert—"

"Bloody *hell*, forget Bert!" Dr. Powell cut in. "That's not important right now! Maria..." She hesitated, then let out a long, frustrated sigh. "I'm sorry, dear, but I don't think I can treat you quickly enough. You've sustained massive trauma, and with the blood loss already—"

"You stabilized her," said Toula.

"I put a plaster on a severed artery. It won't hold for more than a few minutes."

Val's eyes darted back and forth, and I could tell he was running the variables and coming up with the same picture I'd seen. "There must be a way," he said, a note of panic creeping into his voice. "If we keep her together long enough to get to—"

"Hospital?" Bee finished. "With a big iron stake through her chest and severe burns over most of her body? Assuming we could get her to a specialized burn center, and assuming they could stabilize her long enough to operate and cover the open wounds—she's burned down to the muscle in places, Val," she said, lifting her hands helplessly. "*Charred*. She'd need massive skin grafts, which might or might not take, and even then, conservatively, she's going to lose both hands and at least her left arm. They're just *blackened*. Probably her right leg, too. If she ever recovered feeling, it'd be miraculous. That's not the sort of trauma you get over," she said more softly. "And whatever we built around her now to stabilize her or dull the pain, we'd have to break it before we got her close to all of that unshielded hospital equipment."

I glanced down at my unmarred clothing and supple skin, a gift from Ros's imagination, and tried not to envision what Dr. Powell was describing.

"We're not giving up," said Val, vehemently shaking his head. "There's a solution here, there must be—"

"You can't fix her," Ros quietly told him, stopping him mid-sentence. "I didn't bring you guys here to plan her treatment. I thought you'd like a chance to say goodbye."

His face drained of color. "Good…"

"I'm sorry. I'm *really* sorry," she added, turning my way.

"No," he whispered, staring at me. "No, that…that's my little girl, you can't…"

"I'm sorry," she repeated, and stepped aside.

I didn't waste the moments we had left. As I approached, Val pulled me into his arms and held on as if clinging to a life preserver. I rested my head against his shoulder as I'd done so often before, but that time, he shook in our embrace. Only once I felt moisture seep through my shirt did I understand that he was silently crying.

"Guess I should have listened to you, huh?" I joked weakly.

He said nothing, but his grip tightened like a vise.

"I'm sorry," I tried, "I shouldn t have said…"

I knew what I wanted to tell him, but in that moment, the words seemed to fall apart before I could release them. Frustrated and fearing that Ros would send us back at any second, I dropped my mental defenses and murmured, "Look."

Val hesitated briefly, then plunged into my thoughts. But as he did, I discovered that his were open to me as well—whether because he allowed it or because we were all stuck in a place of Ros's making where the rules didn't fully apply. Seizing my chance, I pulled back the curtain.

The initial shock of entering another person's mind is disorienting, and I ping-ponged among his immediate sensations and emotions until I landed on the images closest to the top of his mind: me, but through his eyes.

There I was at twenty, showing off my new magus chain.

At seventeen in my green ballgown, marveling at Firola's lavish home.

At fifteen, glimpsed through my cracked bedroom door while I bent close to Kitty and laughed over our notebooks.

At ten, going through the gate on my first day at school in Glastonbury, looking back over my shoulder and nibbling my lip.

At five, small and scared and sobbing in the moonlit meadow until Val scooped me up and held me close.

And a few months before that, me in his lap, wide-eyed and smiling. *We're family?*

I felt his fear and anguish, but I also felt the overwhelming surge of love that colored every memory.

In my exploration, I hadn't bothered to keep track of what Val was finding in my own mind, but when I withdrew from his thoughts, he was regarding me with fresh panic. "I *am* proud of you," he said in a rush. "I'm so proud, *please* know that. If I made you think—"

"I'm sorry, I was stupid—"

"I never meant to hurt you, carissima filia." His eyes pleaded as they bored into mine. "We chose each other, didn't we? You and me, family. Does it matter how we reached that point?" He didn't bother to wipe his tears away. "You are my daughter, now and forever. Nothing will ever change that. *Marcus* certainly didn't."

I held on to him, feeling quite nearly at peace.

"I love you," he said, his voice finally breaking. "I always will..."

Ros cleared her throat. "Folks, I hate to cut in, but we're running out of time."

At that, Val squeezed me so hard that my lungs—even Ros's version of them—ached. "No. No, please, not yet..."

I kissed his cheek, tasting salt, then extricated myself just enough to see Ros standing nearby. "What about the Hail Mary option?" I asked her.

She folded her arms and made a face. "As I've said all along, that'll almost certainly kill you."

"Well, I'm dead either way, aren't I?" Gently, I pulled free of Val's stranglehold and approached her. "Helen said that Joey took a bolt to the chest and lived once the realm finished with him. What about me? Would it work?"

"You've got a hell of a lot more damage than a single bolt, but the odds are decent," she allowed. "Assuming you survived my tinkering, that is."

I spread my arms. "What do I have to lose?"

Ros thought it over, then nodded. "Hey, Bee," she said as the doctor watched us warily, "are you up for a challenge?"

What happened in the first seconds once Ros sent us back into the flow of time was a well-orchestrated blur. As I gasped like a landed fish once more and tried to scream as pain returned to my torso and lesser burns, Toula opened a gate into the infirmary, and Dr. Powell dashed through, returning with the castle's lone crash cart. She went ahead of us into Faerie—the gate into Val's office remained open—and hurriedly prepared by the couch. "Ready!" she called once her equipment was set up. "Bring her in!"

I felt my body rise from the carpet, looked down, and wished I hadn't. Toula had broken off the end of the rod, which remained embedded in the floor. The stain around it was wide and dark red, and fresh blood spurted from me with every heartbeat. But before I could spend too much time in uncomfortable contemplation, Val guided me through the gate, and the spells Bee had only just cast around me shattered. I sucked at the air with my ruined lung for a few endless seconds until Val replaced that broken spell, and I'd almost taken a real breath by the time I was hovering supine over the couch cushions—quite a bit over them, considering the length of the iron spike still protruding from between my ribs.

"Get it out, Toula," said Dr. Powell.

With a few muttered words, the rod disappeared, and my blood began to flow in earnest. Val maneuvered me down onto the couch, and I fought a scream when what was left of my skin made contact with the leather.

"Move," said Dr. Powell, pushing Val and Toula aside, and quickly established an IV line. As she waved her wand over me and a pair of monitors for cardiac and brain activity appeared in the air beside the couch, I realized with faint embarrassment that my clothing had burned away—hardly the most pressing concern facing me at that moment, but still an unpleasant thought. Before I could attempt to ask Dr. Powell for a sheet, however, the cardiac monitor began to beep, and she stepped back as Ros approached.

"Ready?" Ros asked me.

I nodded feebly and tried not to look at my flesh.

Val moved closer to take my ruined hand. "I'm here," he said, brushing my little remaining hair from my face. "When it hurts, if you—"

"Negative," Dr. Powell interrupted. "Unless you'd like to experience defibrillation."

"What is—"

"Let go of her and come over here," said Toula, pulling Val away. "Can't we give her a shot or something for the pain?"

"No time," said Dr. Powell, turning to her monitor.

"And it wouldn't help," said Ros. She cupped my cheek in her cool hand and smiled grimly. "Okay, honey. Try to hold on."

I heard Val say my name, and then the world exploded into agony.

Every cell of my being felt as if it were simultaneously being ripped apart, stabbed, and incinerated. The excruciating torment made my previous wounds seem like no more than a scraped knee by comparison, and it only grew worse with every eternal millisecond. I wanted to scream anew, but I had no voice left, no lungs, no *body*…

Suddenly, the pain abated, and I felt myself begin to drift in the blissful nothingness that had become my world…until, as if from a great distance, I heard Dr. Powell mutter, "Fuck, V-fib. *Clear.*"

A shockwave ripped through what little remained of me, rending the soothing blackness and thrusting me once more into the jaws of the beast that gnawed at my nerves. Distantly, I realized what had happened, but even as part of me struggled to live, another part yearned for the release from which Dr. Powell's machine had yanked me.

And then, without warning, I was slipping back into the painless void.

"*Clear.*"

Again and again, into a fresh, worsening torture and out for an instant of merciful relief, I cycled through my personal hell until I was voicelessly begging for death, *anything* to make it end.

Finally, the pain faded one ast time, and I knew nothing more.

When consciousness resumed, I was still surrounded by darkness, but the floating sensation had been replaced by a more familiar feeling of weight and gravity. The longer I took stock of my returning senses, the stronger grew my suspicion that I had a body—still? again?—and that it might be horizontal.

Open your eyes.

Ros's voice rang in my mind, though she sounded fatigued. Still, I reasoned that if I could hear her, I probably wasn't dead. Slowly I obeyed and saw shimmering streaks of purple and blue and pink flash and fade above me in the blackness.

My canopy.

You're in your room, said Ros. *Take it easy, you're weak.*

My mouth felt like the Sahara. "Wha—"

You made it through. <u>Barely</u>.

"The defibrillator—"

Six times. <u>Six</u>. We almost lost you on a couple of rounds. You flatlined at one point—Bee did CPR and pumped you full of epinephrine, and your heart finally decided to cooperate. She seemed to sigh, though as she was then speaking directly into my head, I wasn't sure how that was possible. *It was easier with Aiden and my dad—Aiden needed suppression, Dad needed amplification, boom. But you were almost a full-blown wizard, you know? Suppressing <u>that</u>, then amplifying that drop of fae blood...do me a favor, won't you?*

"Mm?"

If you ever have kids, make sure the father's at least a little fae. Working with you was exhausting. Yeah, I know, she quickly added, *hurts you a hell of a lot worse than it hurts me, but it's more than unpleasant. You'll forgive me if I don't manifest right now. Still recovering.*

As my hand reached toward my chest, I found myself swathed in bandages—even my fingers were wrapped.

Bee did it, Ros explained. *I think it offended her on a professional level to leave a patient that exposed. You're intact again, but you're going to be sore for a while, and your nerves may tingle as they finish regrowing. I wouldn't try to run a marathon today. You need to drink as much water as you can. I got your blood volume back to a life-sustaining point, but hydration will help until you make up the difference. In other words, you're probably going to feel like shit for the next day or so, and the scars will take at least a few months to subside.*

I let my hand flop back onto the mattress. "Thank you."

Of course, she replied, sounding warmer. *Pretty sure I still owed Val, if nothing else. He's over there*, she added as the question formed in my mind. *At the table, napping. He's been waiting all day, but I kept you under through the worst of it.*

"All day?" I repeated.

Like I said, working with you was much worse than with Dad and Aiden, and you were in rough shape on top of everything else. You slept all night and day—it's eight-ish Monday night Glastonbury time, I think. And you need food. Food and a <u>serious</u> amount of water.

I didn't bother speaking my questions—with Ros plugged into my head, there was no need to do more than give form to the enquiries.

Toula has things under control. For now, she's pretending that Eva's plan worked. You died in the Archives, your body was brought back here, and they'll have a memorial service for you on Friday. Bert has mysteriously disappeared and is being sought for questioning. He's here, she added before I could worry. *Town. With the rest of the Team and their immediate families—Toula thought anyone connected with the book should be evacuated before Eva figures out it's a fake.*

A thought suddenly occurred to me, and I heard her chuckle. *Yeah, everyone now knows exactly what Frank is. Lakshmi's husband freaked out worse than anyone, really—and*

Allie has been begging Antony to take her to the dragon barn. Mal's planning to sneak her out there if her parents balk. I think the kid has a future on the Team. Hey, wait—go slowly, she warned as I struggled to sit up in bed. *This isn't a race, Maria.*

I grunted, wincing as my new skin shifted, then pushed back the blankets and wished I hadn't. The room was cool with the garden door open, and my bandages, if medically useful, weren't keeping out the chill. I glanced toward the bathroom, where I'd hung an old robe on a hook, and out of habit, I started to whisper into being the spell that would bring it to me—the lazy wizard's trick for getting out of bed on cold mornings. But my lips had barely moved when the robe was flying out of the bath and into my hands, and I stiffened, thrown off my normal rhythm.

You're not casting, said Ros. *Tamp it down, you're approaching it with too much power.* She laughed as the truth of what had just happened registered with me. *Yeah, that's enchantment. Maybe don't try anything delicate until you have some sense of what you're doing, eh?*

"Shit," I whispered.

You may need to reevaluate your career trajectory, she agreed. *But on the plus side, you're alive.*

"This *is* true." Slowly, I eased my robe around me and tightened the sash. "So Toula told everyone that I'm dead?"

For now. She'll probably let Arnold in on the truth, but officially, it looks like Bert killed you in the Archives. He's mortified, by the way.

"What for?"

I mean, there's incriminating video of "him" going around now, and he's tried to be above reproach since that little incident. But he'll get to clear his name soon enough, I'm sure. Toula's plotting. She paused, and I could almost hear her smirk when she resumed. *I popped by to chat with him. Scared him to death.*

"Not you, too," I groaned. "Bert's not—"

Bert has mellowed considerably from when we first met. As have I, she admitted. *He was a smug little prick when he was your age.*

"And I'm certain that you were all sweetness and light," I retorted.

Heh. Hardly.

Sliding out of bed, I tested my balance, then shuffled through the dark room on my bandaged feet until my hand felt the edge of the table. I could hear Val breathing softly, his head resting in the crook of his arm on the tabletop, and I gingerly nudged his shoulder. He bolted awake with a jerk and sat up, and I murmured, "Sorry, sorry, it's just me."

"Maria!" he cried, and waved on the lights—dimmed, thank goodness, though even that made my eyes smart. He stood and pulled me close until I yelped, then released me with a rapid, mumbled apology. "You're still in pain?"

"Yeah," I said, wincing. "Like I was hit by a train and dragged down the tracks."

"Then what are you doing out of bed?" he chided, carefully steering me in that direction.

"I'm fine—"

"Humor me."

I sighed but acquiesced—honestly, I needed little convincing—and he fussed over the blankets while I made myself as comfortable as I could against the pillows. "Really, I'm fine," I insisted. "Don't you have more important things to do than play nursemaid?"

"No." A glass of water appeared in his hand, and I took it gratefully as he pulled his chair to the side of the bed. "Drink that, let's put food in you, and then more sleep. Ros said you should be ambulatory by morning."

"I hate to ask, but could you numb—"

"Certainly." The enchantment was the work of a minute, and he regarded me with faint reproach as he finished. "It's no trouble, carissima filia."

"I don't mean to be a bother."

"You're not." A large pizza box manifested on my lap, quickly followed by a stack of napkins. "Eat, build your strength."

I opened the lid, examined the pie, and smiled. "Ham and extra cheese?"

"Your taste hasn't changed, has it?"

"Not for this, it hasn't. Thanks." I ripped a slice free and groaned with pleasure as I dug in. Mouth full, I mumbled, "I still remember the first one of these you made for me."

"As do I," Val replied, leaning back and watching me stuff my face. "You were so small but your appetite..."

"I was *starving*." Picking up the next slice, I added, "That hasn't changed, either."

For a time, he waited in silence while I tried to fill the black hole where my stomach had been. But once I'd made it through half the pizza and was beginning to slow, he murmured, "Maria, there is something I need you to understand."

I looked up, cheeks puffed with food, then swallowed hard. "What's that?"

He paused to collect his thoughts before speaking again, and when he did, his voice was low. "The reason that I never suggested you call me anything but my name is because you had parents. Their memory has always been dear to you...even if you don't actually remember them," he allowed. "But you know their names, their faces. I...I didn't want you to think that I was trying to erase them."

"*Val*," I began, hastily wiping the worst of the tomato sauce from my bandaged fingers before reaching for his.

He took my stained hand and gently squeezed. "That bothers you about Marcus and me. I don't care what you call me, honestly. Whatever pleases you."

As I comprehended the extent of what he'd seen in my thoughts, I started to flush. "It's...it's not *that*, really, I just..." I floundered for a moment, then blurted, "It's really difficult to compete with him, you know?"

"But there is no competition," he replied, perplexed. "Is there?" He searched my face as I struggled, then tightened his grip on me. "Yes he's my son. And you're the child I tucked into bed and saw off to school and worry about every time you leave. No one could replace you."

My eyes pricked, and Val stood to brush my regrown hair from my face. "I love you both," he insisted. "Ros can rank things however she likes, but neither of you is inferior in my eyes. Different, yes, but not *inferior*." He perched on the edge of the bed, and I pushed the pizza box aside. "Marcus looks up to you, you realize."

"*Me?*"

"*You*," he said, mimicking my surprise. "And why not? He speaks often of you." Val chuckled briefly. "For some reason, it was Toula who told me you'd bested him. I can't imagine why he wouldn't have mentioned that himself. But Maria, I wish you'd *talked* to me before this festered. Please don't be jealous of him. Nothing between you and me has changed—nor will it. This I swear to you, child."

"I know," I mumbled, "I'm sorry, it's stupid—"

"It's not," he interrupted, and carefully hugged me. "You are home. You will *always* have a home. That little girl I found on the street, setting fire to rubbish—you will never be that girl again. Believe me."

"I do, I just—"

"You don't." He tapped my temple to drive home the point. "Maria…it's your life. Do what makes you happy. Run off to that ashram like Toula keeps threatening, if that's what you want. But even if I complain, I would never throw you out. *Never*." He paused, then said, "Do you know what I told Firola after you left that night?"

I shook my head.

"That if she uttered a word to humiliate you again, I would revoke her title, and that would only be the beginning of it. I've not spoken to her since then. Marcus has already informed her that he will not be accepting her invitations."

"You didn't have to—"

"You are so much more important to me than the

court's social calendar could ever be." He held my gaze as if he could stare truth into my soul. "Maria, you have been a daughter to me since the day I brought you back from Glastonbury. I would not consider you a truer child had I sired you myself. What can I do to make you believe that?"

My vision blurred, and when I felt him gingerly wrap his arms around me again, I held on to him as well as I could with my sore body, awash with a sense of relief I'd never known I was missing.

When Val released me, he wiped the escaped tears from my cheeks and smiled. "You will be whole again soon. When you can stand, I'll teach you what you need to know. Helen has already agreed to assist."

"Helen can't enchant," I pointed out.

"No, but she knows what and how you've been taught to this point. In any case, it should be far simpler working with you than it was with Aiden and Joey," he muttered. "They started from nothing. You, now…" He held out his hand, and an orange fireball bloomed and burned in the center of his palm. "Try."

At that moment, fire was the last thing I wanted to play with, but I knew that if I didn't face it, I'd be on my way to fearing it. Hesitantly, I copied his pose and focused on the raw magic around me, thinking of how I would build the spell. But as with the robe, the magic seemed to respond to my desire before I could properly channel it, and another orange flame appeared in my hand…then quickly grew until it engulfed my forearm.

"Don't panic," Val instructed as I began to do just that. "It's under your control. Does it hurt?"

"No…" I said, watching the flames lick at the air just above my elbow. My robe, at least, was unsinged.

"Will it away." He waited until the fire vanished, then laughed softly and shook his head. "You've always had an affinity for fire, girl. I see that Helen didn't train it out of you."

"Sorry."

"There's no reason to apologize." He stood and smoothed the indentation in the blankets. "Training begins when you're ready. With your background, you should be in control of yourself by the end of the week. Plenty of time."

I frowned. "We have a deadline?"

"Well, no, but I assumed you'd rather have a rematch with Eva sooner than later." As my jaw dropped, Val grinned. "I know you, Magus Corelli. Build your strength, I will teach you a few techniques, and then you may loose your fury on her. Not that you'll need assistance, but if you want any, I know that Marcus would love the opportunity. He's rather cross with her on your behalf."

"I'll keep that in mind," I replied, and smiled sadly. "Don't think I'm going to be a magus for much longer. What am I supposed to do with myself now?"

He glanced at the ceiling with feigned innocence. "You know, you could always stay here, find a hobby…"

"Yeah, you've got Marcus for that."

"Not exactly." Seeing my bemusement, he explained, "He very much enjoyed Peru, aside from the altitude and the panic trigger. Ted says he was helpful. Marcus may be sidling his way onto the Team."

"Really? You're okay with that?"

Val shrugged. "His life. And we should have time—I don't plan to drop dead. If he's enjoying himself, there are worse places he could be than with them."

"And Kitty's a solid minder," I added.

He cocked his head and gave me an enigmatic smile. "Is that the word we'd use? I could be mistaken, but I believe the nature of their relationship is somewhat…different."

My eyes widened. "You think—"

"I think Marcus has learned much in the short time we've had together, but he hasn't yet mastered the art of keeping me out of his head. Perhaps you could teach him," he replied, and reached across me to retrieve the cooling pizza. "Are you going to finish that?"

"Of *course*."

"Then I'll replace this one," he said, and took a slice.

CHAPTER 21

Toula's office door was locked from the inside, but still, I kept an anxious eye on it as I paced and waited. Discerning the direction of my thoughts, Bert, who had taken a chair and was bouncing one knee up and down, pointed to the couch on my next pass. "Walking the floor isn't going to speed this along, dear."

"You're not nervous?" I asked.

"Never said that. But save some of your energy for the actual meeting, won't you? You're making me dizzy."

I plopped onto the couch opposite him, but stillness proved impossible. Within a minute, I was opening my hands, summoning fire, extinguishing it with my fists, and repeating the process.

"Maria."

"Hmm?"

"Patience."

I glanced up in exasperation. "You're not the one who just had a memorial service."

I'd floated the notion of attending in disguise, Tom Sawyer–style, but that had been shot down. By then, Val had been relatively confident that I could control myself, but Toula vetoed the plan as too risky. There would be no unnecessary chances taken, she'd insisted, and that meant that everyone would continue to play their roles.

At least Kitty had the decency to give me the highlights. "It was well attended," she'd told me when Marcus hustled her back across the border that night. "Almost all of our year came in for the occasion. And *all* of the magi," she'd added, her voice hardening. "Guess it would have looked weird for Mom to stay away."

I hurt for Kitty. Like the rest of the Team, I'd tiptoed around the slight issue of her mother's treason, but Ted had called a group meeting on Wednesday morning, just before they returned to Glastonbury, to discuss the matter. Since Toula had been busy herself up to that point, the meeting had to be held in the field outside town, as Frank was still very much unensorcelled. I'd been released from training to join them, and though Rodney still kept Lakshmi between him and the dragon, I'd smiled to see little Allie sitting at the base of Frank's neck without a care in the world.

The meeting had been brief and to the point. "All right, look," Ted had told the assembled, "we all know Stanhope's dirty. *That* isn't Stanhope." He'd pointed to Kitty, who'd looked more than a little uncomfortable with the attention. "If anyone has a problem with Ms. Connolly's continued presence on the Team, speak up now."

Silence had fallen over the group, and Ted had nodded. "Thought so. Hear that, Kitty?"

Her eyes had welled, and Lakshmi, leaving her poor husband exposed to potential dragon attack, had hurried over to hug her, murmuring reassurance. Daphne had made it a group hug, and the men had looked at each other awkwardly until Ted piled on.

They had departed shortly thereafter, once Toula had arrived in a flustered flurry and returned Frank to a more manageable size. "Remember," she'd stressed as they headed into her office, "you were evacuated briefly while we secured the installation, the leak has now been patched, we have no lead on Bert yet, so go about your business. I'm your contact magus for the moment."

Arnold Lowe had waited to receive them on the other side, and Bert and I had waved at him through the gate. "Enjoying your holiday?" he'd joked.

I'd pushed up my sleeve to show him the fresh bruises Val had administered that morning. "Loads of fun. Wish you were here."

In truth, training hadn't been horrible, and Val had apologized profusely when he accidentally overloaded my shield. My years of work with Helen and my Arcanum instructors had given me technical expertise—the difference was that instead of channeling a kitchen tap's worth of magic, I was now trying to manipulate a firehose. All of the careful augmentation techniques in which I'd been schooled were suddenly superfluous, but Helen had remained on hand to steer me back into good habits. "Don't be *lazy*," she'd chided during one water break. "No one ever wished in the heat of battle that she didn't know how to amplify."

She had a point. The careful construction skills and attention to detail that I'd had to cultivate as a wizard were far beyond anything the average faerie mastered—there was simply no need. The rules of construction that I'd been taught no longer worked as expected, but with experimentation and suggestions from both of my tutors, I came up with modified versions that focused the already substantial power I was now wielding into something far worse, much like forcing the firehose to flow through a drinking straw. Not all of my attempts were successful— some techniques simply refused to translate, no matter how many times I tried—but the end result was something close in spirit to Toula's more hybridized work, clearly enchantment but far tidier than usual. Once Val had seen that I could amplify my power, he'd begun testing my limits...which, when we got overly excited, had led to catastrophic shield failure and my badly bruised arm. "I'm so sorry," he'd said as he checked for fractures. "The last time I trained anyone, I didn't have the boost from the realm—"

Look, I worked hard to keep her alive, Ros had cut in. *Don't kill her just yet, okay?*

Val had been more careful after that, and when Marcus had half-jokingly suggested a rematch on Saturday, he'd agreed but stood ready to jump into the fray. But even with my occasional fumbling and the month Marcus had had to practice, I'd still managed to throw him from the ring we'd made in the meadow. "She's faster," Val had told Marcus as he climbed to his feet. "It will come in time."

"And then you'll be flattening me," I'd added, offering him a hand.

He'd taken it and dusted himself off, scowling. "How did you dodge—"

"Reflex," Val had interrupted, nodding to me in approval. "The work of years. Don't expect it overnight. And Maria, shield."

I'd thrown one together a millisecond before the incoming bolt struck, and though the blow had nearly pushed me off my feet, the shield had absorbed the surge and recovered. "No," Val had mused, rubbing his chin, "I wouldn't expect much flattening.'

Pointing to Marcus, I'd arched a brow. "Did you overlook the *slight* age discrepancy?"

"Not at all." He'd flicked two fingers to make the ring disappear. "Your power is comparatively slight, yes, but you amplify everything. The net effect is equivalent to a much older person's ability."

I'd frowned in surprise. "Really? How much older?"

"Old enough," he'd replied, "and I'll thank you not to challenge random strangers trying to figure it out."

"But—"

"*Maria.*"

When his back was turned, I'd glanced at Marcus and rolled my eyes, and he'd grinned in conspiratorial sympathy.

Marcus had offered his assistance in going after Eva, but Bert and I declined. This was a Council matter, after all, and both of us had scores to settle.

After a seeming eternity, Toula's wall clock ticked over

to five past ten, and Bert rose. "They should be settled in and at it by now. Ready?"

"Ready," I muttered, heading for the door.

"Don't crisp her until we get some answers, Maria."

"I know, I *know*."

He stopped me with a hand to my shoulder, and when I impatiently turned to him, I saw the fire hiding behind his thick glasses. "Together?"

"Together," I said, and held the door open while he marched into the corridor.

We hurried toward the largest meeting room, where the full Council had gathered for Toula's pretextual discussion of security changes that might be made in the wake of the book incident. When we paused outside the door, I heard her voice through the wood, still running through housekeeping matters—she had left down the privacy ward that day to allow us to eavesdrop. As she wrapped up, I looked at Bert, who nodded. Gripping the doorknob through my new gloves, I ignored the tingle in my hands that warned me of proximate iron and flung the door open.

The Arc 1 magi usually sat in a clump at the far end of the room, and so I had an excellent view of Eva's shocked face as I stormed in with Bert on my heels. "Sorry I'm late," I said over the cries of my startled colleagues. "Recovery time, you know. What were we discussing?"

The confused magi looked to Toula for an explanation—all but Eva, who continued to stare at me with wide eyes and a slack jaw—and as Bert pulled the door closed, Toula smiled grimly and made room at the head of the table. "Magus Corelli, Magus Wold. Thank you for joining us. Was there something you wanted to discuss?"

"You're meant to be *dead*!" one of the Arc 7 magi shouted.

"Well, I coded half a dozen times, apparently, so close enough," I replied, and sloughed off my robe, then the T-shirt beneath it. True, a black sports bra wasn't the most professional of wardrobe choices, but it nicely showed off the pale patchwork of new skin on my chest, arms, and back. "I went into the Archives when I heard that Bert was snooping around after hours. The person I found next to the Erik Niger book was ensorcelled to look like him. I have to assume that person is the same person who opened a gate *in the Archives* that led to the Conclave's compound. As soon as there was enough incriminating evidence on the security video to frame Bert, the real thief dropped the disguise, and I was attacked from behind. Bert had nothing to do with it."

The Council's agitated murmuring rose in volume until Arnold, who was well in on the plan, stood and raised a hand for order. "Do you know who ambushed you, then?"

"Francine Leighton," I replied, keeping my eyes on Eva. "It seems that her daughter's been given access to our network—or gained access on her own, I can't say. But someone within the Conclave—or helping the Conclave— stole electronic copies of books that Bert and I were using for our crafter research, and we guessed that the lure of Erik Niger would be too tempting to keep that person or people away for long." I paused and smiled down the table. "You were hastier than we'd expected, Eva, but I guess I can't fault you for diligence."

The room turned on her as she began to sputter protests. Looking wildly around the table for support and finding only a mixture of confusion, shock, and hostility, she ripped open a gate behind her neighbor's chair and tried to throw herself through.

I took great pleasure in slamming it in her face, and even more pleasure in the thud she made upon hitting the floor.

"Leaving so soon?" I asked as she scrambled off the carpet. "Pity. I wanted to know what you and your friends thought of the book. I mean, personally, *I* found it interesting, but then I read the real thing. Guess you were in too much of a hurry to look at the text of what you were stealing, huh?"

Her chest rose and fell rapidly as she threw together a shield.

"I haven't had to do any quick translations *into* Latin since I graduated," I continued, "so I'm sure I made a few mistakes, but that was my best attempt at *Crime and Punishment*. No? You didn't get any angry calls from Alaska over that one?"

As Eva reddened and fumed, Toula said, "Magus Stanhope, I'm holding you on suspicion of treason and attempted murder. Drop the shield."

She did, but only to free her hands for offensive work. Baring her teeth, she flung a bolt toward Toula, shouting, "*Die*, mongrel!"

Toula easily deflected the shot into the corner, but before she and Eva could properly engage, Eva flew backward and slammed into the stone wall. Pinned, she struggled against her invisible bonds, giving Bert plenty of time to stroll around the table while his spell tightened its grip. "I know we've never been chums," he told her, "but framing me for treason? Really? Low-hanging fruit, don't you think?" He paused outside of the radius of her flailing arms and legs, watching impassively as she fought in vain. "You're not going anywhere. I wasn't made grand magus for my people skills, you know."

It took half the Inner Council, but within ten minutes, Eva had been subdued and bound, rendered powerless by the spells around her. "You're *dead*," she spat at me as I watched handcuffs appear—an unnecessary measure, but still infinitely satisfying. "You couldn't have survived that. I saw you, you were black and bleeding out—"

She fell silent as both of my fists burst into flame. "That's the funny thing about mongrels," I replied. "You people tend to underestimate us."

As eight magi escorted her into the castle's detention cells, I extinguished the fire, recalled that I was still underclothed, and waved my shirt across the room. "I regret to inform the Council that I must tender my resignation," I said once I was decent, finding the shaken magi's eyes on me. "My situation has, uh…changed—"

"Sit down, Maria," Arnold interrupted, and I plopped into my usual chair, which the Council had considerately left vacant.

"Right, then," he said, taking the floor. "Magus Corelli attempted to prevent a theft and stop the parties responsible for leaking Archives materials to the Conclave. She would have died had Dr. Powell and, ehm…Ros Bolin not intervened." While the table muttered, he looked to Toula, who nodded for him to continue. "As a result of those life-saving measures, Maria is, shall we say, slightly more fae than she has heretofore been."

"*How* fae, exactly?" Iris Johansson asked, cutting her eyes to my gloves.

There was no point in dissembling. "Functionally half," I admitted. "I can't cast anymore."

"Of course," Toula interjected, "if we're going to start talking about percentages, I'll remind you that I'm *actually* half…"

"But you can still cast," I pointed out. "Which is why I'm offering my resignation."

"That doesn't seem fair, though," said Iris, frowning in thought. "You were injured in the line of duty. If we started chucking out magi because of on-the-job injuries—"

"This is a little different," I protested, perplexed. I hadn't expected pushback, let alone from an Arc 1 magus.

"And maybe this is selfish of me," Arnold added, "but I was *really* hoping not to have to teach the second-years this term."

"I understand, and I'm sorry," I replied, "but I literally cannot cast." As proof, I let a fireball flare in my open hand. "I'm fairly sure that one of the requirements of this job is proficiency with spellcraft—"

"Which you have," he countered. "The theory side, at least. I mean, you could still look at a student, see how he waves his wand around, and tell him what to do differently, yes?"

This was most definitely not part of the prearranged plan, but Toula wouldn't respond to the looks I shot her. "I suppose I could," I allowed, "but what parent is going to trust *me* with a second-year?"

"Eh, we could spin it," Bert offered. "And if you think you're leaving me with this treatise to write, you're sorely mistaken."

Flummoxed, I looked around the table for help, but none seemed to be forthcoming. "I...uh...look, that's really nice of you, and I appreciate the gesture, but don't you think it would be best if I bowed out?"

Iris spoke first. "If you did, then who would get stuck with the Away Team?"

"Not it," Bert quickly muttered.

The rest of the Council looked slightly queasy as the prospect of inheriting my assignment. "You see," said Iris, "this isn't entirely altruistic. You need to stay. We can work around teaching and papers and whatnot, but *someone* has to look after those lunatics."

"Hear, hear," one of the Arc 4 magi chimed in, and the others murmured their agreement.

I turned to Toula and muttered, "You orchestrated this, didn't you?"

"Maybe," she said, grinning, and tossed me my abandoned robe. "You'll be needing that, Magus."

As I slipped it back on, I tried out part of my new skillset and thought, *Does Val know about this genius idea of yours?*

I may have reminded him that if Marcus continues to hang around with the Team, it would be best to have a contact magus who wouldn't mind dealing with the heir to the court, Toula replied in kind. *Or Mal. Or _Frank_, for fuck's sake. Incidentally, Frank's already told me that if I try to foist them off onto another magus, that person might find suspicious fires in his office. I don't want to encourage arson, but he's very good at it, so maybe you should stick around, kid.*

"All right," I told her aloud, "if you insist, but under one condition."

"And what would that be?"

"I get a brass doorknob for my office." Lifting my gloved hands, I muttered, "These things are going to get old *so* fast."

Sorting my immediate future was only one of Toula's pressing problems. With Eva locked away until her trial—and quite probably for some time after that—something had to be done about her underage daughter.

I was sitting with Kitty in Toula's office that afternoon as moral support when Toula led red-eyed Beth inside and directed her to the couch. She was only thirteen, skinny bordering on gangly, but her honey-blonde hair was still long, albeit unwashed that day. Her mother had been taken into custody before sunrise in Montana, and I supposed that Beth had been pulled from bed with the unfortunate news and hadn't bothered to shower in the interim.

"Beth, you remember Kitty," said Toula, taking a seat beside her and gesturing toward her sister's chair.

Beth lifted her eyes ever so briefly but said nothing.

"The problem we have here is that you can't stay by yourself," Toula continued. "Not just yet."

And unfortunately for Beth, she had no one to claim her. Her parents had been only children, she had no grandparents living, and unless Toula reached out to Beth's more distant cousins, the only family she had left was Kitty.

"You need someone at least vaguely responsible looking after you," said Toula. "So, for the time being, I think it would be best if you moved in with your sister.

At that, Beth's head shot up. "*Her?* She's barely a witch!

She's—"

"A respected member of one of the hardest-working groups in this organization, and you could stand to learn from her," Toula interrupted, injecting a vein of ice into her tone. "Kitty, I believe your flat has a second bedroom, correct?"

She nodded. "Yes, Grand Magus, but—"

"But what?"

Kitty looked at her sullen little sister, then back at Toula. "With the job, and being gone, and, uh…other trips…"

"I'm confident that Beth's mature enough to keep herself alive for a day or three, and if not, Lakshmi or Bob would probably be happy to look in on her in your absence. Or Madison Copeland—Allie's only two years younger, right?"

"Yes, but—"

"Honey," she said, arching an eyebrow, "you have a couch, Maria has her own spare room, and *he* has a bed he can get to at any time if he doesn't like those options. Yeah?"

She sighed softly. "Yes, Grand Magus."

"Good. And since you have a couple of weeks until the school term begins, I'm sure that you two will have time to get acquainted."

Beth could glare daggers all she liked—Toula was immovable, and so I opened gates back and forth to the silo to allow Beth and Kitty to pack and transport. Neither said much until the last of Beth's clothing had been hung and folded away, and then Kitty leaned against the doorframe and folded her arms. "Look," she murmured, "I get it. You're not happy. This isn't how I thought the summer was going to end, either, but we can thank Mom for that."

Beth's face hardened. "Mom didn't do anything—"

"She left my best friend *crispy* and with a pole through her chest," Kitty snapped. "Not to mention the treason bit. So no, I don't have much use for her. If she's good to you…well, great. I've basically been orphaned since Dad died. If you need to talk or something…I'm here."

Before Beth could respond, Kitty and I turned at the sound of a gate opening in the den, and Marcus hurried through. "How did it go with the Council?" he began, seeing us clustered by the spare bedroom. "Successful?" He hoisted a bottle of wine and added, "Do we drink this, or does someone need to be punched?"

Kitty grimaced, then stepped aside, giving him a view of the room's sulking occupant. "Marcus, this is my little sister. Beth, uh…you might want to keep a bathrobe handy. He visits."

As Kitty and I headed to intercept him—and keep Beth from getting too close a look at the stranger who could have been Val's brother—Marcus smiled. "She's visiting you now? That's—"

Beth slammed and locked her door, and Kitty winced. "Complicated. Wine?"

Toula's other, far larger problem, was the Conclave, and the Council spent much of the evening in heated debate over the proper course of action. Around ten that night, with no sign of imminent consensus, Toula brought Carey Jones and Tanner Adler into the meeting to offer perspective.

"It's *bad*," Tanner reported, leaning over the table. "The gate's as large as any I've ever seen, and I'm no spring chicken. The visitors are getting worse and more frequent, and we're concerned that Nath may make a move."

"Nath?" one of the Arc 3 magi scoffed. "She wouldn't dare."

"Oh, let's rethink that," Carey interrupted, pulling her chair closer to the table. "Badger Parsons was the only thing keeping her from mounting an all-out invasion, and

Badger only made her go away in the first place with subterfuge and luck. If Nath's gotten wind of the fact that Badger's gone…"

The skeptical magus frowned. "She died?"

"Gone to Faerie," Arnold interjected. "My cousin's not stupid."

"I know you've retained the Company to watch the Alaska compound, but we've been keeping our own surveillance as well," Carey continued, folding her hands. "Officially, we're neutral in all of this—it would be hypocritical of us to oppose a splinter arcanum, after all— but we've learned from experience that bad things tend to happen to us when you people have internal tiffs."

"Sorry," another magus said, "and you are…"

"Carey Jones. Authorized by consensus to speak for the Minor Arcanum."

A few of the Council bristled, but Toula shot the room a warning glare. "Dr. Jones is here to help," she told the table. "Let's put aside our differences and focus on the Conclave for now, okay?"

The grumbling subsided, and Carey cleared her throat. "We were content to stay out of your affairs until we saw that the Conclave was willing to kill for a damn book. We've been killed for our wands in the past, and we can't afford to let that happen again. I'm here to offer assistance with surveillance while you plan your next move."

"She can get inside the compound," Tanner explained. "It's too risky for any of my people right now. They've strengthened their barrier ward, and we almost lost an operative who got zapped within an inch of her life."

"I'm a sleepwalker," Carey explained to the Council. "I can put myself into a trance, get to the compound, and report on what I see there."

At that, some of the magi perked. "Can you attack them like that?" one of the Arc 5 crowd asked. "Or bring down the wards? Open a gate?"

"No, no, and *no*. The only wizard I've ever known who

could cast in the dream space is Badger, and I can't imagine that she'd be willing to return to this realm for anything short of the apocalypse." Arnold nodded fervently, and Carey shrugged at the questioner. "But I can be your eyes tonight. Tell you how many there are and where they're stationed."

We needed a break, and so we stood to stretch and make tea while the elderly veterinarian slumped in her chair and closed her eyes. Still, like dogs with a much-loved bone, we kept circling back to business while we re-caffeinated.

Part of the Council—largely the Arcs 1 and 7 contingents, though they had supporters from other installations, too—wanted to continue our "wait them out" approach to the Conclave. Many of our number had at least one friend or relative who'd run away to Alaska, and while they agreed that we couldn't allow them to split off permanently, they didn't want to attack. Another part, led by Arcs 3 and 6, favored immediate action in the wake of the euphemistically named "book incident." For personal reasons, I sided wholeheartedly with them. The rest of the Council waffled somewhere in the middle, recognizing that the danger from the Conclave had escalated but reluctant to pull the trigger on our own people.

And then, just as Arnold sent his aide out for more snacks, Carey woke with a gasp and a jerk. Toula rushed to her side to hold her in her seat and offered her a glass of water, which she declined while she caught her breath. "What did you see?" Arnold pressed, sliding into the chair beside hers. "More wards?"

Carey lifted her head and looked around the room as we stood staring at her with our mugs and half-eaten cookies. "They're under attack right now."

"From what? More of those raiders?"

"No. Nath's guard, or people like them. You know, tall, blue, too many eyes. And I saw a few of the smaller, purple ones—what is it you call them?"

"Svartálfar?"

"Yeah, them."

"You're sure?" he asked.

She nodded. "Dark magic users glow blue in the dream space. They've got the compound surrounded, maybe a hundred of them, and that gate is there to fuel them…"

"Right, that does it," said Toula, raising her voice to be heard above the sudden hubbub of the meeting room. "I say we move now. Arnold?"

"I agree," he replied.

"Good. Bert?"

He started at hearing his name called. "Sorry—you want *my* opinion on this?" he asked, bemused.

"You know that place better than anyone here," said Toula. "What's your gut say?"

"That we're going to lose the compound if we don't act."

"Okay," she told the rest of us, "here's the plan. Bundle up, boys and girls, and get security up here. We're going to go see about the damn Conclave."

Toula wasn't the sort of grand magus who shouted orders from the rear. She led the charge through the wide gate opened from the castle's courtyard—we needed the space to fit the Council and the entire installation security team through in a hurry—and was flinging lightning before our forces had completely arrived. While the surprised invaders from the Gray Lands scrambled to regroup, their attempted siege having turned into a battle outside the Conclave's warded fence, Toula dispatched all of Arc 5's forces to seal the massive gate, plus half the security team to help keep the Gray Landers at bay while they worked. The rest of us maneuvered around the outside of the compound, trampling the summer grass and wildflowers as an afternoon shower turned the ground to muck.

Surprise proved to be our greatest asset, though I like to think that the rings of fire I flung as impromptu lassos helped. By the time the gate team finished, we were down to the final dozen invaders, who clumped together in a defensive, shielded knot as Toula held us at bay.

"You know this realm is protected," she said in Fae, and two of the blue creatures perked in recognition. "This is not your hunting ground, and your lady has been made well aware of that."

One of the two stepped slightly away from the protection of their huddle to address her. "Our lady believes that the one called Hannah Parsons has forfeited her claim. There has been no sign of her in this realm for years."

"Badger's claim has passed to the Arcanum," Toula replied. "This is our realm to defend. Your kind are unwelcome here."

The creature—I assumed it was male, though I couldn't be certain—cocked his head. "Then it is true that she has forsaken this realm?"

Toula whispered a few quick words, and a wave of force swept from both sides toward the Gray Landers, crushing them before they could defend against it.

"She's stepped out," she told the frightened survivor as his comrades' mashed bodies dropped into the mud. "But go back and tell your lady that if she wants this realm, she'll have to go through us first."

We watched as he opened a new gate and fled, and Toula and Arnold sealed the hole behind him. Sighing, Toula studied the well-warded compound—none of whose inhabitants had come out to join the fray—then shook her head and ordered us back from the chain-link fence. "I'm getting too old for this shit," she muttered. "Maria, over here."

When I joined her, she pointed to the wards. "Do me a favor. Think you can overload them?"

"I don't know about the whole system," I replied, "but

I can make a hole for you."

"That'll do nicely. Whenever you're ready."

Concentrating, I drew upon the ambient magic around me, applied the amplifying techniques I knew by heart, and flung the resulting bolt in a focused shot at the wards. It penetrated, shattering the system for at least a meter from the point of impact and melting the fence just beyond it.

She patted my shoulder, then stepped past me through the fence and into the silent compound. "Listen up!" she yelled, amplifying her voice with a quick spell. "You *will* come out, you *will* surrender, and you *will* return to Glastonbury with us for processing and detainment as is deemed necessary. You have ten minutes."

With that, she retreated from the compound to our waiting ranks and traded weary looks with Bert. "Not to be a naysayer," he told her, "but I can't imagine that working."

"Oh, I know," she replied, brushing it off. "I just wanted to give us a chance to prep."

When the allotted time had elapsed, the Council was shielded and prepared, and our security forces stood at the ready. There was still no sign of life in the compound, however, let alone surrender, and Toula pushed back her robe sleeves. "So we'll do this the hard way," she murmured, then extended her hands palms up, splayed her fingers, and slowly began to curl them closed.

I knew Toula was far stronger than she should have been for a wizard or a faerie her age, let alone a witch-blood, but until then, I'd had no real concept of the extent of her talent. As the magi around me gasped, the still-warded buildings exploded into rubble, which then rose and coalesced like a cloud of rock and metal above the compound. The people who had been hiding inside screamed at the concussion, then looked up in alarm at the tons of debris hanging over their heads.

"Thirty seconds," said Toula, "or I bury you alive."

It was said later that this was the moment in which

even the staunchest holdouts on the Council were forced to recognize Toula as grand magus. Feet planted in the trampled meadow, robe soaked and dirty, hair flattened to her head with rain and sweat, Toula stared at the Conclave over the Gray Landers' corpses, holding death in her bare hands and daring them to defy her.

And they blinked first. The mothers with young children ran for the hole in the fence, followed quickly by the rest, all scrambling to escape. Last to come through was Francine Leighton, who was immediately subdued by a crowd of guards.

Toula flung her hands away from her, and the debris fell harmlessly into the grass beyond the far side of the fence. "Chan-mi, Paulo, Kaisu," she said, pointing to three of the younger magi. "Go with Bert and see what you can recover, particularly computers. Everyone else..." She turned weary eyes on the rest of the Council, then gestured toward the gate home. "You know what to do."

Two days and very little sleep later, I slouched over the dinner table as Val nudged the rest of the rum cake in my direction. His cook had tried a new recipe, heavy on the rum, and I got the feeling that most of it hadn't burned off while baking. But as I'd barely stopped for meals all week, the temptation of sweets was too much for me to ignore, and I cut myself another generous slice.

"Are the trials scheduled?" Val asked as I tucked in. "If Toula needs additional cells, we can make arrangements here."

"I think she's set on that front," I replied between bites. "And no, they haven't been scheduled yet. Eva and the Leightons have been detained, but IT is still going through the Conclave computers, looking for anyone else involved with the leak. Antony's helping. So is Aiden, actually."

"He does enjoy his machines," said Val, nursing his

coffee. "Why wait on the trials, though? You have three already—"

"And no firm evidence but my word. We're trying to pull a trail from their computers, prove that Bert really had nothing to do with the book heist." I smirked as I cut a bite with the side of my fork. "They found the fake book, incidentally. I'm surprised no one burned it in a fit of pique. Oh well, our gain. And at least now I've got my credentials back, and I've been cleared to give Bert our transcription of the Erik Niger book, so he and I will have plenty to do until the trials, *especially* once school resumes. Good thing I won't be teaching Beth," I added, making a face. "She probably hates me on principle."

"Poor Kitty," he muttered, then paused. "Maria...I may have been, uh...slightly hasty."

"Oh?"

Slowly, and with obvious reluctance, he said, "Regarding Bert. Perhaps."

"I'm sorry, what was that? Are you saying I was *right*?"

He grunted and mussed my hair, and I swatted his arm away. "Don't push your luck, Lady Maria," he chided, though his smile gave him away. "Or it's still Magus Corelli, isn't it?"

"You knew about that, didn't you?"

"Of course. And if Marcus is going to be over there, I would rest more easily knowing you were nearby."

I smiled to myself, and Val's brow furrowed in query. "You do know Kitty lost her guestroom, yes?" I said.

"I've been informed that her couch is satisfactory."

We sat in comfortable silence for a moment while I finished my cake, and then, finally stuffed, I pushed my plate aside. "I guess it's a little of both."

"What is?"

"You asked if I'm Magus Corelli or Lady Maria. I've always been something in between, haven't I?"

"True." Val gestured, and his coffee refilled. "Claim them both, then. It suits you. And if Toula speaks truly, both may be needed before long."

"Nath?"

He nodded. "Toula can posture all she likes, but the only thing keeping Nath out of that realm was her agreement with Badger. With Badger no longer there to enforce it…" He shrugged. "It's a matter of time, I would think."

"Yeah, well, let's hope she has second thoughts," I muttered into my coffee. "Toula may be scary when she puts her mind to it, but *I'm* certainly nowhere near ready to fight Nath."

"This is also true," said Val, patting my arm. "But while we have time, we prepare. Come." He pushed back from the table and pointed to the door. "Show me these lassos Toula mentioned."

I followed him out of the villa and into the meadow, both of us small among the mountains and below the starry dome, and paused to watch the magic swirl around me as Val readied his stance. Faerie was indeed a beautiful place, and the years since my arrival had done nothing to change my impression on that count. Sure, Glastonbury had its charms, and walking through the doors of the castle felt as comfortable as sliding on a favorite pair of jeans, but this place…

No, it wasn't the realm into which I'd been born, but maybe—just maybe—it could be home after all.

"Carissima filia?" Val called, pulling me from my reverie. "Are you ready?"

I picked out his shield in the moonlight, then smiled and summoned the flames.

ACKNOWLEDGEMENTS

Once more, with feeling…

Thank you for coming along with me on this long, strange trip. I'd like to say a special thank you to those of you who've left reviews or dropped me a line with your thoughts.

The Novel Chicks continue to be the best writing group a girl could want. For reasons unknown, Adam Domby continues to work my books into his busy schedule, for which I'm most grateful.

And yes, here's to you, Mom and Dad.

ABOUT THE AUTHOR

When not writing fiction, Ash Fitzsimmons is an appellate attorney and an unrepentant car singer.

Find her online:
www.ashfitzsimmons.com